PIANO PEOPLE

HAPPY BIRTHDAY HERB

I hope you enjoy reading this as
much as I enjoyed writing it.

Best Wishes
Don Burns
MAY 4, 2002

HAPPY BIRTHDAY HERB

I hope you enjoy reading this as
much as I enjoyed writing it.

Best Wishes

Bob Burns
MAY 4, 2002

PIANO PEOPLE

UPRIGHT GRAND · DOWNRIGHT NUTS

by

DONALD A. BURNS

Published by
Sundown Canyon Productions, Inc.
PO Box 572
Grand Island, NY 14072

Editor – Philip Nyhuis
Cover Design – Jim Petrilli
Internal Design – Jacqueline Baker
Proofreader – Kathy Sue Dorey-Pohrte
Forward – Stephanie Camden

FOR INFORMATION CONTACT:
SUNDOWN CANYON PRODUCTIONS, INC.
PO BOX 572 • GRAND ISLAND, NY 14072

FIRST EDITION - MAY 2002

Printed in United States of America

ISBN No. 0-9716030-0-6

Dedicated
to
Ann and Ray

When an author cannot come up with
appropriate words to describe his feelings,
something must be pretty special.

Ann and Ray are the *most special*
people in my life.

ACKNOWLEDGEMENTS

TO: My Dad and Mom for letting me roam around getting a taste of a wonderful life at an early age.

TO: The wonderful people of Grand Island, NY for letting me add some absurdity to their lives without having me arrested or committed.

TO: Veronica Connor, principal of Charlotte Sidway School. A stern disciplinarian with a heart-melting smile. She convinced every student that they could go as far as they wanted and there was nothing we couldn't do. She brought out the best in all of us.

TO: Harry Simpson, Ed Zuchowski and Mel Rupp, Sr. These three people taught me more about observing and working with the public than any textbook could ever do.

TO: Ragtime Bob Darch for hooking me and constantly holding my feet to the fire of music and entertaining.

TO THESE PEOPLE AND PLACES – *Some of the great spots*

TO: John Cirrito – JOHNNIE'S OLD TIMER SALOON – Tonawanda, NY
Stan Zamiara – THE PILOT HOUSE – Spencerport, NY
Ralph Blum – THE HOLIDAY INN OF BUFFALO, DOWNTOWN – Buffalo, NY
Jack Floreale – LEISURELAND – Hamburg, NY

and most of all

Charlotte Guenther – THE BEDELL HOUSE – Grand Island, NY
She let me pull out all the stops, all the time, and she loved every minute of it.

TO THE THOUSANDS OF FANS AND FRIENDS OVER MORE THAN FORTY YEARS

Little did you know that as I played a show for you, you were putting on a show for me. Your unbridled antics, comments and diverse personalities made this book possible. May I now thank you from the bottom of my heart. You're really something!

SPECIAL THANKS

TO: Pel and Betty Bell-Smith – They raised the entertainment bar for ten years and made me keep jumping over it. I thought they were throwing me to the dogs but I later realized that they had faith in me when I sometimes did not. I thank them sincerely for that.

TO: Those very valuable and trusting friends who saw this book as a viable project and lent their support to get it off the ground. Their names have been withheld by request but I will remember them for the rest of my life.

TO: The Taylor family for their continued support of my music and for affording me a great place to work, both on the piano and in the writing of this book.

FORWARD

In the selection process, a publisher looks not only at the book but also carefully evaluates the author. Is the material in the book something the author can convey; does he know about it; does it ring true? Can the author be depended upon to answer for his work and respond to the demands on his time and knowledge?

My association with Don Burns and the people who know him well has proven one very important point. Don knows the material—has lived the life—and it is rumored that he may have been involved in some of the antics in this book. His long history as a storyteller, public speaker and saloon entertainer has shown time and again that he can and does become one with his audience. People who have helped in reviewing this book have repeatedly said, "Reading this is just like talking to him in person."

Throughout the two years of preparing this book, Don gave endlessly of his time and resources. Although this publication is listed as fiction, the twinkle in Don's eye and his hearty laugh when talking about the contents, tells me that some of these situations might just be a bit more than fiction. While the book was being written I came across a media review for one of Don's shows.

DON BURNS - *Ragtime Revue*

"To say that Don only plays ragtime-style piano you'll love to hear is like saying there are only twelve hours in a day. You've missed half the point! He is a total entertainment package that combines fine saloon piano playing with a side-splitting comedy routine. Don will get you going and hold your attention from start to finish. He is a great performer."

Having seen Don work, that says it all for me. Now that his first book is in print, I think we can safely say that he is a great author as well.

Stephanie Camden

Sundown Canyon Productions, Inc.

TABLE OF CONTENTS

PREFACE

"THE PIANO IS A BEAUTIFUL THING"

The piano remains as one of man's most complicated and intricate inventions. It has been in our midst for over 300 years. In that time the working theory of the piano has not changed a great deal. Yes, we have electronics and player pianos but they are essentially a variety of attachments which automate or assist the basic piano functions. The woodworking of piano cabinets can be magnificent. From a few scrolls here and there to breathtaking carvings of people and places—from flat wooden panels to stained glass fronts—piano cabinetry is often unbelievable.

I have been around pianos all my life. We had a player grand piano in our home on Grand Island. No one else in my family was musically inclined but we all enjoyed the piano and played it by the hour. I would guess we had about 300 rolls.

Grand Island also had a lot of restaurants and taverns which had pianos. In my teens and early twenties I expanded my area of travel from our home to the places where people actually played the pianos. I loved them all but even then I began to notice a great deal of behavior inconsistent with that of my family and neighbors. There was something magic about a piano; it changed people. It had the potential—played properly or professionally—to make people sing, dance, cry, or just sit silent for long periods of time.

Many people will tell you that I grew up on Grand Island. It is true that I was there for fifty-eight years, but I never grew up. The piano has kept me young and thirsting for more and more music for over forty years. Although I have played for four decades, this book is not about me. Yes, I have generated my share of commotion in saloons and clubs but my performances pale compared to the zany folks I have discovered. Therefore, in an effort to shed light on those whom you may not meet or hear about in your lifetime, I wish to present a cast of characters conducting themselves in what they feel to be a perfectly natural environment and pattern of behavior. In many cases, you may feel some degree of bonding if you are a "piano person."

If not, just share the experience. For me, the times and people have been just plain hilarious. I hope you find them amusing, as well.

DONALD A. BURNS
Grand Island, NY
May 2002

BUYING THE PIANO

"...and yes, you'll want
the lightning rod attachment
and a quart of touch-up paint."

WHY DO YOU WANT ONE?

Pianos know no boundaries. They are not able to distinguish nor segregate the genders, ages, colors or ethnic backgrounds of their players. They have no political agendas and they don't care about your financial or marital situation. They are simply put on this earth to confuse all of us—some more than others. Why do some pianos have 44 keys, some 65 and yet others 88? Why is middle 'C' not in the middle? Why do we have to learn Italian and Latin to take piano lessons in English? A piano appears as a gorgeous piece of furniture which then lures you to it by making pretty sounds. The more you fiddle with these sounds, the more you think you should fiddle. Soon you are almost convinced that you may be able to extract a tune or melody from this huge wooden mystery box. Now you are hooked! Some of you have likened this experience to learning to pet a shark.

There exists a plethora of reasons and excuses to want a piano in the first place. Some are very valid and lots are not. Think about the following:

1. Your child has just turned four and can hum two songs by heart. He can also play the first three notes of the "Barney" theme song and you now know that he is destined for the conservatory.

2. You have just been to a show where the featured pianist made it look so easy that you have now convinced yourself that you can do it too.

3. You have just been to your new neighbors home and they have a piano and by God whether anyone in your home can play it or not, you're getting one.

4. You are a participant in the runaway economy, running over at the edges with cash and your interior decorator has suggested that you dump $50,000 into the living room by putting in a baby grand to accent the new drapes.

5. Your child has just announced that he wants to play the drums. You sell him on the piano in self defense.

6. You are having problems with your spouse and have decided that a piano will give you a place of solitude so you can retreat when things get out of whack. This thought has never proven logical in history.

7. A gypsy palm reader at the State Fair said you have piano hands and long fingers. Most anyone would tell you that for $20.

8. Your kids keep telling you that all the other kids have a piano and now they want one too. You have six kids and if one piano will shut them up it is well worth the investment.

9.   You were at an estate auction. Money was just burning a hole in your pocket. You really wanted the cut glass hutch or the gorgeous tea cart but they went at prices you could not afford. You now have your eye on the piano because it is rosewood and you like that. Bidding is moving along and you are just not sure what to do and scratch your ear, the next thing you know you are the last bidder. You now own a piano you know nothing about, but at least you bought something. All the way home you just pray to God that it plays and your husband can move it. It has to be removed by 5 P.M.

10.   You are single and dating a knock-out chick who flips over piano players. You figure if you get a piano, you get the girl. Try not to overlook that you can't play one when you are making this very important decision.

11.   You have just had your home equity line of credit go through and you are spending it all this week before they can rethink the deal. Why not a piano? You went for everything else this week.

12.   You have just moved into an apartment complex on a three-year lease and realize that you hate the people next door. Perhaps a piano playing night after night will drive them away.

13.   You visited a piano store on a Saturday. You had no intention of buying a piano. You had been drinking and were in a blackout. Your original purpose was to use the men's room. You have no recollection of buying the piano, your memory does not tell you when they brought the piano and you can't even play a piano. It was Tuesday when you first noticed it in the den.

HEY! A PIANO CAN BE WONDERFUL!

What could be more wonderful than having the guys over for a card game and having your wife practice the piano eight feet away. Not to mention she is also taking voice lessons and throws that in for nothing.

What could be more wonderful than your father-in-law—now eighty-eight and using two hearing aids—sitting at the piano in his underwear at 3 A.M. He is playing German marching songs because he can't sleep. Oh sure, it was fun when he first moved in last year but now it is wearing thin.

What could be more wonderful than waking to the strains of the scale being played incorrectly at 5:15 A.M. on a Saturday morning? Your son is doing this downstairs right under your bedroom. You told him that if he did not practice piano one-half hour every day dire consequences would result. He is meeting the guys at 6 A.M. to go fishing and is making sure that he has his ass covered in case they come home late. The worst part, you can't say a damn word about it.

BUYING THE PIANO

This book does not endorse nor condemn any piano manufacturer. All pianos are made with the intent of making people happy. They are designed to give good sounds through trouble-free components encased in a piece of tastefully designed furniture. There are tried and true old line pianos like Steinway and Baldwin as well as other fine, dependable products. Don't rule out the foreign brands. You are probably driving a car that was made overseas.

If you are shopping for a new piano you have all the options of variety and price at your command. If you are shopping for used pianos, the marketplace does not give you quite as much latitude. A dealer may have more than one used piano available, but if you are dealing with a private seller there is only one piano involved. Here price really does play the uppermost part in your decision, assuming that the instrument plays to your standards.

If you are running over at the wallet you can have anything your heart desires. But be sure not to fall in love with the very first piano you see. It would be to your advantage to look around, play a few pianos, and perhaps have someone come along who is familiar with pianos and how they should sound and feel. It is a big investment and you will probably have the instrument for a long while.

When shopping for a piano, beware of stickers that read:

"If not completely satisfied with this instrument, return to manufacturer."

Do you have any idea how much it would cost to ship a baby grand piano back to Armwash, Oregon so someone can "look at it?" It would be cheaper to fly the whole assembly crew into town and put them up at your home for the weekend.

BUYING FROM A WANT AD:
WHAT THEY SAY AND WHAT THEY MEAN

In thousands of newspapers across the country there appear a glut of advertisements of used pianos for sale. There are all different descriptions and you would be wise to see through the smoke and mirrors before answering the ad.

1. **NICE LOOKING UPRIGHT – RELATIVELY NEW – MAKE OFFER**

   (This indicates the piano was given to them by some relative, they are tired of it, and you can probably steal it.)

2. **OLDER UPRIGHT – GOOD FOR BEGINNER – SACRIFICE AT $75**

   (This means the piano is really old, many of the keys don't work, and that they figure a beginner does not need all the keys to get started.)

3. **BEAUTIFUL BABY GRAND – ONE OWNER – WAS $3500, NOW $2000**

(This is probably a piano which has been in the family for three generations. No one plays it anymore. It never was $3500. They are hoping for $750 and starting you at $2000.)

4. **HANDY MAN SPECIAL – COULD BE GREAT – ORIGINAL FINISH, BEST OFFER**

(This means that what finish is left is original. The pets have clawed it to pieces and some of the worst parts have been thrown away. It could be great if you are an old-world carpenter specializing in scrolled woodwork, creating new pieces and refinishing entire pianos.)

5. **UPRIGHT – GREAT FOR REC ROOM – WITH BENCH – ASKING $300**

(This is a dead giveaway that the piano has been painted by some fool and the colors are so hideous that the only place you would ever think to put it is in a dark basement. The bench has also been painted. They would love to get $300 but would probably settle for $30.)

6. **SPINET – GREAT FOR APARTMENT – PLAYS WELL – HAVE TO SEE**

(This piano actually is rather nice but it is on the eighth floor of an old apartment building with an elevator too small to hold a piano. You will be responsible for the moving charge down eight flights of stairs. Add $750 to the cost.)

7. **PIANOS, PIANOS, PIANOS. MANY TO CHOOSE FROM – GOING FAST – INSPECTION BY APPOINTMENT ONLY 2-5 A.M. MON-FRI**

(The inspection hours tell you that all of these pianos are stolen. The thief only wants you to come over if he can identify you. He doesn't want the cops. Pass on this deal or you'll be playing in the prison band.)

8. **BAR CLOSING – USED UPRIGHT – WITH CHAIR – DID PLAY OK**

(This indicates that the piano was still playing while beer was spilled into it and cigarettes burned on it. The last time it was tuned was 1953. It is now taking up space which they need for the electronic dart board. It is basically trash. *Note: The part about closing is just a come-on for you to hurry up.*)

9. **CONSERVATORY GRADE PIANOS – SEVERAL TO CHOOSE FROM. INSPECTION SAT 6/30. SEALED BIDS ONLY. CALL FRANCIS AT FLAGSHIP ACADEMY MON-FRI 9-12 (555) 543-3456**

(A one hundred-year-old school is going to dump two fifty-year-old pianos which are so bad they can neither be tuned nor repaired. They are considered conservatory grade because they are in a conservatory. Other than that they are plain old pianos. They are asking for sealed bids so there will be no on-site bickering about what this junk is actually worth. The bids are opened as soon as they get two, which is probably more than they had hoped to get. The pianos are also on the third floor which is something they have neglected to mention.)

10. **FOR SALE – UPRIGHT – NATURAL WOOD – GOOD FOR HOME – MUST SELL. CALL FRANK AT P.A.W. - Circle 9-5222**

(Natural wood means the piano has been outside for three years. The finish has been ruined by the sun and rain. Also notice the P.A.W. in the ad. It stands for PALISADES AUTO WRECKING. They used this piano as a doghouse for their German Shepherd. That's what they mean by "good for home." The term "must sell" refers to the junkyard which has been cited for toxic waste and is being shut down by the Feds in 30 days.)

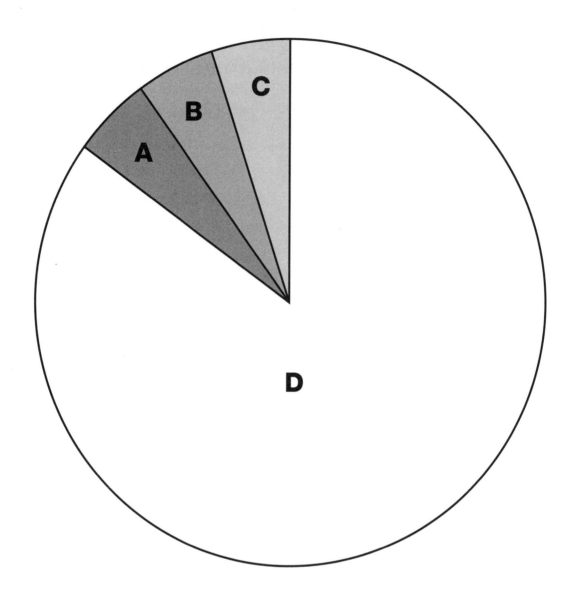

PIANO BUYER'S KNOWLEDGE CHART

A.   People who are totally informed, knowledgeable and savvy when it comes to pianos of any kind.

B.   People who think they know a lot but know only enough to get them into trouble.

C.   People who have been told by someone else that they are piano-oriented.

D.   The totally ignorant and uninformed public who are at the mercy of the industry.

THE PIANO SALESMAN

Piano salesmen are no different than anyone else selling something. They will tell you things you can't verify. They will automatically steer you to the item which brings them the highest commission. Most of all they will tell you anything just to make the sale. Once they realize you don't know what you're talking about, the pitch begins.

"Hi folks! My name is Furd Snidley and I'd like to take you around the showroom here at Tune Town. Let me start by showing you this week's special. It is a hot item and going fast! This beauty is the ROSARIO FORNASIERO MODEL 880 MHE. The MHE stands for Mechanical, Hydraulic and Electric. It is imported from Italy and is of cutting edge design.

"It weighs 880 pounds, has 88 keys, 88 hammers, 88 strings, 88 payments and is available in 88 days. It has only 880 moving parts and it can be tuned to A880 pitch which makes it twice as good as any piano that can only be tuned to A440.

"This model has four pedals as opposed to the usual three. The fourth pedal, located to your left actuates the FROMKISS UTOPIA Note Fan. When engaged it automatically slides two doors open on the piano sides and the fan actually blows the musical notes out into the room for increased audibility.

"The piano has a two-stage hammer greaser and dual wingfaddles not found in any American-made pianos.

"This instrument is self-tuning through a series of mini-winches placed just ahead of the tuning pins. A dial setting from 1 to 88 allows you to select the string that needs adjusting and then you merely engage the red lever at your right to activate the winch—which in turn will adjust the string. Therefore, this piano will never need a tuner.

"Another superb feature is the Model BX DEVONSHIRE Note Coordinator. This allows you to play the black and white keys at the same time in the same or opposing directions. Chords which do not sound right are automatically corrected by hydraulic rams which pop up under the wrong hammers. That stops the note from being played for a while and eliminates mistakes.

"The factory prides itself on the use of exotic woods and materials. The sound board in this machine is made of hand-thatched zeebie weed, soaked in high-density clear epoxy. The cabinet itself is constructed of the finest multi-layered materials. The outer finish is a high gloss solid color as opposed to a natural wood finish which is so overly used in today's pianos. Colors come in red, blue, aqua, beige, tangerine and fuchsia. Black and white are available at slightly higher prices.

"It is equipped with a humidity control unit that takes excess moisture from the air and forces it into a plastic bottle. This is hooked directly to the internal fire prevention sprinkler system actuating at 120°.

"This piano is used widely throughout Italy in wineries, warships and tour buses. It is the overwhelming choice of the Vatican house band, and the original model—Serial #1—is on display in the Mussolini Museum.

"This unit will play American or foreign music. It has stainless steel skids under all four corners to eliminate any caster failure. The backside is equipped with two large flat spots just above a love seat. People who are hard of hearing can sit there with their ears pressed against the soundboard.

"This piano is shipped in a velvet-lined crate with two six-foot lengths of pipe, three-inch diameter, thick walled. These can later be attached to the sides of the crate to convert it into a coffin. Coffins come in natural woods or stains of your choosing. You will also get a stool, bench, chair or hammock with your piano. The Super XXX Deluxe Bench has three layers of foam rubber, an electric vibrator/massager and a Preparation H atomizer for those who suffer but must play on.

"You don't have to buy an expensive warranty program because there isn't any. It comes with a crate of extra parts and a night-light for evening repairs; thus you will never need to call an outside repairman. The owner's manual originally was a hard-to-read booklet but has now been replaced by a CD with the same information as sung by the Boy's Choir of Napoli.

"The Model 880 is priced at a modest $8880 FOB Genoa, Italy. The freight would be additional. Terms are available. This week only I can get you into this rare find for $8000 down and only $10 per week.

"In addition to this factory package I have just described there are, of course, some affordable extras.

1. West Coast-style truck rearview mirrors that allow you to watch the kids while you practice.

2. Electrically heated foot pedals for those cold mornings when you want to practice barefoot.

3. Assorted decals of famous classical pianists or your choice of colored scenes of Italy. These can be placed around the piano on various panels for decoration.

4. Two ninety-six-inch tall marble pillars with imitation electric torch bulbs at the top. These can be mounted on both sides of the piano to give it that extra regal splendor and also throw some extra light.

"To add to this list of exquisite extras, I can tell you that our research division is working on some soon-to-be-released additional features which could be retrofitted to your new instrument. The first feature to be released will be the HUSHPUPPY FIVE Fifth Pedal. This pedal when depressed will totally eliminate all sound coming from the piano when you are playing. This is specifically designed for those who hate their own music but must practice anyway.

"Plus, our dealership here at Tune Town has thrown in yet another extra. All purchasers will receive an 8"x10" black and white glossy photo suitable for framing. It will show you and your salesman signing your purchase agreement with your piano in the background. The customer also has a choice of vertical or horizontal mounting."

ASK THE AUTHOR
—
NO. A426

Dear Don:

I have heard tales that violin strings are made of cat gut. Are piano strings made of the same thing and if so, where do they find cats that big?

~ Strung Out in Stratford

Dear Strung Out:

Today piano strings are made of steel. However, prior to knowing that elephant tusks came in black and white (see Author... #A374), they used zebras to get the black and white hides to cover the keys. The tendons from the zebras were used to make early piano strings (they had to use more than just the hides and it seemed a natural process). It is also rumored that test strings in 1542 were made from some forms of crocodile snot but there is no apparent documentation to support that theory. Apparently no survivors!

INSURANCE FOR YOUR PIANO

In cases where they are available, the salesman will naturally want you to take out the factory warranty extension. It goes beyond the one-year warranty that comes with the piano. It is backed by the firm of Scassafava and DiNiro of Sicily. It is reasonably priced at $73.25 per year.

What exactly are you getting for this additional charge? I have seen pianos that are thirty years old and have still not been played enough to have anything go seriously wrong. After thirty years you will have invested $2797.50 and the piano is still running like a champ. The salesman has since passed on and the piano manufacturer is out of business. The dealership is still going strong but never mentions these things to you, and they continue to send out the owner protection package for renewal.

Since the piano builder in many cases is nothing more than a furniture builder using internal parts procured from other manufacturers, the likelihood that he will stand behind anything other than the cabinet is slim. Therefore you have almost $3000 tied up to touch up the wood. If you want to warranty something, take out some insurance on the vertical adjuster screw on the stool. If you get some fat-ass clown rocking back and forth on that for a couple hours, you'll be looking for repairs and a warranty in a week.

The piano salesman might point out that homeowner's insurance does not cover a piano for theft. Well, duuhh! The reason it is not mentioned under theft is because no fool in his right mind would set out for a night's heisting with a piano in mind.

Jewels, cash, fine wines, silverware and automobiles are logical. Perhaps kidnapping some fine looking chick for a ransom as well, but you know as a one-man theft ring you are not about to invite a rupture trying to stuff a piano into your gunny sack.

It's bad enough you actually have to be part of a piano moving operation—let alone the thought of doing it during a robbery. How many times do you want to take it in and out of your van so the fence can appraise it for your payoff? So, as for theft insurance on the piano, I'd let that one slide.

Also be aware that there are those salesmen out there who want to scare the shit out of you to get you to buy yet another useless item. Through the hocus pocus of double talk and fictitious statistics they will try to convince you that any piano within ten feet of a window is a potential hazard.

The large steel harp and pin frame will attract lightning. When the lightning strikes the piano the heat will travel through the piano down to the steel casters. That heat will surely ignite the wood floor or carpet on which the piano is situated. Therefore you must have the new DEVONSHIRE MODEL LD (Lightning Diverter) to insure your safety and primarily that of your children.

Salesmen always include your kids in these ripoffs since they figure you will bend for the kids. My fellow Americans (and those abroad), may I say to you with complete surety: If a lightning bolt hits your piano, you have no worry about the steel harp or casters. The intense heat of the lightning will torch all the wood on the piano while melting the harp and casters. The floor and/or carpet will be consumed with the rest of the room. The only thing the lightning rod will do is divert the strike to another part of your house where the salesman has cleverly hidden the ground wire. Now, instead of starting at the piano, the fire will start somewhere else in the house and eventually burn up to the piano room with the same results as having no rod. Records through the years hold proof positive that the chances of lightning striking your piano are so unlikely that it should be of no concern.

As a footnote I would tell you that if you are a baritone horn player and lightning strikes your horn while you are playing it, you are probably going to die. In such cases the multi-colored flash at time of impact gives new meaning to the term "LIGHT OPERA." Incidentally, pianos being played under a tree in a rainstorm do tend to increase the odds of an incident. Try to avoid this whenever possible.

BOTTOM LINE HERE: LIGHTNING INSURANCE IS ALSO A NO-BRAINER

The insurance you are really looking for is called **SCRATCH & DENT!** The salesman will not offer it and homeowner's insurance doesn't even want to address it. This is an insurance you wish you had to cover cigarette burns, beer glass stains, and various noticeable marks in the cabinetry of the instrument.

These marks can be caused by any number of child-driven devices. A few things like tricycles, steel dump trucks, water pistols and hand launched aircraft come to mind. Children will use the side of a piano for a dart board or as a target for bow and arrows. If they push hard enough or hammer them, thumb tacks will go into the side of a piano. This so they can mount that ever-endearing finger painting from Grade 2. You know, the one you like so much you wish you had a hundred more for friends. In reflection, however, this might be better than the finger painting applied directly to the piano itself. Car keys constantly thrown on the piano will do a number on it as well. Another culprit is the fat party guest who hugs the side of the piano all night long to help him stand up and leaves a ten-inch horizontal scrape from his belt buckle.

Children who are nervous find great solace in swinging their feet and kicking things while seated at the piano. This is not good. The lower panel will take on the texture of a cobblestone street and will need refinishing. Then there is the first time your young daughter thinks it is cute to tap dance on top of the piano. She saw it on TV while watching "The Barbary Coast" saloon scenes. Now is the time you must decide to stain or buy a throw cover for the whole top of the piano. In fact the throw cover is not a bad idea. It stays loose and the first time she tries to dance up there again she will no doubt fall on her ass and the problem has been addressed.

There are yet other unconscious vandals at work on your piano. Your little cowboy decides to "scale" the piano while dressed in his spurs and boots. There are also those marks left by your teenage daughter who has the latest in three-inch fingernails. They are made of the best and strongest plastic and could easily be used to open shipping crates. These fingernails hit the vertical inner panel just behind the back end of the keys and leave marks that look as though your German Shepherd has been clawing his way into a meat factory.

OK, NO INSURANCE ... WHAT TO DO

Well, the spur marks aren't too deep and the scrape down the side of the leg is only about two inches long. That can be touched up. You are off to the hardware store to get the original "Household Touch-up Kit" for furniture of all kinds and colors. It has about eight or ten assorted sticks in a window package. They are nothing more than stain-colored crayons. They are wax based and you rub them over the scratch after having carefully selected the colored crayon that looks closest to your finish. Only after you have applied it do you realize that it is not quite the same color you had hoped it would be. You color it some more but nothing much changes.

Okay. This is not a big spot. You decide to buy some "liquid satin" stain to clear up this problem. You come home with five small bottles because you couldn't really remember just what color that finish on the piano really was. You apply the paint to the damaged area that you have just colored with the crayon. Now a new problem crops up. The stain will not adhere to that area because you have covered it with wax. The stain runs down the leg to the area with no wax and it does stick to that part. But the stain on that part looks too dark now and besides, some of it has run all the way down to the floor and is dripping on the rug.

Okay. Let's not panic. It's still wet. Should you smear it around with the brush or take a rag and wipe it off and sand that part of the leg where the wax has been applied? Probably best to wipe it off.

Back to the hardware store for some sandpaper. Sandpaper is all the same to you and they have 80-grit automotive paper on sale. You grab a bunch of that and get back to the piano. You rub the leg with the paper and in eight strokes you have bare wood. Not just where the wax had been applied but also four or five inches above and below that spot. Now you definitely have to stain and you do.

You walk away content that this particular desecration has been professionally dealt with. Twelve hours later you notice that you have about ten inches of the leg that does not match. You go ahead and do the only thing that makes sense. Sand and stain the whole outer side of the leg. Turns out nice, even, and glossy. But it doesn't match the rest of the piano. Need I say more? You have done most of this staining in the evenings after work and it isn't until the true light of dawn hits the piano that the real sins appear.

Now you know the inside story about pianos that are blue, red, green and orange or have mirrors or artwork attached to them. Under that camouflage and paint you will find a two-inch scrape.

BOTTOM, BOTTOM-LINE

TELL THE SALESMAN YOU WON'T BUY THE PIANO WITHOUT A SCRATCH AND DENT POLICY. IF HE CAN'T OFFER THAT TO YOU, INSIST ON A SIZEABLE PRICE REDUCTION TO OFFSET BUYING YOUR OWN POLICY. YOU'LL NEVER GET ONE, BUT YOU MAY SAVE ON THE INITIAL PURCHASE.

ASK THE AUTHOR

—

NO. A-374

Dear Don:

I heard a story that white piano keys were originally from the ivory in elephant tusks. If this is true, where do the black keys come from?

~ Curious in Calcutta

Dear Curious:

For many years the white keys were indeed ivory, and the elephant the source. Black ivory used for the other keys came from a farm in New Hampshire owned by Marlon Marketcart. In the 1900s elephants were used to haul coal up from the mines. At some point every one of them developed "Black Tusk" disease and Marlon bought them used. As the elephant was replaced by machines, Marlon went out of business. The black keys on today's pianos are made out of clear plastic resin mixed with licorice pulp and tar.

Note: That is also why there are more white keys on the piano. The black ivory was more rare and expensive.

ASK THE AUTHOR

—

NO. A-380

Dear Don:

I have recently purchased an older model upright piano. I am wondering how I can tell if the white keys are ivory or plastic.

~ Mystified in Melbourne

Dear Mystified:

For a sure-fire solution to this question, take your piano over to a window. Open the window and bring in your garden hose. Let the water run on the keys for about ten minutes. Ivory soaks up water, so in no time the key covering will curl up and fall off. If this occurs, you had ivory.

TOUCH-UP PAINT

Be sure when buying a new piano that you insist on a quart of touch-up paint. Be sure it is for that particular piano. In years gone by this has been a terrific problem. I know a quart sounds like a lot but you may be touching up this piano for twenty or thirty years.

You will find that no major paint or stain manufacturer today can supply "just that color" and you will go nuts trying to mix it yourself. I often wondered why this was so—what made these colors so special? After much research I was able to locate a retired supplier of this product and conduct an exclusive in-depth interview.

In the mountainous area of upper New York State I was afforded an afternoon with Howard Brushbanger. He was a senior partner and C.E.O. of Widdle, Waddle, and Wallow. For eighty-one years this firm was responsible for providing the excellent finishes on the nation's finer pianos.

I cut no corners and went right to the main question.

(DB)   "Why aren't modern paint companies able to duplicate older paint finishes? Their products never match."

(HB)   "Not usin' the right stuff."

(DB)   "What did you use that they don't?"

(HB)   "Whole process at our plant was unique."

(DB)   "How so?"

(HB)   "Today the major companies are all trying to get a good product using synthetic bases. No good."

(DB)   "Would it be out of line to ask what you used?"

(HB)   "Well, since we have sold out the company and I have my money in the bank I guess I can tell you."

(DB)   "I would be forever in your debt."

(HB)   "Up here in the north country we don't have access to a lot of fancy stuff so we created our own blends using what was available. There were only three colors needed in them days. They wanted brown, black and white."

(DB)   "Makes sense. I noticed that those are still the most widely used colors today."

(HB)   "As a base we elected to use bear fur. There were a lot of black and brown bears around and the colors were just what we needed. In addition, the fat gave us a good oil base. Then we experimented and found that ground up bicycle seat covers would give us some texture. We also added fudge brownies without nuts. The frosting seemed to give us the shine we needed and the chocolate acted to neutralize the stink of the bear fat. To get some adhesive qualities to the product we engineered a combination of bubble gum, taffy, tire inner tube repair cement, molasses and owl tears. The owl tears were used to get the proper viscosity. They were probably the hardest thing to procure. Owls don't usually cry unless you tell them they are blind as a bat or you speak rudely about their children. We put all that into a high speed blender for six hours and strained it through nylon panty hose."

(DB) "This is an amazing revelation."

(HB) "At this time we were also dealing with complaints of brush marks left by the piano painters. This of course was prior to the modern spray methods of today. We pioneered a system whereby the finished product coming from the panty hose was diluted with carbonated cola. This added some more color. But first and foremost it allowed the piano companies to set up their first spray operations. We packaged our paints in twelve ounce pop bottles and shipped them that way. All you had to do at the piano factory was pop the cap, put your thumb over the end of the bottle, shake it real good and let it fly! There were some guys with magic thumbs who could lay a gloss coat on a piano in three bottles. Shine so bright it almost glowed in the dark."

(DB) "This is the most amazing and unusual story I have ever heard. Knowing you only had black and brown bears how did you get the white pianos?"

(HB) "Polar bears. But we had to get them from Alaska. The freight charges were outrageous and the fur-to-fat ratio required extra procedures to get what we needed. That's why you don't see many white pianos. Very expensive to paint."

(DB) "What about the occasional, custom color you see from time to time. How did you do that?"

(HB) "Hey, you throw in a couple squirrels or a muskrat and it's gonna give you a new color."

(DB) "What was your biggest challenge while running W.W.W.?"

(HB) "We did a special order for Lady Alexis Trinkwalter Trent of the London Trents. She wanted a yellow piano. We had to grind up 420 canaries, 12 lemons and a school bus fender to get the right mix. Biggest problem was the triple filtering of the canaries to eliminate the beaks, claws, and bones. But I'll tell you this—she wanted a yellow piano and we delivered the color."

(DB) "Amazing. What do you miss most in your retirement?"

(HB) "I would say hunting polar bears and sniffing bicycle seats."

(DB) "I once heard that you made sheet paint. Is this true or just some foolish rumor?"

(HB) "No, that's true. The product didn't last long but we thought we had something good going for us. We put a pile of paint on a table and rolled it into sheets and baked it. Had a nice shine and was easy to package for shipment. The idea was to just cut the sheets to fit the piano and nail it to the case. Eliminated drying time. We ran into problems with bent-over nail heads and seams that didn't match. Occasionally one sheet did not match the next in color either. Stopped that in 1931."

(DB) "Well, thanks for all this information, HB. Do you have any final words for the piano public?"

(HB) "Yes, I do. If you run across an old can of W.W.W. touch-up paint, when you open it don't be surprised if it looks a bit furry before stirring. Hair rises."

ASK THE AUTHOR

—

NO. A450

Dear Don:

Last winter I was given a piano. My husband and I were in the process of remodeling a room for it but it came a bit early. A friend offered to store it in his garage. This spring he cleaned the garage and while burning the trash he also burned the garage down to the ground. He said, "I never dreamed such a thing could happen." Now he wants us to clean up the burned-out piano and get rid of it. He accepts no responsibility. What do we do now?

~ Burned-Out in Beemersville

Dear Burned-Out:

Go over to visit your friend. Tell him you want to talk about the cleanup. Keep him busy while one of you drops a molotov cocktail into his S.U.V. and make sure it's close to the house. When you are sure the house is burning well you can leave, saying, "I never dreamed such a thing could happen." It won't bring back the piano but revenge is sweet and you'll sleep better.

P.S. The fire demolition people will probably take away your piano along with the S.U.V. and the debris from the house.

BUYING AN OUT-OF-TOWN PIANO

In the used car industry many salesmen will tell you: "Hey, this is a Southern car that's never seen snow or salt." Or they may tell you it comes from California or Texas, that it's always been in sunny weather and doesn't have any rust. For some reason buyers are intrigued by something from somewhere else. You know that it is just possible that beneath that shiny, rust-free exterior there lies a car that has had the snot run out of it. Drag racing through the foothills of California or hauling beer across the deserts of Texas at 120 m.p.h. for hours on end. All is never quite what it seems to be.

Believe it or not, people can be convinced that an out-of-town piano is something very special. In one sense this is correct. The thing that is special is that it is very, very far away. Many a piano has been purchased from a photo. Here are some things you may want to consider regarding buying an out-of-town piano.

Typically, you'll find certain things about pianos unique to the areas from which they come. I have chosen a few areas across the United States and outlined a few of the questionable bargains from each.

1. Pianos from California are subjected to constant sunlight. The intense heat will probably dry out all the glue holding the parts together. When it is played it will disintegrate. This instrument could also have been involved in sand and water activities. Water dries but sand is forever!

2. Pianos from the Texas and Oklahoma areas are sometimes used for entertaining crews in the oil fields. They are put inside or near little sheds known as barrel houses where the men gather after work. They rarely get into town while the drilling is in progress. All goes well until the well comes in, then everything for half a mile is covered with crude oil raining down from the skies. This crude oil seems to devalue these pianos while adding a certain unique fragrance at the same time. The pianos become sluggish to play and impossible to wax. If you are buying a piano from this area, beware of the words "SLICK" and "SQUEAK-FREE."

3. Pianos used in and around the logging camps of the great Northwest are apt to be filled with sawdust. They notoriously have ax and chainsaw marks in the woodwork, and the legs may be of various lengths or nonexistent. Be sure to ask if a giant redwood has ever been dropped on the piano at any time. It could make it hard to tune.

4. Pianos from the Midwest farm belt area may contain quantities of grain and may even have nesting grain rats inside. If this piano has been played in the barn

or barnyard it may have an odor which may cause social problems. Pig dung is not an aroma widely accepted at cocktail parties. Unless your housecat is over fifty pounds and a dedicated rat chaser, I would pass on pianos from this area.

5.   Pianos acquired from the Chicago area are specially constructed. In earlier years, especially the 1920s, pianos in nightclubs were forever being destroyed by random machine gun fire. This led to the newer models that were all steel, no wood. This proved to render them virtually indestructible and a purpose was served. However, you may want to make a note that these pianos weigh about three tons. Moving could get expensive and improper care could cause them to rust out.

6.   Pianos from in and around the Wall Street area are all coin operated and are probably owned by the syndicate. Music is secondary to money on Wall Street and nobody wants a piano that can't turn a profit. Be sure you have lots of nickels if you buy one of these; they are all player pianos.

7.   Pianos from New Jersey should be avoided. Anybody who is selling one probably doesn't own it in the first place. The actual owner is probably someone you don't want to get involved with anyway. From the time you send the deposit check until the time you actually show up to inspect the piano, it has probably been crated up and shipped overseas. These pianos give new credence to the term "Family Entertainment."

8.   If you purchase a piano from the Washington, D.C. area you are in for a real tussle. The seller will want to know what political party you are backing and when you made your last contribution. There will also be an added clause in the sales contract (usually thirty-three pages in length) which tells you that the sale of this piano is contingent on the passing of House Bill X4595 which seeks funding for a fish hatchery in Nebraska and a $7 million grant for the research of the night life of the dingo dog. You agree to wait for this bill to pass the President's desk and also agree to be on the steering committee which will eventually travel nationwide to put forth the full revelations of the dingo dog. The piano is red, white and blue and must remain these colors or the sales contract is null and void and you must return it prepaid. You will also pay all legal fees for the drafting of the sales contract as well as the moving of the piano from its current location. You will also agree to display any political signs that refer to the further aspirations of the seller in his quest for any office whatsoever for a period of fifteen years. You'll have to sort this one out for yourself. There must be a better deal somewhere else.

9.   Pianos from the retirement communities of Florida are usually in nice shape. The old folks can't play them very hard and since they are all in bed by 8 P.M. there is little chance that the pianos have many hours on them. The big prob-

lem with these instruments is that many of the seniors who play them are on various medications. Therefore you might find any number of drugs, cigarettes, or needles strapped to the underside or inside of the piano. In the bench you may find some blank prescription forms hidden between the pages of the AARP news magazine. If for some reason you do acquire one of the Florida units and don't make a clean sweep of it with a drug-sniffing narcotics dog, your child or pet could die from an overdose somewhere down the line. On the other hand you may be part of a drug investigation and the DEA might charge you with the interstate transportation of a controlled substance. Therefore, when your piano arrives, don't be surprised to see a car or van from the DEA or Alcohol, Tobacco and Firearms Task Force following your moving van.

ASK THE AUTHOR

—

NO. A356

Dear Don:

I am an amateur banjo player. In my spare time I like to play rolls on my player piano and try to accompany them. Once the roll starts my attention is given to the banjo. Last weekend my daughter's gerbil ran up into the piano and got wound up in the roll. I know this because there is a big bulge in the paper and the tail is hanging out. How do I tell her what happened. It's for sure I'm not going to open up that roll.

~ Rolled Up in Redrock

Dear Rolled Up:

To avoid the pain she might experience just go along with the story that the gerbil somehow ran away or got lost. Do not tell her about the roll. She may want a replacement pet to comfort her. I would recommend a pig, they won't fit in a piano.

BUYING A PLAYER PIANO

When it comes to buying a player piano you are entering a whole new world of confusion and detail. There are thousands of parts on a piano like this, and anything and everything can go wrong. Age is a big factor since pianos—like people—tend to deteriorate with age.

An often asked question is, "How old is this player piano?" Salesmen will tell you that age has no bearing on the condition, but bear in mind it is hard to buy a fender for a 1923 Chevy. Chances are very good that the piano was built in the 1920s. Peak production of the player piano industry came in 1923-1924. Total production for 1923 in the piano industry surpassed 345,000 units and of those—205,000 were players of some sort. The buying public spent over $100 million that year for pianos. The real heyday for player pianos ran from the turn of the century to the Depression 1900-1929. In 1930, sales began to plummet. The advent of radio, talking pictures, and the phonograph cut sharply into the world of the piano—once the home entertainment center. This period also marked the demise of many coin operated pianos in saloons, hotels and other places of entertainment.

People often ask, "What exactly is a player piano and what is the difference between a manual and an electric?"

There is a great difference between manual and electric and if you can get an electric, go for it! Otherwise, you or someone will spend many hours pumping the piano for others to enjoy.

A PLAYER PIANO IS ACTUALLY AN 800-LB. VACUUM CLEANER COVERED WITH SOME TYPE OF ORNAMENTAL WOODEN BOX

If you doubt this statement think about this. In the 1920s, The Regina Company of New York and Chicago was a major manufacturer of player pianos. Today they are known worldwide as a leader in the vacuum cleaner industry.

This contraption plays music but its major function is to inhale dirt and smoke and hide it. I have yet to see an advertisement for dust collector bags for pianos. If you want to know where all that stuff goes, ask the piano tuner; he knows.

Once this instrument is in place, it is impossible to move it unless you schedule a family picnic or hire a professional. If you do not have an electrical piano it means you'll have to pump it with your feet to create the vacuum. The electric motor runs the vacuum pump for you.

So make your primary question prior to purchase: *"WHO'S GONNA PUMP THIS THING?"*

There are physical demands and physical outcomes that must be considered if you are the pumper. First off, you will be sitting for long periods of time. Your feet will get sore, your ankles will swell, and your arches will collapse. Your legs will look like those of an Olympic wrestler. Your butt will balloon so you can only fit on a bench. If you sit on a stool it will actually disappear into the rolls of flesh. You will, however, have to get up and down every time you want to change a roll because the rolls are on top of the piano just out of your reach while seated. This will ruin your back.

Moreover, if you want to master the art of singing along with the rolls you must learn to read vertically, not horizontally as you are accustomed. This is because the words are printed along the edge of the paper rolls and are whizzing by just under the speed of light. The ink is usually faded and in most cases the piano is not located in a well lit area. Therefore you will soon be blind.

You might actually be tempted to learn to play the piano on your own by watching the keys go down and following with your hands. Because you are constantly pushing on the pedals with your feet, you tend to push yourself away from the piano. To offset this situation you hang on to the underside of the piano trying to stay close enough to pump it. Once you figure out how to get your hands on the keys with your arms at full length, you notice that twelve keys are down at one time. No one ever told you that the factory cuts in extra notes. After a while you will lose your mind trying to figure out what to do to play twelve notes.

Once you have found the roll you like the most, it will be the one that will fray most often and the one from which the tab and flap will rip first. It is therefore the one you mend over and over with magic mending tape until you can't understand it anymore or it just won't play at all. This is because all the holes along the edge that you covered with tape used to make it go.

It is also the roll that the makers of new piano rolls no longer stock.

Having given the preceding long thought, you now wonder—if not me, who will play this thing?

Children have the attention span of a gnat. They will tire of the piano in the length of time it takes you to sneeze. You have come to the conclusion that you don't want to put yourself into the position of pumper supreme unless absolutely necessary. WHAT THEN?

Perhaps you have an elderly infirmed relative living with you. They are probably old, dottery and using a cane or a walker. They can't hear well and God knows they can't sing. In many cases they have a feeling of worthlessness or uselessness. Well, here is your chance to solve a problem and be a hero too. Tell them you are buying a player piano for them and that they will be the keeper of the box.

If they are arthritic, tell them it is recommended therapy for their knees and ankles to pump the piano three hours per day. Set up a pill stand next to the piano with water and bourbon. It might be well to include sports cream and oxygen as well. A state-of-the-art electrical blood pressure monitor would be nice—hooked to a siren. This is a good way to monitor their activity for the day. If the piano stops or the siren blows, something's up. Be sure that any bathroom breaks are scheduled to begin exactly on the hour so an intermission will not be a point of alarm. Alzheimer's patients will love this setup because every day the songs will be new again.

Even if you go out shopping, tell them you are in the cellar ironing and you just love the music.

If they complain about the pain tell them that when they get strong again you will convert to electric. It gives them a goal.

You might say this is extreme cruelty. Not so. Hey, they're gonna die from something sometime. Many years from now when you are looking back at the coroner's report, wouldn't it be much more sporting to see:

> CAUSE OF DEATH: RAGTIME PIANO PLAYING, MECHANICAL

If you decide to do this you may want to review their will in advance.

ANOTHER HELPFUL GUIDELINE FOR YOU

If you are looking at a player piano and you see excessive gouges around the bottom of the front legs, watch out. That means the piano is probably very hard to pump and has been used with a set of retention chains. These are chains much like you see on trucks that haul heavy machinery. The chain is placed behind the stool or bench, near the floor, and then fastened to each front leg of the piano. You then adjust the stool or bench to your setting for maximum comfort and leg position. Grasp the chain ends at the piano legs, move the hook along until the chain gets tight, and then hook it back into the chain itself. This insures that the stool or bench cannot slide backwards when you pump. This setup is used when the piano is so hard to pump that you shove yourself away from the piano before any vacuum is generated. It is used in place of locking your hands, palm up, under the piano keyboard until they turn purple or lose feeling.

Another giveaway when you are looking at these pianos is the old "throw rug" trick. If you see a throw rug under the bench or stool, move it aside. There are probably ruts in the floor where the legs have slid back and forth while the pumper fights an endless battle to hold position.

This piano might not be for you.

Note: If the seller mentions anything about using an industrial grade vacuum cleaner to assist you, pass on this piano.

A LITTLE KNOWN FACT

As is always the case when something is hot, others will try to copy a product to exploit the craze. One such item—although short-lived—was the player tuba. A spin off from the player piano era, it was originally conceived by Hans Valvepounder, and briefly manufactured by Heidelberg Wind Works in Germany.

This instrument had a dual mouthpiece. The player sucked in on one mouthpiece to create a vacuum. At the same time he was sucking, he was cranking a small two-inch paper roll which passes over a brass tracking bar. The holes in the roll allowed the vacuum to pull down the proper valve and thereby designate the note. The actual air flow to produce the sounds from the horn was supplied by two compressed air bottles strapped to the player's back. This air was forced into the second mouthpiece. Early on it was thought that it was easier for the player to suck and the tanks to blow. Later it became clear that even when the player wasn't sucking, the tanks were still blowing. Thus the tuba played incessantly until the backpack regulator valve was closed. In final assessment of the invention, aside from the tanks, the whole thing sucked.

The eventual downfall of this system came when some backpack tanks were filled with hydrogen and exploded during a concert. The tubist was killed on the spot, some of the band members and audience were burned, and the horn itself melted away.

SORT OF A BABY HINDENBURG.

OTHER THINGS TO BEWARE OF WHEN BUYING

When buying a piano it is important to look inside. If it is a grand piano, make sure the seller has not nailed the top down for some reason. Shine a flashlight inside if necessary.

FIVE THINGS TO LOOK FOR INSIDE THE PIANO:

1. Strings
2. Hammers
3. Iron harp structure
4. Tuning pins
5. Cleanliness

FIVE THINGS THAT SHOULD NOT BE IN YOUR PIANO:

1. Concrete
2. Fire brick
3. Moss or grass of any kind
4. Body parts of any sort
5. Any creature or critter, living or dead

BEWARE of any piano listed in ads as "handyman special" or may need "some work."

BEWARE of pianos that are not original wood. If the piano is purple, aqua, red, blue, or any shade of orange and has PEACE signs all over it, it may have been refinished.

BEWARE of pianos that are attractively priced but are located in an area that just had a major flood.

BEWARE of salesmen selling old player pianos with a voice track. Old roll pianos cannot sing.

BEWARE of a player piano that can only be operated when hooked to an industrial vacuum cleaner running at full speed—also any player piano that begins to smoke after the third roll.

BEWARE of pianos that have worn keys. The white keys could have a leading edge sharper than a Wilkinson sword and the black keys are probably "dished" from excessive use. Also check to see if the last tuner left his business card inside. If it is dated in Roman numerals, forget that piano. If the front panel above the keyboard is a wood carving of the Last Supper the piano is old. Look on the bottom of the stool legs. The feet should be claw type construction holding glass balls. If the feet are holding marble, the piano is too old.

BEWARE of a salesman who tells you this piano is a fine antique. This is a fancy term for very old. If you are a bona fide collector or a dealer in period furnishings, you may find some success in dealing with these items. If you are merely trying to get a piano at a reasonable price, this field is not for you. Any story that might crop up about this instrument is usually a fabrication designed to stimulate your imagination and inflate the price. You should equate buying a piano from these people with buying fresh fish from a truck with Nebraska license plates.

BEWARE of pianos known as "signature pianos." These are pianos that may have been played or owned by anyone your salesman can convince you was a celebrity. They may further try to convince you that this piano may have been connected with a certain event, movie or play. The player or celebrity may have signed the inside of the piano after such an event and thereby increased its value. There are those who are mesmerized by celebrities and willing to pay much more than necessary to procure the piano.

These folks are akin to the guy who buys a rotted out DeSoto for $17,500 because forty-nine years ago Marilyn Monroe sat on the passenger seat for a ten minute ride in a movie. Some people are prone to paying preposterous prices for nostalgia. DON'T GET HOOKED.

In some cases, pianos used by celebrities are returned to the factory and rebuilt, eliminating the possibility of someone making a fast buck on that rig. If in fact you do stumble across a "signature piano" or an "event piano," here are some things you'll want to keep in mind.

1. Who signed it? Are they really that important?

2. If the signature is accompanied by a date, make sure the person was alive on that date.

3. If the name of the celebrity is misspelled, watch out!

4. If the name is printed in crayon you're probably getting screwed.

5. Check the serial number of the piano. If it was built in 1980 and signed in 1952, watch out!

6. If the signature is smeared or worn down so it is no longer legible and some salesperson or owner is telling you what it says, it probably doesn't say that at all.

7. If they tell you the piano is pre-1700, forget it. The piano wasn't even invented yet.

8. There was no piano in the employees' lounge on the Mayflower.

9.   No pianos survived the Titanic.

10. George Washington did not authorize a piano to be used for troop moral while crossing the Delaware.

11. No pianos survived Hiroshima.

12. No pianos came out of the burning of Atlanta.

13. No pianos from the Mustang Ranch in Virginia City, Nevada are available. The government sold them at auction and they were snatched up by other brothels.

14. Any piano that supposedly was played by Harry Truman should be destroyed. It has gone through enough.

15. And last but not least, be sure the person you are dealing with is reputable. Check their business card. If they also sell ferris wheels, solar flashlights or vacant land in New Jersey, pianos may not be their main interest.

Let me tell you about some of the most recent piano sales scams. These situations may not be real and neither are the pianos which were purportedly involved.

1.   If you come across a piano with a missing chunk, filled with seaweed and other ocean species, even though they say it is signed by Roy Schieder, avoid it. If you look closely at the original Jaws movie when they open the belly of the shark, no piano came out. Even though they are telling you this is the one, it is more likely the badly abused piano from somebody's pool-side bar.

2.   If you come across a piano with bullet holes supposedly signed by Clyde Barrow, remember that Bonnie Parker and Clyde Barrow did not begin a relationship because she admired the way he played jazz piano. This piano was probably in a hunting camp down South. It rained all weekend and the eight guys who were holed up in the lodge decided to have a few drinks. They then proceeded to see who could shoot the most stuff inside the building without killing anybody. Avoid this piano.

3.   Be very careful not to buy any piano made by Arlene and Frank's Piano Company in Flintlock, Mississippi. You are surely dealing with the bottom of the line. We know of only six that were ever built so the serial number should be short. There is another dead giveaway on these units. The outside wood still has the bark on it. Also, it is a rumor that their factory, located on the edge of a swamp, had a noticeable slant to the entire floor. All their pianos were built level to the slant so if you do get one and you take it home and put it on a level floor it will lean three inches to the left.

Four of these pianos have 88 keys, one has 83 keys and the remaining one (s/n unknown) has 76 keys and a cup holder to fill the void at the right end of the keyboard. We are not sure whether this was a math problem, a material shortage, a Friday-produced piano or just a stab at some subtle new innovation. It is unique.

It is well to note that on these pianos all pedals are from 1973 and 1974 Pontiacs (probably to make people feel more at home). All six are of the upright configuration and all the benches are covered with alligator skin. We have pointed out this particular series of pianos as a DO NOT BUY item because the factory has since been turned into a full-time still and we fear you may have trouble getting parts and/or service. You should purchase at your own risk.

NEVER buy a piano that has been stamped "FACTORY SECOND." That is like buying a car with no engine and having the salesman tell you it is very special because only a few of them got out of the plant that way. Your "FACTORY SECOND" piano will probably have no strings or hammers.

FINANCING THE PIANO

*"You don't pay...
it goes away."*

FINANCING THE PIANO

You and your wife have made the decision to buy a new piano. It is a major investment akin to appliances or new furniture, and at $7200 it may even be as big as that used Plymouth you recently purchased as a second car. But you have three talented daughters who all show interest in music. They are 8, 9, and 11 and old enough to take lessons and know what the teacher is saying. Secretly you might even take a whack at the piano yourself.

This money thing needs some talking out. You have a savings account and a checking account but taking this much from either one would inflict a severe reduction and your plan for rainy day emergency cash would be compromised. You also have a modest stock portfolio but you don't want to disturb that because it may be the stepping stone to college for the girls. Therefore, you consider the next alternative—financing. Since your accounts have been at FIRST CONSOLIDATED MORTGAGE, SAVINGS AND FINANCE (FCMSF) for almost twelve years, your instinct tells you to go there. As a depositor you should get some kind of help on your deal.

Rodney Zippernipper, your piano salesman, had mentioned some "in-house financing" available through the Piano Manufacturer's Guild but you cannot believe that he could come up with a deal as appealing as the one put forth by your own personal bank. You arrange a time for meeting with the bank. They will see you this Friday at 2 P.M.

Friday turns out to be a beautiful day, and you and your wife arrive at the bank at the pre-arranged time. You had a nice ride over there and are very upbeat about this meeting. You are met by the young lady seated at the front desk "up on the platform." She is apparently the receptionist. That area called "up on the platform," refers to the area in the bank which is eight inches higher than the rest of the floor. When you step up there you are led to believe that you have entered some kind of magical kingdom of the super intelligent and forceful hierarchy of the banking world. In fact, the only reason that area is raised is because they have all the wooden desks there and they want to protect them in case of a flood. The carpet is there because the bank tried to cut costs when they built the facility and the raised area was built with used lumber. When it was done it looked like shit. The solution: Some indoor/outdoor carpet to cover it up. It's cheaper than new wood.

The gal at the reception desk is a recent high school graduate. She knows nothing about banking and did not have an academic record enabling her to move on to college. Her uncle Harry is the security guard and his wife Myrt used to be a teller in the bank. She took early retirement on disability after she accidentally set off a dye bomb placed in a "bait bundle"—a cash package given to robbers during a holdup. Her vision is shot and her face and hair are permanently purple. She and Harry used some leverage to get their niece this job.

You take a seat next to her desk while she is on the phone. As you read her name-plate you hope that it does not forecast any upcoming events for the day.

It reads, "KREATA KRISIS" - RECEPTIONIST

She completes her call and gives you her best smile.

"How may I help you?"

"Mr. and Mrs. Needlerammer. We have a two o'clock appointment to see someone about a loan."

"Certainly, I'll see who is available."

She once again lifts the phone to her ear, pushes a button and relays your message to someone on the other end. Placing her phone back on the cradle she flashes you another of those smiles—the kind you see in toothpaste commercials when they hire a girl who doesn't have to say anything.

"If you will follow me please, I will show you to our loan department."

As you and your wife follow her, you notice that she has all the right clothes in all the right places and her long legs add to the fashion statement as well. Your wife gives you a jab in the side.

"For God's sake Arnie. You're staring at her like you never saw a pair of legs like them before in your life."

"I was just thinking the same thing," you answer with a smile.

You arrive at a cubicle with four-foot wooden walls topped off with three additional feet of frosted glass. Miss Krisis directs you to be seated in a pair of leather arm chairs positioned across from the empty seat at the desk. She turns on heel and you watch her stride off majestically as she returns to her post.

You have a few moments to take in the appointments of the office. One filing cabinet, one desk, one computer station, one credenza, four chairs, and an endless theme of golf throughout. There are trophy cups, photos of all sizes, and a golden golf club mounted on some sort of wooden plaque that decorates the wall behind you. There is even a golf ball ashtray. On the top of the credenza there is a tray with a glass water pitcher and four glasses. They are all adorned with the crest of THE SUNNYWOODS GOLF CLUB under which is a banner that reads TOURNAMENT ALL STARS 1999. They are resting on a patch of bright green imitation grass placed in the tray. A good looking man of about sixty strolls through the doorway into the office. You know he did not get that suntan by driving to work with the top down. Quickly you identify him as the man in the photos, surrounded by dignitaries and golf pros.

"Hello folks, my name is Oswald Fundgrabber. I am a senior loan officer with this branch and I'll try to help you."

In twelve years with the bank you have never heard of this man. He has your banking records in a file folder that he opens up on his desk. Peering through a pair of low riding spectacles, he spends a minute perusing the information therein. Everything seems to be in relatively good shape and he asks, "What can I do for you today?"

You pull out your envelope from the piano store and hand it to him. At the same time you tell him that you would like to finance a piano. In the next thirty seconds he quickly reads the notations on the piano forms and appears to become just a bit nervous. You try to make idle chit-chat to level the playing field because you are nervous also.

"I see that you are an avid golfer."

"Yes, I am very involved in the game. Since my wife passed on it has become my passion in life. Do you folks play?"

Neither of you has ever swung a golf club and there is no use trapping yourself in a lie.

"No, I'm afraid not. With all the rigors of my job and raising three children we have never had time to get involved in golf."

Any avenue of communications which you may have had with Mr. Fundgrabber has just closed. All he knows about or cares about is golf. You two don't golf so now you are just two bodies taking up his time. There are several reasons for him to feel on edge.

1.   It is a beautiful 80° summer afternoon. The only reason he is sitting here with you is that he has been filling in this week for two people on vacation. This will end in two hours.

2.   His main prowess in this branch is the underwriting of mortgages, industrial loans and some auto loans. He views a piano loan just as he would a powerboat, a motor home, a jetski, a motorcycle or a skidoo. Just another toy that will have to be repossessed in a short period of time as the novelty wears off.

3.   Finally, he'd rather be golfing. He is not going to tell you, but frankly he doesn't care if this deal flies or not. For the little commission he might receive it is a pain in the ass. He runs his hand through his combed back gray hair.

"A piano loan, eh?"

"Yes sir. A brand new Clapsaddle 88 Spinet," you say to him proudly.

"I see. Give me a minute to put a few things together."

He spins around to the computer and types in a few things. Some ledger configurations appear on the screen. He scans your dealer's letter and then types some more. He punches up the printer and a form comes out. Your price at the dealer was $7020 for the piano. You notice here that the face value of the loan is in the amount of $8000. You look over the breakdown sheet.

FCMSF - FORM 433

NO DOWN PAYMENT LOAN BREAKDOWN (Value $8000)
ITEM: 1999 CLAPSADDLE 88 KEY SPINET PIANO   s/n CS8444X

ACCOUNTING OF CHARGES TO BE APPLIED

ITEM AND DESCRIPTION	COST TO BUYER (This you see)	COST TO BANK (This you don't see)
1. Piano	7300	7020
2. Shipping	175	100
3. Administration	110	50
4. Graft (shown as GR)	200	–
5. Kickback/Dlr. (shown as KB)	100	50
6. Bad debt Cushion	90	–
7. Miscellaneous	25	–
	$8000	$7220

You pass this paper on to your wife and continue your dialogue with Mr. Fundgrabber. Not wanting to rock the boat just yet, you ask him what terms are available.

"Oh, on things like this the bank is very liberal. We can stretch the payments out to ten or fifteen years. It'll make it very affordable."

That word affordable makes it sound nice so you ask him to draw up the agreement. Also you mention to him that you'd like the weekend to think this over.

"Why certainly. Why don't you have a seat in the reception area? I'll get right on this and you should have papers in hand and be out the door in about fifteen minutes.

You and your wife make your way back to the reception area to wait for your contract. "Legs" Krisis is there and she flashes you yet another all-American smile as you take your seats. Her desk has a full cover on the front and you realize from where you are you can no longer see her pretty legs. Your wife makes note of that as well. YOU BET SHE DOES! Having little else to do you look at the document that he gave you in the office. You have a feeling he has already jumped on your bones for $780 but you will hold that thought aside until you see the full proposal.

As promised, the paperwork arrives at the front desk. It is not delivered by Mr. Fundgrabber but rather by a clerk showing complete neutrality on the issue.

"I have the Needlerammers' proposal here. Are you they?"

"Yes, thank you."

Since you will be reviewing this over the weekend there is no rush to look at it right now. You take the envelope, smile at Miss Krisis and are on your way. As you shut the door behind you your wife speaks up for the first time.

"You know that club-swinging faggot is sticking it to us, don't you?"

"Now dear, let's not be hasty to judge until we have seen the whole proposal."

Friday night after dinner you have a chance to open the package. The first thing you see on top is a big thank you slinger showing two hands clenched in a handshake. The caption reads: "PARTNERS IN YOUR EVERY NEED!"

Under that there is a fluorescent banner which proclaims the news that every person who receives a loan also receives a gift.

> LOANS TO $10,000 . . . . . Wall calendar and pen set.
>
> LOANS OVER $10,000 . . . . 12-volt electric toaster which can be plugged into your car's cigarette lighter for doing bagels or muffins on your way to work or play.

Attached to the slinger is a handwritten note which reads: "From the desk of O. U. FUNDGRABBER." Written is: "Given your long relationship with F.C.M.S.F., you have earned the status of preferred customer. For that reason I have selected three separate proposals for your review. I hope you will find one of them to be within your budgetary guidelines and that F.C.M.S.F. will be favored with your new business in the very near future." It is signed: "Best-O.U.F." On yet another piece of paper with bank heading you find the following:

RATE STRUCTURE – NO DOWN PAYMENT LOAN – VALUE $8000 – PIANO

> Item 1: 10 years at 10% . . . . . 120 pymts . . . . . . $105.72 ea.
> Item 2: 12 years at 11% . . . . . 144 pymts . . . . . . $100.28 ea.
> Item 3: 15 years at 12% . . . . . 180 pymts . . . . . . $ 96.01 ea.

You go to your little desk in the front hall and pull out the pocket calculator. Punch a few numbers. HOLY SHIT!

> DEAL #1 = $12,686   DEAL #2 = $14,440   DEAL #3 = $17,281

Having seen this as the opening salvo you cannot imagine what else could be in the agreement, so you and your wife read it.

PURCHASE AGREEMENT – PIANO

THIS AGREEMENT, MADE THIS_____ DAY OF_____, 20 _____ BETWEEN

THE LENDER___F.C.M.S.D.___ AND THE PIANOEE:

NAME_____ SS#_____

ADDRESS _____ PHONE _____

CITY_____ STATE_____ ZIP _____

SHALL CONSTITUTE THE FULL AGREEMENT AS SET FORTH HEREIN.

F.C.M.S.D. reserves the right to do anything they want to, any time they want to. Pianoee agrees. Piano at all times shall be located at the pianoee's address. Buyer agrees to install and maintain an electronic leg monitor on the piano to insure lender that the piano shall not leave the premises. Pianoee agrees that piano will be operated by competent persons in a professional manner and further agrees that any and all maintenance and/or repairs shall be solely his responsibility. Buyer also agrees that once each year (annually) the loan officer may summon the piano to his home on any date he decides. Pianoee agrees to deliver and pick up said piano within 500 miles of his domicile having been served with a 24-hour notice to do so. In the event that said loan officer cannot coordinate use of the piano at their residence, the pianoee agrees to hold a party at his residence with 24 hours prior notice. The group to attend shall not exceed 250 persons and said function shall not exceed 72 hours. All food, beverage, catering, valet service and janitorial requirements shall be borne by the pianoee. Said pianoee further agrees to hold harmless the loan officer and any and all persons attending said function any damage, police action or theft. In the event of a major fire, lender agrees to reimburse pianoee in a sum not to exceed $100 (one hundred dollars) to help offset the deductible on the homeowner's policy. Said policy will be on file with lender at all times in an amount not below $1 million. Loan officer further stipulates that F.C.M.S.D. shall at no time incur any moving charges. Upon default of payment, a monthly late charge of $375 per month shall apply.

Failure to make payments for a period of 90 days or more shall be grounds for repossession and pianoee agrees to underwrite all legal and moving charges associated with same. Monthly payments of $_____ shall commence 30 days from the date of this agreement whether the piano has been received or not.

F.C.M.S.D. _____ PIANOEE _____

DATE_____ DATE_____

CO-SIGNER #1_____

CO-SIGNER #2_____

CO-SIGNER #3_____

CO-SIGNER #4_____

CO-SIGNER #5_____

THIS CONTRACT WAS BROUGHT BEFORE ME BY THE ABOVE-SIGNED PIANOEE WHO DID SWEAR THAT HE IS THAT PERSON TO WHICH I HAVE AFFIXED MY SEAL OF NOTARY PUBLIC TO ATTEST TO SAME.

NOTARY _____ DATE _____

MY TERM EXPIRES ON _____

NOTICE: THIS AGREEMENT SHALL BECOME BINDING ONLY AFTER REVIEW AND RATIFICATION OF THE CONTENTS BY THE LEGAL FIRM OF:

FLINTPICKER, SAPSUCKER, MOTHERGRINDER, TANNENBAUM AND SMITH.

NOTICE: A .05% INCREASE IN THE CONSUMER PRICE INDEX GIVES THE LENDER THE RIGHT TO MODIFY ANY INTEREST RATES INCLUDED IN THIS AGREEMENT WITHOUT NOTICE TO PIANOEE. PIANOEE AGREES TO PAY SAID MODIFIED INTEREST WITHOUT CONTEST.

NOTICE: THIS AGREEMENT DOES NOT APPLY TO BENCHES OR STOOLS WHICH ARE CONSIDERED A RISK ITEM AND ARE DEEMED "SEPARATE EQUIPMENT" AND ARE UNDERWRITTEN UNDER A SEPARATE AGREEMENT WHICH CAN THEN BE AFFIXED HERETO. INTEREST RATES ON STOOLS AND BENCHES MAY VARY FROM THAT WHICH APPLIES TO THE PIANO PROPER.

It is clear to you both that Mr. Fundgrabber is really trying to hustle you. It is apparent that he thinks when it comes to buying a toy, the average Joe will sign anything just to get that item into his possession.

When looking at your loan agreement you begin to ponder. You have had your checking account and savings account at this bank for twelve years. They have been paying you about 5% on your money. You have decided not to disturb these accounts in case of an emergency and now you are looking for a loan. However, it is evident that while F.C.M.S.D. has been paying you about 5%, they are now offering it back to you at 10-12%. Why does this bother you? Does the word RAPE flash into your mind? One full night with no sleep can often alert you that something is wrong. Could it be that Mr. Fundgrabber thinks you are dense? Could it be that sometime in the past he made an improper loan and is trying to use you to recover funds, or is he just plain practicing paper prostitution? And what is this little pink Stick-It paper on the second page of the contract? "BE SURE TO GET YOUR SEPARATE PAPERWORK ON THE BENCH!" What's that all about anyway?

The absurd wording of the contract combined with the very high payback schedule now motivates you to see if the piano guy can get you financed. On Saturday you call your salesman, Rodney Zippernipper, to see what can be done to improve your position. He tells you that all their finance agreements go through the Piano Builder's Guild. They have a specific agency which handles all that type of work. He would be happy to set up a meeting to see what can be done. Unfortunately, when you were berating the bank you mentioned that they were loaning you $8000.

Later that afternoon Mr. Zippernipper calls back and has arranged for a meeting. Since you already took a half day off on Friday he has honored your request for an evening meeting on Monday. The appointment will be at the Atcheson Bar & Grille on Second Street. You know the area and agree.

After what seems like a twelve-hour day at work filled with flashbacks of Mr. Fundgrabber and his dumb-ass golf trophies, you arrive at the meeting place at 5:45 P.M. Mr. Zippernipper is there with two other men. One of whom is N. Zero Farnsworth Jr., branch manager for Razzledazzle Guarantee. For some reason you identify him almost immediately. Ah yes, recent news coverage of his sketches. These were not sketches that he did, but rather those of a courtroom artist during the Farnsworth trial. It seems that he was recently accused of armored car robbery. He did not steal any money, just the armored car. He told authorities he thought it would make a nice motor home for his brother-in-law. In subsequent arrangements Farnsworth agreed to clean the judge's swimming pool for two years free of charge. In return for this, the felony charge of "grand theft auto" was reduced to a traffic violation of "following too closely."

Mr. Farnsworth introduces you to a well-tanned Southerner, Ronnie Bob Shortwit. Mr. Shortwit will be in charge of your account should you decide to go with this loan company. Mr. Shortwit begins his dialogue about the loan firm. The parent company was founded in 1874 in Utah to help finance a fleet of birch bark canoes for some Indian uprising. Through shrewd management and proper loan practices, the company has now gone nationwide. It is a front runner in the financing of hot air balloons, portable rest rooms, public fountains, toxic waste processing equipment and pianos. It is no secret that they want your business and that they can better the bank's proposition. If you are interested, the papers can be drawn up and signed this evening. Their law firm is located in the very next block and is open until 8 P.M.

The Jack Daniel's is flowing, the bottle is on the table, and you knock back a few with the group. Besides being tired, you just want to get this whole deal behind you so you agree to meet with the lawyer and see the package. Mr. Shortwit smiles showing his eighty-five perfect teeth and now takes off his aviator sunglasses and pops them into the pocket of his lime-colored leisure suit. Add to that the three rings on his fingers and the dark green alligator shoes and you have the portrait of a salesman. As weird as it sounds you feel more at home already. He tells you how happy you will be with the loan company while he continually runs his comb through a pile of sun-bleached blonde hair. He has yet to make eye contact with you since removing his glasses, but at this stage you really don't care.

"Drink up and let's get this done," he announces.

About this time Mr. Farnsworth is approached by an over endowed and apparently undereducated young lady. She whispers in his ear and he excuses himself and accompanies her to a spot at the bar. This indicates to you that his priorities have changed and he feels no further involvement is needed on his part. In less than a minute you and your two remaining friends are passing through the doorway into the night. You walk a short block past closed shops and a drugstore. Now you are in front of a very old red brick building—obviously of landmark status. You enter and climb the stairs.

Out of breath, you arrive at a pair of tall, wide oak doors with frosted glass windows. Professional black and gold lettering tells you that you are about to enter the nerve center of the law firm of Waterford, Waterpick, Waterslide, Waterman and Cavanaugh. The two men with you enter first, even though you are the customer. Just a minor indication of their social graces. It is after 7 P.M. and all the desks in the reception area are deserted. The absence of ringing phones, office machine noises, and people milling about lends an eerie feeling to this setting. Half of the lights above your head are turned off in an alternate pattern which only furthers the shadowy effect of everything in the room.

You look around for some stately man in a three piece suit to enter the picture. Instead, you are greeted by a short Chinese man named Ling Fong. He is attired in dungarees, tennis shoes, and a T-shirt which reads: "Class of '88 - Canton University." You can only assume that this does not refer to Canton, Ohio. You know his full name is probably not Waterfong and you wonder how he ever got into the firm. He is smiling ear to ear and the rest of his face is covered with a pair of oversized black rimmed glasses.

You are escorted down a hallway to a small conference room with a circular wooden table and six chairs. In the event you take the deal, Mr. Zippernipper has already faxed all pertinent information ahead and the loan agreement is on the table at various locations. You are shown to the seat where the original copy has been placed. Mr. Shortwit scans the one-page contract, Mr. Fong is still giving everyone a big smile, and Mr. Zippernipper excuses himself to the men's room as you start to read the agreement.

Seeing that you will save a few bucks with this deal as opposed to the bank proposal of last Friday, you nod to Mr. Shortwit. He nods to Mr. Fong, who then nods to you and says, "Please, you sign three places."

This is the first time he has spoken and you will not hear much more from him tonight. On the last line of the contract there is a notation—subject to the approval of the law firm. You ask him if someone is here to approve it tonight.

Mr. Fong smiles, nods and says, "Please, you sign three places."

LOAN COMPANY AGREEMENT

DATE:_____   CONTRACT NO._____

WE/US:_____RAZZLEDAZZLE GUARANTEE_____

YOU: _____

AMOUNT: _____$8000_____   REPAY: _____$10,099.44_____

MONTHS: _____72 at $140.27_____

INTEREST RATE:__Doesn't matter, you'll like it._____

LATE CHARGE:__Physical_____

ITEM: _____Piano and stool, brown_____

AGREEMENT:____We own it 'till you buy it. You don't pay, it goes away.__

FOR RAZZLEDAZZLE:_____

DATE: _____

YOU: _____

DATE: _____

WARNING:	FAILURE TO MAKE TIMELY PAYMENTS COULD RESULT IN UNSCHEDULED ORTHOPEDIC INTERVENTIONS.

OUR MOTTO: **PROMPTNESS IS WELLNESS**

APPROVED BY: _____

LAW FIRM: WATERFORD, WATERMAN, WATERPICK, WATERSLIDE
             and CAVANAUGH

Mr. Shortwit intercedes with this swashbuckle approach and says to you, "No sweat, my man. Sign on the dotted line and first thing in the morning, Mr. Haverstraw, the senior legal man, will rubber stamp this ASAP."

There is little else to do. You are going for it and you sign three copies as asked. You slide them over to Mr. Shortwit, he scribbles his name on the bottom and slides them over to Mr. Fong. Mr. Zippernipper is apparently out of the loop since he never sat down again. Fong looks at the signatures and with a full faced smile looks at you and says, "Okay, Joe." Your name is not Joe but you figure it would take all night to teach him to say, "Thank you Mr. Needlerammer."

All parties rise and as you glide towards the door Mr. Fong bows to you and says, "Thank you for signing three places, please."

Just before exiting into the hall you notice a large glass-covered photo poster. It must be three feet wide by four feet tall. It is of the mysterious Mr. Fong. On top he is shown in the kitchen of some restaurant, surrounded by people all dressed in cooks uniforms, as he is. In the lower half you see him in a suit, standing in front of the White House with a small American flag in his hand and that big disarming smile. Under these pictures is the inscription: "You've come a long way, baby."

You trundle down the stairs behind the other two. Outside the building you ask Mr. Shortwit when you will get your funds.

"You'll never actually see them. They go directly to the piano store and they will call you when the deal is in place."

Mr. Zippernipper and Mr. Shortwit exchange comments about how well the deal went and they decide to go back to the Acheson Bar & Grille. Mr. Shortwit thinks there is some early evening action. It is evident that you have not been invited and you begin to wonder how much you would have had to spend to get "in with the guys." They bid you good night and thanks as they stroll away down the street at a pace guaranteed to distance themselves from you in short order.

You walk slowly back to your '86 Plymouth. You gaze at it and smile. If all goes well you'll soon have two cars and a piano. It is a moot point that your car is worth only half the price of a new piano. You head for home knowing that you have some of your own Jack Daniel's there. And you won't have to share it with anyone.

On the drive home you can't help but wonder if perhaps, through some sort of wartime mix-up, there may have been a Ling Waterfong.

After arriving home and informing your wife that the deal is now in place you both kick back on the couch with some Jack Daniel's on the rocks. Although it is summer you can't help but enjoy the fireplace. After all, you're burning the agreement from Mr. Fundgrabber. What could be nicer?

THE MOVERS

*"Excuse me, ma'am,
does your husband have
a chain saw?"*

THE MOVERS

The piano was invented in 1700. It was heavy then and it's still heavy today.
Thus, piano movers have been at their craft for 300 years.
But some people still think they can beat these guys at their own game.

After the first 200 years piano moving became simpler. A device called "The Atwood Piano Loader" was sold as an attachment to the Model T Ford. You removed the rear seat from the touring car, laid the piano on its back and strapped it down. The idea was a simple one, patented in 1917. You backed up to the backside of an upright piano, strapped it to a couple of the posts, and using a crank and two cables, rolled the piano up onto the deck of the car where it laid flat. One person could do this in a jiffy and piano salesmen could now take their pianos anywhere. Just pull up on the driveway or lawn, unload the piano to its upright position and you could demonstrate it right there.

So who did away with this rig? The unions? The truckers? Nowadays you have two or three guys on a $50,000 van using all sorts of ramps, blocks, dollies and straps. Hydraulic liftgates are also a popular item. In the days of that Model T gadget you could buy the Model T for $400, the attachment for another $65 and you were in business. Today, if you want a piano moved you will pay $100 and up. That means in five moves you could own the Ford and the Atwood free and clear.

Note: There was also a competitive loader put out by the Bowen Company in North Carolina, but it cost $95. Granted, it did come with a fine waterproof moving cover.

Since the Atwood and Bowen loaders are history, let's peek in on the mover of today.

The professional mover has an enclosed truck. As previously stated, this rig is equipped with ramps, piano boards, dollies and straps. There are also moving pads and tie-down arrangements inside the van to secure the piano while in transit. It is a properly equipped vehicle.

The moving man is either an independent who makes his living moving all sorts of things or he is operating a truck owned by the piano store itself. He will usually have one helper and, when circumstances warrant, may have two. The professional mover is a seasoned veteran of the trade and knows all the tricks of how to get the big and heavy objects into the most challenging places. He is even able to do piano "hoisting" when the piano must go through a window many floors up. This person has been educated through on-the-job experience and knows the risks as well as the tricks of the trade.

I have hired many piano movers in my lifetime and have met some excellent men—courteous, efficient and reasonable. It has been a pleasure to do business with them and interesting to watch them work.

After hiring that many piano movers I can tell you that some movers are just experimenting with your piano, hauling pianos around on rigs that in some cases defy description. Let's outline some of the things you should watch for when hiring your piano mover. The first time you see your piano mover might be the day he pulls up to your driveway. Be sure to look at his truck! It's IMPORTANT!

CHECK THE TRUCK

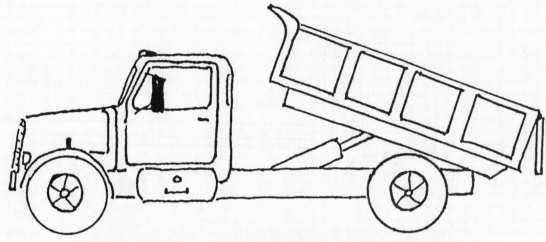

This is a DUMP TRUCK!
Wrong Application

Dump trucks are used for the construction and road-building industry. They also work in landscaping and highway maintenance operations. They have no place in the piano moving business because once they dump your piano on the driveway it will need to be rebuilt. You will also have to shovel up whatever else was in the dump box before they put your piano in there.

CHECK THE TRUCK

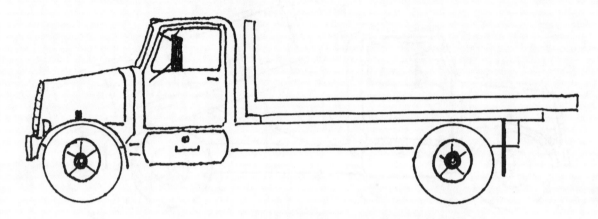

This is a **FLAT TRUCK!**
Not a Hot Setup

Flat trucks are used to move all sorts of things (except pianos). They haul stuff like heavy machinery, steel, pipe, lumber, etc.

NOTE: There are no sides and no protection from the weather. The piano will probably have to be laid down and chained to the deck. Not ideal for high-gloss wood finishes. Unless there is a ramp, your piano will get shoved off the rear and drop four feet to the ground. You may also encounter grease and other contaminants from the deck.

CHECK THE TRUCK

This is a TOW TRUCK!
Totally Wrong

Unless you are trying to get your piano delivered for free by charging it to your auto club emergency service card, this truck has no place within a mile of your piano. The tow truck is also known as a wrecker! The piano maker has made no provisions for a hook. These trucks deal in brute force using cables and chains. However, it might be okay if you are lowering your piano into a thirty-foot pit to play for a snake convention.

CHECK THE TRUCK

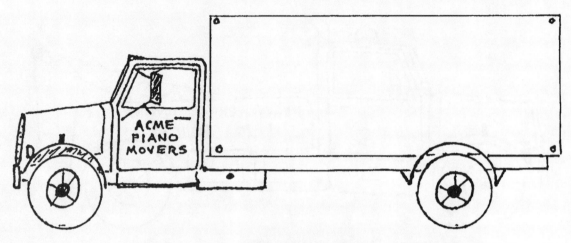

This is a MOVING VAN!
Now You're Talkin'

This is an enclosed, clean, weatherproof van; the choice of thousands of piano movers worldwide. Your piano can be hauled in a professional manner, oftentimes on air ride suspension, and delivered unmarked to your home. The cargo body has ample room to carry all the equipment necessary to handle the move after the van arrives. You are heading in the right direction if you see this type of truck delivering your piano.

CHECK THE TRUCK DOORS

Many times just reading the company name and/or advertisement on the cab door will give you a hint of their specialty. Be sure to do this before the delivery starts.

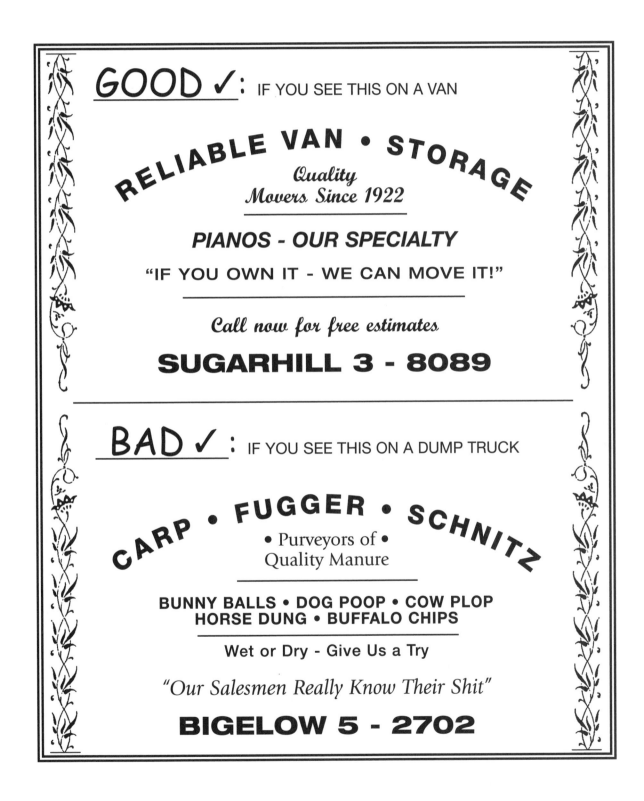

GOOD ✓: IF YOU SEE THIS ON A VAN

RELIABLE VAN • STORAGE

Quality
Movers Since 1922

PIANOS - OUR SPECIALTY

"IF YOU OWN IT - WE CAN MOVE IT!"

Call now for free estimates

SUGARHILL 3 - 8089

BAD ✓: IF YOU SEE THIS ON A DUMP TRUCK

CARP • FUGGER • SCHNITZ

• Purveyors of •
Quality Manure

BUNNY BALLS • DOG POOP • COW PLOP
HORSE DUNG • BUFFALO CHIPS

Wet or Dry - Give Us a Try

"Our Salesmen Really Know Their Shit"

BIGELOW 5 - 2702

You know if your piano is in the back of a U-Haul trailer or a pickup truck that the mover is either just beginning or is in the last stages of bankruptcy.

Movers are usually dressed neatly in a uniform or jeans. Some, however, prefer to expose a wide range of tatoos and chest hair as well as pony tails, beards, mustaches and sideburns. I count the appearance of the mover as 25%. The language and conversation that occurs goes for another 25%, and the actual technique and efficiency will make up the last 50%. In all fairness, the customer sometimes provokes a situation by doing things which actually hinder the piano delivery.

1. Mopping and/or waxing floors half an hour before the delivery.

2. Buying a piano which is just too big.
    (On one occasion I overheard a couple in a piano store. They were looking at a big old upright piano. The husband said, "Before we buy this maybe we should go back home and do some measuring to see if it will fit through the doors." "What for?" she asked. "That's the mover's problem.")

3. Asking the movers to take a piano into a basement which is going to be a rec room but currently has no electrical service or lights.

4. Asking the movers to rearrange the entire living room five times while the customer decides what location is best for the piano.

Most movers will tolerate a lot. They are skilled and do this routinely. Some have even been in competition to hone their craft. Each year the U.S. Piano Cartel holds its annual convention and competition in Birdstall, Ohio. Teams of movers from all over the United States and Canada converge to compete in all sorts of contests. This event takes place in an abandoned five-story warehouse owned by the Cartel and is geared to test even the best of movers. Movers are tested in the categories of parking the truck, loading, unloading, stair climbing with weights and hoisting pianos. They compete to see who can stuff the most merchandise into a twenty-six-foot van body and who can catch the heaviest object thrown from the roof of the building. The latest event challenges the movers to take an upright piano 300 feet over a new hardwood floor without a dolly, leaving no marks. Any scratch or scrape disqualifies the contestant. First prize is a trophy shaped like an upright piano with the names of the team members engraved into a brass plaque. There is also a very special glass trophy shaped like a man's arm with the muscles bulging. This is awarded to the person who moves the most weight alone. Last year's winner, Vito Trundlerump, carried his one-ton delivery truck across the parking lot. At a mere 400 pounds and sporting size sixteen shoes, he made it look simple.

We have established the existence and credibility of the professional mover. They are available and most of the time you will be pleased with their workmanship. Of course, there are some others who are just learning, don't know, or just don't care. As a cautionary exercise, let's visit this group. For openers, we'll look at an advertisement.

The moving company of CHIPPENDALE & DOOLITTLE recently ran an ad seeking an apprentice moving man. The ad read:

**INDUSTRIOUS PERSON TO LEARN SKILLED TRADE
REQUIRING O.J.T. THROUGH JOB EXPERIENCE
SUPPLEMENTED BY RELATED INSTRUCTION. APPLY
IN PERSON. C&D VANS; 345 BELFAST RD; 9-4 MON-FRI**

This sounds like a real professional position with a big firm. Following is the text of the application presented to those who showed up.

WELCOME TO C&D VANS

We are not a non-profit organization and we intend to keep it that way! Please read this carefully or have somebody read it to you. Your application must be filled out in English and in ink. Your name must be your most recent (nicknames will not be accepted). For your information we have set forth some basic qualifications, conditions and regulations pertaining to the position advertised.

1. You don't have to know anything. We'll show you.
2. The on-the-job-training for the first seven days is at your expense.
3. You must have no physical defects below the neck.
4. You must be strong enough to throw a garbage can full of cement over an eight-foot high fence with either arm.
5. You must have no love for wood, carpet, paint or floor tile.
6. You must be strong enough to force large objects into areas which are physically not large enough for that object.
7. You must know at least one foreign language and speak it fluently to insure the customer that you do not know what they are telling you.
8. You must have a work shirt with a name other than your own to confuse any claims about who did what.
9. You must be able to endure long truck rides with two other people in confined quarters with gymnasium-type orders.
10. You do not have to know how to tell time or wipe your feet.
11. Previous knowledge of ropes, chains, knots and power saws is a plus.
12. You must have completed sixth grade in less than ten consecutive tries.
13. You may be subjected to loud noises from falling objects.
14. If you are a boozer or a user you must do your drugs during lunch and in the truck cab. (We do not encourage this but we know shit happens).
15. Tardiness will not be tolerated unless it pertains to the customers.
16. Women applicants will be subject to a wet T-shirt test and arm wrestling auditions.
17. For your own safety, no one over seventy-five need apply.
18. You will be expected to show some degree of aptitude for reading maps, bridge clearance markings, and street signs.
19. You will also be tested on house numbers and phone numbers.
20. Those with their own truck will receive special consideration.

NOTE: If you cannot write, you should get somebody to fill out your application.

C&D VANS
EMPLOYMENT APPLICATION

NAME _____ AGE_____

ADDRESS_____

CITY_____ STATE_____ ZIP _____

PHONE _____

DATE YOU CAN START _____

PAROLE OFFICER PHONE _____ LAST ARREST DATE_____

COULD YOU KILL A DOG?   YES___   NO___   HAVE YOU? YES___   NO___

DO YOU HAVE MORE THAN ONE SET OF UNDERWEAR?   YES___   NO___

LAST DATE YOU SHAVED_____

LAST DATE YOU SHOWERED_____

DO YOU OWN YOUR SHOES? YES___   NO___

IF YOU ANSWERED NO, WOULD YOU BE WILLING TO BUY A PAIR?
YES___   NO___

HAVE YOU EVER FALLEN FROM A MOVING VEHICLE? YES___   NO___

DO YOU THINK YOU COULD? YES___   NO___

DO YOU OWN A FIREARM? YES___   NO___

DO YOU THINK YOU CAN SHOW UP FOR WORK MORE THAN ONE DAY
IN A ROW? YES___   NO___   IF YES, HOW MANY?_____

* *

THIS CONSTITUTES THE ENTIRE APPLICATION. PLEASE GIVE THE COMPLETED
FORM TO THE DISPATCHER ALONG WITH YOUR ATTORNEY'S NAME AND
PHONE NUMBER.

This application would lead one to believe that this company does not offer top notch service. It probably means that some of their methods are questionable as well.

Piano movers don't want you in the room when they are moving your piano for the same reasons an orthopedic surgeon puts you under before he pulls out his power saw, electric drill and hammer.

Did you ever wonder why nurses in the orthopedic surgical ward are wearing smocks with an embroidered logo for a major tool company? Did it ever seem weird to you that just before the doctor put you out there was a Sears salesman in the operating room? He was telling the nurse that he was delivering a new ax to replace the one that broke during the last operation.

Well, movers have the same basic tools to work with on your $35,000 grand piano when things get tight. While they are there, the best advice to you is to go next door or to the corner saloon and have a few beers. Hopefully, when the mover has completed his task he will call to tell you that the "operation has been a success."

Another very important rule is never to think you have a few minutes to do something before the mover arrives. Never leave the house. Do not step into the shower or tub. Do not tie up the phone or throw in a load of wash in the basement where you might not hear the doorbell. Avoid all other forms of personal grooming. Because when you least suspect it the men will be there while you are on the sofa in your underwear with Kleenex between your toes, holding a battery-operated hand fan to dry your toenail polish. Movers don't "come back later." They reschedule. It could be tomorrow, next Friday, or who knows when. In some cases they have casually dropped the piano off outside and continued on their way.

YOUR NOTE FROM THE MOVERS

Flamboyant Moving Works, Ltd.
100 Canal Street, W.   Nip, Florida   N⁰ 8121

• SORRY WE MISSED YOU! •

8/26/99

Dear Ms. Fudgekeister

Due to a heavy work schedule we had to make your delivery at this time. Your piano is in the back yard 10 ft. past the end of your dogs chain. Due to the rain we put the blue vinyl cover over it. (The one that was on your compost pile.)

Dave
10:40 am

This situation leads to what the company refers to as a "call back." That would be you calling them to see if they would mind bringing your piano into the house. This, of course, generates a surcharge and puts everyone on edge during this second move. Some customers have even attempted to move their own piano inside to avoid the second charges. Later in this chapter we will tell you how that usually ends.

Above all, when and if the movers do come back, don't try to tell them their business. They do it day in, day out and if there is any way to do it, they will.

Sometimes things happen either at the warehouse, in transit, or at your location. Since piano movers are generally not English majors, they will usually express themselves in point blank terms when they have something to say. Here are some of the lines you may encounter:

1. Did you know that the aluminum awning hanging over your driveway was lower than our van? (Key word: WAS)

2. Oh, that grass will grow back.

3. That cracked blacktop will flow back together this summer when it gets hot.

4. While we were unloading in the street your next door neighbor backed over your piano.

5. Too bad about the broken concrete. We probably should have left the truck at the curb.

6. If your cat doesn't come down off the van's roof we'll have to leave with him up there.

7. A few wheelbarrows full of dirt and your lawn should look like new.

8. I must say your son is quick to pick up new language.

9. I think your cat was sitting on the engine fan when we started the truck.

10. Your piano fell down the elevator shaft at the warehouse but the boss says it still plays real good.

11. Probably best to put the side with the scrapes next to a wall.

12. The guys at the warehouse are still trying to find the other leg for your piano. They sent along this four-by-four in the mean time.

13. Someone lost the keys to your keyboard cover so we pried it open with our crowbar so you could play it now.

14. We had a small fire in the van, but that smell should go away in a few days. Throw a couple bars of soap in the piano or some stick-up air fresheners.

15. Do you mind if Harry climbs on top of your piano to take out this top hinge pin on the door?

16. We've come a long way out here, can the three of us use the toilet before we offload?

17. We picked up a dead deer along the road. Can we lay it on your porch while we unload the piano?

18. Are these cockroaches yours or ours?

19. Don't worry, lady. By the time you get dressed we'll be done.

20. Pardon me, ma'am. Do you have homeowner's insurance?

Movers sometimes depend on unorthodox methods to move pianos into your home. Watch out for the piano movers who flop the piano end over end. They will try to convince you that it is easier than lifting it and the casters will not scratch the floor.

If the initial entry to the house proves to be a tight fit it is proper to remove the door and perhaps even some molding. It is not proper for the mover to grease the sides of the piano and try to push the piano into the house using the rear end of the van. Also be sure they don't shear off any door knobs or handles. This causes the door to lose some of its performance qualities.

When moving grand pianos the legs are usually unscrewed and removed. Do not allow your mover to use a chain saw for any part of this process. It is the sure sign of an amateur.

Having pointed out many of the shortcomings of some movers, we must now deal with the alternative.

ASK THE AUTHOR

—

NO. A-351

Dear Don:

*I am a middle aged man with a moderate weight problem. I am 4'8"
and weigh 430 lbs. (down from my original 450 lbs.). My arms are
short and when I sit on the bench my stomach hits the piano before I
can reach the keys. Please help me.*

~ Dieting in Delancy

Dear Dieting:

Get rid of the bench. Get a bunch of pillows and sit cross legged on
the floor (if you can). This way your belly will stick under the piano.
Get yourself up so your chin is about level with the keyboard; you
should be able to see the keys. Put your arms over your head and
play that way. You'll get use to it after a while.

MOVING YOUR OWN PIANO

There is that certain something in the logic side of our brain which derails or shorts out when it comes to saving money. People will do anything in this mode. Men are more prone to this phenomenon when it comes to physical and mechanical things. No matter what the task, the male mind equates this challenge to a "right of passage." It is the "I can do anything" attitude which sets the scene for thousands of would-be piano movers to engage in an act for which they have never been trained. It is the age-old art of trying to beat a craftsman at his own game just to save a few bucks. In this case it is the "mover."

Many times it starts with a casual comment at home. The husband is trying to impress his wife while bolstering his male ego. "Well dear, don't worry about the moving charges on the piano. We can save some money if I move it myself. Gunner and some of the guys down at The Flat Rock Cafe offered to give me a hand this Saturday after the pool game. It'll cost me a few beers.

"We think we can strap it to the roof of our station wagon. After all, it's got that strong luggage rack on top, and we should be able to strap it to that. And besides, the guy at the warehouse at Max Grundoon's Piano World is a pal of Gunner's. He says if I sign a release he will have the guy on the fork truck set it up on the luggage rack for free."

At this point no mention has been made of how the piano will get back down from the roof. Gravity enters the wife's mind but the visions are scary.

"We were going to use Bronk's pickup but he's got two car engines, a racing sulky, and a refrigerator still in there from moves he's been doing for three days."

FACT: Piano moving does not have a magic formula which says: "The more beer you have, the less people it takes to move a piano."

FACT: Regardless of the collective alcohol consumption of the participants, the weight of the piano remains constant.

FACT: You can get a hernia even if you're drunk.

Okay, this guy has a mental image that he is a piano mover supreme. His friends have encouraged him and they tell him that they are as good as any piano moving crew around. After the pool game he has bought them three cases of beer and everyone is going to Piano World to get this project started. He takes his '88 Chevy Caprice wagon and they follow him in a van. After arriving at the warehouse, the buyer (we'll call him Buzz Off), meets with the warehouse manager and mentions the deal with Gunner. Done deal. The piano comes out the door of the warehouse on a fork truck. The operator carefully sets it down with its back laying flat. As he places it on the car, the luggage rack collapses and folds into the roof. Maybe this wasn't a good idea.

"No, wait!"

"Hey Buzz," one of the guys shouts, "you don't need the luggage rack. Let's just run some ropes through the windows and up over the piano. That should hold it."

Seems like a good idea, so the fork truck guy lifts the piano up again and places a few two-by-fours under it so when he lets it down this time he can pull the forks out. The piano is in place. You hit the power window buttons and roll all four windows down. The boys have good strong nylon boat ropes which they throw through each pair of doors, front and rear. One guy gets up on top and ties the knots and it looks pretty foolproof. Everyone agrees that you are set. Nobody has noticed that your tires are flattened halfway to the rims. But what does that matter anyway; it's not like you're going to be speeding with this thing. Okay, all set, let's go. Whoops! The doors are all tied shut by the ropes going up to the piano and everyone laughs because they all know they screwed up. One guy suggests that you open the tailgate door at the rear and crawl over the seats. You opt to prove your real NASCAR bravado and slide through the driver's window into the seat.

Okay, this is a go. You pull out of the parking lot very carefully with your crew behind you. As you make the first turn onto the busy two-lane road you realize that this car is super top-heavy and you'd better be extra careful. At 20 m.p.h., you quickly build up an angry crowd behind you. Your guys in the van are giving you the thumbs up and waving for you to pick up speed. The few people who have been able to get past you have given you signs with one finger or the rotating index finger to the side of the head to indicate that you are nuts. This has upset you and you decide that 35 m.p.h. is not real fast on this level, straight road. At 35 m.p.h., the car is more like a boat rocking in the water, sort of floating along with the waves.

Here comes the first signal. If you play your cards just right you can beat it and avoid a stop. You accelerate just a bit and then it turns yellow. Should you run it or stop? Coming down the crossroad to your right is a huge tractor trailer carrying a piece of construction equipment. Black smoke is pouring from his exhaust stack and you can tell he is gunning for the green. That's it, gotta stop. You try to do this incrementally but you are running out of room and you stand on the brakes. The car responds and stops quickly, the piano does not. The person who originally tied down the piano had not figured any ties from front to rear, only side to side. It neatly slides forward on the two-by-fours, through the nylon ropes, down over your windshield and onto the hood. You can't see a thing and lots of cracks have shown up in your windshield. You can also see by looking up that the light has now turned green and you hear lots of horn blowing behind you. The piano is just balancing there and you wrestle with the idea of whether or not you should move the car at all. One of your pals from the van comes running up and stands beside your open window.

"Hey, Buzz. Don't lose it, buddy. Watch my signals and I'll get you pulled over onto the shoulder."

He walks beside the car telling you what to do as you very gingerly clear the intersection and pull to the side of the road. A string of traffic comes by, some tooting, some laughing, some just mad. You feel like a real ass just about now.

The van has pulled ahead of you and your pals are looking things over while you sit behind the wheel. One of them leans in the window and says, "Hey Buzz, I think we should go back to the saloon and try to round up a pickup. You okay sitting here?"

"Yeah, but hurry up. I'll sit with it," you reply. The fact is though, you're so weak in the knees right now that you couldn't crawl out the window if you had to.

Your crew roars off in the van, no one making any attempt to stay back with you to lend moral support, and you are still tied into the car. Shit, the least someone could have done was to untie the damn ropes. Traffic is passing you in both directions and the responses are pretty much standard. Except for the sheriff who's coming down from the other direction, spots you and swings around in the intersection. As he pulls up in front of you it seems that your day is about to be complete.

As the officer approaches your window all you can see at first glance is a pair of gray pants, a brass buckle and a holster with a small cannon in it. He leans in your window, a young man with a big round face and a thick neck, probably a football jock you guess. His brown eyes are big and his cheeks are rosy and he is smiling at this point. Not foreboding so far.

His opening comment, "So, how's everything going here today?"

"Not so good I'm afraid," you answer.

"I got some time. You got a story to tell me?"

"I'd rather not get into all that just now," you say.

He leans in a bit farther and says, "Okay, let's start with number one. It's against the law to operate a motor vehicle with the doors tied shut. Number two, your windshield is not safe for driving with all those fractures in the glass. Number three, your tires are very overloaded and unsafe to drive on and number four, you are on my highway with an unsecured load which is also obstructing your vision. That should set you up for about $300 in fines and thirty days in the can. What are you intending to do with this half-ass moving van?"

"My buddies took off to get a pickup, they shouldn't be long. We're going to load the piano on that."

"Well, lad, here's the story. I'm feeling real generous today. I'm going to leave now cause you got your hands full. I don't want you to move this car one inch with that piano out there. I'll come back in about a half hour and if this pile of junk is still on my road I'm going to hang enough paper on you to do a wall in your bathroom."

69

"Thanks, officer. I understand. We should be gone by then."

Before leaving, the cop slides the rope around so the knot comes down to the window and says, "You seem to have some time on your hands. Untie this and get yourself out of that deathtrap." With that he gets into the patrol car, makes a U-turn and is on his way. You proceed to untie the knot with your sweaty hands fighting you every second.

Soon your crew is back with the van and a black Chevy pickup that looks almost new. The kid driving swings the pickup around in the road and backs up to your hood. The others park the van ahead of him and make their way back to your car. The game plan is to let the gate down on the pickup, stand the piano up on your hood and roll it down into the pickup. This kid is as thin as a rail and appears to be a nervous, almost hostile teenager with a bad haircut. He is wearing an orange and white baseball cap from Hooters which is on backwards. He is introduced as Gunner's nephew. He was at his girlfriend's house when Gunner got hold of him to do this favor. He's not real happy. In fact his mood seems to swing from testy to nasty. He just wants this over with. He also made the opening comment, "Anybody scratches this truck, I'll kill you."

The guys are up on your hood now and, although the piano has already inflicted sufficient damage, they are adding to it. Pushing and lifting, they stand the piano up and the casters make two real scrapes in the hood, right down to the bare metal. But there's no time to complain about that now. You and another guy are in the bed of the pickup and two more guys are on your hood. The kid is just watching as you gently work the piano into the bed of the pickup. It's an eight-foot bed so the piano can go to the front with three feet to spare behind it.

"There, that's good," you say. "Let's tie her down."

"You ain't tying nothing to this truck," says the kid. The tone of his voice is convincing. "Why don't somebody ride with that thing so it don't move?"

Nobody seems to want to ride back there with this kid driving but one guy says, "Hey, we could use those two-by-fours on your hood for blocking. We'll put them behind the piano." All agree and the piano is blocked, sitting lengthways in the center of the bed. They cannot move it to either side because it may scratch the fender wells or the sides of the bed.

"Hey, with those two-by-fours behind it and all that weight, that piano is surely not going to roll anywhere," says another guy. "It should sit right there."

The kid is obviously in a hurry and he is already in the cab with the motor running as the tailgate is closed. He has been told where we are going and it is assumed he will follow one of you and the other vehicle will follow him.

That was the assumption. The kid looks in his side mirror. There is a string of about a dozen vehicles just starting toward him from the light and he decides to beat them.

70

Little streams of stones and dust fly from his tires as he accelerates into the traffic lane from the shoulder. Immediately the piano is moving like it was on rollerblades. Pushing the two-by-fours ahead of it over the slick metal floor, it slams into the tailgate and now there is a definite bow in the gate. We have traveled about 300 feet and he is back on the shoulder again, and he is pissed off big time.

"Nice blocking, you asshole," he shouts to one guy.

"Yeah, nice driving, Mr. Andretti, you slimeball," is the reply.

"Hey, I'm not out here for the afternoon," says the kid. "Do you want to move this thing or not. I don't give a rat's ass either way."

"Yeah, we want to move it, but not by air freight. You got to take it easy with it."

The tension is mounting with everybody. This simple moving job is not the piece of cake you had envisioned. And you have yet to get this piano into the house. Another crew member, Dan, now speaks to the kid.

"Hey kid, would you let me drive the truck? I drive for a living and it's only five or six miles. I'm not gonna hurt your truck."

"Nobody's ever driven this truck but me," says the kid. "You put a scratch on it and I'll kill you."

"Okay, okay, cool down and let's get this done."

It is decided that one man must ride in back with the piano. Since it is your piano you feel responsible to take that position. Harold will drive your car, Dan will drive the pickup, and Nicky will drive the van. You just want this move over with. One end of the piano is up against the front of the bed and the other end is facing the tailgate. You decide to stand behind the piano to avoid another incident with the tailgate. The convoy pulls away at a reasonable pace and once again your piano is on the move. You've come less than a mile and a half in an hour and a half. It's going better now and soon you are crossing that familiar little bridge near your home. You are leaning with your back against the piano watching the traffic behind you and looking at your partially destroyed wagon as it follows the pickup. All that's left is a left turn onto your street and it's home sweet home.

For some reason the pickup does not slow down completely for the turn and as the truck makes its move so does the unrestrained piano. This time it falls over onto its back against the side of the pickup bed, denting it in two places. The kid hears the thump and looks out the rear window. He is freaking out and you don't care to make eye contact with him at this moment. There is no way you're going to stand this up alone so you make a futile gesture by resting your hands on it. Soon you are at your driveway and the pickup is backed up to your garage door. The kid jumps out and in language fit only for the WWF wrestling ring he screams that he wants that #@**#!* piano out of his truck this second.

So do you. Everyone scrambles onto the truck to right the piano and get it unloaded. The tailgate does not come down very easily because it is sprung pretty badly; once the piano is lifted off the side of the pickup the damage is rather visible. The kid is ranting and raving that he wants cash to repair his truck; you tell him to get an estimate and you will be happy to settle up with him. He screams in your face, "If you screw me on this I'll kill you!" With that he burns $40 worth of tires off on your driveway, tears out to the road and flies off at breakneck speed.

Everybody is laughing at his childish exit except you for this has not been your funniest day so far, and the task of moving the piano is far from over. You never mentioned to the guys that this piano is heading for the basement which you are doing over as a rec room. When you tell them, the smiles disappear and a serious decision-making process begins. Who's going to lift what and when? "Well," you say, "let's do some looking and measuring."

The four of you go into the house through the garage. The basement door is off the hallway just past the laundry room. At least you won't tear up the house, the door is only fifteen feet from the garage. You have all the piano dimensions on the pad and Dan has the tape. Okay, the piano will fit through the garage side door opening by removing the door. The piano will also go down the hallway; that's good. Now you're going to swing the piano 90° to line it up with the cellar stairs but you are sixteen inches short there, the hall is not wide enough to swing it. That's number one; number two is that the door to the basement and possibly some mouldings will also have to be removed. It's going to be a tight squeeze but you feel confident that it will work if you do this. Next the conversation turns to who will be on the bottom end lifting the piano down the stairs?

"You guys are gonna love me for this," you say. "I have thought about that for most of the week and suddenly I had a brainstorm. I called Butch, the guy who drives the big delivery truck for Ant Farm Cookies, and he brought me two of those long aluminum roller tracks that he uses to roll big boxes down from his trailer. We can lay them on the stairs and set the piano on top of them and that sucker will roll right down. They're right outside along the garage wall."

A sigh of relief comes from everyone, knowing that the lifting has been eliminated. Next it appears that the handrail along the basement stairs must also be removed and you get your little tool box from the garage and give Nicky the job of taking off the door and handrail while you and Harold go outside for the roller tracks. They are light and easy to carry and there must be 200 little rollers on each one. Once in the hall you measure them and find that two side by side will not fit in the stairway, so you take one back out to the garage.

Your wife has come by to take a look and seeing the door and handrail laying in the hall she shakes her head and heads back for the kitchen. Your loud but hollow assurance that you have this project covered brings her little comfort.

Now the engineering begins in earnest. First you must lay the track on the stairs. It is twelve feet long and it never occurred to you that no way is this thing going to turn and go down the stairs. Damn it. Nicky comes up with the idea to take it outside and shove it into the basement through a window. Hey, that's top-notch thinking. You and he scurry out to the rear of the house and notice there are three windows in the back wall, the center one appearing to be approximately in line with where the stairs should be. You and Nicky go back into the house, grab the track and Dan and Harold go into the basement to open the window. It is in a steel frame and pulls inward, but it has sliders on the sides which only allow it to open 45°. The window has to come out. The slide rails have rivets in them that are fastened to the frame so Harold cuts them with a hacksaw. Now the window drops down to a flat position and you guess that it better stay that way instead of messing up the hinges by removing it completely. The aluminum roller track is pushed through the opening and laid on the basement floor; with that accomplished—everyone returns to the garage.

Now let's see. We can't swing the piano in the hallway so it will be necessary to stand it up on its end and turn it. Everyone agrees that this can be done. Nicky observes that the casters might catch on the roller track and you observe that the top is flat so the piano will have to go down the roller track upside down. The top overlaps the outside edges of the piano sides so it will do the trick. Since no lifting will be required on the bottom end, Nicky will be in the basement to guide it, and Harold and Dan will help you wrestle it into position and start it on its way. You're going to need something on that slate floor to spin the piano around. Without mentioning it to your wife you go into the bedroom and grab a wool blanket from the bed. That should do it; let's get the piano.

Everyone to the garage. Gee, this thing seems heavier every time you move it. The first time the fork truck did the work; the second time you were just sliding it down off your hood into the pickup truck; the third time you dropped it down off the pickup truck, but now you actually have to lift this thing. There are a pair of big wooden grab handles on the backside but only the piano cabinetry on the front. You all wheel it to the door as if you were wheeling a coffin into church and at the doorway you set it up on the little step and start it into the hallway. It becomes evident that there is no room for anyone beside the piano as it rolls down the hallway; you'll have to work from both ends and there are no lifting devices on either end. Nicky and Harold have to go around to the front door and come through the house to the hall while you and Dan are at the rear in the garage. Nicky is more agile and younger so he squats down to pull on a leg. Harold is the beefy one with the big beer gut hanging over the front of his Levi's and he squeezes along the wall to get a grip on one of those lifting handles.

An 800 pound piano can test anyone's strength, but the sheer bulk of it and lack of adequate lifting points while it moves down the hall increases the challenge. You and Dan try your best to lift and push while the other two guys pull. It moves slowly into the house, the caster wheels leaving two very nice white streaks along the slate floor, while Harold's metal suspender clips draw a line down the walnut paneling as he squeezes along the wall. Now the piano is at the doorway and it is time to stand it up. You and Dan take your best grip and it feels like the piano is bolted to the floor. Better get Harold around here to help. He parades back through the house and out to the garage. The three of you strain as the piano comes up on end and Nicky throws the blanket under it before it lands. Good thing you weren't three feet further along the hallway or you'd have probably cleaned off the ceiling light.

Now the main event is about to begin. Nicky goes to the basement and grabs the roller track. He lays it in place and it is four feet shorter than the staircase. That's okay, you guys can "feed" the piano onto the track as you push it through the doorway. Easy now, let's turn this piano. The blanket was a good idea, and the piano slides around fairly easily. Now, with the casters toward the open doorway you carefully inch the piano to the top of the stairs. The next thing is to slowly lower the top side of the piano back toward the wall across from the doorway. This will allow you to "walk" the piano over the edge of the first step. Alright, nice and easy, let's lean it back. It is coming down nicely but getting very close to the wall in a hurry—better feed it over the stair top. Now you jointly give it a shove and the blanket is still doing its job but the piano breaks loose and starts sliding. "Hold it, hold on to it!" you shout. "Let it down some more, it's getting away from us."

Now the piano is down and sliding along the stairs and you have no way to raise the lower end to get it up onto the roller track. The piano hits the track butt end and continues down the stairs shoving the whole roller track ahead of it. Nicky is stepping lively just to get out of the way and in seconds the piano has hit the concrete floor and stopped. Most of the piano is still on the stairs and there is no way Nicky is going to lift it off from there alone. You start down the stairs with the other two but the two of you barely squeeze into the stairwell shoulder to shoulder. Harold is too big so you and Dan shove the piano while Nicky pulls. The leading edge at the bottom slides along the concrete floor taking the finish and just a bit of wood off the edge of the top. Since all you can do is push, the piano drops from stair to stair for the last four stairs and is finally sitting on the floor upside down. You still have to push it some more to make room to get around it. Not too much, just enough to scrape most of the finish off the top as it slides flat across the concrete.

This is wonderful. The piano is now in the basement and all you have to do is stand it up on its wheels and roll it into the corner until you finish the rec room. You figure one guy to push and the other three of you to catch it as it comes over onto its back. One, two, three... push! Alright now, grab it, it's coming over. If the bottom edge hadn't started to slide along the concrete floor you'd have had it made but

Nicky couldn't stop it. It gets away from you and this time it drops on the concrete floor on its back with a sensational ringing sound from the interior. Oh well, it did not drop that far. Pianos are tough, no harm done you guess. Well, let's stand it up. Hmmmmm. It's now on its back and the lifting handles are facing the floor under the piano so there is no place you can grab to lift it. Harold looks at it and says, "Gotta drive some sort of wedge under it to raise it and get a grip. Wood will probably split; we really need something steel."

You go up to the garage and get a crowbar and your ten pound sledgehammer and a couple of short two-by-fours. Back in the basement you hold the chisel end of the crowbar against the bottom edge of the piano while Harold taps it a few times to start the bite. As you release your grip he gives it a woodsman's wallop and the crowbar flies out and hits you in the shinbone. This is getting to be no fun in a hurry and you are starting to get aggravated. The next try succeeds and you are able to place a two-by-four under the edge. All hands work to raise it and as more space opens up all four of you get a good grip and start to lift it up. Two thirds of the way up the casters hit the floor and you all chase the piano across the floor until it hits the wall and you can stand it up.

"Just swing it around so the keyboard is facing out and let's have a beer," you say.

Everyone agrees that this is a good idea; the piano is turned around and Nicky goes up to the garage for four beers. Oh yeah, the roller track still has to go back out the window. You get it lined up but it needs to be raised to a flat position so it will slide out the window—you need to raise it to level. Dan grabs a small table and stands on that, hoisting the track and shoving it out the window. That works great and all you have to do is go over by the wall, shove the last few feet out and shut the window. You take the table over by the window and since they are usually rather stiff to move, you give it a good yank. Without the guide sliders hooked to it the window flies up into position as a pane of glass hits the basement floor. A comment seems in order so you say, "son-of-a-bitch!" as you lock the window into place.

Well, the piano is moved into place. It only took four and a half hours start to finish and look at all the money you saved.

After three more rounds of beer in the garage, the guys leave and you are left to your thoughts. What a day this has been, but by God you got it done without paying the movers a dime. As you sit in the garage you now notice that the door is still off which means so is the one in the hall, along with the railing for the staircase. Well, you'll have to put them back yourself, or maybe your loving wife will help you now that you have saved the big bucks with your moving project. Oh yeah, and don't forget to grab the roller frame around from the back of the house, too.

A week has passed and now it is time to see how Buzz, "the piano mover," did with his crew.

COSTS:

3 cases of beer at $9.50	$ 28.50
Repairs to the Chevy Pickup (including a new tailgate)	612.00
Windshield for the wagon	282.00
Luggage rack and roof repair	375.00
New hood and paint for same	510.00
Scrapes in the slate floor that would not come out (15' new floor)	440.00
Scrapes from suspenders too deep to cover up (2 new wall panels)	77.00
TOTAL	$ 2324.50

The piano will need either a new top or major refinishing. Plus, there was major damage to the wood at the end of the top. One other thing that did not show up right away: probably as the piano fell from the roof of the car or for sure when it hit the concrete floor, it cracked the soundboard. The piano will be junk forever.

Note: The mover quoted $200 delivered into the basement.

ASK THE AUTHOR
—
NO. A217

Dear Don:

Last month my car was parked at the curb. A piano moving crew was hoisting a piano into a third floor apartment when the rope broke and the piano flattened my Yugo. The policeman who investigated was new to the force. He said that because the piano had no license plate, this was a matter for my homeowner's insurance and I should sue the rope maker. How come the movers were not included in this matter?

~ Crushed in Corona

Dear Crushed:

Since the piano, in theory, fell from the sky it would be considered an act of God. Therefore, if God is on the side of the movers your chances of winning are slim to none. You go get a new Yugo. This time you may want to have your auto "PIANO-PROOFED."

ASK THE AUTHOR

—

NO. A230

Dear Don:

Several weeks ago the movers brought our new piano. In the process they scraped the moulding on a doorway and also put a six-inch mark in the hardwood floor. The man said not to worry, he'll send an estimator over next week. It has now been three weeks. Do you think he is coming?

~ Waiting in Walla Walla

Dear Waiting:

No.

ASK THE AUTHOR
—
NO. A-383

Dear Don:

I am fascinated by the piano hoisters and would like to get into that line of work. I have found no school that teaches this type of thing. Can you help?

~ Hoping to Hoist in Harlem

Dear Hoping:

I have no information about any school since most of the art of hoisting is learned on the job. No matter where you apply they will always tell you the Cardinal Rule of the hoister:

> *Before you throw the piano out the window make sure you have enough rope.*

Perhaps you could start by lowering your furniture out the window to see if you have the knack for it.

MORE ABOUT MOVING YOUR OWN PIANO

DO NOT TOW YOUR PIANO

Even if you only live a short distance from the point of purchase to your destination, DO NOT ATTEMPT TO TOW YOUR PIANO. Piano casters are made for very short moves measured in feet, not miles. Going slowly with the car does not count. A tow job of several miles will destroy the casters and as they disappear the bottom of the piano case will come in contact with the road surface. The abrasive nature of the road will heat up the wood and set your piano on fire. For this portion of the trip you will be trailing a cloud of smoke and eventually some flames. When the wood has gone far enough the next thing to come in contact with the road will be the harp and pedals—these are steel and will not burn. They will, however, set off a trail of sparks which at average speed will parallel or exceed any good Fourth of July spectacle you can recall. All during this road adventure your piano is getting shorter in height and it smells terrible. You now have lost six inches of wood, four caster wheels, all the pedals and part of the harp and sound board. As long as you are on a roll, keep going until you reach the City Dump.

DO NOT TAKE YOUR PIANO ON A BUS

Despite the very affordable fares and the huge size of a bus, DO NOT ATTEMPT MOVING YOUR PIANO BY BUS. Even if you have been encouraged by a demented bunch of friends who are whacky enough to help, this is not a good plan. Even the newer buses that "kneel" at the curb for wheelchair access were never intended for piano moving. The piano might fit into the door opening but the first time you try to turn it you are screwed. Now the piano is half in and half out of the doorway. You are inside and everyone who has helped to push it is outside. You can't push it back out alone and they are telling you they can't get in to help you. (No one has thought about the rear door of the bus during this crisis.) The driver can't get out of his seat and he is commenting on your mother and the passengers are mad because of the delay. They will not volunteer to help because they assume anyone nuts enough to bring a piano onto a bus must also be a mental case and therefore they could be killed. In the end, this bus move can only create a bad day.

IF YOU STILL WANT TO...

If you are still determined to move the piano yourself, there are a bunch of proven facts that you need to study. It will be very rewarding as you undertake this most mysterious of endeavors.

It is probably best that you use a pickup truck. It is open and readily available without renting. Lots of guys have them and for a few beers they'll probably pitch in to help with the move.

If you rent a truck you will find that the only truck they have left for you on this day is a twenty-four-foot van with a lift gate. It is also twelve feet high and the odds are pretty good that before the day is out, you will hit a bridge, snap off some tree limbs, or rip an appendage off the outside of your house. You will also spend $135 in hidden charges when you return the truck.

If you rent a trailer and you don't have a hitch, the rental company will install one. That takes about twenty minutes to do but two hours until they can get around to it. The hitches are pretty much foolproof and work well. They also have safety chains which are there in case the ball comes loose. It is the electrical portion of this operation that causes grief. You rent your trailer on a Saturday and the kid who is in the yard doing the hookups has come from an all-night beer blast just in time to change clothes and get to work. He does not want to be there and you are regarded as the enemy. Because of you he has to work as opposed to lying down on a pile of moving blankets to sleep off his buzz. When he has completed his masterful task of rewiring your vehicle, you use the left turn signal and the headlights come on. To activate the right turn signal the radio must be turned on, and every time you step on the brakes the horn honks. Let's assume you can deal with this and you pull the trailer to the site of the move.

You are now ready to back in and load the piano. Backing up a little trailer, however, is not as easy as it might appear. Trailers are subject to very rapid changes in direction. If you have an open trailer you can't see it from any of your mirrors, inside or out, until it jacks around to a 90° angle to the car and stands up on one wheel. Once in a while someone will volunteer to stand up in the trailer so you know where it is, but that someone is usually the smartass who has had a few beers and thinks it is cute to walk from side to side in the trailer while you are backing up, just to confuse you. In the other scenario you may have the "box," or closed trailer. This offers you a full view of the trailer at all times. It does however, completely block your view of anything else, and if you're not a good judge of distance you will probably ram your house. You can also figure that with this blind operation you could also back over a hedge, a mailbox or even a fire hydrant.

It is also a proven fact that 90% of the people pulling a trailer can't back it up because they can't get it through their heads that for the trailer to go left you have to steer right and vice versa. If you doubt this and want to see confusion at its peak, just go to a public boat launching ramp on a hot Saturday or Sunday. Everybody wants to be first in and nobody has time for the guy ahead to learn how to back up. I once saw a guy so frustrated that he took a high speed forward run down the ramp with his car and went out far enough into the pond that the boat floated off the trailer. Then he called AAA to pull the car out. He figured by the time he was done fishing for the day the car would dry out and the guy from AAA would have figured out how to get the engine running again.

But back to the pickup.

Modern pickup trucks are so gracefully styled that many people find them attractive enough to use as their personal vehicle. But remember, good looks mean no hooks.

There is virtually nowhere to tie a rope unless the pickup is equipped with a bed liner with some steel rings fastened to it. Therefore, good judgment would dictate that one or more persons are going to wind up riding "shotgun" in the back of the truck with the piano. If you are one of those chosen few there are some things for you to remember.

First and foremost, check the weather. If you think it will rain, stay home. If it is cold, consider the chill factor. This is the temperature that occurs when people in the cab forget you are out in the back and they are going 55 m.p.h. in 20° weather. That puts you somewhere around 75° below zero and probably a corpse by journey's end. Banging on the cab roof to make them slow down will probably not work because the radio will be at full volume to make the trip more fun. The best thing you can do to protect yourself is wait until they come to the first traffic light or stop sign and hop out the back. Let them figure out what the hell happened to you when they get there. Also, if you fall out of the truck going around a turn and are not badly hurt, you may want to call ahead to the drop point and leave word that they need to come get you. Sometimes they will let you ride back there with a dog. The dog was put there by someone but he is probably looking at you and wondering why anyone in their right mind would voluntarily climb into the back. And finally, on this same subject, there will be that one person who will defy all these warnings and tell you: "I have come prepared for anything. I have three pair of pants, five shirts and am wearing my snowmobile suit over that."

One of the laws of moving states that the need to go to the bathroom is directly proportional to the amount of clothes you are wearing. That means if you are out in back of the truck with four layers of clothes on your body, you won't make two miles. Bear in mind that the driver will not stop for this either.

A piano which is about to be moved has a certain demonic quality. There is an overwhelming gravitational pull which makes one believe the piano could actually be fastened in place. The piano is constructed so that the weight is not centered and anyone who has moved pianos knows that you should be on the keyboard side. You are dealing with 600 to 800 pounds and the piano seems to have a mind of its own. It can cartwheel over the side of a pickup truck, fall over on its back or roll over your foot—all in a split second. Some people, after moving a piano, have actually called in a priest to conduct an exorcism to remove the demon within.

Note: The acceleration rate of an unrestrained piano going down a flight of stairs is zero to sixty in two seconds.

Also a word about the casters or wheels on a piano. They are usually about one and one-half to two inches in diameter and made of steel. They were no doubt designed by the same people who invented diamond cutters. A caster wheel is under that piano for just one reason: to cause trouble. It will mark a floor, hook on a rug, and start to skid as soon as it hits a gum wrapper, hair pin or dust ball. It certainly was never designed to support the piano. Just compare the size of the caster wheel to the size of the piano and figure the load it supports. It's like putting a roller-skate under a Mack truck. Another pleasant feature of the caster is that many times the caster wheel is mounted to a vertical pin about four inches long. That pin is then inserted into a hole or pocket on the underside of the piano. Since the caster is fixed to that little shaft, the shaft itself does the rotating in the pocket as the piano changes directions. It also means that since the shaft is free to rotate in that pocket, if you lift the piano more than four inches, the shaft slides out of the pocket and the wheel falls off. You will either step on it and damage your foot or you won't notice it at all until the piano is at its destination and it won't sit straight. That means you will have to shore it up with a block of wood to keep it from rocking.

When moving a grand piano the wheels or casters are a moot point. Why? Because they are bigger and will roll along nicely until you hit a snag and then the leg will break off. This you will not be able to correct with a small block of wood. You're going to have to build a pile of concrete blocks, bricks or cord wood to go from the floor to the keyboard, then throw a shawl or cover over that end of the piano to make it look decorative. It is well to note that a builder's supply store does not stock piano legs so don't be disappointed when they are not able to show you to Aisle 17, rough cut lumber, plywood, studding and piano parts.

With these few things in mind, let's talk about the move. If you bought a piano that has been sitting in the same spot for years, make sure you look behind it with a flashlight. The dark area behind the piano lends itself nicely to nesting areas. Be sure to ask the owner if he has ever seen the piano move when he was not near it. If you see small lights back there, be careful; pianos *do not* have small lights back there. Those are critter eyes staring at you. You may want to refer to the Marlin Perkins "Wild Kingdom Piano Mover's Guide" to tell you what to swat, what to net, what to trap, and what to run from. An often-used technique is to tie a rope on the leg of the piano, move back twenty feet, and jerk the piano from its resting place. This establishes a buffer zone which enables both you and the critters to run. Once you are convinced that all wildlife has exited the rear of the piano you can start to wheel it. If you hear a great deal of squeaking it is probably not the casters but rather a piano full of mice. You can set traps, fumigate or take them for a ride. They usually don't get around much and they would probably enjoy the new location when you get to the drop-off point. In summer homes there have been reports of yellow jacket and hornet nests in pianos so you may want to wear a beekeeper's suit when doing that kind of move.

Assuming you are ready to transport and have chosen the pickup truck as your vehicle of preference, we will now get you underway.

1.   The truck should have enough fuel.

2.   The driver should be reasonable and attentive to the needs of anyone riding in the back.

3.   Make sure the tie down ropes you use are quality grade and new if possible.

4.   Do not allow anyone to convince you that a little rain won't hurt the piano. *It will*.

5. Make sure any plastic or fabric cover you use is also tied down.

6. Do not drop the piano from a multiple story building directly into the bed of the truck.

7. Be sure to take along the stool or bench.

8. Empty the bench before you start to handle it. (You bought the bench with the piano so anything in it is yours. Do not be intimidated by or feel sorry for any person who starts crying or yelling about something they left in there. That's their problem.)

9. Do not back the empty pickup truck over a soft lawn to get at the piano. Once you've got the piano loaded, the truck will sink into the ground up to its frame.

10. ***Most important, bear this in mind:*** There are those people who will tell you, "No need to tie this piano down. It is so heavy it can't possibly go anywhere." *Oh yes it can.*

Getting the piano ready for transporting is probably more important than the actual hauling. On new pickups you can throw a rope under the truck, put some blankets against the outside of the bed and bring the ropes right up and around the piano. Be sure the person in charge of tying the ropes is not wearing loafers because he can't tie his shoes. Knots are vital. There have been occasions when a piano was tied into a closed twenty-foot van, secured to the front bulkhead. Over the period of the ride the knots worked loose and the piano became free. Upon acceleration from a stopped position the piano has flown out through the rear overhead door and both piano and door have fallen into the street in front of the next vehicle in line.

Let's assume the worse-case scenario and say you cannot tie the piano anywhere. Remember that this thing is off balance, the weight is all in the backside where the harp and soundboard are located. Pianos do not like riding and they have a thing for jumping out of moving vehicles. Never load the piano into a pickup truck with the high side facing the street. The first sharp turn you make will actuate the phenomenon. At the most inopportune moment the piano, without warning, will lurch over the side of the truck. For some unknown reason, our studies show that pianos being moved through the city usually fall over the left (driver's) side into oncoming traffic only to be run over by a 20-ton garbage truck or something bigger. Pianos being moved through the country will lurch over the right side. They will always land in the deepest ditch within five miles, one that is filled to the brim with green slime and moss. This is the same green stuff you see on the Discovery Channel when scientists are experimenting to isolate a rare virus, some new mutations or other forms of life. No need to retrieve the piano from the ditch, it will slowly bubble out of sight and sink to the bottom as surely as the Titanic hit the ocean floor. All the while you are watching it sink you might ponder the thought that you are not insured to move a piano and whatever happens, it is your kiester.

If your piano falls out of the pickup truck into traffic be sure you have the receipt with you. The police will need that to make out the accident report when the car behind you plows into the piano.

For example:

```
┌─────────────────────────────────────────────────────────────────────┐
│  KISSLIPS, DEL.     POLICE DEPT.     ACCIDENT REPORT                   │
│                                                                       │
│  DATE_____    BADGE #_____     INCIDENT #_____    │
│                                                                       │
│  VEHICLE ONE:   1993 Buick Skylark, 4 door    VIN _____    │
│                 Color - White                                         │
│                 Operator:    Miles Furnblat, Jr.                      │
│                                                                       │
│  VEHICLE TWO:   1933 Baldwin Upright          VIN _____    │
│                 Color - Mahogany                                      │
│                 Operator:    N/A                                      │
└─────────────────────────────────────────────────────────────────────┘
```

This accident would be charged to the piano as a hit and run since there is no driver at the scene who will actually admit to driving the piano. If you paid $25 for the piano and the damage to the Buick is $2745 you are best to haul ass out of there and find yourself another piano. Your original piano is now trashed and if they get your plate number the worst you can be charged with is leaving the scene of an accident.

Just a couple of words about hoisting pianos in and out of high buildings.

HIRE SOMEONE.

We have all seen the comedy routines in the movies with Laurel and Hardy and others where they are going to lower a piano down to the street. The block and tackle is rigged and a rope is taken down to the street and hooked to a donkey. He will be the counterweight and he will back up slowly to lower the piano down. They shove the piano off the third floor balcony, it crashes to the ground and the donkey winds up in the balcony.

My opinion on this is: "ONE ASS IS ENOUGH. JUST SAY NO."

POINT OF GENERAL INFORMATION

Probably the very worst time you can call on a mover is when you have an upright piano half way down your basement stairway; it is jammed into the ceiling on a 90° turn and will not move up or down; and there are two people now trapped in the basement below with no way out. Your phone call radiates panic, you tell them you need them immediately and price is no object at this point.

———◆———

FINAL COMMENT

Movers are great fellas and gals with bills to pay and families to support. Do yourself a favor and give them the work. You'll sleep a whole lot better and you can use the money you won't need for your hernia operation to take your wife out to dinner.

**ASK THE
AUTHOR**

—

NO. A-415

Dear Don:

When I first started playing piano my teacher said my left hand was much weaker than my right. Therefore I gave much more attention to it. Now it is so strong that when I play ascending scales my left hand runs right over my right hand. How can I fix that? It really screws things up.

~ Cross Handed in Caledonia

Dear Cross Handed:

Congratulations on your fabulous left hand. Stride pianists in the twenties and thirties had this problem. Many on low income just tied a brick to their left arm to slow down the speed. If you are playing in dressy conditions you could slide a length of six-inch sewer tile over your arm. It will fit under a suit coat and no one will be the wiser.

THE TUNER

**Your goldfarb is
hitting the fricken and
the wallyfrass has some
frayed wiring.**

"...the piano has to go to the shop!"

PIANO TUNING:

*Definitely not a field for the mechanically inept
or those of diminished patience.*

WHO IS THE PIANO TUNER?

The piano tuner is that rare breed, both male and female, who can stand to hear single piano notes played over and over thousands of times each year. Piano tuners are gifted with the patience of a saint and the uncompromising and relentless determination to overcome the illnesses which befall the music-making machinery of the piano. It may be something in the piano that has broken, come unglued, or simply reacted to temperature, the moisture or moving. Or it may simply be some foreign object belonging to the owner which has found its way into a spot not visible to the untrained eye. In cases such as this the tuners—while feeling that you have not been vigilant enough to stop the intrusion of debris—must make light of it and move on. Piano tuners deal daily with people ranging in age from the young who can barely crawl to the senior who is having trouble walking. Their air of diplomacy would surely secure them an exalted position with any government as an ambassador of peace or a finely tuned negotiator. Although many tuners play the piano very well, they are always courteous to a fault in complimenting you when you sit down to test the tuning and repairs. They answer hundreds of questions which they already have been asked thousands of times. They respond with interest and without burying you in technical rhetoric. Tuners must have the hands and steadiness of a surgeon while working with small parts in dark places. Their hearing ranks with some of the most acute in the human race.

Thousands of men and women are engaged in this highly specialized trade and my hat is tipped to these real technicians. They keep America and the whole world singing and dancing. But like every trade there are a few hustlers bouncing around out there who have falsely labeled themselves as tuners and rebuilders. From these people you must retreat or better yet flee. Some tell-tale signs are found on the next few pages along with some examples of modern day testing.

The task of finding a new tuner who is reputable is quite similar to finding a new doctor. You have to ask around. Piano tuning is like brain surgery. It is a field that should not be open to those who are practicing at your expense.

The first thing you must realize is that you can rarely arrange for an emergency tuning. The piano technician has an automatic three-week calendar. Therefore if you call on the 8th, your appointment is automatically scheduled for the 29th. Any deviation might incur a surcharge.

A piano tuner might hone his craft by means of an apprenticeship. That is to say they have been taught on the job by an experienced piano tuner. Still others may attend classes to gather knowledge and to work on test pianos furnished by the schools. There is yet another group who are the "Match Pak Marauders." They have taken a correspondence course which was advertised on the inside or outside of a pack of matches.

> **"YOU TOO CAN MAKE BIG MONEY IN THE FIELD OF PIANO TUNING. 6 TOOLS - MANUAL - PROFESSIONAL HELP - ONLY $195. FIND YOURSELF EARNING BIG BUCKS IN THREE MONTHS OR LESS. ASK ABOUT OUR SPECIAL PROGRAM FOR THE DEAF. THIS PROGRAM PROVEN SUCCESSFUL NATIONWIDE - DIPLOMA GUARANTEED!"**

The advertisement says three months but by the time you send your money, your check clears and you go back and forth in the mail to get your assignments graded, your diploma finally arrives sometime after the six-month mark. How a company in Fogbank, Montana can issue a diploma to a person in Winnepoo, Maine without hearing how they tune—or seeing how they do repair work—is a mystery to me. But this is happening every year.

Never just glance at a tuner's diploma. (If you should ever be fortunate enough to see it.) Read it all very carefully. You might be surprised what you find there. Also remember that certain initials on that paper or on the tuner's business card may give credence or warning to the new customer depending on what appears.

GOOD INITIALS: R.T.T.   P.T.G.   R.P.T.   C.A.P.T.
NOT SO GOOD: A.F.U.   D.O.A   I.O.U.   I.R.S.

If the tuner has actually attended a school it is usually a two-semester course – about four to six months.

THE FIRST SEMESTER

One learns to expect what's inside the piano. Things the maker has put there as part of the manufacturing process. Pins and hammers, dowels and rods, screws and bolts and the manufacturer's stamping in that big steel whatchamacallit.

Not included as factory original equipment and yet often found within are hairpins, gum, marbles, cat hair, coins, pens, pencils and dead critters of all types, flies, gnats, all forms of small rodents, and an occasional stray turtle with the little decal still on its back. Some are still living!

At the tuning school the students are brought into a dark room where the instructor leads them to the piano and instructs them to run their fingers around inside. Various things have been placed there by the staff and it's amazing how fast the student learns to distinguish between the quick and the dead. It is also this course which outlines the various means of dealing with the animate portion of the class. Unlike police personnel who rely a great deal on mace, pepper spray and tear gas, the tuner has a completely different bag of tricks. His aerosol cans usually all have a skull and crossbones on the label. The basic ones are DDT, chloroform, and RAID. Shellac is also a great spray tool. Whatever is in there can't run or fly if it is stiff. The main theory instilled in these students is SPEED. Once you have disturbed whatever that critter is, you may rest assured that it is pissed off. If you don't get it first, it will get you.

THE MOTTO FOR SPRAYING THESE THINGS

"SOME IS GOOD, ENOUGH IS BETTER, TOO MUCH IS JUST RIGHT"

Usually when the piano is suspected of containing living things the aerosol containers are to be worn in a holster to allow for the "quick draw" effect. Fumbling around in your tool case could cost you a finger or two or at least garner you a nasty sting or bite. Having completed the first semester which is usually referred to as "Mechanics" or "Technical One," the student is moved along to the second and most important part of the course.

THE SECOND SEMESTER

Because this phase deals with two distinctly different areas of education it is split into parts A and B.

PART A - LEGAL   Although space prohibits a complete summary of this segment, a few of the more pertinent topics can be revealed.

1. What is the responsibility of the piano tuner to the owner if the tuner actually finds something of value inside the piano? Can he keep it? Should he return it? Does he need a lawyer?

2. What is the best defense if you kill a child who will not stop asking questions while you are trying to tune the piano?

3. Is it legal to dismember a child if you catch them with their hands in your tool kit?

4. What are your rights and options if you are seduced by the lady of the house who whispers that her VISA is maxed out and hopes that your charges are negotiable. If you accept, do you finish tuning first or strike while the iron is hot?

PART B - MATHEMATICS   This is the most important part of the second semester and some will say of the entire course. It does however, give ideas to the sinister element among the tuners. It tells you how to figure charges and make up an invoice. It basically walks you through the art of charging for tuning time, parts, shipping, handling, phone calls, waiting time, travel time, weather reports, invoice paper, phone orders to parts houses, cleaning clothes soiled on the job, aerosol can replacement costs and burial services for critters that may have been pets. Note that a recent ruling by the Fourth Circuit Court of Wisconsin states that when flushing things down the toilet you may charge the travel time to and from the piano to the bathroom. The customer has already paid for the water and tissues. If you want to make a buck on your vacuum cleaner you should haul it on a trailer. That way you can charge for it as a piece of industrial equipment. Acceptable charge is an eight hour minimum plus trucking charges in and out of the site. You could also slide in a fuel charge if the customer fails to notice it is electric.

In the event that the tuner is scratched, bitten, stabbed or otherwise injured on the job by children or pets the invoice may also include estimated medical expenses, either immediate or projected.

When the tuner must remove the piano from the premises for a major rebuild or when another piano is sold by him to the customer, the course will instruct the student on the proper construction of a finance agreement. This item is a point stressed highly since interest collected by the tuner is a windfall. Ironically, people hate to pay with cash because they can physically see you taking it from them. But tell them they can put it on their credit card and immediately they feel as though they haven't spent a thing. It is further taught that interest rates should be kept under 30% to insure repeat business and referrals.

At the conclusion of the course there are, naturally, exams to be taken to insure that you have absorbed the curriculum. On the next few pages we have a random sample of some of these tests. There is also a diploma for you to review. The tests are from the well known albeit questionable **CANARVIS & SCHWARTZ HOME TUNING SCHOOL.** Although they do have an actual course in a school setting they are far and away the top Match Pak educators in the field of piano technology.

"EDUCATE BY MAIL – NO WAY YOU CAN FAIL"

**CANARVIS &
SCHWARTZ**

FINAL EXAM – #P8

PIANO TUNING

Course Instructor
Tondeleo Badwhiff

Rance Snotgrab

STUDENT

FINAL EXAM – P. 8 • REMINDER PAGE "A"
10 THINGS YOU DON'T SAY TO A CUSTOMER

1. This is a lot simpler than I thought.

2. You're in luck, I've got all the parts with me.

3. This piano is excellent – I'd leave it alone.

4. You're a new customer – I'll only charge half.

5. This needs to go to the shop but I'll pay for the moving.

6. If you give me a hand I'll knock off $35.

7. I'd be glad to help you with your warranty forms.

8. Sure. I'd love to play for your house party.

9. If you get me referrals I'll rebate you.

10. Don't worry about the money. I'll bill you later.

FINAL EXAM

CANARVIS & SCHWARTZ

PART A

SELECT THE CORRECT LETTER AND ENTER AT THE LEFT

1. WHAT IS THE ACCEPTABLE MARKUP FOR PARTS?

____ A) 3%   B) 23%   C) 107%   D) 255%

2. WHAT IS THE MAXIMUM CHARGE FOR TRAVEL MILES?

____ A) $.22/mile   B) $.45/mile   C) $1.35/mile   D) No Limit

3. WHAT IS THE FURTHEST DISTANCE YOU CAN SHOW FOR TRAVEL?

____ A) 10 miles   B) 25 miles   C) 50 miles   D) 1500 miles

4. WHAT CAN YOU CHARGE FOR FREIGHT ON PARTS?

____ A) $10 minimum   B) $25 minimum

     C) $14 for each part   D) Anything

5. IF YOU ARE LATE FOR AN APPOINTMENT, WHEN SHOULD YOU CALL?

____ A) 1 Hour   B) 4 Hours   C) 12 Hours   D) Never

CANARVIS & SCHWARTZ

FINAL EXAM

6.   IF A CUSTOMER GIVES YOU A CHECK UP FRONT, SHOULD YOU RUN TO THE BANK BEFORE TUNING?

____   A) Yes   B) Sometimes   C) Probably   D) Always

7.   IF YOU HAVE UNDERESTIMATED YOUR CHARGES, SHOULD YOU STEAL SOMETHING VALUABLE FROM THE CUSTOMER TO MAKE IT UP?

____   A) Maybe   B) Probably   C) Generally   D) Always

8.   IF YOU KNOW THE JOB WAS SHITTY, SHOULD YOU...

____   A) Confess   B) Come Back Again

     C) Dummy Up   D) Grab the Cash

9.   IF YOU FIND SOMETHING VALUABLE INSIDE THE PIANO, SHOULD YOU:

____   A) Tell Them   B) Take It   C) Take It   D) Take It

10. IF YOU KNOW THEY ONLY PAID $100 FOR THE PIANO AND IT NEEDS $800 WORTH OF REPAIRS, SHOULD YOU:

____   A) Do It   B) Dummy Up

     C) Fix It   D) Go For It

FINAL EXAM – P. 8 • REMINDER PAGE "B"
TO OVERCOME YOUR INEPTNESS,
10 THINGS TO SAY TO YOUR CUSTOMER

1. Has anyone been working on this piano lately?

2. I've never seen anything quite like this one.

3. I hope you bought the warranty package.

4. Normally this type of job is done at our shop but I'll try to do it here.

5. Holy shit! What's this?

6. Usually this doesn't break under tension.

7. Golly, I didn't figure on this problem.

8. There's a lot more parts in these older models.

9. I may have to come back again tomorrow.

10. We may have to review my original quote.

YOU HAVE BEEN ISSUED YOUR MANUAL OF STANDARD PIANO TUNING TOOLS. <u>WITHOUT</u> REFERRING TO THE MANUAL, IDENTIFY THE TEN ITEMS WHICH BELONG.

1.	Creeper	11.	Bearing Puller
2.	Band Saw	12.	Lt. Wt. Hammer
3.	Flashlight	13.	Bolt Cutters
4.	Chainfall	14.	Timing Light
5.	Glue	15.	Screwdriver
6.	Wire	16.	Magnet
7.	Cutting Torch	17.	Skil Saw
8.	Felt Pads	18.	Tuning Fork
9.	Pipe Wrench	19.	Air Wrench – 1"
10.	Pliers	20.	File

FINAL EXAM

CANARVIS & SCHWARTZ

PART C

YOU HAVE BEEN ISSUED YOUR PIANO REPAIR MANUAL. <u>WITHOUT</u> LOOKING THESE UP, PICK OUT THE TEN PARTS WHICH ARE FOUND IN A PIANO.

1. Crankshaft
2. Damper Felt
3. Blower
4. Beater
5. Trap Rod
6. Frammus
7. Conneaut
8. Hammer
9. Shank
10. Diddler

11. String Crank Rod
12. Compensator Liftrod
13. Driveshaft, Upper
14. Pin Block
15. Flame Arrester
16. String
17. Hitchpin
18. Whippen
19. Finch
20. Spoon

WATERCREST INSTITUTE

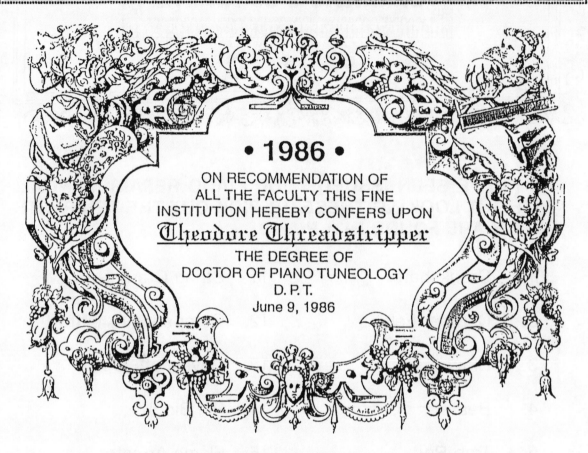

• 1986 •

ON RECOMMENDATION OF
ALL THE FACULTY THIS FINE
INSTITUTION HEREBY CONFERS UPON

Theodore Threadstripper

THE DEGREE OF
DOCTOR OF PIANO TUNEOLOGY
D. P. T.
June 9, 1986

**STUDENT HAS SATISFACTORILY PURSUED THE
REQUIRED STUDIES AND TESTS AND IS THEREFORE
PRONOUNCED A CERTIFIED D.P.T.**

with all rights, privileges and honors pertaining thereto.

We do not guarantee his work and will not be responsible for work not up
to professional standards. Grades achieved were within the guidelines for
promotion but we have no evidence that the graduate did not cheat on the
test, purchase test material for advance study or pay to secure his diploma.
We do not know if the person who took this test was actually the student himself.

We will certify that his tuition check was good, our main and only concern.

Now the graduate is out in the mainstream soliciting work from the general public. That's you.

He has a list of things with numbers that he rattles off whenever he has the chance. Two pedals, 3 pedals, 20 tons pressure on the strings, 44 keys, 65 keys, 88 keys, 230 strings, 440 pitch and $500 for repairs. Pianos have basic parts like keys, strings, hammers, etc. But you might be told about hammer butts, retention springs, bridges, keybeds, coil locks, plate bushings, pin blocks, actions and dampers. This is usually all bullshit! In fact the new piano tuner has memorized these parts and if you asked him to point them out he wouldn't know any more than you do. Tell him, "I just want the thing tuned – can the sermon!"

Piano tuners usually come in casual clothes with a small case similar to a brief case. On occasion there might be a metal tool box. Their tools are small and the work they do is relatively quiet except for the sound from the notes being played on the piano. Average time is one to three hours. The average charges without parts range from $40-$75 and the work is most often completed in one visit.

Beware of the "would-be tuners" out to rip you off. They show up in a 26-foot diesel van truck marked "INTERNATIONAL MUSICAL DIAGNOSTIC INTERPRETATION AND CORRECTIONAL SERVICES OF AMERICA LTD." There are usually three men in coveralls who come into your home with tarps, lighting plants, and big rolling tool boxes similar to those you would find in a NASCAR garage. Within fifteen minutes they tell you something like: "Your goldfarb is hitting your fricken and the wallyfrass has some frayed wiring leading to the rotating commutator." They then tell you that the piano could explode if you play it above middle 'C' and it would be best for them to take it to the shop for repairs. The estimate will be somewhere in the neighborhood of $1000 (excluding moving) but they will let you know if they find anything else once it is at the shop. They will ask for your credit card number as well. Once that piano has left your home you will never again know what has happened to it. It is probably best to report it stolen and replace it. If they ever do get back to you it will become apparent after further diagnosis that your deedle-banger is worn out and has left all the hammers in the piano with severe damage on the fromkiss. New estimate is $2000 and they will ask if someone can come by and have you sign a charge slip for the first $1500 so they can proceed. Now is the time you must ask yourself if it is prudent to sink $2000 into a piano for which you paid a total of $125 delivered.

Although the fear of a dishonest tuner might be in your mind, PLEASE, DO NOT TRY TO TUNE YOUR OWN PIANO! The strings altogether exert a huge strain on the mainframe. If you increase this strain through misinformation or stupidity the piano will explode and kill everyone in the house. Perhaps the parts will rocket up through the chimney and roof. Homeowner's does not cover stupidity.

Of course, there are telltale things to watch for when you are employing a tuner. Many of these can be early warning signs which will tell you to be wary and ever vigilant throughout the entire tuning process. I am not saying that you have to spy on this person every moment but IT IS YOUR MONEY! And your piano as well.

BEWARE: Of a tuner who arrives with a three day beard, rumpled clothes, a large cooler of beer, and his tools in a plastic bag. He may not be your best bet for this job – at least not today.

BEWARE: Of the tuner who arrives in a limo wearing a smoking jacket, patent leather pumps, striped trousers and a money belt. He may be smoking a pipe and he will tell the driver to wait. He will not drink or take drugs in your presence but instead will return to the limo MANY times during the tuning. There is a young blonde lady in the back, often referred to as his travelling secretary or parts clerk.

BEWARE: Some tuners are not rebuilders. There is a difference. There are about 3500-4000 parts in a regular piano. Given this fact, there must be a million in a player piano. If the tuner is working on your player piano, observe what is happening. All the parts in a player piano are old, dry, non-replaceable, and not numbered but necessary. If your tuner has created a pile of parts on the floor which now exceeds his height, you are in trouble. The dead giveaway is when he looks at the pile of parts and says, "I'll have to come back tomorrow." You are now on your own. Unless you think making a novena might help, you should shovel up all the parts and throw them in the trash. Burn all your old piano rolls and use the piano cabinet for a planter. Odds are the piano would never have been the same again anyway. And for sure, HE AIN'T COMIN' BACK!

BEWARE: TUNING IN BARS, CLUBS, AND OTHER WATERING HOLES.

BEWARE: If your piano tuner is tuning the piano in your barroom and he spends two hours trying to hit on the barmaid. You should not be charged for that time.

BEWARE: If the tuner buys a round of drinks for some gals at the bar while he is working and adds that to your bill—you are getting taken.

BEWARE: If the tuner asks you for a napkin at the end of the job so he can write you out a receipt.

BEWARE: If at the end of the job someone has to pack his tools for him and he cannot physically write out the receipt because he can't remember what he did fifteen minutes ago. He may have been over-served and you must scan the bill or write it out yourself.

BEWARE: If the tuner laughs a lot, falls down or cannot get up from a kneeling position without help. If he constantly refers to your piano as the box, crate, rig, or manual entertainment center he may have had just a wee bit too much to drink while doing his work.

BEWARE: If the tuner gets behind the piano and does not come out for more than an hour there is a problem. Basically there is nothing back there for him to work on and he may have passed out. You may opt to let him sleep but be sure that this time is not reflected on your invoice.

BEWARE: If the tuner is using an electronic device to impress you and it is not plugged in. Electrical things do not work well without power. Also, if he repeatedly pounds on the electrical devices with a hammer his equipment may not be up to par.

BEWARE: Do not use a tuner who has a tape deck on which he is playing some other tuner's work from which he is trying to get some hints. There may be a problem here.

ASK THE AUTHOR
—
NO. A-308

Dear Don:

We have an upright piano which has been in the family for four generations. A while ago I had the front off to clean dust from the interior and my 5-year-old broke off six hammers and then flushed them down the toilet. The tuner says there are no new parts available for this piano so two weeks ago my husband had the cover taken off of the septic tank and sure enough, there were the hammers. Can we use them over again?

~ Flushing in Fargo

Dear Flushing:

Basically I would think that would be up to the repairman. He is going to handle them. They should be boiled in a solution of root beer, linseed oil, salt, garlic, and rose petals. Many of the very old uprights sound like crap anyway so I can't see where this re-use could hurt.

ASK THE AUTHOR

—

NO. A432

Dear Don:

We have an upright piano at our lakefront summer cottage. People tell us that in the winter months the piano will pick up excessive moisture and the strings and pins will rust. I know it always needs tuning each spring but what about this rust thing? It's a neat piano and I want to keep it.

~ Rusting in Riverside

Dear Rusting:

It is true, strings and pins can rust. Try spraying the inside with WD-40. If rusting persists, open the top cover of the piano and stand on the keyboard cover. Dump a five gallon pail of 10W30 motor oil into the piano, making sure to spread it the full width of the keyboard. You may also want to paint the back of the piano with roofing tar.

For maximum protection, try wrapping your piano in a "fat man" body bag from the coroner's office.

P.S. There is a unit called the "Devonshire Model BH800" which is a butane/propane fired heating device. It is self contained and needs no electric. It will keep your piano at 250° 24/7/365 as long as you have the propane tank full. Costly but effective.

ASK THE AUTHOR

NO. F-1

Dear Don:

A while ago I had my piano tuned. Although the tuner was an average looking man I found the tuning process erotic. Each strike of the notes seemed to further excite me. By the time he was done I was so horny I could hardly write the check. What can I do?

~ Horny in Hannibal

Dear Horny:

Music in any form can stimulate, excite, or provoke human emotions. My advice: next time the tuner comes compensate up front and take him to bed before he unpacks his tools. Both of you will be able to relax during the tuning. When you get the bill, be sure the amount is much lower than for previous tunings. Do not believe the tuner when he says your piano should be tuned twice each week from now on.

ASK THE AUTHOR

—

NO. L-74

Dear Don:

I recently needed to get a new piano tuner. I was told that blind people are very good at this type of work and then last week somebody also told me of a local deaf piano tuner. What is the story here? I would love to help the handicapped.

~ Dumfounded in Dallas

Dear Dumfounded:

Deaf piano tuners have not made great inroads into this trade. They may exist but are both rare and questionable. Piano tuners who are blind are very good tuners. It seems that nature provides extra acute ability for someone who has lost another sense. It is wise however to stay in the rear of the house until the tuner has parked his car, even if he has a white cane stuck out of the driver's window. Some assume that once their vehicle has struck your house that they have arrived. Try to overlook these little things.

ASK THE AUTHOR

—

NO. A-114

Dear Don:

I am very new at this piano game. I have just bought a used piano and have only been playing a few months. How do I know when my piano needs tuning?

~ Confused in Cleveland

Dear Confused:

Easy fix here. Most automobile horns are tuned to the key of 'F.' Pull your car alongside the house and push your piano over to the nearest window. Have one of your kids or a neighbor go out and lean on the horn. If you can duplicate the car horn sound by play-ing the proper 'F' on your piano it does not need tuning just yet. For those of you with pianos in a high-rise situation, go out and put your ear against the grille of the car. Have someone blow the horn for fifteen seconds. That should ring in your head for an hour. Go upstairs and check it out.

THE PLAYER PIANO REPAIRMAN

A player piano repairman can tell you so much crap that you have no idea what he is talking about. It would be like your first day at computer school. Names of parts and pieces that do not ring a bell with you at all.

He comes over to your house and sits at the piano. Runs a few scales on the piano manually and then opens his box and brings out a roll. This is a "test roll" he brought along with him. It is pre-screwed up. The notes do not play at any equal volume and there are skips when no sound comes forth. It tends to start re-rolling in the middle of the tune and you never knew your problems were so great.

He begins by telling you that the piano has to go to the shop. This is akin to taking your elephant to the Vet. He pulls out a book and shows you a piano builder's factory diagram of the entire player piano system and you draw a blank.

Next item is that your tubing is failing and you will need a tubal ligation. He does not know what that means either but he saw it on a hospital show on the Learning Channel. It sounded important.

He becomes vulgar when he tells you that most player pianos are supposed to suck and he feels that your piano blows. You want to swat him in the head for being so vulgar and crude but then he goes on to tell you about the vacuum system and what happens when your bellows rupture. He also tells you there is a good chance that your timing chain is worn to the point it is rubbing on your snotfluter and that the main hose from the primary blower is also a problem. It seems that this hose is servicing the shiny brass bar with all the holes in it. That's the one the roll passes over right in front of you.

The problem is that the rig is picking up all kinds of dust and mites and blowing them into your face.

Having said that he tells you that for $2500 he can bring this piano back to original and you probably won't die. The deposit would be $500 and the job would take six to eight weeks because he has two pianos ahead of yours. He has to order the parts and they come from Pakistan but he'll try to kick that along. Secretly he is hoping that he can stay sober that long.

Hey, aren't you glad you had this little chat?

Note: He did not mention that his wife beating case comes up in court in four weeks and he might go to jail while your piano is in his shop.

ASK THE AUTHOR

—

NO. A314

Dear Don:

Recently I was operating our player piano. I had a cigarette going and when I blew smoke at that brass bar which the rolls pass over, it seemed to suck the smoke in. My question is, where does that smoke go? I ran around behind the piano to look and none came out.

~ Smoking in Sandusky

Dear Smoking:

All player pianos have smoke converters. Any smoke which is taken in is turned into dirt. The dirt created is four times the smoke entering the piano. Therefore, if you blew a whole pack in there the dirt pile would be the size of four cigarette packs. Many heavy smokers empty their pianos annually, usually in the Spring so they can use that dirt on their gardens. If you don't empty the piano periodically the dirt will get so deep the keys will stop working.

Note: Conversion for cigars is two to one. If you smoke a box the pile will be the size of two boxes.

THE LADY TUNER

Ever put the top down and lay on top of your piano?

As the preface of this book indicates, not all the people in the piano-associated professions are men – quite the opposite. There are great women all along the chain. These gals have added a much needed flair to the industry: salespeople, teachers and female entertainers are all a welcome addition. There are also those women who have entered the technical side of the piano business. They work in the fields of design and manufacture and a natural progression has taken them into the world of tuning and rebuilding as well. People generally conjure up the image of a piano tuner as a middle-aged male or perhaps even a senior citizen. The customer's impression of his skill is often tied to his age, the older the better. Well, not all these theories are etched in stone. Some startling exceptions are on the loose – let's look in on one.

You are a man in your sixties, a widower of three years, residing in a nice neighborhood. Your home has retained its appearance inside through the weekly efforts of a cleaning lady and your grand piano in the living room still has its sparkle thanks to her. In keeping with your annual ritual you have decided it is time to have the piano tuned. A few months ago your piano tuner of twelve years was involved in a serious accident which left him disabled. He has moved from the area to live with his daughter and you are faced with selecting a new tuner. You know no one else and are now flipping through the yellow pages. An advertisement catches your eye:

FINESSE PIANO TUNING SVC.
313 Victoria Ct. • Sledgewater 8-3333

**"SERVICE WITH A SMILE - ONCE YOU'VE HAD US
YOU WON'T WANT ANYONE ELSE"**

This ad just seems to make you want them in your home. You grab the phone and dial them. After a few rings a low feminine voice answers the phone.

"Finesse Piano. How may we help you today?"

You are put at ease from the very start.

"Hi, this is Percy Knowlittle. I am in need of a piano tuner. Would someone be available?"

"We are always available."

"That sounds good. How soon could you make it?"

"Where do you reside, Mr. Knowlittle?"

This voice is really disarming you, it's fantastic.

"I am on the culdesac off Benedict Arnold Parkway over near the lake. It is called Bearwhizz Park. I am number twelve."

"Great. We will be working your area this Friday. Can someone be home to let us into the house?"

"Certainly. I will be here personally. What time might you arrive?"

"Well Mr. Knowlittle, it looks like three o'clock would be my best guess if our other appointments go as planned. Would that time be convenient?"

"That would be super, and please, call me Percy."

"Okay, Percy. Someone will be there Friday around three. And thank you for calling Finesse Piano."

You hang up the phone and find yourself experiencing a warm fuzzy feeling. You are confident that you have just talked to the greatest secretary or receptionist that you can remember. You somehow wish that tomorrow was Friday but that day is still five days away. The appointment is duly noted on your big wall calendar in the kitchen and you go about your business knowing that the piano tuning has been dealt with for now.

The week has passed without incident. You have put in your part-time hours at Reuben Bros. Electric Company where you are a counterman. It is just something to keep you busy in your retirement and does not pose any real challenge. You have taken off at Noon on Friday to insure that you will not be late for the tuner. After lunch at home you go next door to collect some money from your new neighbors—Rafael and Carmen Finnegan. They moved in several months ago and her first attempt at operating a twelve-horse power riding mower was a wipeout. First she hit their car and then in a panic swerved away just at the right angle to plow through your flower beds and return to her yard via your new hedgerow. They figured since no one got hurt that "I'm sorry" would work. You figured that $500 would work a lot better and they have been putting you off until today. You spend a few minutes with Carmen and are happy to leave this issue behind as you walk back home with five crisp $100 bills in your hand.

As you return to your front door you spot your computer teacher on your front step. He has walked over to your house from his home down the street. Oh yeah, you almost forgot that you told him you might be home early today. He is going to set you up to be able to trade stocks over the internet. This will help to pass the afternoon while you wait for the tuner. It is 1:30 P.M. and you feel there is ample time to get this done so you usher him through the door and into the den. The computer is already running and he gets to fooling around with it to get the program he wants you to study.

Your teacher is Vladimir Bitchalot. You met him a few months ago at a block party. Russian by descent he has been in the United States for about forty years. He is a retired professor of economics from Helen Keller University in Natchez. A confirmed student of the Andrew Mellon School of Finance, he loves money, worships the computer and the internet and still has his first dollar framed at home. To say that he is frugal would be the understatement of the year. It is a safe bet to say that he would not pay five cents to see Jesus tap dance on Lake Michigan. He is dark of feature, sporting a well-trimmed gray beard and mustache and he is wearing his trademark wire-rimmed glasses. At a height in excess of six feet he carries himself very well for a man in his seventies. Although his speech still reflects his native tongue to some degree, he does have a command of the English language.

As he proceeds into his presentation, his loud and very authoritative voice is in sharp contrast to the soft and sexy voice that you are now secretly hearing in your subconscious. You have had recurring thoughts about that since Monday. You are keenly aware that the minutes are ticking away toward the three o'clock mark.

At 2:45 P.M. you tell Vladimir that you have the hang of it now. This despite the pleasant recollection of that soft voice saying, "Three o'clock Friday" has distracted you to the point that you have missed half of what he has been showing you. Now you just want him gone so you can spend some quality time with the tuner when he arrives. You don't want just any old jerk working on your $40,000 Steinway grand. Vladimir accepts his dismissal with the air of a man destined to much more important chores and he is gone in a flash.

You shut down the computer and walk about the house to make sure things are in order. Don't want this piano guy to think you are a slob. Suddenly the doorbell chimes. You glance at your watch, it is 3:02 P.M. These folks are prompt, that's a good sign. You swing open the front door and your pacemaker draws full voltage. This is no guy standing here. No, indeed! Before you stands a lady. A beautiful young, smiling, breathtaking tall lady.

"Hi, I'm from Finesse. Are you Percy?"

In your current state of shock you are not sure of the right answer to the question.

"Hmmmmm. Percy. Oh yes, that's me. Won't you please come in?"

She glides through the door as if propelled by a breeze. You close the door and feel yourself helpless not to stare.

"Are you the piano tuner?"

"That's me honey. Here's my card.

FINESSE PIANO TUNING SERVICE
MS. COPPA FEEL – Technician
R.P.T.   C.A.P.T.   P.T.G.

First take on your part: She is EASY, BREEZY, BEAUTIFUL. The unblemished clarity of her skin and its apparent softness is striking. Her perfume is just right. Not overpowering. Just an enchanting fragrance which invigorates you at once. You suppose that Elizabeth Arden has already given this scent a name. If you were naming it you would call it "My Place or Yours." It is wonderfully aromatic. Engulfed by it, you take a moment to look at her.

A flawless look. She is dressed in a man's blue business suit with a faint white pinstripe pattern. It is set off by a white blouse opened at the neck. In each hand she is carrying a suitcase, one larger than the other. To relieve her of these you show her across the thick carpeting to the piano bench. She places her bags beside the bench and sits down. Glancing around she says,

"You have a very beautiful home here. Your family must be very happy with it."

You reply, "Oh I have no family. I'm a retiree and a widower and I live here alone."

Her face lights up like Macy's best store window at Christmastime.

In her seated position her trouser cuffs have risen to reveal her suntan hose, spotless black high heels and an eye-catching diamond ankle bracelet. The ankle bracelet is only the beginning of her elegant jewelry. Her necklace, earrings, watch and arm bracelets are all part of a polished collection. She sparkles from head to foot.

"Well, Percy—you don't mind me calling you that do you? It was noted on the order that you told the office you wanted it that way."

"Oh hell no. Feel free to call me Percy."

Her soft voice reminds you of the Monday phone call all over again but this time the speaker is in living color.

"Tell me a bit about this piano of yours."

"Well, I believe it is just thirty years old. We, that is my wife and I, bought it at an estate auction about fifteen years ago. She was quite an accomplished pianist and since her passing I have learned to entertain myself on it although I am nowhere near as proficient as she was."

"I see. I am sorry to hear of your wife's passing. How long has she been gone?"

"It will be four years in February."

"I'll bet you still miss her."

"Yes, that's why I find great solace in the piano. When I play it seems a part of her is still here."

My goodness. Here you are talking to this goddess in blue as if she were your psychiatrist. She has been here less than five minutes and you are feeling warm all over. You'd tell her anything she wanted to know at this point.

She swings around, places her hands on the keyboard and begins to play a classical piece of music. It is dreamy and her playing is that of a well trained student. In a way this song reminds you of your wife's playing and you wish this gal would just do it for an hour. You are becoming more and more relaxed and she is rapidly stealing your heart. The music stops and you come down off your cloud. She spins around on the bench and says, "You have a very beautiful instrument here. You have taken great care of it over the years. The Steinways are one of my favorite line of pianos. When was the last time you had someone tune it?"

"I think it was about this same time last year. I'm not exactly sure. My tuner of twelve years is gone away. He kept the records and he would automatically call me when it was time to do the tuning."

"May I ask who did the work?"

"Sure. His name was Clive Fortnight. They called him Magic Hands. Perhaps you have heard of him."

"No, I can't recall hearing that name."

Now she looks straight into your eyes while she stretches her beautiful long fingers in your direction.

"Percy, when it comes to magic hands these babies have done more magic in twenty-six years than Houdini did until he died."

There is a lightness to her voice, perhaps even a hint of laughter. You stare at those beautiful hands and fantasize. WOW!

"Well, we'd better get started." She rises to full height. In heels and with her brunette hair pulled back on her head she stands fully four to five inches taller than you. Of course this is no mean feat since you have never measured over five-foot-five. In a swift motion she places both of her cases on the bench. Now she lays another trip on your mind as she opens one up.

"I'll just need a few minutes to change into my work clothes and I'll get right to work."

"Oh sure, the bathroom is right down this hallway on your left."

"Nonsense," she says. "I don't want to mess up your bathroom. I can change right over here by the piano. It isn't like I'm going to be buck naked or anything. Besides, you look like a guy I can trust."

HOLY SHIT! She's going to strip in your living room!

"Okay, sure. If you think that's alright you can do your changing wherever you'd like. I can go into the kitchen while you're doing that."

"Well, whatever you'd like, Percy. It'll only take a jif."

She grabs a plastic bag out of the larger case she had opened and walks around to the far side of the piano. With the top of the piano in the raised position she is partially hidden. Your best intention is to go to the kitchen but you find yourself damn slow getting to it. You are thinking as fine a tuner Mr. Fortnight was, he never came close to this show.

Now composing yourself and wanting to be every bit the trusted man she has said you are, you wander into the kitchen. You seem to be very warm and your heart is palpitating some. Maybe a blood pressure pill would be good right now. You took one this morning and generally that is it for the day, but this is a very special occasion. As you palm the pill and go to draw some water it occurs to you that a short drink might relax you. In one of the cupboards is your limited supply of alcohol. It is not your big thing. You choose a bottle of Crown Royal leftover from Christmas and pour two fingers into a rock glass. The liquor is gone in one swig and the pill has been washed on its way. The warming effect of the drink is immediate. Boy, this is really turning out to be a very different day than you would have thought. You step to the kitchen doorway and holler,

"How ya doin' in there?"

"Great, I'm all set, thanks."

"Do you mind if I come back in there?"

"Percy, I'd love it. Come on back in here, honey."

Honey. WOW! That's neat!

Braced up by the oncoming glow from the Crown Royal you re-enter your living room. HOLY SHIT all over again. Ms. Feel is parading around in a pair of red leather hot pants and her shoes are gone. In addition she has a skin tight T-shirt sporting the caption across the front:

"EINSTEIN'S THEORY WAS REALLY E = F FLAT"

Given the size of her chest the F flat part was a glaring contradiction. This setup could well have been for a Playboy photo shoot. You are warmer now than ever. You move towards the piano and something else catches your eye. You remember that Clive Fortnight always walked back and forth to his attache case to get his tools. This gal has a crimson colored leather tool belt around her waist. It is riding high on her curvaceous hips and half a dozen chrome tools are hanging in small loops on each side. The sunlight coming through the window lights them up as she moves around. Now in your mind you can picture her wearing two six guns and a cowboy hat. Boy, is this lady starting to rent a lot of space in your head.

You are now at the piano bench and both cases are atop it and opened wide. The smaller one has a selection of tools which are not on her tool belt. The other case—the larger of the two—is however a real revelation to you. You can't help thinking that this is some really exotic tuning equipment. At a glance you see several bottles of pills. There is a fancy flat glass container about the size of a compact and it is full of some sort of white powder. There are three boxes of condoms, a pair of hand-cuffs and some feather gadget. Rolled in one of the corners you spot some clothing which you make out to be black lace panties and a bra. Next to that is a small paper-back book entitled *The Foreplay Report 1998*. There is also a videotape there. You have to crank your head around to be able to read the title, "PONIES, DOGS, MEN, WOMEN, & FUN." Topping off the contents there is a flat metal box that you run credit cards through to validate a sale. You are now starting to pick up a new vision. Percy, this ain't no run-of-the-mill piano tuner.

She is over by the side of the piano leaning into it and working some sort of tool. She definitely has been watching you scope out the open cases – after all, she left them open just for that reason. You are ever more aware of your heart beating and think it might be advisable to open the front door and let some breeze in through the screen. While doing this you notice for the first time that this lady has arrived in a brand new snow white Mercedes. Percy, now you know she is no ordinary piano tuner.

You have a flashback to Fortnight's beat up station wagon, an Oldsmobile you think. He always backed it into the driveway so the Auto Club could get the hood up to jump the battery when it wouldn't start. Now another thought has popped into your head. If Fortnight drove that beat up crate all of those years and could never afford an upgrade how does she at age twenty-six afford a new Mercedes? You steal anoth-er glance at her and hope it will take forever for her to tune that piano. You guess it is time to ask what it is costing to do this job since it never came up in Monday's call. You wander over next to her and clear your throat.

"Say, Ms Feel, how much are you charging these days?"

"For what, Percy?"

"For tuning the piano, naturally."

"Oh that. Well, the basic tuning is about $60 if we don't need any parts. And this piano is super nice so I don't think it should need any repairs."

She grabs you gently by the waist and pulls you to the side of the piano.

"Here, take a peek. This baby is as clean as the driven snow. Your last tuner did a very thorough job. Probably he went beyond his normal duties. But then, so do I."

The way you feel at this second she could probably tell you it cost $5000 and you'd tell her to do it twice.

"So, you figure I'm about at the $60 level for today?"

"Well, Percy, there are all sorts of money plans with our group. You can pay the $60 if you like or I can charge you $100 per hour and that way I can expand your services and toss in the tuning."

Yes, Percy, you're right. She's coming on to you. Now you suddenly feel inadequate to play in her league. You had expected a man tuner so basically you are dressed down. Baggy casual pants and an old beige shirt. Knock around loafers that have seen better days. And what's this? Is there a bead of sweat on your glasses?

She gives you that little soft laugh and says, "You don't have to decide this second. I've got some time to go here."

Slowly she slides her hand across your back as she pulls her arm from behind you and returns to her work. You move away a step or two and then tell her you have to go back into the kitchen for a few minutes. It's either that or drop dead from a heart attack right here in your own living room. You waste no time beating it back to the kitchen and you wonder if another blood pressure pill would be good for this anxiety you are feeling. NO. Better not, you've already had two. But another little glass of Crown Royal wouldn't hurt. This you do in haste. Now a ridiculous thought comes to you. Maybe you should change your clothes. To you this seems important. To her clothes are just things to take off. In the next moments you are in your bedroom dressing up for the piano tuner. Much better slacks, a polo shirt and your best shoes. You glance in the dresser mirror and decide you better butter up your chapped lips and comb what hair you have left. Nothing you can do about the balding area and it would look like over kill to come out in a hat. Your libido is kicking in for the first time in years and as a final male upgrade you stuff a rolled up sock into the front of your jockey shorts. That should ring her bell.

As you exit the bedroom and return to the kitchen you wonder if she might like a drink. You move to the living room archway and ask. "Can I get you something to drink?"

"Sure Percy, that'd be great."

"What is your pleasure?"

"Got any Scotch?"

"Yes. I've got a nice bottle of single malt Glen Baywatch."

"Perfect. I'll have some of that."

"What would you like for a mixer?"

"Not necessary. On the rocks is fine."

"Coming right up."

You skate back to the cupboard and grab the Scotch. Pull down a rock glass for her and pop a few ice cubes into it. She's a big girl so you probably should give her a big drink. Three shots over ice should be just fine. This booze on the rocks sounds good to you so you also pour three shots of Crown Royal over some ice for yourself. You really never drink this much but it would be insulting to ask your guest to drink alone. You return to the living room with both glasses. She spots you and puts down her tools. She comes around to the bench and sits on one end of it, one leg tucked under her and the other stretched out for your review. You really don't need a review. You've been thinking about them since the first time you saw her. She has purposely left ample room for you to join her and that is your next move.

As you two sit there sipping your drinks you are the first to speak.

"Tell me more about this alternate charge plan."

She looks right into your eyes. Hers are blazing blue. Somehow with all this Crown Royal you're pumping into your system you figure yours are probably blazing red. You know for sure that they are watering a bit.

"Well, for the $100 per hour service I not only tune the piano but I will show you some other things to do with the piano. And I will play some more songs for you if you'd like."

"Know any jazz or ragtime?"

That was a stupid question. What the hell difference does it make if she plays Twelfth Street Rag or Theme from Swan Lake as long as you can sit next to her while she is doing it?

"Sure Percy. I love jazz. Fats Waller is my favorite."

"Give me a sample. My interest is piqued."

"Okay. Here, hold my drink."

She passes the drink to you and you can feel your whole body going weak. This is getting to be one fast moving show you are involved with. She places those gorgeous hands onto the keys and starts out with a moderately paced version of "Ain't Misbehavin." All the chords are full and it sounds great. As soon as she finishes that she turns to you and says, "You know, Fats Waller wrote some great music. His vocals are outrageous. Listen to this."

She plays an introduction that you do not recognize and now she is singing a song entitled, "Find Out What He Likes and How He Likes It" (and give it to him just that way). Any doubts you had about this afternoon's program are fast disappearing.

Song completed, she swings back around on the bench. This time she is sort of leaning her back against the keys and both legs are stretched right out straight. Her Einstein T-shirt is also stretched out tighter than shrinkwrap on a boat in for winter storage. You hand her back her glass of Scotch and you both take another drink.

"So, did you like those tunes?"

"I loved them both; you are a very talented lady."

"Thanks, I'd like to think that's true."

"You mentioned other things you could show me about the piano. I have been around pianos for many years and although I can't play as well as you do I feel I do know a considerable amount about them."

"Ever been under one?"

"What?'"

"Have you ever taken the time to slide under a piano like this one and gaze at the underside. It would be great on this rug."

"No, I can't say I have."

"Ever put the top down and lay on top of your piano?"

"My God, no. This top's never been down."

"Percy my man, I can take you under and over this piano and show you things even Steinway didn't know about a grand."

"This is all very interesting." Secretly you say to yourself: Interesting, bullshit. This is downright fantastic and overwhelming.

"Now, Percy, we also have another option which is geared up for those not faint of heart. For $500 I can call one of our stretch limos and you and I can go to dinner. After we have dinner we'll come back here and I'll spend the night with you. That way I'll be here in the morning to check out your piano once more to make sure it stayed tuned."

About this time that rolled up sock in your shorts is really starting to get in the way. She has that genuinely arresting smile and soft laugh about her and you gulp the rest of your drink. She follows your lead and downs hers. You take her glass and she stands again. She says, "Well, I got to get back to work now. Thanks for the drink."

"Don't mention it. I'll just take these glasses into the kitchen."

You are so revved up you can't even get a good grip on the glasses – or yourself for that matter. Here you are, a sixty-six-year-old man going through the first proposition of your lifetime and you are half shit-faced already and falling apart at the seams. You stand there listening to the notes of the piano being struck in the other room knowing that this lady will soon want a decision. You walk out the back door onto the patio and plop yourself down at the picnic bench. It's time to get your thoughts together. This afternoon has taken you by storm and it would be well for you to review the facts.

Your take-home pay from your part-time job is about $106 per week. That means if you go for the $500 deal you will have to work five weeks just to pay for it. She is twenty-six and you are sixty-six; that's quite a spread. You have a pacemaker and you are sure she doesn't. A roll in the hay with her could easily kill you. Is it that important? You can always call the same company again and next time maybe you'll have the courage to make all these choices. You sit outside far longer than you realize and suddenly she is standing at the back door.

"Percy, honey, I'm done tuning. Do you want to come in and play a tune to see how it sounds?"

"Oh yes. That would be swell."

She holds the door open and you pass by her. She makes sure there is not enough room for you to enter without brushing against her breasts. The heat is starting all over again. You both go to the piano and you sit down to play. While you are preparing to do this she is standing right behind you. She places her palms on your shoulders and begins to massage your shoulders and neck. You play a song that you know very well and because of her you make a dozen mistakes. You finish the song and decide it is time to pull the plug. You stand up and move away from the bench.

"The piano sounds great, Ms Feel."

"Thank you, Percy."

"You've done a wonderful job. I would like to explore your other offers but I just realized I have a dinner party to attend at six o'clock tonight and time is running short. How much do I owe?"

"Sixty-eight-fifty with the tax, Percy."

"Perhaps you'd like to change while I get your money."

"I'll do just that, thanks."

You go to your bedroom and find your hands trembling as you peel off one of the $100 bills you got earlier today. Think about this Percy. Think what you are letting out the door. You wrestle once more with all your options and then your mind is made up in a second. There on the dresser is a picture of you and your wife. She is smiling and you know she would want you to be happy in her absence. But perhaps this is TOO HAPPY.

Back in the living room your tuning goddess has redressed into her suit and is looking every bit the part of a Madison Avenue lawyer. She has a bill printed out for you and as you take it from her you hand her the hundred.

"Please keep the difference. You've given me quite an afternoon."

"I'm glad you enjoyed it. Thanks for the drink."

"Oh believe me, the pleasure was all mine."

"Well, if you need me again you have my card. Give me a call. By the way, I like what you did to your pants."

"Thanks, be seein' ya." You are beet red, she did notice the sock.

She walks out to her Mercedes, puts her bags in the trunk and is out of the driveway in a minute or less. What an afternoon... HOLY SHIT.

You shut the door and turn inward. One glance at the piano and several things race into your brain.

1.   You never even heard the piano when you played it.

2.   You couldn't give a shit if she even did anything to it.

3.   Seems like a year is too long between tunings—should get her here about every three months.

4.   Imagine if you had been having her over for the last twelve years instead of good old Fortnight.

5.   NO GOOD. Your wife would have only let that happen once. And twelve years ago Ms Feel would have only been 14.

Time to hit the couch and let the Crown Royal paint your fantasies until slumber becomes the victor.

In a moment of bravado you hope the neighbors saw her leave.

TEACHERS

The world's "PIANO FARMERS"

"Only they can plant the seed to grow a star."

THE TEACHERS

Perhaps the one most critical person involved in the piano industry is the teacher. People can design, build, sell, tune and move pianos, but the piano remains a useless piece of furniture until someone learns to play it. It is through the undying devotion of the army of teachers that we hear the gorgeous tones and tunes of the piano. Our hats are off to the teachers—the backbone of the piano world.

A piano teacher is endowed with a special gift, a drive to help others learn what he or she has already discovered. The piano is an endless tool of experimentation, eclipsing other instruments which cannot by themselves produce its rich harmonic blends. Millions have attempted to conquer this fine instrument and many do arrive at some degree of proficiency during their lifetime. With the exception of prodigies born to the music, the struggle to understand and conquer the piano's complexities is only aided by one person: THE TEACHER.

Teachers who are educated at top level music institutions can invest $100,000 or more to receive their diplomas. A person has to be determined to keep their nose to the grindstone for a long while to recover such an investment. In essence, the teacher sets out on a lifetime journey; planting seeds and hoping for a flower. Teachers sort through the diverse agendas of thousands of students, playing the role of everyone from John Wayne to Mother Teresa to motivate that student.

They must be able to convince even the most skeptical that hard work, willpower, and determination will see them through. Further, they must paint the picture that piano keys are the keys to a kingdom of entertainment and enjoyment. In this sometimes thankless occupation the teacher faces many adversities and challenges. From the first day a student starts the teacher does not set out to be an intimidating force nor do they expect to be worshiped. What they do hope for is to be understood and trusted. No one ever knows when a child is born anywhere in this world what musical ability might lie within. It is the teacher, the person I call the "Piano Farmer," who will plant that seed, nurture that child and pray for the strength that they may teach well and not derail any students from their aspirations. Those students who master and achieve are the flowers of the "Piano Farmer."

Do teachers ever cry?
You bet they do. Just catch one when they are at a recital and they think no one is watching. You will see eyes water up in an outpouring of emotion and sheer enjoyment.

Do teachers ever pray?
Of course they do. They pray for the students to practice.

Do teachers seem too hard on the student?
Not at all. The student may think so but they have missed the twinkle of an eye or the silent smile that just happened behind their back.

Are there whacked-out teachers?
You know there are. Let's take a look.

1947

PIANO TEACHER
FREEDOM OF
INFORMATION
—— ACT ——

1947

In the spring of 1947, a meeting of teachers from all over the United States and Canada was convened. The purpose of this assembly was to hammer out certain issues and to draft iron-clad rules concerning the teacher-student relationship. After months of horror stories by teachers, the Piano Teacher Freedom of Information Act of 1947 was passed by a vote of 432 to 6. The drafting of this most valuable document insures that hardships heretofore endured by teachers will no longer be tolerated nor expected. Since the actual text is lengthy, we present here a brief overview.

In the conducting of business between students and teachers there must be formed some common bond. There must be a trust by the student that the teacher is knowledgeable not only of the material but also of the necessary means of conveying that material to the student. Likewise, the teacher must have some feeling that he is not whiling away the days and months trying to insert music into a rock. Although the personal lives of the student and teacher are just that, it seems that the teacher—not knowing any of the past history of the student—has the right to expect some degree of revelation concerning matters which might directly enter into the learning process.

It is safe to say that no two of us are alike when it comes to medical things. Our bodies are all running at various speeds and we are experiencing varying degrees of health. Only the student's disclosures to the teacher about various maladies can prepare the instructor for what otherwise could be an upsetting event.

If you are taking some sort of medication, it may be to your advantage to inform the teacher. That way, if you fall off the bench in a coma, he may be able to speak on your behalf when the 911 people arrive on the scene. It seems that in today's rat race, most of us are on some sort of medicinal trip. Some of the more common ones are:

Exlax	Cod Liver oil	Visine	Ritalin
Prozac	Viagra	Alcohol	Darvon
Sterno	Decon	Ludes	Codeine
Crack	Valium	Ecstacy	Cocaine
Marijuana	Kaeopectate	Suppositories	Speed

These and a host of other chemicals could alter your performance, cloud your mind and/or vision or impair your hearing.

It is a further courtesy to relate what effects these products may generate so that your teacher may be forewarned. If you think you will sneeze, fart, belch, cough, sway, sweat, convulse, shake, tremble or faint, let him know. If you are prone to honk, hurl or spew, it is well to have the necessary equipment on hand to minimize that effect as well. If you are on dialysis it is only proper that you schedule your lesson when you are not on the machine. If you have artificial arms and one is out being repaired, you may want to reschedule.

IN ALL CASES - DO NOT RESORT TO DECEPTION AND CHICANERY - IT COULD WORK AGAINST YOU IN THE LONG RUN.

TEACHER PROTECTION

In most cases, the teacher who calls at your home to give you a lesson has the right to expect some privacy and safety. If you are a person going through marital problems and your spouse is currently stalking you and prone to breaking into your home and taking pot shots at you with a handgun, you MUST tell this to the teacher. It would be most considerate of you to at least provide a flack jacket, bullet proof vest or Lexan shield for him. You may want to go a step further and provide the teacher a spot in another room or even the basement where he can monitor your playing over closed circuit TV without the danger of being murdered.

MEDICAL ETHICS

If you are terminally ill and expect you might die during a lesson, it is normal and expected that you pay in advance.

ECCENTRICITY AND TEACHERS

From time to time someone will label a teacher as an eccentric. This may be a misunderstanding of that person and is often unfair. After all, what is the definition of eccentricity?

Webster's defines **ECCENTRIC** as:
Deviating from the recognized or customary character, practice, etc. Irregular; erratic; peculiar; odd. One engaging in eccentric conduct.

I submit to you that almost everyone I know has some sort of eccentric behavior. To berate the teacher—just because they happen to be in the spotlight—does not seem fair. I would imagine that thousands of people are happy that no one knows their quirks, hobbies and endeavors. Just because someone travels a road not often trod by others does not make them eccentric. It may, in fact, make them bold trendsetters who take no joy in the mundane lifestyle and behavior of the masses. They seek to push the social envelope, test boundaries and get their kicks by doing something extreme. They know that life is a one-time deal and you'd better make of it what you will while you can. Before you label someone eccentric, review your own situation. You are probably either doing something eccentric yourself or are just sitting on your ass day after day listening to the grass grow and watching your car rust.

The following cases have been labeled eccentric behavior but I can only surmise that these folks love life and are just doing their thing. You may want to think about looking at them in a whole new light.

CASE NO. 1: FLANNERY FRICTIONBARK – SKATER/ACTRESS/TEACHER

Mrs. Frictionbark and her husband, Granger, live just north of Hugwillow Hollow. Mrs. Frictionbark is sixty-one and a former gold medal figure skater and movie actress. She has retained much of her youthful beauty and generates both a sunny and carefree image. She has strawberry blonde hair piled atop a 5'8" frame which is physically very well maintained. Her bright blue eyes look as though they may have been snatched from a store doll. For many years she studied piano and voice and now in her retirement she has become a part-time piano teacher.

Mr. Frictionbark is a retired commercial artist with over one hundred magazine and book covers to his credit. He was most noted for his portraits of famous Americans.

The Frictionbarks are far from destitute and have spent a considerable amount of money to pursue a dream. On their twenty-five-acre estate they have erected an indoor ice rink larger than a football field, complete with grandstand seating. This year-round ice palace is where Mrs. Frictionbark does her teaching.

The student enters the arena and is seated on a large float mounted on runners. The piano is bolted to this. All around the rink there are mannequins. Fifteen hundred in all. These were purchased at store closings around the country and then decorated to detail by Mr. Frictionbark. This is for the edification of Mrs. Frictionbark and usually scares the hell out of her students who think they are in a huge recital hall all the time.

Once the student is seated, Mr. Frictionbark begins to tow the float around the rink. He is dressed in a purple and pink snowmobile suit and is driving an electric blue Zamboni with portraits of angels all over it. On the Zamboni he also has an electronic control panel. From this he is able to activate speakers all over the building. Your piano lesson is being played to Mrs. Frictionbark as she skates behind the float. She is all gussied up in her beaded tutu and diamond spattered skates. As she listens to what you are playing, Mr. Frictionbark is also playing a skating song done on a huge pipe organ. This is so Mrs. Frictionbark can do her performance at the same time as your lesson. A remote control spotlight focuses back and forth from you to her (but mostly her) and when you have finished a piece of music, the Zamboni stops. A sound system broadcasts loud cheering from all over the grandstand area. The student is stunned as Mrs. Frictionbark skates to center ice and does her super spin and then a bow. The cheering slowly subsides and the float begins to move. She returns to the rear and once again skates along with you, singing her own song and telling you how nicely you are doing.

The students who have written about her have these complaints:

1. Object to carrying winter clothing to lessons in summer months

2. Zamboni does not stop for bathroom calls

3. Inability to perform difficult fingering with mittens on

4. Loss of concentration on lesson plan while overhead speakers are blaring skating music

CASE NO. 2: DUNCAN TRICKLEPEE – FIREFIGHTER/TEACHER

Mr. Tricklepee is a thirty-year veteran of the firefighting community. He is now fifty-six and still physically fit for his age. Thrice married, his latest wife has recently divorced him and all his children have grown and moved out. He owns his own home on a spacious lot. He became proficient at playing the piano during thousands of hours of "stand-by time" at the fire station. Finally getting serious, he pursued that talent, went to night school, and received a teacher's certificate. In 1988 he began teaching students after his retirement from firefighting. Our information regarding his supposed eccentricity leaves us wondering if he isn't still living his days on the job. Students report as follows:

Upon arrival for your lesson you push the button which would be the doorbell on any normal house. Here, a siren goes off and Mr. Tricklepee responds by sliding down a brass pole in a large glass tube just east of the door. (Rumor has it that as he first drafted students they were required to climb a ladder up into the third story window and slide down the pole with him but that practice was discontinued as young boys gathered to watch young girls slide down the pole). Next, Mr. Tricklepee opens the door, hands you a fire safety pamphlet and reminds you that this is a non-smoking area. After removing your jacket, sweater, etc. you are fitted with a Scott Air-Pac. You need this since Mr. Tricklepee also insists that all his students go through fire drills. You never know when that will be, but randomly he will throw a smoke bomb under the bench. This is followed by a deafening bell clanging over and over. He instructs you to "hit the floor," activate your air supply, and crawl out of the rear door to the side yard. You will usually wait there until he has shut off the bell and declared the structure safe for reentry.

Several times a year he also hauls tree stumps and wood from demolition jobs into the side yard and builds a huge fire. Well soaked with kerosene prior to ignition, by the time you get to see it, it is as high as the house with flames. He will then come running into the house yelling "FIRE, FIRE!" and the student is expected to jump into rubber boots and coat and rush with him to the fire site. The duration of the fire is not too long but during that period you are instructed in hydrant hookup and hose folding. At times you are also asked to take a walkie-talkie and go around to the opposite side of the fire to report the progress of the firefighting efforts. You are usually about fifteen feet away from him, can see him, and could probably yell the message over to him, but the walkie-talkies turn him on.

Mr. Tricklepee drives a red Chevy Blazer with all the roof top lights you might expect. His blazer and helmet carry the initials T.V.F.D. (Trickleepee Volunteer Fire Dept.) He is restoring a 1948 Ward LaFrance ladder truck in a slightly modified two-car garage at the rear of the house. That building also has indications that at one time or another it had either caught on fire or was set on fire. He has eight Dalmatians and the entire first floor of his home is a firefighting museum. Basic complaints from the students:

1.   Lots of dog poop around the piano and yard

2.   Students do not like playing while wearing steel helmets and air packs

3.   Parents often complain of students returning home stinking of smoke

4.   Teacher has scanner running on top of the piano at all times and often will run from the house and drive off when he hears about a nearby fire or accident

5.   Piano lessons are often held on an old upright piano in his garage while he works on this fire truck; female students complain of greasy hands and clothing when asked to stop playing and hand him tools

CASE NO. 3: TREVOR WHISKERMUFF – NATURALIST/TEACHER

Mr. Whiskermuff lives on forty acres in upstate New York. He is 100% dedicated to the preservation of everything in the world. It is thought that he would save a fart if he could get it into a jar. While searching for a remote home to further his preservationist efforts, Mr. Whiskermuff came across some railroad real estate for sale. Thirty-nine plus acres with a double track, siding, workshed, and five abandoned rail cars. He literally stole the property and equipment at an auction. He has, over some time, revamped some of the cars for his personal use and living quarters. A concert pianist in college, he now instructs those who choose to come to his estate.

The setting is rather unusual. A stone service road takes you a quarter mile back from the main road to the five rail cars that are attached and connected to each other with covered walkways. Great effort has been taken to cover them with vines and other sorts of foliage so they are virtually undetectable from the road. About an acre of grass has been cut and electricity strung back to the cars. Plumbing is quite another matter. An outhouse near the caboose is apparently the only area of relief and for that reason winter lessons are suspended. Bottled water inside the cars is available for general purposes.

Mr. Whiskermuff is a bit of a recluse, funded by a family trust fund and not noted for his social contacts. He travels to the nearby town in his restored Dodge three-quarter-ton Army surplus Power Wagon. It is still olive drab in color and you can't see that back in the woods either. Once he has cashed his monthly check, purchased supplies, and stopped at the local pub for his update on the gossip, he disappears back to the camp for the rest of the month.

Students report that one baggage car is filled with dozens of old pianos. Each in various states of repair with parts strewn about. The other baggage car is "the studio" and there are six pianos in there as well. Two or three of those are non-functional as he repairs them from season to season. There are steel stairs leading into the studio car and they are the main source of entry. Most students never get beyond that car. A few have made it to the dining car which is a combination storeroom, kitchen area and dining room; the caboose serves as a den and TV room. The pullman sleeping car is at the far end of the five-car setup and stories about it abound. It supposedly has a sensational décor but no one seems to know if any student has ever shared it with him. Perhaps he has chosen to spend time there with someone not associated with his piano work and therefore we are not privy to firsthand information.

In summer months, Mr. Whiskermuff has the main sliding door on his baggage car open as weather permits and he encourages all sorts of wildlife to come aboard. He routinely feeds everything that comes around and therefore it is not unusual for students to have several birds perched atop the piano or an otter or muskrat brushing at your feet. Although he does have his own pet black bear in the car at times, most bears, deer, and large animals are content to "dine at the door." They will however seek shelter in bad weather and some days it does get a bit crowded in the studio. Main complaints and comments from students:

1.   Poor lavatory conditions including poison ivy, bees, bats, mosquitoes and skunks

2.   Occasional power outages; no lights in the studio

3.   Distance from home to lesson averages fourteen miles one way

4.   Mr. Whiskermfiff occasionally sits in the open door of the studio car firing his shotgun at tin cans and bottles

5.   Pianos in general are out of tune, dusty and in poor repair

6.   BEST FEATURE: Lessons are $5 per hour (he doesn't need the money)

ASK THE AUTHOR

NO. A-477

Dear Don:

My teacher, Pitney Jingletramp, is an aging man. He's a good teacher but sometimes crabby. He has two big rabbits in cages on top of the piano. At almost every lesson Pitney passes gas and then always says the same thing when the sulphur smell comes around. "Goddamn rabbits, gotta move them somewhere else."

Don, I know it's him but it would be awkward to say so. This isn't much fun, taking lessons in a gas chamber. Help me, please.

~ Gassed in Gainesville

Dear Gassed:

If you want to stay with this teacher you will have to confront him and address the situation. I agree you must be tactful. The next time he blames the rabbits, tell him he is wrong. Advise him that you went to a pet shop and they told you that bunny farts smell like carrots, not sulphur.

ASK THE
AUTHOR
—
NO. A441

Dear Don:

Our son is 14 years old and taking lessons from a young teacher here in town. She is very attractive to say the least. Lately Kevin has had nausea, migraine headaches and failing grades in music. He says it is because the teacher conducts lessons while clad in miniskirts, bikinis or less. She even told him she does her housework in the nude. We have never discussed sex with him and although she is a good teacher, I think she is derailing my son's musical education.

~ Skingame in Stromsburg

Dear Skingame:

I think it is time to move your son to another instructor. But, before you do that, I would like a few photos and perhaps a name, address and phone number of this teacher. (It is strictly for reference, you understand.)

P.S. I would be happy to pay for film and postage.

ASK THE AUTHOR

—

NO. A448

Dear Don:

My teacher, Mrs. Hefferstench, has a bunch of birds and they fly all over the house during my lesson. Last Tuesday, one landed on my head and pecked a hole in my forehead. When the blood started running in my eye I started to cry and asked for a Band-Aid. My teacher told me to stop crying, that the bird was only playing and the reason the blood was running in my eye was because my eyebrows weren't fully developed yet. She also said that if I stopped picking at the hole it would clot before the lesson was over. I'm scared of these birds. What do I do?

~ Pecked in Pemberwick

Dear Pecked:

1. You may want to rent a deep sea diver's helmet so you will be covered down to your shoulders. You can open the glass face door to see your lesson, and the music should also drift in.

2. Have your family get you a mature outdoor cat – fifteen to twenty pounds. Place him in a comfortable cage and stop feeding him two days before your lesson. When you arrive at your lesson, throw the cat in first. The birds will not bother you as they will be very busy with their new agenda.

ASK THE AUTHOR
—
NO. 470

Dear Don:

I am a young man of 24. I take lessons from a divorced woman in her fifties. Although I love the piano, I am also a biker and a member of a motorcycle gang. I have a mustache, beard and sideburns. I ride my bike to lessons and am usually wearing my black leathers. When I strip to my shirt she flips out over my tattoos. Two weeks ago I came to my lesson and found her dressed in black leather too, with spikeheeled boots and spike choker collar and bracelets. She had so much makeup on it was coming out her ass. I think she's coming on to me. The last thing I need is a fifty-year-old "Harley Harlot." Advise me at once.

~ Biking in Belfast

Dear Biking:

There are two roads to ride here:

1. Invite her out. Take her to the biker bars and your gang's clubhouse. Get her really drunk and make sure she gets a few tattoos. It's a crapshoot but she might wake up and act her age.

2. Next few lessons you dress in a different costume each week. Frogman, Indian chief, chef, bank guard and transvestite. It will take her a week to get her outfit to match and by that time you'll have a new one. In 3-4 weeks she'll either get straightened out or go nuts.

ASK THE AUTHOR

—

NO. 455

Dear Don:

I teach in a town in Wisconsin. In winter the parents drop off their kids five minutes before the lesson. I have to help them out of four layers of clothes, boots, mittens and hats. After ten minutes of their lessons it is time to dress them up again. I'm tired of it. What can I do?

~ Weary of Winter in Wisconsin

Dear Weary:

Fight fire with fire! Buy yourself a nice snowmobile suit and some warm boots. Open a few windows in the house and keep it at 34° (just so the pipes won't freeze). Lay a plastic runner from the door to the piano to save your rugs. Then let them take their lessons fully dressed, boots and all. You're a piano teacher not a nanny.

P.S. With all those clothes on they might not want to go to the bathroom as much—you may actually gain lesson time.

THE SCHOOL PLAY

"Did you just whack my beaver?"

In the grooming process for teachers there are standard channels of education. There are also many various extra assignments and experiences which help to shape the new teacher. Situations which may, for a brief period of time, divert the student from their pre-conceived path of endeavor. Although 99% of these experiences are musically related, they often test the mettle of the individual. The following story shows one of those unexpected curves on the road toward success.

I would like to thank the author for allowing me to share this experience in the hope that it will open the eyes of aspiring music teachers. My name is Lolita Loopfiddle. I am a woman of thirty-one years. I was raised by an average American family in a town with 15,000 people. For as long as I can remember I have been fascinated by the piano. My grandfather was a saloon piano player and whenever he came to our house he would play for hours. I listened to him every time he played and just loved it. While growing up with two younger sisters I was always the one to seek out music—be it day or night. As we went through high school, my sisters were the brainiacs, cheerleaders and sports nuts. That was not my bag. I wanted to be anywhere there was music and most of all I wanted to play the piano and do it well. I started my instruction in high school from Mrs. Beachfrump. She was the only full-time music teacher in the school. Other people worked part-time in band instrument training but Mrs. Beachfrump did all the voice and piano teaching. I loved my lessons and she recognized that. At times she even had me come to her home where she gave me extra instruction. It was my dream to graduate from high school and go directly to a music college with the full intention of becoming a music teacher for piano.

As fate would have it, during my senior year my Dad and his brother had a business failure, but not before all the money set aside for my college education had been spent trying to save the business. Therefore, when I graduated from high school I just became another thread in the tapestry of working stiffs. My musical aspirations had to be set aside and I felt that I might never achieve my goal. Although I bounced from job to job, my teacher never gave up on me. I continued to see her weekly after graduation, faithfully taking my lessons and greatly improving my skills and knowledge over the next few years.

Five years ago, without my knowledge, Mrs. Beachfrump sent a tape of my playing to a college near our town. They have a large music department of some renown and I was summoned to appear there for an audition leading to a possible scholarship. I performed the audition and to my surprise was accepted. In addition,

Mrs. Beachfrump and I worked for another year and secured a grant for me to take a full four-year program at the Cinnamon Grove Conservatory, a part of that school. Wow! A full music education only sixty miles from my home. I was in heaven and my discipline over the years had been rewarded.

My love interest over a five-year period, prior to going to this school, was a guy named Mickey Sudsguzzle, a rambunctious red-headed Irishman. He was lots of fun and I guess we really never got very serious about anything—we were just together all the time. He was a frustrated actor who never made it. His field was ventriloquism and although he did it well, no big breaks came his way. He still lived at home with his Mom. His Dad, an out-of-work stagecoach driver, died from being out of a job for twenty-eight years and hanging out in bars, so Mickey felt his Mom needed him at home. He spent his weekends working in a funeral home and during the week he was an over-the-road beef jerky salesman. His favorite pastime was making the corpses talk which scared the shit out of everybody. When I told him of my plans to go to Cinnamon Grove Conservatory, he was elated at first but then seemed to quickly cool to the idea. I had to make a decision and it was a no-brainer. Nothing was to stand in the way of my musical advancements so I let him down easy and dumped him.

The next four years were spent in school and I worked my fanny to the bone. Although I was close to home I often spent weekends doing extra music projects at school and keeping my eyes and mind focused on my goal: TO BE A MUSIC TEACHER. I studied a great deal of classical music by choice and faithfully did all the other work dictated by the school. At the beginning of my senior year, Mrs. Beachfrump announced that she was going to retire in a year and was recommending me as her replacement. What a wonderful thought. A full-time job doing what I loved and had trained for—and in my home town. I was on cloud nine. With this new dream in view I was determined to do my most exceptional work in this, my last year. Somehow, Mrs. Beachfrump had pulled some strings at the high school and they told me that if I graduated in the top third of my class they would hire me with no further credentials.

Over the years at school, I had worked one-on-one with younger students, studied choral directing, played in quartets, quintets and orchestras and even took some classes in composing. I was comfortable with it all and my immediate superior at the school, Professor Kirby Zippowick, was gearing me for that job at the high school.

One course requirement I had not yet fulfilled was an off-campus assignment to compose for and help direct a play, show or major choral event. This had to be done soon and I was shopping for a venue. Once again Mrs. Beachfrump came through. Her longtime friend and patron of the arts, Hannah Handleyank, had hooked up with a budding young novelist named Cliff Hanger. He had written a book which had been recently converted to a stage play. It was a cabaret-type story set in 1930s Germany and was called "Mein Schottzie." Mrs. Handleyank was funding the premier stage presentation of this play and needed someone to work up the music for it. There would be a cast of a dozen or so and I would have full responsibility for the musical part of the show. What a perfect setup. The premiere would take place in my old high school—the very place I hoped to take up residence next year. Mrs. Handleyank was a very wealthy woman and I had heard through the grapevine that she had been instrumental in helping to secure my grant for music school. What a great way for me to silently pay her back.

Although I knew this would mean some grueling hours and lots of driving, I agreed to take the position. To my surprise Professor Zippowick arranged for me to get a thirty-day leave from campus provided I submit a daily log and copies of all the musical work I did while back home on the project. I figured I would use that time to study the storyline, formulate my approach to the music, and meet the players. I was thoroughly excited. It would be my first chance to actually meet the kids I would some day be working with and teaching. Although I had visions of teaching students one-on-one, this new twist of fate had me excited about group work and I felt it was within my grasp and ability. Mrs. Beachfrump, Mrs. Handleyank, and I met for the first time at Mrs. Handleyank's estate, "Hummsong" on September 28. The author, Mr. Hanger, was also there.

Mr. Hanger struck me as a kept man who was using Mrs. Handleyank to climb the ladder of success. He had a face like a collapsed lung, drank like a sand dune and appeared to be a man who had never worked a day in his life—except for the project we were about to review. I am a woman of discipline and one who loves people. I do not, however, tolerate arrogant people and I could sense that Mr. Hanger and I might not mesh well.

The book had been converted to a stage play by someone named Piedmont Hosenozzle whose address was a Post Office Box in Harlem. He was not present but I did not rule out that someday he might surface.

I had come to this meeting for many reasons. I loved and respected Mrs. Beachfrump and I knew Mrs. Handleyank was a capable backer and interested in the arts. I would also complete another requirement for my graduation and in the back of my mind I figured if this were a successful endeavor, I would ride into my new job at the high school with a feather in my hat.

While conversation was bandied about over cookies and tea (except for Mr. Hanger who preferred Manhattans), I was able to scan the basic script. The more I read it, the more I knew it. About halfway through I realized that this was nothing short of a duplication of "Cabaret." There were a few variations but with a lot more overlap than originality. It further confirmed my suspicions that Mr. Hanger probably never had an original thought in his life. I was feeling a swiftly rising disenchantment with him and a suspicion about Mr. Hosenozzle for his part in this obvious "theft of art."

I was drawn back into the conversation when Mrs. Handleyank asked, "What do you think? Can you do it?"

Hannah Handleyank, at age ninety-seven, had a reputation for being a direct and controlling person. She was still in pretty good health despite being an incessant smoker. I think Glenda (Mrs. Beachfrump) told me Hannah was doing about sixty cigarettes a day because I remember asking, "You mean three packs?" "No, sixty cigarettes," said Glenda. "She doesn't buy packs, she rolls her own. Bull Durham, I think. Gets up at 5 A.M., rolls sixty and puts them into a plastic storage bag that never leaves her side. Still uses those wooden kitchen matches to light them too. Says lighters are not dependable."

Anyway, I was a bit taken aback by Hannah's question. I had only taken about ten minutes to scan the script and she wanted an answer. I was also a bit disarmed when I noticed she was cross-eyed. If my chair hadn't been separated from the rest I wouldn't have known who she was looking at. But I had to be professional about this.

"I haven't seen all the script but I'm sure I can come up with something."

"Good," she said. "I told Cliff you were the best."

What she actually meant was the cheapest. Since this was a school project for the college I could not charge for my services.

Hannah rose from her chair and her long black dress with giant white polka dots hung far below her knees. She wore black, block-heeled shoes with laces, the kind the nuns used to wear in the '50s. (You know, the ones they used to kick you in the back of your lower leg with when you were not moving fast enough in the cafeteria line.) Also, I was surprised that at her age she did not wear glasses. She looked at Glenda and said, "Let's get this show on the road. I'll call Forbes and get some keys."

I immediately wondered, who is Forbes? I leaned over to ask Glenda. When I did, Hannah snapped at me. "You got a question? Ask me. I'm the answer lady on this project. What do you need to know, Missy?"

"Uh, my name is Lolita, Mrs. Handleyank, but my friends call me Loopy. I was just asking who this Forbes person is."

"Forbes Doofus owns the Imperial Playhouse. It has finished its summer run and he is going to let us rehearse there."

"I see. Thank you," I said.

"Anything else buggin' you, Missy?"

"There is one other thing," I said. "When do you expect to start auditions and casting calls?"

"All done," she said. "Cliff and I have people all picked. The dancers, singers, stageman, wardrobe lady, choreographer, and lighting man are all in place. I'm the director, you're the music lady and you'll answer to Glenda and she will answer to me. Anything we can't work out will be resolved by Mr. Hosenozzle by fax, E-mail or phone. He is working on a new play and won't be here until we get further along."
140

I just sat there, head spinning. It seems I was the last one in on this deal. Oh well—onward and upward.

"This is Saturday and tomorrow being Sunday I figured everyone involved would be available. I am having a catered get-together party at the Imperial to have everyone get acquainted."

There followed a silence you could cut with a knife. The only sound in the whole room came from Cliff as he added ice to his glass. Apparently we were dismissed.

As I walked out with Glenda, I was still in a fog. This was a fast-moving show alright. Knowing Hannah by now I figured she'd probably want the whole score in place by Monday. I said to Glenda, "If this is a school play how come we're doing the rehearsals at the Imperial?"

"Several things came up. First, you can't smoke in the school and Hannah needs her cigarettes. Second, she wants to rehearse on weekends and they wouldn't open the school just for her. Third, I think Cliff persuaded her to use the theater so he could drink there. And fourth, for years Hannah has bailed Forbes out of trouble when he has had a bad year at the playhouse so he owes her big time."

"Wonderful," I said. "Just wonderful."

Glenda and I hugged and left in separate cars. I went to my parents' house where I would be staying for the next month while the play took shape. That night I told my folks how I felt about the obvious copying of "Cabaret." They both said to do what my conscience told me.

After a restless night I called Professor Zippowick. I told him the story and he said, "Loopy, I would not compose any music for that play. Use songs that have already been done and give credit to the composers and artists where necessary. You must protect yourself from any involvement in this scheme. You will become just the arranger but it sure beats jail or a court battle."

"I think you're absolutely right, but what about my credit for composing?"

"I think we have enough of that from last term to pull you through, don't worry about that now," he said.

We said goodbye and I hung up the phone and pondered his advice. I reflected on my third year at school. I had composed a group of songs called "Suite of the Swamp," tunes reflecting the creatures of the Everglades swamp. I had spent all summer perfecting my opening fall concert of Beethoven's Pianoforte Sonata in A Flat, Opus 26 and had given a flawless performance my first week back this fall. That took care of my yearly dose of culture. I guess the professor was right. Just carry on and do the best I can with this thing. As an arranger, using other people's songs, how hard could it be? I felt much better now. After all, I am not a prima donna looking to pounce on anything I find wrong. I am an aspiring teacher about to embark on a career and following advice from teachers to get there. I like to help folks and working with these young people in this play might just be good training. I'll give it my best. Glenda will be there too and that will help.

Soon it would be 2 P.M. and I'd meet everyone and get in the groove. I put on a nice suit, makeup, sensible shoes and told my folks goodbye. The day was sunny and I was upbeat.

After a twenty-minute drive I reached the Imperial Playhouse located on the edge of town. It was a renovated barn and the outside looked the same as it had when it was part of a farm. There were half a dozen cars there and I parked and went inside. The exterior certainly did not prepare me for what I saw there. The whole place had been gutted and remodeled. It had a main stage with tall velvet curtains, a small band pit, some rather bland dressing rooms and community bathrooms for the actors. The seating was in two levels with the balcony seats located in the area previously used as a hay loft. The temperature today had climbed to 63° and it was rather comfortable inside. Glenda was just inside the door and we hooked up at once. We came across the stage area together toward Hannah and Cliff who were there with another elderly lady. A man in a white chef's outfit was laying out food and beverages on a long white linen covered table. There were twelve or more chairs scattered about but at this point everyone was still standing. Glenda took me by the hand and we moved to the side of the lady whom I had not met.

"Loopy, I want to introduce you to Mackenzie Wrenpoop."

Then Glenda looked at the lady and said, "Mackenzie, this is Loopy Loopfiddle. She's going go be doing the musical work on the play."

"Hello my dear," said Mrs. Wrenpoop. "Pleased to meet you."

"Mrs. Wrenpoop has quite a colorful history in show business," said Glenda. "She worked with some very big names in her day."

Mrs. Wrenpoop laughed. "Yes, Glenda, but that was a long time ago."

I noticed a definite shaking in her right hand and arm as though she might be in the early stages of Parkinson's disease but I said nothing.

At 2 P.M., the stage started to fill with people in all sorts of wardrobe. Guys and gals, some coming in alone, some in pairs or groups. Soon it was apparent that Hannah was ready to roll. She pounded a rock glass on the table and said, "Listen up, everybody. Let's get started."

The various conversations stopped one at a time and soon it was quiet.

"I've got some sheets here with everyone's name on them and I'll pass them around so you can see who's who. Then I want you to mingle and introduce yourselves. In about fifteen minutes I'll tell you all what's going to happen from here on. Help yourself to the food and drinks."

Hannah moved around handing out 8½" x 11" yellow sheets. I thanked her when she gave me mine but it brought no response. I looked at the lineup. What a rogues gallery we had here.

```
                "MEIN SCHOTTZIE" - PERSONNEL


       HANNAH HANDLEYANK . . . . . . . . . . . . . . . .PROMOTER/DIRECTOR

       CLIFF HANGER . . . . . . . . . . . . . . . . . . . . . .ORIGINAL STORY

       PIEDMONT HOSENOZZLE . . . . . . . . . . . . . .STAGE PLAY

       MACKENZIE WRENPOOP  . . . . . . . . . . . . . .WARDROBE MISTRESS

       LOLITA LOOPFIDDLE  . . . . . . . . . . . . . . .MUSICAL DIRECTOR

       GLENDA BEACHFRUMP . . . . . . . . . . . . . .MUSICAL ADVISOR

       FALLOPIAN NOONBANG . . . . . . . . . . . . .CHOREOGRAPHER

       HUMPHREY LOINRUBBER . . . . . . . . . . . .STAGE/PROPMASTER

       LINCOLN LOGG . . . . . . . . . . . . . . . . . .LIGHTING/SOUND

              DANCERS - VOCALISTS - ACTORS

       SUGAR BRATCHILD               COLEY FLAPYAP

       THROBIANNA COTROCKER          HELMUT LOCKPICKER

       BAILEY BOTTLESWIG             KELSEY NIPDAISY

       FONTANA FLANGEPANTY           STONE ROADROLLER
```

I looked at the list several times and then looked around the room. I have always been one to take music over sports and movies over rock concerts but as I looked at what we had to work with I'd have rather been at Rockingham rooting for the NASCAR drivers. I even wondered if Hannah might have paid these people to show up.

Glenda would be my only lifeline right now since she knew a lot of the kids from school, as well as the other players from around town. I was feeling strangely alone just now. Lots of young people, a few old people, and me in the middle. The only two people in my age range were Ms. Noonbang and Cliff, the author, whom I was giving a wide berth.

Glenda did her best to whisk me from person to person and introduce me, but fifteen minutes for introductions hardly left any time at all for individual speaking. The girls stayed in one group, the boys another, except for Stone Roadroller who seemed to be very intent at staying at Hannah's side. When the allotted time had passed,

Hannah pounded on the table with her rock glass and asked everyone to be seated. I noticed that Mr. Loinrubber had a hard time getting into his chair. Glenda informed me he had a wooden leg. I was seated between Glenda and Mackenzie as Hannah began to speak from her position at the head of the table.

"Alright, I guess you all know why we're here. This is my own special project and you have been selected to get it done. The rehearsals will be on Tuesday, Thursday and Saturday for the next eight weeks and our planned performance will be the first weekend of December at the high school. This Tuesday we will be assigning parts and Mrs. Wrenpoop will then measure you for your appropriate costumes. As you know, we have arranged for those of you in school to leave one hour early on rehearsal days. Be sure you have a ride here and are prompt. I have a great disdain for tardiness. Any input you might have as we progress should pass through me. I am the director. Mr. Hanger will be here to guide us for the full length of the rehearsals. The first rehearsal will be 3:30 P.M. Tuesday and you should allow two hours for the rehearsals. That's all from me, now a word from Mr. Hanger."

"Hi, all. I'm Cliff Hanger and I wrote the book from which this play has been derived. I'm thrilled to see my book come to life on the stage and look forward to working with you all. Mrs. Handleyank has spoken highly of you and I'm sure we will put together a cohesive working plan in short order."

Cliff took a moment to down half a Manhattan and continued. "Mr. Hosenozzle has captured the very meat of my book and I'm sure you will find the text of his script entertaining."

It should be, I thought to myself. Cabaret has been doing very well for years.

"In addition," he continued, "since we are doing this for the first time ever, it gives us the latitude for rewrites, improvisations, all sorts of tunes and special attention to the needs of each performer. Thank you."

Cliff sat down and I couldn't help but wonder what "special attention" meant. He was looking right at the girls when he said that.

Hannah spoke again. "Are there any questions? If not you may continue to enjoy the food and beverages until 3 P.M. or you are all free to go."

The young people and Ms. Noonbang were gone as if someone had put a giant vacuum cleaner to the barn door and sucked them from the building. In five minutes there were only five of us left. Hannah, Glenda, Mackenzie, Cliff and Myself. Stone Roadroller was hanging out over near the door having a smoke. I don't know why he was over there, Hannah was smoking like a brush fire right under a two by three foot red and white NO SMOKING sign on the wall near the table. According to Glenda, this Stone guy chauffeured Hannah around a few days a week. I'm sure that was a lot better than letting Cliff behind the wheel.

I had half a turkey sandwich and a diet soda and asked Glenda, "Anything more to do here?"

"No, I think this is pretty much it for today. Let's get going."

We said our goodbyes and as we made our way to the cars I said, "You know, that wasn't very productive in my opinion."

"Yes, well, Hannah had a chance to tell everyone she was the boss and to get them to the barn for the first time. Also, the schedule is now in place and nobody seemed to balk at it."

"Probably scared shitless to say anything to her," I said.

"Could be," said Glenda. "We'll know a lot more Tuesday."

"Okay, I'll see you then. Have a great day."

I rode home thinking how nice it would have been for Hannah to give me a copy of the script to study but she had not said a word about it and neither she nor Cliff offered me anything.

On Monday I went to a music store and bought the soundtrack tape for Cabaret. I wanted to get the feel of the music so I could think about similar tunes without stealing any of the originals. I felt a challenge coming but had to remember Professor Zippowick's comment "do the best you can."

Tuesday afternoon I was at the Imperial at 3:15 P.M.. There were five cars when I arrived. It looked as though there were a few spots up near the door but I cruised up there to look and they were Handicapped Only zones. I went back down the row and parked. As I got out of my car a red Jeep Cherokee with three people in it whizzed by me and pulled in front of the door. When I walked up I saw Sugar Bratchild exit the driver side and I said, "That's a handicapped zone, dear."

"I got a toothache. Does that do it for you?" she shot back.

"Oh yes, crippling I'm sure," I said.

"Yeah, it's got me like all freaked out."

Two other girls now emerged from the other side of the car and one appeared to be walking a dog. This observation was to change when I got up close and discovered she was walking a beaver, a cute thing about three feet long including that big scaly flat tail. I recognized the beaver walker as Throbianna Cotrocker.

"You got a neat beaver," I said.

"Thanks. I take him everywhere and people love him."

"Does he have a name?" I asked.

"Yeah, I call him Damit."

The third girl I recognized from Sunday but I could not remember her name until someone inside said, "Hi, Fontana." Then I remembered. Fontana Flangepanty.

Inside the barn, people were milling about. I did not know just what to bring for this startup session so I had my briefcase and some writing paper and sheet music. Glenda, Cliff, Mackenzie and Ms. Noonbang were in a huddle. Stone was hanging nearby alone. At 3:30 P.M. sharp Hannah hollered, "Everybody line up for roll call." As she waited, she lit another cigarette.

Boy, this sounded military to me but what the hell, it's her show so I took my place in line. The balance of the people hurriedly joined the line with a few stragglers running to "make the muster." All names were called from the roster list we had been given on Sunday. The only absentee was Bailey Bottleswig and Hannah made a note on her sheet.

"Okay," said Hannah. "Glenda, you and Missy take two of the girls over by the piano and let's see who can sing and who can dance. Cliff and Fallopian, you'll take the rest of the gang on stage and start to explain the storyline. I want everyone to pass by me here and grab a copy of the play out of these boxes.

Glenda and I grabbed our copies and walked over to the piano with Sugar, Throbianna and the beaver on our heels. I sat on the piano bench at a 45° angle with the keyboard while Glenda drew up a chair to my left and sat down. The two girls just stood there. Okay, here I am with my first-ever students. My opening ice breaker question was, "Tell me, girls, just why do you want to be in this play and what are the special talents that you bring to this rehearsal?"

Sugar spoke first. "I'm telling you now I'm so like bummed out about this. Like I am so not interested in this but my Mom says I gotta do it for Mrs. Handleyank. I really am here because Throbby is my best friend."

"Thank you for sharing," I said. "Do you intend to participate?"

"It's like not on my 'A' list but I'll give it a shot."

"Fine," I replied. "Now, Miss Cotrocker, what do you do?"

"I took three years of dance when I was in grade school. I quit when I was twelve. I guess I can bring it back again."

"Well, that's a start. Tell me, how did you come to this project, anyway?"

"I'm dating Stone Roadroller and he told me this would be a good way to skip some classes and have some fun. I told Sugar about it 'cause I don't have a car but she already knew about it from her Mom. Sugar's grandmother and Mrs. Handleyank were good buddies."

"Well," I asked, "did anyone conduct any sort of voice or dance audition with either of you?"

"No," they answered in unison.

"Great," I said. "Am I to understand that virtually this whole cast is just a bunch of buddies and that no one's been tested?"

"That's about it," said Sugar. "We went by Mrs. Handleyank's one day to see that book writer guy, Cliff whoever, but he was passed out on the couch in the sunroom so we like blew it off."

"Okay," I said. "I'm Ms. Loopfiddle and I'll be doing the music for the show. Currently there is none and frankly I have to establish a starting point. I was under the impression that all the people here had been tested and were capable performers to some degree." I turned to Glenda and said, "Do you know anything about how these kids were chosen to be here?"

"Not a whisper. Hannah said the casting was set and I just assumed that a process had taken place."

I looked back at the girls and said, "Look, I want to work with you if you want to do this play. If not, let's not make this an uphill run."

"Hey, we're here," said Sugar. "But so far nobody seems to know shit about anything. At this point we don't even know what this freakin' play is about."

I felt something happening under me and I saw the beaver starting to sample the leg of the bench. Throbianna saw him at the same time and hollered, "Stop that, Damit." The beaver moved a few feet away and just sat there.

"Is he going to be with us all the time?" I asked.

"More than likely," she said. "I usually take him to the lake every day after school but with these rehearsals I guess I'll have to bring him here."

"Alright," I said to the girls, "let's us get a table and some chairs. Glenda, I want to sit with you and these girls and get a thumbnail profile of just what the hell we're working with on this thing. We might be sunk before we leave the dock."

We left the piano and went backstage where there was a small lunchroom. Two pop machines, two tables with four chairs at each and a countertop with a coffee machine. Glenda and I sat down but before I could begin my inquest the two girls asked if they could have a can of pop. I agreed and they moved to the vending machines.

I looked at Glenda and said in a serious tone, "What the hell am I getting into here? I'm trying to become a teacher, not a lion tamer. I'm beginning to think there's not an ounce of music between these two, or possibly in the whole cast. God only knows what's out there on the stage."

"Yes, Loopy, you've got a challenge here. I wanted you to get into this to prepare you for what is coming later down the road. Teaching is not all a bed of roses. I've been at it over forty years and generally I can tell you that your schooling only teaches you the music. You also have to be a psychologist, psychiatrist, mentor, taskmaster and guidance counselor all rolled into one. You will find some students with whom you can make great strides while being as gentle as kitten paws treading on a beach. Others will progress so slowly and be so upsetting that you think the only way to shape them would be to throw them into a blacksmith's furnace. When you got them red hot you could then mold them using an anvil and a ten-pound sledgehammer. And then there are the rebellious few who you know are hopeless and going nowhere. They are wasting your time and theirs for numerous bogus reasons. These are the ones you'd like to toss into an industrial size bug zapper. You hope that once you hear that cracking noise they'll never be back again."

"You know, this is a rude awakening," I said. "In all the years we've been together I've never heard this side of you."

"Well," answered Glenda, "I'm getting tired. I don't have my whole heart in this project and now that I hear what these two girls have to say I believe Hannah deceived me when she said they had picked the cast. The more I sift through these names the more I see a group of friends just out for a good time. You are the one they are depending on to pull this thing together. On the other hand, if you don't see some daylight by week's end don't worry about me if you want to bail out. Let's just talk to these kids today and see what light can be shed on this situation."

"Glenda," I said, "I really want to be a teacher more than anything. I'll try my damnedest to rise to this occasion and put something together but thank you for leaving me an escape hatch. I just hope I don't have to use it."

After a few minutes the two girls had returned to the table and we began to chat. I took out my pad and the roster sheet and said, "Okay, let's run right down the sheet. If anybody can shed some light on anyone on this list, please do so. Your comments will not leave this room and nothing you say will change the way you are treated here at these rehearsals. Also, Glenda, whatever you know would also be a help. I'm sure the girls know that privacy is the key word here and that they must be discreet. Let's start with Hannah. I know she's got the novelist staying at her house and he's a lush. I know she's ninety-seven and a power freak with lots of cash. What else?" I asked.

Glenda said, "She's also scared to death that this might be her last project. Secretly, the doctors have been telling her that all this chain smoking is killing her. She's chosen to turn a deaf ear on them. My personal opinion is that she's grabbing at straws to push a lousy project at breakneck speed just to get her name in lights one more time. She's overlooking a lot of stuff at other people's expense."

Then Glenda looked directly at the two girls. "You must understand that Ms. Loopfiddle here has her hands full. For whatever reason you have come here you should either decide to work with her or get out. Any attitudes from either one of you is not what we need. I'll put it point blank going in, you throw any shit in the fan and I'll guarantee you I'll see that it blows right in your face."

I was shocked to hear her say this but it really did set the tone and these girls knew it.

"Alright," I said. "Now on to Mr. Hanger. I peg him as a lush and a loser who's taking Hannah for a ride. I have looked at the script and basically he's stolen the storyline from "Cabaret." I don't have a good feeling about this guy."

"Well," said Throbby, "I know that when Hannah goes to bed, some nights Cliff takes her car and goes to Poncho's to booze it up."

"What's Poncho's?" I asked.

"Basically it's just a Mexican food joint where we all hang. They have a DJ and dance floor and on the weekends we just dance there. There's not supposed to be any drinking but there always is and somebody always has drugs in their car and now they've even got that Ecstasy shit. It scares me to think a guy like him could get his hands on that stuff."

"Yeah, he's like freaky enough without it. He's tried to hit on me already and I'm like so bothered by him," said Sugar.

"Alright, we know he's a loser and a lounge lizard and he has to be watched. Whatever is between him and Hannah we can't know just now." I checked his name on my list and put a star there as well.

"Next one here is this Piedmont Hosenozzle. Where does he fit into the picture?"

Glenda said, "I believe he's an African American person who lives in New York City. I've heard Hannah and Cliff speak of him but I've never seen him in person, or even a photo of him for that matter. He's a mystery right now."

"Fine," I said. "Out of sight, out of mind. Let's move on. Glenda, you know Ms. Wrenpoop, fill me in here."

"Well, she is pushing eighty and lives alone. She has never been married and most of her career days were spent in California in the movie industry. She was head of wardrobe for many companies out there and did her last eighteen or twenty years with CHRO-MAG STUDIOS. They were a 'B' type film company but they turned out a lot of stuff and kept her very busy. She returned about five years ago and bought a small house here. The last year or so she seems to be failing, healthwise. She's got the shakes and I suspect a touch of Alzheimer's as well. She's a very tight friend of Hannah's and that's why she's here."

Throbianna chimed in. "She must be a sugar freak too, cause she's always eating cookies."

"They're not cookies, my dear," said Glenda. "They're Milk Bone dog biscuits. She eats them all the time to keep her teeth white. She shakes too bad to floss or brush."

"Dog biscuits!" exclaimed Throbby. "Holy shit, what a gas."

This revelation also prompted Sugar to lose her composure and she burst out laughing uncontrollably. Glenda gave her a no-nonsense stare that cooled her instantly. All was quiet again.

"Okay," I said to the girls, "I'm next on the list and for your sake I'm thirty-one years old and just now in my senior year at music college with a projected graduation as a music teacher. This project is required of me and I'm going to try to do it. I really wanted to start my teaching work off on a one-to-one basis but if I have to tackle this herd for openers, I'm going to do it. I want to extract the best things from you both, and to help where I can. I expect your respect and cooperation or I'll have to snuff your candles."

The two girls looked at each other and then back at me and nodded. I wouldn't have thought to say that if Glenda hadn't fired the first salvo earlier in the meeting.

"Glenda here is a seasoned veteran in the music field. She has been the head of music at the high school for many years as well as conducting private tutoring at her home. You probably already know that. Have either of you ever studied with her?"

They both shook their heads no.

"Well, I have. For many years we have worked together and she is a wonderful woman and is also worthy of your respect. Next is the choreographer, Miss Noonbang. Who knows of her background?"

"She started showing up at Poncho's about six months ago," said Throbby. I don't know where she came from but she's going overboard to be a kid again. Makes an ass of herself on a regular basis trying to score with all the young guys. If she does make a hit she takes them out to her Winnebago and has her score right in the lot."

"Many years ago she had a crush on Hannah's youngest son," said Glenda. "When he married someone else she left town. She's been gone for many years and like Throbby said, she just popped up again about March of this year. She visits Hannah on a regular basis, they're still friends. I've seen her there. She's got a hell of a figure for her age and dances like a gazelle. She worked for years as cruise director on a ship called The Sweetheart. It was based in Ecuador and finally sunk in port a few years ago. She was very active in that business but they chose not to reassign her. They alleged that she threw her ethical business practices out the window in exchange for endless repetitive pleasures with her male group known as the Engine Room Glee Club.

"I know one thing about her," said Sugar, "she wears a backpack with an air mattress in it. That's like so not conventional."

"I think you call that being a hooker," said Throbby.

"So we know at least she can dance and possibly that glee club thing means she might be able to sing," I said. "That's a positive note here."

The door to the coffee room opened and Hannah stuck her head in. "So this is where you all are hiding out. Seems to me no music's gonna get played on a soda machine. What's the plan in here, Missy?"

She was really starting to get to me with that Missy crap but I decided not to push it today.

"I thought it necessary to interview people to arrive at a start up point for the score and Glenda agreed. We thought sitting around a table might be a bit more comfortable," I said.

"Well, don't get too damned comfortable, Missy, we've got a lot to do and Fallopian says she can't do any dance stuff without music, so the ball is in your court. Let's get something going here."

As she closed the door I exchanged glances with Glenda and one of the girls said, "What a bitch."

Since she said it, I didn't have to. But I thought it.

"Let's continue," I said. "This screening is most important to me before I get with the other people. We're doing well so let's go on. Next person on the list is Mr. Loinrubber, the prop man. I know he's got a wooden leg but I don't know the story behind it."

"Okay," said Sugar. "I can tell you a few things. Humphrey is older than us. He graduated from high school and then went into the Army. He got hurt there and has that leg thing. He like works for the school part-time and he's like the hired stage man at our things. He's always dressed in that camouflage stuff like we're going to war and that hair of his always looks like sagebrush in one of those old Westerns."

Glenda chimed in with her two cents worth. "I am led to believe that he was in the Culinary Corps, you know, a cook. He claims the enemy planted explosives in a turkey and it exploded in the oven. The oven door blew across the kitchen and severed his leg up near the hip. He received the "Purple Ham" for bravery and now he thinks the world owes him a living for his supreme sacrifice in the line of duty. He's still reeling from the revelation that doing two years as a chef in Arkansas does not make him a war hero. He's quiet and moody and very often displays an inferiority complex about that leg."

"Holy cow," said Throbianna. "Any half-ass freakin' cook should be able to see a bomb in his turkey. This guy must think he's Norman Schwatrzkoff from Desert Storm. What an ego trip he's on."

"Enough said about him, I think," I said. "We've got a lot of ground to cover, let's keep moving on." For all that had been said so far I could not see any huge swell of theatrical talent racing over the horizon.

"Lincoln Logg, lighting and sound man. What's up here?"

"Link is just Link," said Throbby. "He does what he's told and he's pretty smart in school. I don't think he's ever been in plays or stuff like that but he's been around the auditorium and theater when things are going on and I know he's helped out with different stuff backstage."

"I haven't run across him at all," said Glenda. "Can't help you on this one. I'm not sure how he got picked."

"I know," said Sugar. "His brother is like dating Bailey's sister so he probably got in by association. It surprises me that her sister isn't here too, like we need that bitch along on this journey."

"As long as we're on the subject and not to jump out of sequence, where do you suppose she is today? This is the first meeting and she is a no show," I said.

Glenda said, "I think Miss Bottleswig has a substance abuse problem as relates to alcohol."

"Substance abuse, my ass," said Sugar. "She like prides herself that she outdrank every guy in the ALPHA ZED fraternity on Toga Night. She's a lush, for God's sake. She's a whiz in science and chemistry and she's studying to be a brewmaster. To that end she says she's always testing beer."

"Yeah, and retaining water too," said Throbianna.

"Look," I said, "if this girl is going to be a problem from the very start, maybe we should replace her."

"She's just always like so out of it," said Sugar. "Like she's always queasy and sweating a lot. She always says she's like really parched and in need of replacement fluids."

"In my association with her," said Glenda, "I found that she had energy in spurts but she was primarily lethargic and listless. Clothes are not her priority and she appears virtually the same every day. A pair of sweat pants, sneakers, and a sweat shirt with some slogan on it."

I remembered the one she wore last Sunday. It said: "BEER. Helping bashful people have sex since 1862."

"I guess whether she makes the cut or not is Hannah's call, but I don't want her dragging the project down. I'll watch her, assuming she ever shows."

I passed over the names of the two girls at the table. I figured to get their stories from another source, and colorful I'll bet they'll be, too.

I took a moment to get a glass of water and Glenda got up for a coffee. We said nothing but merely looked at each other and smiled about the absolute lunacy of this interview. This was not a musical cast, it was MASH or Cheers. A group of total misfits thrown together by fate and association to do whatever. I couldn't wait to hear what else these two had to contribute. Apparently slamming people was something they felt comfortable doing, and they did it well.

Once seated I began again. "Next in the barrel is Miss Fontana Flangepanty. I believe she travels with you two."

"Yes," said Throbby, "F.F. is a blast. She's a sports freak and the big favorite of the football team. She is also a great swimmer. She got a gold medal in the breast stroke last year."

I remembered the build on this girl from Sunday's get together. She was very, very well endowed. I, of course, did not know anything about this swimming medal until now. I am not a sports person but I theorized if the size of your breasts is somehow equated to how well you do the breast stroke, she should be able to do 35 m.p.h. without breaking a sweat. Just an observation, mind you.

Sugar said, "She's like just an all around good friend. She's always 'on,' loves to dance and never misses a thing. She's got lots of ambition and she loves the guys. I'd call her a flirt—very affectionate."

I put two stars after her name when I heard the word dance.

"Alright, ladies. Now we'll do the guys. I want you to be as constructive as you can. I'm trying to get some good points to work on here. What about Flapyap?"

Glenda said, "I know him. He's a frustrated actor and singer and he never shuts up."

"I remember him as the lanky, kind of neurotic one with that flashy, wide tie. Is that the guy we're talking about?"

Just then there was a crash as the beaver tipped over the trash can. I had forgotten he was around.

"Get out of there, Damit!" yelled Throbianna, and the beaver ran to a neutral corner to await any punishment that might come his way. I could see he would be a constant interruption for this whole program.

Glenda continued, "Yes, that's the guy. I had him in class for two years. He is prone to uncontrolled outbursts of screaming and when he talks to you he is almost always talking in someone else's voice, you know, impersonations. He's very competitive and although his language needs some cleaning up, he is eager to learn. His main objective as I see it, is to outdo everyone else on stage."

"Sounds as if I can use him, if I can tame him," I said.

"Helmut Lockpicker by name must have a soiled past. Does he belong in this group?"

"Helmut is a dork" said Throbby. "He's in love with himself 24/7/365. He's on parole for burglary and possession of stolen goods. He thinks he's cool because he has colored spiked hair and a few piercings and his motorcycle gang is supposed to be tough."

Sugar gave her a look that could kill. She said, "I asked Helmut to come with us. Like he's okay but some people just don't understand him. I think he's got some good qualities and like I don't think he needs to be slammed for past mistakes."

"Geez," said Throbby. "Are you from another planet? Grow up. Let's walk this one through. Helmut is just hanging around with you because he knows he can get laid and you have a car. He's not going to have his license back for three years and if you ever shut him off he'll drop you like a rock. The train has left the station on this one."

"Well, pardon me, Miss Perfect. At least I don't store up sex like a camel and then dish it out sparingly to every guy at Poncho's. I think you got no room to mumble about me and Helmut. You're a pretty good lounge flounder yourself. At least I've got one steady guy."

"Alright, girls. Let's cut this short. I'm going to mark him 'X' because we don't know what he can do yet, at least what we can show on stage."

"Let's move on to Kelsey Nipdaisy. Any potential here?"

Glenda was first to speak on this one. "Kelsey's been around the stage since freshman year. He's a great dancer and I do think he can sing a bit. I would pair him up with Fontana if it were up to me. I think they are your two best dancers."

"Last year he played a girl in a play and no one caught on for all three shows," said Throbby. "If you ask me, he and Fontana could do a sister act if you stuffed two melons in his shirt."

"Yeah," said Sugar. "Like he's a bit of a swish."

"His whole locker door is plastered with pictures of Juliet Prowse," said Throbby. "He'd give his left nut to have a dance with her."

"Great," I said. "There's promise here I think. We're doing just great and we are on the last name, Stone Roadroller. I have a feeling deep down, that he is tied to

Hannah someway. I did hear through the grapevine that he acts as her chauffeur some times. Does he have any show biz qualities?"

Glenda said, "Stone used to work around her home doing the lawns and trimming— once in a while some painting. He always complimented her on her beautiful '57 Buick. She kept that car in A-1 shape and lots of times he washed and waxed it for her. At some point in time she asked him to drive her to the store. I guess he must have done alright because she's had him on call a few days a week ever since. I know he has the pallor of a dead tree and he comes on like an airhead, but deep down I think he's a good guy who's willing to pitch in and help."

"I tried dancing with him at Poncho's one night," said Throbby. "You know, there is a saying that you can tell how a guy is going to be in bed by the way he dances. If this is a fact, that dude is going to be dancing alone and sexually self-sufficient for a long time."

"So I assume you're saying he can't dance. Is that true?" I asked.

"Reminds me of one of those guys in a log rolling contest," she said.

"Okay, girls, that wraps things up on this deal. Let me see," I said as I checked my watch, "we've got forty-five minutes. Let's go back to the piano."

The girls rose and so did we. They were smiling to think they had used up over half of the rehearsal doing nothing but I, on the other hand, had amassed a great profile of my brood.

As we got to the piano I said to Throbby, "Might as well get Fontana over here too so I only have to go over this once."

She looked over at the stage and then turned back to me.

"I think Bailey showed up and she's with her. She doesn't look great."

"Very well," I said. "I'll go over there with you and let's see what's what. We need to get them over here."

Glenda said, "You're asking for it now, Loopy."

"Hey, I gotta get my feet wet sometime, why not now?"

Throbby and I went up on stage with the beaver in tow. She approached Fontana who was consoling a weeping Bailey.

"What happened to her?" asked Throbby.

"She slid by Poncho's after school to have a couple beers. Said she needed something to level her off for the rehearsal. She ran into a bunch of iron workers who had just topped off a nearby building after nine months work and they were celebrating the completion. She had a couple shots of 151 rum along with ale chasers and that was all in an hour. It caught up with her quick."

"Well," said Throbby, "Miss Loopy wants all of us over at the piano so I guess we better gather her up and help her over there."

As this conversation was taking place, Mr. Loinrubber was seated on a folding chair nearby. He was reading over the prop and scenery schedule for the play. The beaver had enough rope to get to him and smelling the wooden leg he deemed it necessary and fitting to have an afternoon snack. He started chewing on Humphrey's pants leg to get to "the meat" of the deal. Although the leg itself was devoid of feeling, Humphrey felt a tugging on his pants. He looked down and seeing this action, he reacted immediately by whacking the beaver on the head with his clipboard. As the beaver recoiled, Throbianna got a glimpse of that move by Humphrey. She moved immediately to him and cupped her hands around his face and chin. Looking straight into his eyes she asked, "Did you just whack my beaver?"

"Yeah, the son-of-a-bitch was chewing on my leg!"

Now Throbby reacted, turning her nails inward and drawing three lines down both sides of his neck. Rivlets of blood filled all six slots and he let out a scream.

"You little whore. Look what you've done to me. I'm bleeding to death."

"Nobody whacks my beaver. You got that you flag-waving nerd?" She left him as he scrambled for a rag.

"What am I supposed to do now?" he hollered. "Look at all this blood."

"Call the V.A.," she hollered back over her shoulder. "Tell them you need a medic."

Fontana, Bailey, Throbby and I returned to the piano with Damit in tow.

From the other end of the stage Humphrey screamed, "I'll kill that oversized rat, you little whore."

Fallopian heard Humphrey calling somebody a whore and she spun on her heels to see who might be cutting in on her territory. She thought she had that part covered.

The harmony among the cast members which I had hoped for seemed doomed on this, the first rehearsal day. I had prayed that these young people could find room in their hearts to elevate their behavior to a near-adult level but apparently this was not to be.

"What was that all about?" asked Sugar.

"General Patton over there whacked my beaver so I cut him a set of trolley tracks to remind him never to do it again," said Throbby.

I watched him stamping around on the stage with a T-shirt wrapped around his neck.

"Alright, let's see who can sing here," I said.

"Aw, shit. Do I have to?" asked Bailey. She was already in a chair with the back of her head leaning against the piano.

"When it comes your turn, yes you do. I'll make you last to give you time to collect yourself and hear what we're doing," I answered.

I tried each girl individually to see if she could sing the basic scale. The results were less than earth shattering and Bailey was a waste of time. The rehearsal time had run out and we all left. Sugar and Throbby led the pack with Damit in full stride behind them. The object here, I assumed, was to outrun Humphrey and get clear of the place as fast as possible.

I had to come up with some music by Thursday. Like it or not, Hannah was right—the ball was in my court. At home that night I tried to figure out what I'd do. My Dad was mostly into Dixieland jazz and at first I had excluded that from my field of choices. Then I heard something coming from his den which mirrored the flavor of the music from Cabaret. I went in there and asked him what he was playing. He said it was a tape of a German jazz band. The song I had just heard was their theme song and that plus two others on the tape were originals that were created by them. In a moment of desperation and flat out piracy I decided to make a tape of those three tunes. What the hell, they were from Germany. How many people could possibly know them here in the states? This would give Fallopian something to choreograph and I could always give credit to the German band in the program.

Besides, I had this feeling. I am not a psychic or a mind reader and I don't believe in fortune tellers. Somehow, though, I had an inward feeling that this play would never see its opening night so my gamble was not that big. Call me crazy, but that was my premonition.

The dance music having been addressed, I moved my thinking to the songs we'd be needing. Here I had quite another problem. In basic testing of all eight actors I found five with no idea of pitch at all, a few who would maybe be okay, and one pretty good one. Fallopian could also sing but as choreographer she could not be in the actual show. During auditions I heard comments like: "I'm so like not into this," "Are we going to have to learn more than one tune?" "What is my motivation?" "Is he going to be singing in my ear?" and "Is there any money coming our way for this deal?"

I know that for a powerful performance there should be ensemble singing. One tune for sure and maybe two. I made a decision to call in a favor. I picked five songs at random to use in the show and then called a friend of mine at college. Maxine Jamsticky was the director of the school choir and also was into women's barbershop through the Sweet Adelines. I told her I needed vocal recordings of the songs I had selected. I told her how many voices to put into each song, ranging from one to eight, and asked her to record them at the school. Now all I had to do was to get my crew to memorize the lyrics so they could lipsync them. Fallopian, on the other hand, had to really teach them to dance. You can't "footsync."

With the basic music in place, we started to buckle down at rehearsals. Time really started to fly. Although we were making meager progress and from time to time tempers flared and people stamped their feet, we still inched forward. I was also getting to know the cast. I had asked around about Sugar and Throbianna and now had a profile on them too.

Sugar Bratchild was just that. An unruly brat who was just spoiled rotten. She was rude, pushy and rich. Her mother was actually the one who met Forbes at Hannah's request and was able to secure the Imperial for rehearsals. The catch was that Sugar was to be in the play. She was indeed dating Helmut because he was a loser and she had him dancing on a string. It made her feel powerful.

Throbianna Cotrocker, was her best friend and was apparently known all over town for her beaver. She was also currently on parole. She was trying to tie a cherry stem into a knot with her tongue while it was in some guy's mouth and that wound up turning into a class A felony. She was also on heavy medication, a new drug with unpredictable side effects ranging from blindness and insanity to nymphomania and dysentery. She apparently loved it and had four cases at home. She was a vixen of sorts and enjoyed taunting any male in her path. She was tall, talkative and witty and unable to control her impulses concerning men. She was prone to shutting guys down after exciting them to near climax, sort of a double edged love/hate sword.

As the fall weather came upon us and winter neared, the temperature during the daylight hours was now not much over 45°. I asked both Cliff and Mr. Loinrubber to see about turning up the heat a bit. Then I learned that since the Imperial was a summer playhouse, it had no heat. You really get a lot colder when you know there is no way you're going to get any warmer. Your mind automatically tells you that you are going to freeze to death. Cast members were now wearing heavier clothes and it was interfering with the dancing and general movement on stage. Some of the girls had even taken to wearing mittens and gloves. Although I thought that was overkill, I said nothing.

Cliff and Hannah were jointly coaching the actual dialogue for the play. Not many of the kids were good at that either. Memory lapses, forgotten lines, bumbled cues, and onstage horseplay all dragged forward progress at a snail's pace.

Cliff had moments of incoherence brought on by his usual state of intoxication plus his disagreement with some of Mr. Hosenozzle's apparent digressions from his book's original storyline. Hannah, who daily sat following the script, had problems of her own, brought on entirely by her chain smoking.

I am no medical person so I don't know what it is like to read when you're cross-eyed and you can safely bet I never asked her. Given that it would be a possible if not probable handicap, she was compounding that with smoke curling up into her eyes as her cigarettes hung from her lips. That made her eyes water and of course, the script became blurry. At times, tears even fell onto the script itself. Add to that the ashes which also dropped onto the script and you get the picture. Ashes that were brushed away left gray streaks through the copy and ashes that were not noticed had burned holes right through the paper and those lines had "gone up in smoke." Therefore, she was continually correcting people when they were right and she was wrong, or just guessing.

Fallopian was really trying to get the guys to dance. Her big problem was Helmut. He had an attitude and was not about to have anybody "direct" him. He wore a pair of heavy black leather motorcycle boots which were absolutely not conducive to any form of dance. When asked if he could wear another type of shoe he said he wears nothing else and at times has even slept in his boots. Every time he tried a step or twirl he left a big black mark on the stage. It was as if he were wearing a pair of all-weather radials.

His attitude spilled over into Mackenzie's wardrobe assignment too. The script called for a clown scene. It was advised that the clown be the tallest person, for effect. That made Helmut the candidate for that part. Mackenzie told him she was going to measure him for a clown outfit. He started with his bravado tough guy routine, parading around in his black leather jacket with his thumbs hooked in the front pockets of his Levis. "Hold on, Granny. You ain't fittin' me for no bullshit clown outfit while I'm still breathing. You can just forget that item. File that under never."

"Whoa, wait a minute! Who are you calling Granny, you sawed-off piss pot?" said Mackenzie. Helmut was actually a full foot taller than her but she stood right up to him, "I don't know who you think you are but I worked with Marlon Brando and you wouldn't even make a rash on his ring finger. I worked with James Dean and Henry Winkler, too. They were men compared to you. If I were in charge of casting I'd shitcan that black jacket and make you Snow White or Mary Poppins. You remind me of an envelope. Big name on the outside and nothin' on the inside. I don't think you've got a hair on your ass and if you don't shut up and let me do my job I'm gonna take my scissors and convert you from a clown to the lead soprano. Now get over here and let me take your measurements, little girl."

Activity on the stage ground to a halt as everyone stood and watched the air rush from Helmut's ego balloon. He was redfaced, shocked, scared and hurt all in an instant. This Miss Mackenzie should have been with General Custer. He might have had half a chance.

At the end of the fourth week and early into the fifth we thought there might be some hope for this play. My thirty-day leave of absence from the college had expired and I was forced to drive sixty miles each way for rehearsals plus resume my normal work load at college. This was time-consuming and expensive. Gas prices had passed $1.65 per gallon and even my mid-range car was using an ample amount of fuel for three round trips weekly.

We had resolved some more of the problems and the bickering. Throbianna had found someone who wanted to play with her beaver three afternoons a week. Hannah had ordered Damit removed when Humphrey threatened a lawsuit over the neck attack.

Stone and Coley had located a huge kerosene heater in a boat storage warehouse and brought it to the Imperial to give us some warmth. It really did make a lot of warm air but it roared like a jet plane. They moved it out to the doorway and although the noise subsided somewhat, the fumes quickly filled the entire theater making everyone sick and forcing cancellation of rehearsals for that day. We finally settled for a pair of electric heaters in the coffee room which we used from time to time during the day.

Hannah and Mackenzie decided that she was not really up to making all the costumes from scratch, so Hannah told her to go to the Salvation Army and Goodwill clothing stores. "Buy something close and we'll make it work," she had told her.

In a gesture of partial cooperation and face saving, Helmut got measured for the clown suit and was now dancing in a pair of hunting socks.

Bailey had virtually dried out and was able to make all the rehearsals on time and in a coherent condition. She was really trying to make something happen on her part. In short, we actually had the beginnings of cohesion among the cast members and staff. Then I arrived on Thursday, and although everyone was present, the air was thick and silent. Glenda came over to me and said, "We've got some bad news."

"What's that?" I asked.

"Apparently Mr. Hosenozzle was gunned down in his apartment in Harlem. The newspaper account said it stemmed from a lover's triangle gone bad."

"Oh my goodness," I said. "Where does that leave us now?"

"Well, the big bombshell went off when Cliff heard the news," she said. "He screamed out, 'NO. NO. NO. I was his lover. He loved me. Only me always.' Then he passed out on the floor. Hannah's trying to pull him together but he's a wreck."

"Great. This is just great. Are we going to try to rehearse? I just spent an hour and fifteen minutes on the road getting here. The least someone could have done is buzz me on my cell phone."

"We didn't find out until ten minutes ago," said Glenda.

I went over to get a look at Cliff. If I had to rate his color on a scale of one to ten I'd give him a zero with an option to reduce that to a minus two. He was sitting on the floor with his head in Hannah's lap and babbling. She just kept repeating, "Yes, dear. I know, I know it hurts."

I looked at her and said, "Under the circumstances I think we should cancel rehearsals for today and start up again on Saturday."

Hannah nodded and said nothing. I told the cast to leave and drove back to school.

On Saturday I came into town about 11:30 A.M. and went to my parents house. There was a phone message from Glenda. I returned her call and she said, "I think we have a new and more serious problem. Can we have lunch before the rehearsal?"

"Sure. Where?"

"How about the Wishing Well? It's just down the road from the Imperial so it will be handy."

"Alright," I said. "How about 1 P.M.?"

"Fine, I'll see you there," she answered.

"Glenda, you don't want to give me a hint, do you?"

"No, I think I'd rather lay it all out at lunch."

"See ya soon," I said and hung up. What the hell could be wrong now, I wondered. Did I just blow another 120-mile round trip?

The Wishing Well was a rather pleasant place and did a brisk business. It was a cut above your average hamburger joint and the trade was more adult. Glenda was waiting in the foyer as I entered and the hostess showed us to a table near the windows. I could no longer contain myself. "What's up?"

"Well, you know, about Piedmont and that tragic thing in New York."

"Sure, it was an absolute shocker," I said.

"Well, Loopy, try this one on for size. Thursday night Cliff stole Hannah's car and went out on an all-night bender, probably over this Piedmont thing. He got really drunk and was coming back toward her house at 10:30 A.M. Friday. He apparently was speeding and cutting in and out of a funeral procession on a two-lane road. He cut into line to avoid an oncoming car and rear ended the hearse at 40 m.p.h. He shoved the hearse into the rear of a police motorcycle that was escorting the procession. The cop was thrown from the bike onto the shoulder and the hearse stopped on top of the motorcycle. Cliff cut out and fled the scene, but the hearse driver had the presence of mind to get his plate number and call 911 on his cell phone. At that point the cop thrown from the motorcycle may have been okay but the flower car swerved onto the shoulder to avoid Cliff and the hearse and it ran over the cop. The cop is now in intensive care!"

"Holy shit, you couldn't get this on TV," I said.

"Wait, there's more."

"What more could you add to this?" I asked.

"Well, from the 911 call the cops ran the plate; it gave Hannah's address and they got Cliff and the smashed-up Buick about a mile from her place. Apparently the radiator had been damaged, all the water ran out and the car overheated and quit. Cliff was in it—passed out. They arrested him and charged him with D.W.I., reckless driving, leaving the scene of an accident and possible possession of a controlled substance. They towed the car and impounded it, and he's behind bars. The cop in intensive care may live or die which means Cliff could get wrapped up in a vehicular manslaughter charge as well."

"God, Glenda, this is tragic. What does Hannah have to say about all this?" I asked.

"Well, that's the frosting on the cake," she said. The cops called her at Noon and told her they had her car and that it was damaged and impounded. They also told her that Cliff was the driver and was now in jail. They told her the charges and said he would be arraigned today sometime after 11 A.M.

"About 3 P.M. yesterday the rescue squad got a call to go to Hannah's. Apparently she suffered a stroke or a mild heart attack. Now she's also in intensive care and there's no word of her condition."

My premonition of the demise of this play came rushing into my mind. "What are we going to do now?" I asked.

"I don't have the foggiest idea," answered Glenda. "You know Hannah. This project was all her idea—her money—and she deferred authority to no one. We virtually have no authority to proceed nor do we have any funds to do it if we need them. I think we might have to call a halt to it all. She's in no condition to make that decision right now and who knows what the outcome of her hospitalization will be."

I looked at Glenda with what I knew to be a blank stare. I was feeling empty inside, sorry for this rash of events and probably a little selfish that my efforts seemed now to be dashed on the rocks. "I sure hate to see this all go to waste but I think you're right on this one," I said. "She is the director, and without Piedmont, Cliff is the only other connection to this project. I guess we better bring down the curtain on this one today."

"I'm sorry," said Glenda. "I know I got you into all this and you worked like a Trojan horse to get it to go, but we've got to be realistic."

"I know," I said. "Don't beat yourself up on my account, there's no way you could have seen anything this bizarre coming."

When the gang gathered at the Imperial, Glenda took the stage to act as spokesperson. Mackenzie was obviously very upset and she and Fallopian were trying to comfort each other. Stone appeared very shaken as well but I didn't know if it was over Hannah and Cliff or the Buick. Glenda told everything just as it had happened to avoid the inevitable rumor mill that would start grinding out stories. I listened and wondered how much wilder a story anyone could dream up to top the actual facts.

There was a general milling around and finally someone said, "Let's go to Poncho's. I think this is a wrap."

We shut down the theater and everyone left. Glenda, Mackenzie, Fallopian and I stood outside the door as they all passed by. Then Glenda turned the key in the door and we started to walk to the parking lot. I gave the other three the eye and asked, "Anyone for Poncho's?"

In the deepest moments of tragedies some great relationships are born. The four of us spent a few hours at Poncho's. I learned more about them and a lot about myself as we hashed over our lives and the project. Ironically, in this kid's joint, with our newfound cast members around us, we did not feel the least bit out of place.

Of course, we knew that some of the kids were glad it was over. But there were also those who, after some encouragement and guidance, were able to see the challenge and the fun that we had set up for them. For those few I felt genuine sadness. I was aware after only a month or so of this play that you can't take a handful of butterflies, put them in a plastic bag, and expect them to all adjust, fly and live just because you say it's going to be that way.

I reflected on my education to date. By graduation the cost would be over $85,000 for four years. I had been tutored by some of the very best teachers. We had studied not only music but history, science, humanity and language. Textbook cases and situations had been presented time and again. I know now that much had been overlooked regarding adolescent behavior patterns. The natural behavior patterns of that age group, the rebellious attitudes and weekly mood swings, the cliques which develop and the continual seeking out of both acceptance and independence. I do know that I was able to show them that I had some experience and expertise. I did not try to become one of the gang, but I did, from time to time, tell them that I understood their frustrations. Over a month's time I was able to get their attention. I also learned very quickly that at their age, whatever crap they couldn't dump on their parents ran downhill and wound up on their teachers.

On the up side, these kids, despite school activities, some part-time jobs, love interests and more, were tireless. They were energetic, humorous and multi-talented. As I sat in Poncho's I wondered if I had had each one individually to teach and to guide, what I could have done.

Once I saw all of them kick back in their own environment, they were neat people. They were relaxed knowing that there was no net over their heads. Anytime they wished, they could open the door and split. Sugar, Throbby and Fontana came to our table several times that afternoon. They offered to buy us a drink and I think they were sincere when they said they were sorry the play had gone sour.

One bit of irony came from this chain of events. Hannah never came out of the hospital and the very day she had hoped to open the play, she died. Her name never got up in lights but it did make the headlines of our newspaper:

HANNAH HANDLEYANK, PATRON OF THE ARTS, DEAD AT 97.

ASK THE AUTHOR
—
NO. A-209

Dear Don:

My eighteen-year-old daughter and her male piano teacher went to the music store in the plaza. The teacher said he needed a special piece. They've been gone five months. How long should it take to find a special piece?

~ Wondering in Waverly

Dear Wondering:

If your daughter has been with that piano teacher for the last five months I would say he has found his special piece. Rent her room, give her clothes to the Salvation Army and get on with your life.

ASK THE AUTHOR

—

NO. A-309

Dear Don:

I have been taking lessons from an elderly lady in my neighborhood. She's a friend of my mom's and a nice person but I think she's getting senile and perhaps blind. When I make a mistake she points to someplace on the music which is not at all where we are. How do I confirm my suspicions?

~ Suspicious in San Pedro

Dear Suspicious:

1. Offer her a cookie. If she has to feel around her face to find her mouth before eating, she's losing it.

2. Next time you know a piece well enough to play it without the sheet music, turn the music upside down. If she doesn't say anything your probably right.

3. Another test for blindness is to observe her sitting on the piano bench. If she points with her left hand and has her right hand laced through the harness on a German Shepherd there is 94% chance she has a sight problem.

ASK THE AUTHOR
—
NO. A-372

Dear Don:

I am a capable teacher with a good list of credits to my name. I want every student to move forward with interest and excellence. It seems some of my male students are bogging down and losing interest in the lessons. What can I do to rekindle the flame of learning?

~ Flickering in Flagler

Dear Flickering:

Get some old Playboy magazines and tear out the centerfolds. Place them strategically in the lesson book. Tell the young men they can "have a peek" only when they have mastered the music up to that page. Be sure that book stays with you and that they practice from a duplicate. You will find new learning and speed that you had heretofore never imagined. It is the old "dangling carrot" approach.

ASK THE AUTHOR
—
NO. A-404

Dear Don:

I am a fairly young teacher and love my work. One of the hardest jobs I have is to keep students from over-pedaling the piano. The damper (slang term "Loud Pedal") should be used sparingly and many times not at all. How can I break this recurring habit?

~ Pedaling in Patchin

Dear Pedaling:

I know your frustration. Several ideas are at hand:

1. Hook your pedals to a 12-volt battery. It will generate a shock acting like a cattle prod and reduce pedaling.

2. Handcuff the student's legs together at the ankles. The extra effort required to use both legs to pedal will tire them soon.

3. Tape each of the students legs to the legs of the piano bench with duct tape. Soon they will agree to stay off the pedal just to avoid the groin pain.

4. Take a torch and cut off all your pedals.

**ASK THE
AUTHOR**

—

NO. A-408

Dear Don:

As a teacher of piano I do not propose to know about teaching voice. I have one young lady who insists on vocalizing with all her tunes whether there are words or not. She can't sing on key and it is distracting to me as a teacher. How can I stop this annoying habit?

~ Offkey in Oakdale

Dear Offkey:

The next time your darling student opens her mouth to vocalize, take an aerosol can of Black Flag or Raid and give her a generous shot down the windpipe. It will be quite some time before she warbles again, and even then she will remember you in a whole new light.

Dear Don:

I am an aging male teacher. I feel I am losing touch with my younger students. Can you give me any hints on how to get rebonded.

~ Disconnected in Dixfield

Dear Disconnected:

Adolescents often go through a time when "gross is in." You may want to lean that way. Throw a block of limburger in the piano. Chew tobacco and spit on the floor, the piano, and on the student once in a while. Wear no shirt at all, shower once a week, braid your armpit hair, keep your teeth out and be sure your diet is loaded with garlic and onions. Wear the same clothes for a month. Kids love body odor, farts, mucus, zits, burps and bad breath. Shaving and haircuts are out. If you do have to shave, divide your face down the center and shave only one side. Remember when blowing your nose, no hanky. Put your thumb against one nostril and blast air through the other. It's effective.

THE CONSERVATORY

"A day without **TURTLETURD** *is like a goat without a canoe."*

It was May of 1998 when young Colin Crapperpacker was discharged from the U.S. Air Force. He had served for four years, filling many roles in both the United states and abroad. His dad had passed away some years back and his mom and two sisters now lived in Cincinnati, OH. As a boy he was drawn to the piano and over several years he had taken lessons from three different teachers as his family could afford it. He secretly hoped someday that he could be a teacher himself. While in the Air Force he used his spare time wisely—playing in officers' clubs, small bands, and once in a while at places off base as a solo pianist. He religiously studied music and theory and had a photographic memory for printed music. It was therefore natural that Colin should seek out a school to further his musical training.

Many thousands of would-be musical artists dream of a time when they will attend a prestigious school such as the Eastman School in Rochester, NY or the Juilliard School in New York City. Colin was no exception, but because he had regularly sent money home to his mom during his years in the military, he was now seeking champagne on a beer budget. The big schools demanded top credentials just to get in and their tuitions exceeded $20,000 per year. Colin figured that he did not have a chance in that arena so he opted for a more moderately priced venue to begin his studies. He had heard of a place in the Midwest while he was in the service and now he made it his business to track it down. It is known by the name of TURTLETURD ACADEMY and is located in Hijinx, NE. It is here that we catch up with young Colin in the midst of his second year as a piano major.

The following description of the school and its people gives credence that there is always a place where those of lesser talents or financial problems may attend in comfort and at a reasonable price. It is good to know how this school came about and who got it off the ground. Not everyone begins on Broadway or in Hollywood or Las Vegas, so why not hone your craft in an unusual setting full of unusual people in a great little town in central Nebraska. Here you've got no place to go but up!

TURTLETURD THEATRICAL CONSERVATORY & ACADEMY

3131 Cornhusker Way • Hijinx Corners, Nebraska
CO-OWNERS: SUSAN D'LERIOUS AND PEARL DIVER
SCHOOL MOTTO: "Life without Turtleturd is like a goat without a canoe."

HISTORY: Bradley D'Lerious, a land owner of some notoriety, agreed in the 1960s to enter into an agreement with the local Game & Wildlife Preservation Authority to deed over thirty-five acres of farmland. It was to become a nature preserve and fish hatchery. Six acres of the land were cleared and the hatchery built thereon. The rest of the land was fenced off and bit by bit was stocked with animals. Since the whole thirty-five acres had been corn fields, the only animals that could live there were those that fed on corn. The nature preserve fizzled out in the second year but the fish hatchery flourished.

Bradley's brother, Lyndon D'Lerious, was put in charge and seemed to have the knack for breeding and hatching fish. The output exceeded the demand however, and soon the place had thousands of tons of frozen fish waiting for somewhere to go. In twelve years the hatchery closed, a victim of its own success. It lay dormant for ten years, during which time the state returned the land and all the structures to Bradley. Lyndon passed on in 1973 and Bradley put the place up for sale.

A woman from Oregon heard about it. She was a deepsea diver and underwater photographer named Pearl Diver and she wanted a place to set up a school to teach that type of thing. She met with Bradley and his wife, Susan, proposed that the hatchery be converted into a seaquarium, and with her financial aid and direction it happened. In the fall of 1983, the Pearl Diver Aquatic Academy opened for business. It was a most impressive structure. Glass walls rose sixty feet into the air and while onlookers were treated to the sight of many species of fish, the young students were diving in the waters and photographing all the various underwater creatures. But trial and error proved that all fish are not compatible—something that Pearl had evidently not thought through. Some of the large fish busied themselves eating the smaller fish. No way to control water temperatures was another factor. In the hot Nebraska summer of 1984, many of the frail fish actually cooked. The costs of restocking soared, and in three years Pearl found that she could no longer underwrite the losses. The D'Lerious family were landlords but had no interest in the seaquarium business, so Pearl finally had to admit that her venture was doomed. The final nail in the coffin for the seaquarium came during the harvest season when a young man accidentally backed a harvesting machine into the tall glass walls. In minutes a wall of water filled with fish rushed into the fields. It was a disaster of major proportions.

Pearl was devastated but Bradley, ever the entrepreneur, saw a buck in this. He held a two-day marathon fish fry. He advertised over radio and television telling folks that for one time only they could have all the exotic fish they could eat for $5 per person. People tramped through the muddy fields by the thousands. Since there were no tables or chairs, those attending ate standing at hay wagons. The fish were cooked in mortar boxes full of charcoal. Normally haddock is a pretty good fish for dinner, but imagine having your choice of shark, marlin, porpoise and octopus for $5. It was a runaway success for two days and then it was over. The remaining fish and all the related debris were plowed under and there sat the remains of the vacant seaquarium. What to do with this white elephant?

Enter the savior Jeremiah Turtleturd. A lifelong student and professor of music, he had long envisioned his own school for the theatrical arts. At just the right time he came into a large amount of cash. He had sold his patent on the "Piano Bench Fart Arrester" to the Devonshire Piano Equipment Works. He approached Bradley, Susan and Pearl with a deal, which they happily accepted. In return for naming the school after him, Professor Turtleturd agreed to pump his cash into the remedial work required to turn the place into a school. He was to be the headmaster.

The seaquarium became an all-glass theater for the arts and opened in the early '90s. It was a most unique setting and offered everything in the show business field. A brochure which was circulated contained in part the following information:

The school took off at once. The negotiable tuition meant that the students paid as they were financially able and the work program allowed them to split their education time with an outside source of income. The student body and faculty grew rapidly and Professor Turtleturd could not have been happier.

The admissions process was very fair. It was the DART METHOD. All applicants had their names printed on six-inch round cardboard discs. These were glued to a corkboard wall in the conference room and each August 2, the Professor and his staff would enter the room at 11 A.M. They all drank until 1 P.M. then everyone was blindfolded and given two dozen darts. The darts were then randomly thrown at the corkboard wall and the discs receiving the most hits identified the persons to be admitted. In the event not enough hits occurred, the balance of the round discs were taken into the parking lot. There they were sailed like frisbees and the ones that travelled the farthest identified the additional people to be admitted.

Enrollment started with nineteen students in the first year and by the time Colin Crapperpacker arrived, it had passed 200. The old buildings where they used to freeze fish had been converted to dormitories. In his first semester Colin was rooming with a boy from Germany whose uncle had been a busboy on the Hindenburg. Although there were few rules at the school, the students were not allowed to have cars on campus—they were allowed to have tractors and horses. This helped with the annual corn harvest which helped to support the school.

Colin enjoyed his time at TTCA and he was an outstanding pianist. The students often performed in the "Rotunda." That was the huge glass-enclosed area which had been the seaquarium. This venue gave onlookers a full view of everything while at the same time protecting the students from having things thrown at them. Loudspeakers outside the glass walls provided the sound for the spectators who were seated in bleachers. The big shows usually coincided with the Hijinx Corners Tractor Pull and once the Professor agreed to allow dogs and beer in the stands the crowds swelled.

While working on a story entitled "MUSICAL MADNESS AND MERRIMENT IN THE MIDWEST," we interviewed Colin and in the following story he recalls two of his most memorable times at TTCA.

The first situation was a real stickler. Colin was chosen by computer to be on a panel that was assembled to decide on the ability of Professor Turtleturd to remain as headmaster. The event that triggered this panel to be formed came during a national television show being broadcast live from TTCA. It was a documentary showcasing the Professor and his school. As was only right, he was the first scheduled performer. He had selected the famous "Rhapsody in Blue" for his number—a widely acclaimed and famous work by Gershwin which lent itself to the piano very well.

As the cameras began to roll on this live performance, the Professor took the stage, bowed to the camera and seated himself at his prized nine-foot concert grand piano. He proceeded to adjust the bench to his liking and then sat motionless for four minutes after which his head nodded down. The cameras were halted and school personnel immediately removed him to the dressing room for attention. He awakened about ten minutes later completely oblivious to the events that had occurred. The show continued with acts by the other scheduled artists but he never returned to the stage.

In the weeks following, it was discovered that the Professor suffered from nar-colepsy and Alzheimer's disease. On the night of the show he spent those four minutes trying to remember the tune and when it finally came to him he fell asleep. It had often been reported that he dozed in class which was always attributed to extreme fatigue. In other cases he would approach members of his own staff in the hall, extend his hand and say, "Hi, I'm Jerry Turtleturd. Are you new here?"

The panel decided that as headmaster and namesake of TTCA, he should not be removed. He was allowed to stay on but relieved of his musical chores. They bought him his own tractor and told him he was to work outside; the fresh air would do him good.

Subsequent to that decision it was further discovered that prior to establishing TTCA, he had lost several jobs due to his narcolepsy. In one case, while acting as a volunteer nurse, he fell asleep and drained three gallons of blood from a patient.

This did not set well with the next of kin and they filed a $5 million lawsuit against the hospital. In two other cases the Professor was relieved from his job due to the narcolepsy. On the job, while employed as an armored car security guard he slept with the rear door of the truck open while four young men methodically unloaded $6 million into their Pinto and sped off into the big city. In his other job as an over-the-road tour bus driver he was discharged for routinely taking the bus through field and stream as he dozed at the wheel.

These revelations only served to further reinforce the decision of the panel.

In his second and probably most memorable event, Colin was asked to perform as the accompanist for a visiting opera singer. In his time at TTCA he had often played for singers. This time he would be tested since there was to be no rehearsal and he was expected to play onsight whatever music the singer produced. It was in essence a test of his reading and performing skills. Oddly enough he felt confident about this. He had become a master reader and since the job was at the school in the Rotunda, he felt at home with the surroundings and the big grand piano which he had played so often. He had never met the singer and little was known about her by anyone at the school.

The following is an account of that performance as told to me by Colin himself.

It was a Sunday evening, June 27. The hot sun had kept the air conditioners whirring at full speed just to hold the Rotunda at 75°. The big tractor pull was going on up the street and would be ending soon so I knew we'd have people. I dressed in my black tie and tails for this affair and I was wandering around the dressing area when a most attractive young lady approached me. I figured her to be in her early twenties and for a moment I wondered if she could be the singer.

"Excuse me, I'm looking for a man named Colin."

"That would be me," I said.

"Oh good. Then you are the man who is playing for the opera number tonight."

"Yes ma'am, that's correct."

"Well, my name is Honey Dipper, I'll be working with you tonight."

"That's fine. You look very young to be an opera singer."

"Oh, I'm not the singer," she said. "My grandmother is going to sing. I'll be your page turner at the piano."

"Well, Miss Dipper, just where is your grandmother now?" I asked.

"She's in her dressing room and she asked me to find you and have you come there."

"Okay, let's go and meet the diva," I replied.

We made our way along the hall to the master dressing room reserved for stars and premier performers. Honey tapped on the door and a booming voice said, "Come on in, it's open."

I entered the room behind Honey. Her grandmother was seated on a couch. Honey turned to me and said, "Colin, this is my grandmother. Her name is Belinda Bargebottom but you probably know her better by her stage name, Sunflower McBride."

At first I thought it would be a nice gesture to sit next to Ms. McBride but there wasn't any room on the couch. She took up the whole thing. She was eating tuna fish out of a quart tin using a tablespoon and washing it down with port wine. On the table next to her a cigar smoldered in the ashtray.

"Take a seat," she said. "I'm just having a snack here. I'll be done in a minute."

I grabbed a chair for myself and pulled another up for Honey. "I'll just sit here for now," I said.

In an effort to keep a conversation moving, Honey spoke next. "Gram has been in this business for a long time. She has performed all over the United States and Europe. She studied in Italy under the tutorship of Roman Holiday, a well known voice coach."

"How very interesting," I replied. "And what brings you to our lovely school this evening?"

"Gram is hoping to retire and Professor Turtleturd said he may have a spot for her on the faculty of the voice school."

During this conversation, I noticed that Ms. McBride was hoisting tuna fish into her mouth like a finely tuned conveyor. Next she reached behind the couch and came up with a gallon bottle of the same red wine she had been slugging. She refilled her glass, threw the tuna fish can and spoon onto the table, picked up her cigar and relit it.

"Gram likes to relax a bit before a show," said Honey.

I looked at her and said, "I can see that. And nothing calms you down like a tin of tuna fish, some port wine and a fine cigar."

Then Ms. McBride stood up and began to talk. Her voice sounded like she had just swallowed a Brillo pad. If I had closed my eyes I might have believed I was talking to Jimmy Durante.

But I couldn't close my eyes. I think I was being very courteous when I rated her size as ample. Ample that is if I were constructing an igloo for a family of ten. She was wearing a huge white silk outfit and had a black bun of hair on top of her head. That was just what I envisioned: an igloo with a derby hat on its roof. The outfit was layered and there was silk everywhere. The sheer sight of it sent my mind racing back to thoughts of my stint in the Air Force. The last time I saw so much white silk in one place I was rigging a parachute to drop a two and a half ton truck out of a cargo plane.

Her shoes were silver satin and they fit so tightly that her chubby little feet puffed out of them like two loaves of bread rising from a pair of tins in the oven. She had everything a man could ever want. Broad shoulders, husky arms and a mustache.

"I have my own arrangements here," she said. "Take a look at these and see what you think." She handed me a pile of single sheets of paper that looked as though she had sat on them more than once.

"Did you do this arranging yourself?" I asked.

"No, Dearie. A guy named Chester Moistmuffin from New Jersey did these. We worked together one summer at the Love Canal Contamination Festival in

Niagara Falls. That was back in '88 when he did them. He was a great arranger—died way too young."

"Heart attack?" I asked.

"Naw, he got his head crushed in the liftgate of a rental truck when we were moving a piano. Couldn't save him. Gone in a minute. Started with his tie and just sucked him in."

"I am sorry for your loss," I said.

"Thank you. Do we have time to go over this music?" she asked.

"Well," I said, "there's a practice piano down the hall in one of our student rehearsal rooms. It's only a spinet but I do know it's right in tune. Would you like to go there?"

"Sure. Come on. Honey, you should go with us."

"Okay, Gram, whatever you say," replied Honey.

The three of us went down to the practice room. It is not a room made for three people and with Ms. McBride in there it was not even a room made for one person.

"Let me just glance at the music. Perhaps I have done this opera before," I said.

"I think not," she said. "I wrote it myself."

"Oh, I see," I said. "I noticed on the front page that some of the notes were blurred as if they had gotten wet a time or two."

"Yeah," she said, "shit happens."

"What are these arrows pointing back and forth to these different chord symbols?" I asked. "Just reminders to me from another rehearsal. Ignore 'em."

"My Italian is really not up to par," I said to her. "What is the title?"

"Questione di Attualita Palpitante," she replied. "It means Burning Question."

"I certainly have never seen it," I said. "I see it starts off in 'D' flat. Nice key, very bright."

"Yes," she said, "but I have been singing it in 'D' lately. I guess you'll have to transpose as you go."

I'm thinking now that in a song I've never seen she wants me to go from five flats to two sharps and God knows what else further on.

"Okay," I said. "Let's try a few lines."

I rolled a first arpeggio and as soon as I got into the next measure she cut loose. Her voice sounded like a tugboat horn in the Jersey Harbor. I couldn't believe it. Thank goodness this was a rehearsal. At the end of the first page I just couldn't stand being in the room with her anymore and besides, I was supposed to do this number with no previous practice. I also recognized that the perfume she was wearing was actually either Ben Gay or Deep Heat.

"Fine, Ms. McBride. Let's call this a wrap."

I got up off the bench and we all went into the hall. In actuality, half of her had been in the hall anyway. I looked at Honey and handed her the sheet music charts and told her to go to the Rotunda and place them on the grand piano so at least we didn't blow that part. She grabbed them up and scurried down the hall while Ms. McBride trundled off in the direction of her dressing room, puffing on her cigar.

I remember saying to her, "I really think you should put out the cigar. They frown on people smoking in the school."

"Screw them," she said. "I'm the star here. What are they going to do, throw me out?"

She entered her room and slammed the door. It was ten minutes until show time and that should have given her time to down the rest of the wine. I figured it was best to check on Honey so I headed off for the Rotunda. She was talking to our Irish exchange student who was currently head of staging and lighting, a likeable chap named Mad Dog Cafferty from a place in Ireland known as Listowel. He claimed to have had a drink in every pub in Ireland and now that he was in the United States it seemed he was shooting for a new title as well.

It appeared that the music was in place. The next logical and professional step was for the three of us to meet backstage and enter together. I couldn't stand the thought of being next to Ms. McBride again. I could only hope that she had popped a few dozen Tic Tacs to dull the cigar breath. I strolled over to take my place at the piano and Honey came to my side.

"Do you want me to stand at your right or at your left?"

"Stand on the left," I told her. "If you stand on my right the audience will not be able to see me."

"Oh yeah, I forgot."

I glanced out the huge windows and could see the audience filing into the bleachers. It was becoming a sizeable crowd. There were people from the school and people from the tractor pull. Their hats pretty much told the story of who they were. In one area the hats were marked BALDWIN, YAMAHA, STEINWAY and WURLITZER. In the other half it was pretty much CASE, JOHN DEERE, ALLIS CHALMERS and INTERNATIONAL HARVESTER. The outside floodlights had come on as dusk approached and I could see two Indians on horses. Right down in front was Professor Turtleturd seated on his new Oliver tractor, which was attached to a fully loaded manure spreader. I could tell that in his mind this was indeed a formal event. He had his black bib overalls on over a white shirt with french cuffs. He had a black bow tie and completed his wardrobe with his dress black cowboy boots. He was casually sipping from his pint of brandy.

The stage lights came on and I could tell by the vibration in the concrete floor that Sunflower was on the move. In an instant she was standing in front of the grand piano and had picked up the microphone. She smiled at the crowd and then turned to me and nodded. The opera began. I was transposing like crazy and I had agreed with Honey that I would nod my head every time she was to turn another page of music. Old Granny McBride was belting it out. Page 2, good. Page 3 and we're on a roll. I looked out the window for just a second to see a few folks leaving. Back to the music. So far, so good.

Next Sunflower started moving about and going through all sorts of gestures to spice up her presentation. As she backed into the curved side on the grand piano, her dynamic bulk forced it to move away a bit. Not too much, just enough that I could not reach the black keys. I quickly moved ahead to the leading edge of the bench and regained my position on the keyboard. I nodded and Honey turned another page. What was this I wondered? There is no continuity here, there must be a page out of place. I knew that Honey had turned three pages and as I looked at the top right of the page facing me I spotted the number fourteen. I was lost for a second and took one finger and pointed to the fourteen so that she could see what had happened. She nodded and took all of the music off the piano and began to shuffle through it—looking for the right sequence. Sunflower was now winging it acappela and giving me the look of death. She tried to look casual but the beer cans and tomatoes smashing against the glass windows were a bit unnerving. Driven by natural instinct, she recoiled backwards and this time she backed into the piano with force. It rolled about two feet. Now I had to stand up and move the bench forward and Honey thought she should help me, so she dropped the music on the stage and grabbed a corner of the bench. I turned to her and shouted for her to pick up the music and find the right place. She apparently took that as a reprimand and started to cry. With all the tears in her eyes she couldn't see anything after she picked up the music sheets and I figured this was fast turning into a comedy—or perhaps a tragedy.

I walked around the end of the piano, hoisted the top a bit so I could remove the topstick and lay the top down flat. I jumped up onto the piano top and started to dance the tarantella.

As I turned and faced the window I saw Professor Turtleturd looking at me and running his index finger across his throat. I knew that meant that either the show was over or I was expelled. Even the sight of the German Shepherd peeing on his tractor tire could not relieve my horror. Having nothing more to offer this show I jumped from the piano and ran into the wings. Honey ran after me and we stood in the doorway of the Rotunda as Sunflower kept singing. When the number was completed she came rolling off the stage as if nothing had happened.

She looked at her granddaughter and said, "The Professor loved it. I just know I nailed the job."

Then she looked at me and said, "Sonny, I could swear you messed up somewhere. We probably should have rehearsed more."

That's the last I ever saw of those two. I know to this day that she has never been appointed to the staff and that's okay with me. As for my performance, I got a 'D'. It would have been an 'F' but they had to give me something for showing up.

P.S. The dancing teacher said my tarantella rated a 'B' but unfortunately it was not a dance recital.

Colin Clapperpacker

THE OREO RATWARBLER STORY

Profile of a Winner

New teachers, follow your dream, be persistent.

Oreo Ratwarbler came from modest beginnings—born and raised in the Minneapolis-St. Paul area. Her dad worked in a plant making slots for coins to be used in vending machines. Her mom was a plain woman, dedicated to her family and staying at home to raise Oreo and her two younger sisters. In her spare time Mom also ran a small bomb-making operation in the basement. In good conscience she never let the children play with the bombs but they were allowed to box them for export.

Oreo started to play piano at age eight. She practiced on a grand piano given to the family by a Mafia representative in return for some crates of "MOMS-BOMS" (the trade name for the basement bomb-making activity).

Oreo soon realized that she liked to sing and found herself leaning toward piano sheet music with lyrics. She became quite proficient in the higher range vocals. Her mom even gave her a dollar a week to scream if the police came near the house. Encouraged by her friends and teachers she continued piano lessons for a few years but economic hardships forced her to stop. By this time she had set her sights on the fields of opera and gospel singing. She often rode her bike to the Spring Valley Baptist Church to hear her idol, Astoria Thighpacker, a soprano of great renown. They sometimes met after church and a bond was formed which would have surely pushed Oreo into an operatic orbit. Miss Thighpacker unfortunately was in an orbit of her own and was sent away for selling drugs. She is doing seven to ten years at Flemflinger Women's Correctional in Sandstone.

Oreo then turned to the music of Maria Callas and Barbra Streisand but at age twenty-two, tragedy befell her. Her dreams of a career in opera were dashed by a freak accident. Late one night she was playing golf with three blind friends. Apparently the blind folks don't care whether it's dark or not so they often played at night when the rates are best. One man did not realize she was standing so close and he hit her across the throat with a nine iron. Her voice would be changed forever.

The injuries to the voice box and vocal cords were devastating and would require major surgery. She engaged the world-famous voice surgeon, Dr. Irving Flupasser of Oxnard-on-the-Hudson. He was determined to have her speak again but told her that despite gargantuan efforts and a very controversial procedure, she would most likely never again sing in public. The rebuilding of the voice box was critical. It had been driven into the back of her neck and turned 180°. It was decided to leave it where it was, and although Dr. Flupasser was successful in getting vocal response, he had to rework the vocal cords. In a landmark nine-hour operation, he shortened the cords and cut a small speaker hole in the back of her neck.

As she went through recovery Oreo could speak but it sounded as though she had marbles in her mouth. She had to look away from people and speak through her hair. If she faced someone and spoke, it sounded like the guy behind her was talking.

After the accident she decided her love for music would shift to the piano. She had some formal training in conjunction with her singing and now decided she wanted to be a piano teacher. This, however, is not something one does on a whim. Thousands of hours of instruction and practice precede the acceptance of even the first student. It is akin to the hundreds of Olympic hopefuls who, year after year, put aside many of life's pleasures to work endlessly toward those final few minutes of glory. Both the aspiring teacher and the Olympian will not know until the end of training if all will lead to gloom or glory. The sensational thing is that thousands do risk it and many succeed.

A patron of the arts, Florence Greatbutt, of the very elite social family the Palm Desert Greatbutts, read about Oreo's unique surgery and her relentless pursuit of music. Through a Greatbutt Foundation Grant, Oreo was sent to study piano at Turtleturd Academy in Nebraska, a dream come true.

Four years at Turtleturd produced a great musician and a reassured and confident woman. Oreo graduated Magna Cum Okay in 1997 and has been teaching in the small town of Short Valley since then. She is the resident pianist for the St. Sophie's School for the Deaf in Knudesport. Her accomplishments prove that all adversity can be overcome if you have faith to carry on.

Note: Oreo has even given speeches to groups using her own invention. It is a 'J' pipe made from plastic tubing. She holds the short end against the back of her head and then puts the long side forward. The sound coming from the rear speaker travels through the tubing to the front which she places against the microphone. It sounds a lot like she is in a reverb chamber but it gets the job done. She has even designed a black 'J' pipe with diamonds on it for formal speaking engagements. Necessity is indeed the mother of invention.

Medical Note: Although Oreo cannot blow her hair out of her eyes she can blow out the back and get it off her collar.

RECITAL

A musical or dance program given by a soloist, soloists or an ensemble.

Actually it is a showcasing of the unwilling to an audience of the uncaring by an instructor who is being paid to do it and can't wait for it to end. The instructor is as sure of the upcoming performances as is the lion tamer entering the cage for the first time with eight new cats.

Each performance is likened to watching a NASA rocket leave the launch pad. Its initial fire is bright—but anything can happen seconds into the flight. Backstage the teacher seems totally relaxed. Three bowls of Prozac for breakfast will radiate that effect. Also, behind the scenes the teacher is dealing with fright, nausea, amnesia, rage and defiance. On stage meanwhile, the children are dealing with concentration, memorization and disintegration. They are either totally wrapped up in their efforts, looking around the theater or hall to see who has come to hear them play, or falling apart a note at a time since missing a note in the first two measures. The melodies roll from the fingers on little hands—these newly drafted entertainers only hoping to get to the other end of the song—each second seemingly taking an hour. Short children scramble to regain position after falling from the front of the bench while trying to reach the pedals.

Relatives and friends are there because they either want to see the student screw up (much like people go to NASCAR races to see a wreck) or they have been promised something afterwards. It could be a great meal with lots of drinks, the forgiveness of a longstanding and overdue debt, or even just the hope that the proud parents will remember your attendance and continue your name in their will.

The student has been prepped over and over again on one piece. Generally the performances go well. That this student has grown to hate this tune from six months of practice, coupled with the fact that they will never again play this selection after the recital, is of little or no importance.

Piano recitals are to the musical parent as Little League is to the jock. Rude comments about other children in the recital should be avoided. Just because the child is as attractive as a bus wreck and may have even pooped their pants onstage does not mean that they have no talent. Don't get too smug about how ugly someone looks until you have reviewed your wedding album and yearbook. It is expected, that those in attendance will refrain from coughing, burping, farting, sneezing and loud unwrapping of lozenges while the performers are onstage. You must remember that every student wants to play first and get out. The longer they are backstage the more nervous they become. It is a saving grace that they cannot hear the audience giving someone the raspberry when they goof up on stage. If you are one who thinks this is cute and are having a great time embarrassing those onstage, just be glad there was no audience the first time you had sex.

ASK THE AUTHOR

—

NO. A333

Dear Don:

My piano teacher has false teeth. I know because they rattle when she talks. Last Tuesday she got a fit of sneezing and blew them into a fern near the piano. I started laughing and could not control myself for the rest of the lesson. She was embarrassed and mad. I am sorry for my conduct and do not want to lose her as a teacher. Should I buy her a gift?

~ Sorry in Salem

Dear Sorry:

Great idea. Next lesson take her a big box of taffy. Insist that she eat it during your lesson. You will hear no more rattling and if she does sneeze while her mouth is full of taffy, those choppers are going nowhere.

ASK THE AUTHOR
—
NO. A-340

Dear Don:

I am a fairly new teacher—two years into the game. I have a ten-year-old girl student who is becoming a discipline problem. Whenever I ask her to stop and start over she screams at the top of her lungs. I can't take much more of this. Please advise A.S.A.P.

~ Teaching in Tacoma

Dear Teaching:

Try the goodies game. Offer your unruly student a marshmallow; kids love marshmallows. When she has finished the first, offer her a second and substitute a golf ball. As she puts it in her mouth rap it gently with a hammer. Not too hard – there is a difference between gagging someone and a "hole in one." At the end of the lesson a quick Heimlich maneuver should pop it right out.

Note: Some teachers have used a double wrapping of duct tape around the child's head but they usually have to cut off all the kid's hair to get the tape off.

Dear Don:

As a teacher of long tenure I have learned tolerance and compassion for my students. However, I now have three students who seem listless and are very slow in their movements. I have tried everything to motivate them but to no avail. I am befuddled and need help.

~ Befuddled in Bristol

Dear Befuddled:

You may want to try a "quick start unit." They are used by the automotive industry to charge and jump batteries. Plug it into your normal house current and wheel it to the bench. Hook the red cable to the left arm and the black to the right. Set the control knobs to 12-volt "High" or 24-volt "Hot" and flip the switch to "ON." The change in arm and hand movements should be visible at once.

ASK THE AUTHOR

—

NO. A249

Dear Don:

I am a piano teacher, eighty-four years old. Recently I have noticed that I can't hear my students as well as before. I have lots of hair in my ears and perhaps a wax buildup. I live on a very tight budget, cannot afford a doctor and am afraid to go poking around in my ears myself. Can you help me hear?

~ Going Deaf in Detroit

Dear Going Deaf:

Although not approved by the medical community, I do have several remedies to suggest:

1. Get a butane cigarette lighter, turn the flame up to high and blow it in your ears. The hair will disappear and if you can stand the heat the wax should melt.

2. If the heat is a problem, the next time you sneeze keep your mouth shut and hold your nose. The internal pressure should blow the wax out with such intensity that it will rip the ear hairs out as it passes.

ASK THE AUTHOR

—

NO. A411

Dear Don:

I recently played the piano for a funeral. The piano music was a prelude to the service and I was located very close to the grieving widow. Amidst the sobbing and crying I heard her say, "I could use a rag," so I played the Twelfth Street Rag and she went berserk. The Parson fired me on the spot and told me I was insensitive to the proceedings. The lady actually meant she needed another hanky which she called a "rag." Do you think I can sue for my job back?

~ Ragging in Richmond

Dear Ragging:

There are certain things one must not do at a funeral – like hitting on the widow for a date, bringing beer or dogs into church, laughing for any reason, and playing up tempo music. Your misjudgment of the lady's meaning of "rag" gives you good grounds for reinstatement, but remember to stay with the solemn music from now on.

STUDENTS & LESSONS

Lesson No. 1

"Middle 'C' isn't in the middle!"

STUDENTS & LESSONS

The dictionary defines a student as: *a person formally engaged in learning.* It gives no specifics as to age, gender, ethnic origin or locality as it pertains to this learning process. Therefore, the student could be anyone, anywhere, anytime.

Given that seemingly endless population of candidates, what are some of the various motivations or situations which start people off as piano students?

1.   A natural part of formal schooling, i.e. school music class

2.   Private interest by parents to educate their children in the arts

3.   Specific children who take an exceptional interest on their own

4.   Children forced to do what their parents could not

5.   College students pursuing specific studies which include knowledge of music

6.   Busy people looking for an avenue of relaxation

7.   Lonely people trying to fill a void in their lives

The student can take up the piano at any of these various stages of life and for any number of reasons. The need for music in one's life is never ending, thus the saying, *"Of music man never tires."*

Whether the student will stay with the piano or switch to another instrument is also a variable. The piano can be an intimidating and challenging instrument at first and many students fall by the wayside early on. The teacher must feel out the motivation, degree of determination and interest, and the level of each student's ability. Furthermore, for piano lessons to work, the student must work hard, be honest and constantly believe that "the best is yet to come."

The interaction and trust that is built between the teacher and the student will play a great part in the success or failure of the study process. Not all associations between student and teacher are compatible and changes may be required to attain the specific results desired by the student.

Regardless of the teacher, practice will be the first and foremost ingredient for success.

On the following pages we will discuss the various helpful hints and ideas behind a successful lesson program. Many things tend to interfere with practice and we must find ways to deal with them. Practice, after all, is like a chain. To be of any value to the student, it must be uninterrupted.

We will also discuss the things a student must be aware of when starting out. There are pitfalls in every endeavor of our lives and piano lessons are no different.

Finding a teacher is probably the most important first step of the learning process, so make sure you select a reputable person who will take interest in you and guide you on your way.

Your first decision is whether you want to go to the teacher's location or have them come to you. Prices may be slightly higher if they travel to you. If the teacher travels by limousine and charges $100 for the first half hour, keep looking. Do not hire a teacher whose picture appears at the Post Office, especially on pedophile bulletins. Most teachers who give lessons in a bar room are not dependable and if your teacher arrives in the backseat of a police cruiser and the cops wait for the lesson to end, think about another teacher.

Newspapers often have ads for piano teachers in the classified section. You may also want to ask around the neighborhood to see if anyone else is being instructed by a good teacher. Referrals are a big part of the teacher's student base.

Remember, if you sign up your child to go to a teacher, you will be responsible for taking them and picking them up. Sometimes this gets to be a pain in the ass. If your child is under ten years of age, the police will not condone your letting the child drive your car just because you don't feel good. If you choose to wait in the studio while the lesson is in progress, you may NOT smoke, drink beer, eat fast foods or listen to the radio you brought along. You should also refrain from singing along with the lesson or continually reminding the teacher what a gifted child you have.

Not all teachers take on private tutoring. Some teach only in schools, theatrical settings and camps. They may also have a specific age range for their students. Therefore, your search may take some time, but it will be time well spent.

Watch out for the piano teacher who always has something to sell. It is normal to expect them to have books and sheet music for sale. That is part of learning and essential to the process. Be cautious, however, of gadgets which are touted as necessary tools for a greater advancement or advised as required. Some of the more common ones are:

1. THE SIMPSON ELECTRONIC FINGER STRETCHER
    They will tell you that this two-piece device (one left and one right) will lengthen your fingers and therefore the size of your hands over a period of six to eight months. It is a 110-volt unit, applied to each hand and worn at night while you sleep. The average price for the set is $212.95. Some reported problems have been: electrocution of people with sweaty hands; blanket fires caused when people roll over in bed and pull the wires loose; and mostly, no results at end of the time period.

2. THE SEXTON-DEVONSHIRE AUDIO DIVERSIFIER
    This invention consists of a pair of very sturdy head phones. When you put it on and turn it up it is supposed to change the key you are playing, so that even though you are totally inept at playing the piece as written, you will hear it correctly. It really doesn't work but the teacher will tell you you're doing great

because with the headphones on, you can't hear how bad you really sound. Actually, the teacher has programmed the piece on tape and you are hearing him playing it. Priced at $165, it is best to avoid this item.

Note: The first clue that this item is bogus will be that you hear the song you are supposed to be playing even when your fingers are not on the keyboard. (Take the $165 and spend it on the lottery. The odds are almost equal that your chances of winning the lottery and playing as well as the teacher will become reality.)

3. THE DEVONSHIRE-PROCTOR FART ARRESTER MODEL BM
This invention looks like a tractor seat. You mount it atop a bench or stool. It has a vacuum pump inside the piano with a hose running to the underside of the seat. As you pass gas, the vacuum system sucks the fart through a rubber tube and forces it up to an ornamental gas lamp with a live flame. The methane gas is consumed by the flame. You can tell when the fart is gone because the flame goes from green and blue back to orange and yellow. This unit also has an optional bell pedal that you can depress. It rings loud chimes to cover up the noise of the farting. In certain cases overly active people have taxed the system beyond its capacity and caused explosions resulting in fires and also personal injury from flying glass when the lamps have exploded. Prices on this rig also vary a great deal depending on the upholstering of the seat, the size of the pump, and the degree of ornamentation used in the lamps. For those of you who know you are very gassy, dual lamps and tubing are available. Priced from $122.50 to $749.95.

4. AIR PAGE TURNER - by CLINT CRAPFIDDLE (Patent Pending)
This brainchild is not only dangerous but borders on the useless. Basic operation is to mount a nozzle, much like that on a garden hose, to the right edge of your piano. A high pressure hose goes through a control block on the floor and onto a fitting attached to a compressed air tank. The theory here is that when you want to turn a page without lifting your hands from the keyboard, you simply depress a pedal on the floor and an air stream blows the page over for you. In theory that would be nice but many problems have arisen from the use of this item.

Air pressure regulation is the big factor. The supply tank, when completely filled, has an internal pressure of 1500 psi. Unless you know just how to adjust the nozzle and work the pedal you may easily "over-air" the unit. The initial air burst has already been known to blow a 200-page book through a plate glass window. In one case recorded in Vermont, the air release was so great that it ripped the nozzle from the piano and blew it around behind the pianist, striking him a fatal blow on the back of the head.

Another report from Texas stated that the air supply tank was accidentally filled with hydrogen and when activated, the player's cigarette ignited the gas and blew the practice room and piano through the third-story roof.

We definitely DO NOT advise purchase of this apparatus under any circumstances.

ATTENDING LESSONS REGULARLY

Once you have made a decision on when and where the lessons will be given, it is important to gear up to meeting that commitment on a regular basis. There will be times when you or your child do not want to go to a lesson. It could be that on that particular day other things just seem to be more fun or more important. Another big reason for not going (ducking the teacher) is lack of preparation. You know you can't fool the teacher if you have not done your practicing.

Then comes the issue of the phone call to tell the teacher you're not coming. Remember that the piano was invented in the spring of 1700 and lessons started shortly thereafter. Can you imagine how many excuses have been used up in over 300 years?

One teacher told me that she encountered the following excuses in just one week:

1.   STUDENT ARRIVES WITH ARM IN SLING
      "Fell down the stairs."

2.   STUDENT ARRIVES WITH FOUR FINGERS BANDAGED
      "Injured while disarming a bomb in an abortion clinic."

3.   STUDENT ARRIVES WEARING DARK GLASSES
      "Temporarily blinded watching a solar eclipse."

4.   STUDENT ARRIVES TOTALLY UNPREPARED FOR LESSON
      "Attended a one-week funeral in France."
      "Dog ate the lesson book (142 pages)."
      "My piano had to go to the factory for tuning."
      "Too hot to practice."
      "Too cold to practice."

It is also well to note the irony when all deaths in the family occur on lesson day. It is even stranger when one of the family members dies for a second or third time— and each time in a different city. If you are an adult canceling by phone because you are home ill, be sure the caller ID does not show the number of a tavern or massage parlor.

There is a multi-faceted series of things which occur when you cancel a lesson. Most teachers collect fees on a monthly basis to cover these last minute cancellations. If you miss that time reserved for you, you still must pay.

RESULT #1 - The teacher gets paid for doing nothing and you are out the dough.

RESULT #2 - You spent the whole week thinking up a really great excuse instead of practicing. This is as futile as trying to tell a twenty-five-year veteran of the state police a new reason why you were speeding.

RESULT #3 - You are as dumb as you were a week ago and you paid to stay dumb.

GETTING STARTED

It has been proven over and over that in order to take piano lessons you should have a piano. GET A PIANO.

Place the piano somewhere in your home which is not in a high traffic area. Four rooms to rule out are the bathroom, bedroom, kitchen and attic. The garage is also a last resort location due to temperature fluctuation which is bad for the piano and carbon monoxide which is bad for the student.

Be sure to have a comfortable seat for your piano. If you are a fatass, get a bench. A stool for you would be a hardship. If you want something different you might use a beer keg, two piles of concrete blocks with a sheet of plywood across them or if you are a Yuppy you may want to use the driver's seat from your BMW. In any case, realize that you will be spending hours at the piano and being fair to your fanny is first and foremost.

The keyboard cover on your piano may have a lock. Despite the size of the piano, the lock is small and the key is even smaller. There is usually only one key and the first time you lock the cover will probably be the last time you can ever find that key. Wire the key to a two-foot length of three-inch steel pipe. That way you have a chance of finding it again. Never think that you can hide the key in the piano bench. Six months after you get the bench there will be so much shit in there you could lose a dog team and sled.

You may want to fix up your piano so others do not fool around with it. A car alarm or fire siren would be effective and running 220 volts of electricity through the keys will discourage even the most ardent player.

On older model upright pianos, the keyboard itself can be locked by a device on the piano located to the right and under the keyboard. When you pull on the small knob, a rod slides out and locks all the keys in the "up" position so they cannot be depressed. Adults will usually give up when the keys won't go down. Children, however, will find a way to make them go down anyway and you may want to ponder on just how they will do that. Think about small feet jumping on the keys. That should set your mind in gear.

WHY THE NEED FOR LESSONS?

To preface this section you need only know that pianos are so confusing that even teachers are still taking lessons. In other words, many of them are teaching you stuff they don't know. I will tell you, or try to tell you from fragments of old historical information, just how all this teacher stuff got started.

Note: Information herein may be only partially correct. Since we got it on tape and it happened in 1700 we have reason to believe the tapes were reenactments. This reasoning is based on the fact that the first wire recorders came out in 1898, tape much later.

In 1698 a lady clerk-typist supposedly came to Bartolomeo Cristofori with a problem. She said when it was cold she had to wear gloves in the office while typing. The keys were too close together and she made many errors. She had seen his harpsichords and wondered if he could make a typewriter using the harpsichord keyboard. He agreed to try but two years of experiments failed. The type was too big and the paper would have to be thirty-six inches wide. The pedals used for upper and lower case changes as well as the carriage return did not always work fast enough. The unit was bulky and weighed over 800 pounds. In late 1699 he decided to abandon that project and start on something new.

Cristofori soon combined his harpsichord technology with new ideas and came up with a rig called a "GRAVICEMBALO COL PIANO E FORTE" that over many years has come to be called a piano. He knew what he had invented and his inventor friend Garibaldi Freminetti had figured a way to produce these in mass—but how could they market this new invention and who would show people how to play the piano?

In June of 1700 Cristofori got together with four others at the Appian Way Steak House and Cigar Bar outside of Padua, Italy. Our tapes tell us that the four guests were:

1.   GARIBALDI FREMINETTI - Talented friend and inventor

2.   GINA GREATRACK - Harpsichord teacher

3.   VINCENZO BACALA - Publisher of music in Rome

4.   SAM FELDMAN - New York City advertising mogul

At this meeting they discussed how to market the piano. Surely no one would buy it unless they had a method of learning to play it. Here are some excerpts of that conversation.

"Guys, we gotta think of a way to move these pianos. I already have two built and by year's end I'll have four. I'm up to my ass in pianos," says Freminetti. "I think I speak for Cristofori as well."

Feldman says, "Gotta have a gimmick."

"How about this?" asks Gina. "With every piano we throw in a few lessons. I can teach a few folks to do that much in basic instruction. That will make folks think they can play."

"What are you going to use for reference tools to learn?" asks Freminetti.

"We'll get Vincenzo to print up a lesson book. Hell, we've had printed music around since 800 A.D. He should be able to put something together."

"What about it, Vince?" asks Gina.

"Fine idea, but what if the pianos start going out of the country? How many languages you want?"

198

"Screw 'em," says Feldman. "There's the gimmick. While you learn to read music you also have to learn to speak Italian. Print all the books with Italian directions and if they don't learn the language, bingo, they're screwed."

"How are we going to pay these teachers?" asks Freminetti.

"Build some of the expense into the cost of the piano and once we get them hooked, tell them it's their expense from here on in," says Gina.

"I can sell that," says Feldman.

"Good," says Freminetti, "then it's all set. We'll build up an army of these teacher folks to suck 'em in and the race is on."

"Where's Cristofori?" asks Feldman.

"He's in the crapper," says Vince.

"Okay, someone let him know what we're doing," says Feldman. "I have to get the next ship back to New York to set this up. Tell him to have his people get in touch with my people and we'll do lunch."

THE INSTRUCTION BOOK

Over a period of a year, Vincenzo Bacala and Sam Feldman wrote to each other continually to exchange marketing ideas and to discuss the text of the instruction book. Gina travelled to Rome monthly to advise on certain technical and musical phases for the new instruction book. Some parts of the letters that went back and forth are set down hereunder:

Dear Vince:

Don't ever teach them enough so they can become independent.

Dear Sam:

Gina and I are hard at work making this book and the initial learning process hard enough to confuse them so they keep coming back to the teachers.

Dear Vince:

I feel we should expand the size of the keyboard from five octaves to seven or eight so the little kids can't reach the end keys. That way they'll have to keep coming back until their arms get longer.

Dear Sam:

We're going with Gina's idea to use a setup called "staffs." She wants to assign letters to a bunch of lines and spaces and have one for each hand. You know—A, B, C, etc. She also is kicking around the idea to assign different letters to the bottom one so that they're different just to screw the student over a bit. We'll use the A through G thing on both but on the bottom they won't be in the same order.

Dear Vince:

Had another brainstorm. Tell Gina that once she gets the students to memorize the lines and spaces we should start drawing lines and spaces below those staff things. That should turn up the heat on the come-backers.

Dear Sam:

Gina says okay on the extra lines; it's a can-do. Now she has an even better idea. Let's have two or three different ways to identify the same note. Could be pluses and/or minuses – she's talking about something called sharps and flats (more on that later).

Dear Vince:

Be sure you are the only one who is going to publish that instruction book and that I do the marketing ideas from here. Also, be sure they can only buy the book from a teacher and with one of our pianos. By the way, I want to be the piano dealer over here. Check with Bart.

Dear Sam:

The book is coming along great. We are really on a roll. Gina has dreamed up lots of other shit to throw into the music to keep it fresh and mystifying. That way the students will keep coming back to see what's what. Dots, lines, arrows, vertical bars, various things called signatures and lots of those short Italian words telling them how to play what's written. Gina has a whole bag of tricks for this and she's also on a kick talking about things like rests, values, something called a coda and even some periods stuck in the music somehow that tells you to play it over again. Wow, talk about a broad with imagination, she should be in New York with you.

Dear Vince:

Just got my copy of the bar tab from the Appian Way. I think they screwed us over on the price of the ale. Have the owner tweak those numbers and get me a revised bill – I am holding my check 'till then. Also, in your last letter I got some scribbling from Gina about subdominant something or other and tonics. Is she on drugs? Also saw some Roman numerals thrown in there. Don't think I can sell that idea stateside. The Italian language is already giving me some problems in the Irish bars. Also, look into a rumor that Gina has hooked up with a guy named Albert who wants to build a thing called a clarinet and name the system after himself. We gotta keep a handle on things, Vince. We just can't have every looney running around cutting into our music program. This teacher thing is catching on really well over here. May need as many as six new pianos in March.

Dear Sam:

I told Gina what you said about Albert. She was really hot about it and now I think they've run off together. We may be on our own for a bit 'till I can get someone else. Since you are now a dealer, what do you think about other colors for the pianos? Could be black, white, or whatever. Could charge more for those too. Freminetti is really up on the idea. Write us ASAP.

Dear Vince:

Tell Freminetti I don't give a goddamn if he paints them with polka dots, I can sell anything. Right now I have a bigger problem. One of the last pianos fell off the ship into the harbor. It was serial number LXVIII. We dried it out but three keys wouldn't play. A blacksmith near the port tried to fix it and now eighteen keys won't play. Is Bart going to make a service call? How much? When?

Dear Sam:

Bart says not to sweat it—he'll work something out—just keep on selling. Bart wants to know how you're doing with the teachers, need any? Fortunately Gina trained a lot here before she and Al split.

Dear Vince:

Got lots of good teachers here now—to hell with Gina. One of my gals, Hilda, has one up on Gina's stuff. She came up with a story about some Greek guy named Pythagoras and some twelve-note bullshit. On top of that, she even named all the keys. Do, Re, Mi and like that. I'll send you her notes. More mud for those students to wade through.

Dear Sam:

Bart thinks you should kick your ad campaign into high gear to move more pianos ASAP. Please advise me and cc Bart and Freminetti if you want.

Dear Vince:

The ads are running. Full page ads in four colors in the following: BETTER TENTS AND TEEPEES; COLONIAL HOMES & GARDENS; BRITISH MUSICAL REVIEW; and CARRIAGE TRADE QUARTERLY. Get this, Vince, Madelline, one of my teachers, started sleeping with some of her students. If she keeps this up I could use one hundred more pianos real soon. In fact, I might even start taking lessons myself.

Dear Sam:

Just got your order for that sequin piano. Are you sure your customer is playing with a full deck? Advise.

Dear Vince:

Regarding the sequin piano. I got the cash, build it!

Dear Sam:

The latest and most complete instruction book is done and we are shipping one hundred copies to you. It starts off pretty easy but toward the back it gets so screwed up it looks like a snake crawling through a three-ring pretzel. I think you'll love it and the students will be with us forever. There's no way they're ever going to figure all this shit out by themselves.

SUMMARY

And so as you, the student, embark onto this new frontier, 300 years of chicanery and marketing hype will swirl through your brain. Oh, sure, the beginner's book is a snap and tells you nothing. You are gliding along, picturing yourself on the Tonight Show or up onstage alone at Carnegie Hall. Wait until you see Book #2.

Note: You might like to know that on some older sheet music when the piece required four pages, Feldman dreamed up the idea to leave the center pages unstapled to the rest. He figured about 30% to 40% of the students would lose the middle pages and have to buy the music over again.

THE LESSONS

In this new millennium of the electronic age there stands one basic tool of musical learning and listening pleasure: THE PIANO. I speak not of the new CD players and electronic keyboards, but rather of the old stoic wooden music boxes that are the 100% manual, acoustic pianos. Although we do not exclude or discard the player piano, we will shelve them for the moment. Our main focus will be directed to the plain, straight piano and the people who, single-handedly (or two handed for the actual pianist), use this wonderful invention to make the music come alive.

To learn the piano, the art of booting up, locating icons, buttons, programs and menus is laid to rest. You need have no computer know-how and no electric or phone lines. The only "mouse" in the house may sit back and secretly watch you play, or better yet establish residence inside the piano for better sounds. You will not be sending or receiving e-mail on this fine instrument. The only mail you might expect when you first set out to play is a certified letter or court order to cease and desist playing after 8 P.M. These are usually generated by the neighbors and over time they will either adjust or move. Software, hardware and hard drives are replaced by soft cushions, underwear and hard work. The confusion about what to do if you do make a mistake is very simple to address. Lift your hands off the keys. There! You're clear to start over. The only upgrades needed on your piano will be an occasional tuning and a coat of furniture polish from time to time. Even the polish is optional. You do not need night courses or tutoring to get started in a piano playing business.

HOW TO GET STARTED

Push down one key. Now a second. If your ear tells you that they don't sound good together, leave one the same and change the other. When they do sound good together you add a third note. When all three sound good together you have a chord. After that, all the rest will just be a lot of different chords at different times. And you thought this was going to be difficult!

Lots of folks spend thousands to get started in computers and constantly scurry to update every time something new comes out. When speaking of the basic piano it is well to note that although the piano celebrated its 300th birthday in the year 2000, pianos of the last hundred years all do the same thing. You can physically play the same thing on a fifty-year-old piano purchased for $200 that a concert pianist can play on a brand new grand piano purchased for $50,000. Granted the tonal quality may be a bit different but the basic outcome will be the same. So it's up to you – $200 or $50,000!

Updating is at your convenience and is not dictated by a newer model with more keys, memory or speed. YOU are the memory and the speed. Relax, it's going to be just fine (probably).

Note: Your piano can't crash. When the power goes off you'll only need a candle. The computer freak however, may need clinical help.

PRACTICING THE PIANO

A king was once quoted as saying, "I would much rather be a peasant in a cottage playing my own piano than a king in a palace dependent on others to provide my entertainment."

Once you sit down at the piano you have pulled onto the highway to musicland. As a beginner you may find yourself caught in a tangle of detail but the teacher will usually try to make the learning process actually pleasurable. You need only remember, "HEARING can never take the place of DOING." As you sit at the keyboard discovering new tonal beauties you will slowly master the art of taking time to live. Your heretofore misspent leisure time will be filled with peace and harmony.

Practicing the piano is perhaps the most important part of learning music. It is the thing the student should want to do most. IN MOST CASES IT ISN'T.

There are as many excuses for not practicing or having interruptions while practicing as there are stars in the sky. Children invariably just don't want to practice. Adults, on the other hand, would like to play but are forever bothered by things and people around them.

We cannot stress enough the importance of being comfortable at the piano. Whatever it takes, do it. I have seen vibrator benches and benches wide enough to accommodate life sized blow-up dolls. People like to have their favorite celebrity or model at their side while playing. There are square shallow tubs so people can soak their feet in them while playing. (These are placed just behind the pedals.) I have even seen a piano with stirrups. God only knows what that's for. People use all sizes of cushions and pillows and those with back trouble often resort to using high-back chairs. Rocking chairs are not advised.

On hot summer days, if you have no air conditioning, you may feel uncomfortable. Or perhaps the air conditioning makes you too cold and you would prefer a fan. A fan is okay to a point but let's think this through. It may give you some relief when turned up on higher speeds, however, it can complicate your practice session. If you have long hair it will tend to blow-dry your hair and mess it up. You may want to wear a hat, bathing cap or scarf. If you are a smoker, the breeze will make your cigarette burn faster, blow ashes in your eyes, blow ashes into the piano and also blow burning cigarette butts into the piano which could start a fire. It will also blow your sheet music around, turning pages before you are ready or just blowing the music onto the floor. If you do not have air conditioning or a fan, even though you are hot, unless you are alone or in some very good company, avoid practicing in the nude. If the children are home they'll catch you.

Having a portable TV, computer screen or cell phone anywhere on the piano is not a good idea. If you're that busy on the computer, forget the piano. Anything on TV will in fact distract you and in the end you have accomplished two things: First, you will not remember what song you are playing; and second, you will not completely remember what you saw on TV. In other words – A WASTED HOUR.

For the man or woman who may wish to drink while practicing the piano, I suggest buying a used player piano. (The player part does not have to work.) Gut the electric motor and bellows system from the bottom and the roller assembly from behind the sliding wooden doors. You can then install a small compressor, a quarter keg of beer in a cooling box and run a line up to where the roller used to be. Install your tap and glass rack behind those doors and away you go. Cold beer at the ready! Since the piano was electric to begin with, no one will question the cord sticking into the wall plug. If you find that you are stopping a lot to have a "taste," you may want to set up a hospital-style intravenous beer needle arrangement. Be sure to keep your keg filled with this type setup. If your veins start sucking air you're in deep shit.

Again, we stress comfort. You should strive for a casual, comfortable wardrobe. While it is true that hookers often dress in special costumes for their johns, the student-teacher relationship need not take on this added dimension. Sometimes it starts during practice sessions, while you're alone and just for a lark. Then people start to think if they appear at the lesson dressed as a cowboy, Indian, astronaut, bus driver, fireman, boy scout, girl scout, fan dancer, airline steward, nurse, or anything connected with the Olympics enabling them to wear a bogus gold medal, the teacher will be impressed and their grade for that lesson might go up. It never seems to work out that way. In fact, the teacher may scribble a little note in her personal "student profile" book. Something like: "I think Mr. Jinglefrink is a little light in the loafers. Got to watch for more signs."

I know, as you're reading this you're saying, "Yeah, but doing those boring scales over and over and over, I need some way to stimulate my mind." Well, here are a few games to play with your brain while you endlessly repeat the scales. Try reciting the names of all the state capitals in alphabetical order. If that is too short or you master it too fast, try reciting the names of all the cities and towns in the United States that have illegal and toxic waste dumps. (That should keep you busy.) If you need a short list to get started, you may want to memorize the names or titles of all the repealed tax programs in New York State. That won't take long. You could actually write down all of them inside a match pack cover using a paint roller.

Far and away the biggest complaint from adults regarding practice interruptions has to do with children. Mommies and daddies all over the country write to us in volumes about the child problems. We all know that parents love their kids, or so the experts say. The letters we get here, however, take it a step further. The love is conditional in many cases.

1.   I love my kids when they're sleeping
2.   I love my kids when they're outdoors playing
3.   I love my kids when they're at school
4.   I love my kids when they go to visit Grandma for a week
5.   I love my kids when they're at camp

All of the above denote a continuing love which is elevated by absence. The love and tolerance ratio between the parent and the child is in inverse proportion to their proximity with each other. That ratio is also affected by the frequency of physical contact.

What can we tell you about skirting your parental obligations while trying to practice? It is evident as we look in on more and more families that the remedies are wide in scope and depend a great deal on number and age of siblings, social position, the size of your living quarters and degree of continual aggravation.

Very young children just don't understand why mommy and daddy can't be with them every waking moment. They have "selective amnesia" when you remind them that just five minutes ago you told them that you would be busy practicing at the piano and they should go play. You could be living in a 4300-square-foot home and children will insist that the only suitable place to play is under the piano bench. Children who are a bit older want to bring their friends in to watch you practice and teenagers will stroll past and drop a line on you like: "Yo, Mom, you're like freakin' me out with that same song over and over. Don't you know anything else?" If you do succeed getting the kids to bed you can't practice anyway because now they appear next to the piano and say, "Mommy, I can't get to sleep. Can you stop playing?"

Some parents are actually blessed with home alone time and can get a decent practice session completed now and then. For others, it is just a matter of time before drastic and very real battlelines are drawn. Sorting through our mail we picked out a few of the most popular solutions:

1. Enroll your kids in the "deluxe" sixteen-week summer camp.
2. Erect an eight-foot high chain link fence with barbed wire top around the piano and put a guard dog inside the fence.
3. Build a bullet-proof, sound-proof, air-conditioned shell over the piano.
4. Dig a moat through your living room and fill it with piranha fish—also electrify the liftbridge.
5. Build a separate building behind the house—put the piano in there and be sure that you have the only key.
6. Move the piano to a separate address and don't tell anyone in the family where that is.
7. If the above measures are beyond your finances you may have to resort to basics. If your piano came in a big shipping crate, don't throw it away. It is a perfect place to stash kids while you play. Stain it or paint it with brightly colored paints. Tell the kids it is a playhouse and make sure there is a way to lock it once they're in there. If you don't have the crate perhaps you could get an airline "large animal" shipping box with ventilation holes and accomplish the same thing.

It is well for you to know that people across the country are doing such things so you can defend yourself in court when the child welfare people bring you up on charges.

CHILDREN AND PIANO LESSONS

When it comes to the other side of the coin – the child taking lessons and practicing – the rules shift dramatically. A whole new set of guidelines falls into place and your tolerance level will be tested even further. You and the teacher will, of course, set down guidelines for practice. Things like: time of day; minutes per session; and material to cover. That will be for the amusement of you and the teacher because immediately the child will have none of it and their lifelong ambition will be to change everything about the plan. They will swear to their grave that you never said anything about any of that plan and expect you to believe every word they say.

If you are taking your child to an amusement park on Saturday and you tell them what time you are leaving, they can read a watch or clock right down to the sweep second hand. If you tell them a time to practice they will deny ever having been told how to tell time. They will also have their own time increments: ¼ hour = 9 minutes, ½ hour = 21 minutes and 1 hour = 45 minutes (tops). If you insist on five minutes more from them they will say something like: "If you push me beyond my physical limits I could have a stroke and become a cripple. Do you want that on your conscience, Dad?"

ONE CARDINAL RULE FOR CHILDREN'S PRACTICE – NO EXCEPTIONS; Do not eat sticky foods at the piano while playing. You will sooner or later transfer the peanut butter, jam or pizza onto the keys. Moreover, when cleaning the keys, wipe from front to back, not sideways. If you wipe sideways you allow all that crap to seep between the keys and eventually they do not return from the down position. This is called "FUNK" or "JAMMI." If this situation is allowed to go on for an extended period, a fetid odor will drift over the premises as the food products rot between the keys. At this stage two things happen. One, you will never be able to spray enough air freshener around the piano to overcome the stench; and two, you will develop piano rats. They will clean the keys for you but in time you will have no piano left. They are worse than termites. The only way to get rid of piano rats is to run a hose from your car in the garage into your house and put the nozzle end in the piano. Twenty-four hours of continuous rich carbon monoxide should kill them off. Be sure to tell the family you're doing this as carbon monoxide is not an "selective poison."

THE TOP TEN FOOD PRODUCTS THAT ARE NOT TO BE USED AROUND THE KEYS:
1. Peanut butter and/or jelly
2. Chocolate of any sort (especially in warm rooms)
3. Mayonaisse
4. Tuna fish
5. Pasta sauces or gravies
6. Ice cream and milkshakes
7. Yogurt, puddings, jello, and anything with frosting
8. Creamed vegetables of any sort
9. Pizza in any form, especially with double cheese
10. Duck l'orange with extra sauce

These items will bring about a non-reversible cessation of key activity known as "schtuck down." You will also notice that no matter how many times you wash your hands after eating this stuff around the piano, the keys will remain sticky forever.

Note: When a key has become stuck in the down position, the old wives tale which says "Whack it with a hammer and it will loosen up," does not apply. Also, if you try to pry that key up with a screwdriver you will inevitably come away with the white ivory or plastic covering but the key will remain down. A piano technician is recommended for this job.

When it comes to lesson time there are things you should know. If your child is going to a teacher's home or studio, be sure she has her music book and any money that is due. Most of all, be prompt. The lesson cannot run over if the student is late.

If the lesson is to be given in your home, that is another matter. The child can spend the whole week gearing up to make the lesson less than enjoyable for the teacher.

Starting fifteen minutes before the teacher arrives, conduct a complete strip search of your child. Look for snakes, frogs and small rodents that the pupil may be planning to turn loose at lesson time. Once that is completed you may scout around for other things. Kids like to lay plastic vomit on the keyboard or place ceramic dog crap on the rug in front of the teacher's chair. Another favorite is to remove the lower front panel of the piano and place dead fish or limburger cheese, or both, in that area. Some even put an elevated dish in there with a lit can of Sterno under it. The resulting odor will surely shorten or cancel the lesson.

Check the lesson book to be sure it is there and look inside to be sure the pages for that day's lesson have not been ripped out or defaced. Let your child know that if he decides to go to the bathroom during the lesson, you're going with him. This will insure that he doesn't waste time or lock himself in there for the duration of the lesson.

These hints fall in the category of common sense, security and discipline. There must be a degree of discipline for the lessons to succeed.

You must not, however, go overboard with the discipline. DO NOT hit children across the knuckles with a ruler every time they play a wrong note. This punishment can result in deformities which will, in the long run, prove detrimental to good technique (i.e. club hands.) Also, slamming the keyboard cover on a child's hands can cause that child to develop bad traits that could be detrimental to your well being. Do not offer special incentives to children for playing well, things like a beer with Dad or staying up late to watch a porno flick. Money is the answer!

All in all, lessons, properly arranged with a good teacher to monitor them, can be fun.

GO AHEAD. DO IT. YOU NEVER KNOW WHAT YOU'LL LEARN.

In conjunction with your lessons you may be asked to commit to memory some of the more famous teams of musical composition. Learn these to dazzle your teacher.

1. Lerner & Lowe
2. Rubinowitz & Rubinowitz
3. Sissle & Blake
4. Sears & Roebuck
5. Gilbert & Sullivan
6. Rogers & Hammerstein
7. Hansel & Gretel
8. Burns & Allen
9. Helter & Skelter
10. Waller & Razaf
11. Amos & Andy
12. Story & Clark
13. Rodgers & Hart
14. Mork & Mindy
15. Porgy & Bess
16. Proctor & Gamble
17. Cheech & Chong
18. Pomp & Circumstance
19. Simon & Shuster
20. George & Ira Gerschwin
21. Abbott & Costello
22. Angelus & Mascagni
23. Hallet & Davis
24. Mason & Hamlin
25. Simon & Garfunkle

You will be quizzed on names of the great composers. Commit these important ones to memory.

1.	Audubon	26.	Liszt
2.	Bach	27.	Mascagni
3.	Beethoven	28.	Mattoide
4.	Bisquick	29.	Mendelssohn
5.	Bunker	30.	Moskowski
6.	Cartwright	31.	O'Brien
7.	Cellophane	32.	Ostinato
8.	Clampett	33.	Pawtucket
9.	Chatterly	34.	Rigonfiare
10.	Chopin	35.	Ruebenstein
11.	Debussy	36.	Scarlatti
12.	Dessau	37.	Schubert
13.	Fibich	38.	Sleezebag
14.	Giocherellare	39.	Sousa
15.	Gounod	40.	Strauss
16.	Greig	41.	Suppe
17.	Haydn	42.	Tortolini
18.	Handel	43.	Throtmorton
19.	Humperdink	44.	Wagner
20.	Idiota	45.	Watershed
21.	Jefferson	46.	Widesaddle
22.	Khachaturian	47.	Verdi
23.	Kolopinski	48.	Victrola
24.	Letterman	49.	Vilmente
25.	Lieberman	50.	Zapalowski

All students learning from the Italian-Latin Method will need to operate from a basic glossary of words and terms. Here are some for the beginner.

GLOSSARY

	WORD/TERM	NOTES:
1.	Affettuoso	
2.	Agitato	
3.	Al Capone	
4.	Al Segno	
5.	Andantino	
6.	Aria	
7.	Arpeggio	
8.	Azzawrong	
9.	Brassiere	
10.	Cantabile	
11.	Contralto	
12.	Correctamundo	
13.	Crappola	
14.	Crescendo	
15.	Datzanice	
16.	Dimaggio	
17.	Diminuendo	
18.	Dolce	
19.	Dolt	
20.	Elscratcho	
21.	Elstinko	
22.	Permata	

WORD/TERM	NOTES:
23. Fettuccini	
24. Finale	
25. Fortapache	
26. Fortepiano	
27. Guido	
28. Gusto	
29. Incorrecto	
30. Libretto	
31. Maestro	
32. Marcia	
33. Mosso	
34. Notestupido	
35. Nunzio	
36. Operetta	
37. Opus	
38. Pedalnonest	
39. Pianissimo	
40. Pomposo	
41. Quaver	
42. Rallentando	
43. Ravioli	
44. Rebach	
45 Reversio	
46. Scazzafava	
47. Segue	

GLOSSARY - Page 3

WORD/TERM	NOTES:
48. Seminole	
49. Semitone	
50. Senza	
51. Sforzando	
52. Slickly	
53. Sotto	
54. Sostenuto	
55. Stopanow	
56. Tacet	
57. Tenuto	
58. Tricycle	
59. Troppo	
60. Tutti	
61. Vivaci	
62. Voluptuous	
63. Watercress	
64. Whazzadis	
65. Zamboni	

COMMENTS AND REFERENCE PAGES

ASK THE AUTHOR

—

NO. A418

Dear Don:

I have been told that many years ago the ragtime piano players used to slice the skin webs between their fingers to increase their span on the keyboard. Is this true? I tried it with a butcher knife and my thumb fell off. How do you do this type of thing?

~ Nine Fingers in Nyack

Dear Nine Fingers:

I have also heard that rumor about the web cutting. I would equate that mentality to slicing your armpit so you can reach a higher shelf in the kitchen. Not a good idea. For best results, sell your cutlery today and buy yourself the Devonshire Finger Stretcher (Model 98). You are apparently surgically challenged and should not do this again.

ASK THE AUTHOR

—

NO. A375

Dear Don:

I think my metronome has a rod knock. When it is set on the slow meter there is a distinctive extra beat and when it is on the top end the thing hammers and smokes. What can I do?

~ Knocking in Kanona

Dear Knocking:

If the knocking is coming from the metronome itself you probably have the manual or electric model. It may be low on lubricant. On the back there is a tiny dipstick. Check to see if it is below "add." If so, fill it to the full mark with a mixture of castor oil, vaseline hair tonic and bee's pollen. If knocking continues, replace the metronome.

On the older pulley-driven diesel models the noise would come directly from the engine. Add 10/30 non-detergent motor oil to the full mark. In extreme cold this could also be a fuel knock.

Note: Diesel models should be vented to the outdoors.

Note: When starting your diesel metronome in cold weather, never spray starting fluid (ether) near a burning candle.

ASK THE AUTHOR

—

NO. A429

Dear Don:

I am learning piano at age sixty-six. I was told it would be good to tape my practice sessions. I borrowed my sister's tape machine but can't get any sound. I am using a brand new roll of 3M three-quarter inch magic tape. It seems a bit wide and it's sticky. It won't rewind and I had to beat that little trap door shut with my shoe to make it fit. Am I doing something wrong?

~ Recording in Rhode Island

Dear Recording:

It is well to note that 3M makes a lot of different tapes. Three-quarter inch magic tape is not recommended for recording. It will gum up your machine and yes, it won't rewind. It will be okay for taping stuff in your scrapbook. I suggest you contact someplace like Radio Shack for the correct tape. Also, you may want to look into a new recorder. I don't know how you got the three-quarter inch tape in there but I can only assume the recorder has taken a dump.

Dear Don:

I am a good-looking middle aged woman. I have decided to start piano lessons next month. My teacher is a young man recently graduated from a music conservatory. I am not sure how to dress for my first lesson. Can you give me some tips before I start? I'm feeling nervous about this.

~ Novice in Newport

Dear Novice:

This is very common with ladies taking lessons from younger men. It is understandable that the first lesson can be and usually is a nervous undertaking. It is however recommended that if you are wearing a sleeveless blouse or dress you must refrain from putting maxipads under your arms. Various arm movements at the piano could blow your secret all to hell. Also, stuffing your bra full of toilet paper to impress your male instructor is not a good idea. If you do it once, you'll have to do it forever. You may want to reflect on the gal who decided to have a smoke at the piano and dropped hot ashes into her breast area. The ensuing fire caused a madhouse of activity and the termination of a girlish scam. Breast fires are not pretty. Neither are skin grafts. Dress for comfort. He'll set the wardrobe from there.

ASK THE AUTHOR

—

NO. A366

Dear Don:

I am a fourteen-year-old girl taking lessons from an old man who smokes way too much. He coughs all the time and once in a while stuff flies onto the keys. Should I carry a hankie and wipe it off or ignore it and play through it? It's his piano so I really don't care. I just want to do what's right.

~ Sticky in Steubenville

Dear Sticky:

Your teacher may not know this is happening. Therefore, the next time he does that, stop playing, point to the problem and ask him, "Hey, what is this stuff?" If he refuses to acknowledge its presence you have three choices:

1. Stop everything and wipe it off

2. Play through it and after the lesson soak your hands in a hot bucket of Pine-Sol

3. Change teachers

Note: A fourth option would be to ask him to wear a welder's helmet during the lesson. Nothing should fly through that and he can still see your hands through the little glass window.

ASK THE AUTHOR

—

NO. 349

Dear Don:

I am a concerned parent. My nine-year-old son is taking lessons. His teacher is a stern disciplinarian and besides verbal reprimands, he hits my child's knuckles with a ruler when he makes mistakes. Should this treatment be tolerated? His knuckles look like plums.

~ Swelling in Saranac

Dear Swelling:

As with all endeavors, a certain amount of discipline is in order. The child must understand this but there should also be a code of fairness. When he makes a mistake he must know that the ruler is coming. However, when he plays the piece without a mistake he should be allowed to whack the teacher over the head with a steel pipe. Once this avenue has been opened his playing will improve 200%.

ASK THE AUTHOR
—
NO. A390

Dear Don:

One of my girlfriends said if I can't drive a standard shift car, I can't play a three pedal piano. Is this true? I've always driven an automatic and I'm scared to start lessons.

~ Scared in Syracuse

Dear Scared:

I have been with many women drivers in my lifetime and I have made one observation. If they can hold that right pedal on the floor, they don't care what the other two are for. Go for the lessons.

ASK THE AUTHOR

—

NO. 184

Dear Don:

I am just seven months into my piano lessons. I am a man who loves music and am eager to play. My problem is the loneliness when I practice for hours. Someone suggested I put a life sized inflatable woman on the bench next to me. What is your opinion on this?

~ Lonely in Laguna Beach

Dear Lonely:

Men are prone to activity and showing off. It is not normal however, to have an inflatable doll of any sort on the bench or even in a chair for that matter. At minimum you may be prone to hugging or fondling the doll, which takes your hands from the keyboard and interrupts practice. In a worst case scenario, if you are smoking you may in fact ignite or explode the doll. This could lead to a panic attack, soiled shorts, heart attack, or just a rotten smell in the piano area while the latex burns to the ground. Also, you could burn the house down completely. I do not advise this!

ASK THE AUTHOR

—

NO. A368

Dear Don:

I am a sixteen-year-old girl and pretty well developed for my age. Recently I switched piano teachers and now take lessons from a guy who just graduated from the conservatory. He is just starting out and his piano is in his spare bedroom, along with a bed. Lots of times he tells me to sit beside him on the bed so we can chat. He dresses in shorts but tells me to wear those leather boots which come halfway up my thighs. He tells me the bedroom is drafty and these will keep my legs warm. My first teacher let me pick a gift from the piano supply catalog each year. This one lets me pick anything I want from the Victoria Secret catalog every two weeks. What is going on here?

~ Bootsy in Babylon

Dear Bootsy:

Sounds as if the boots are warming *his* legs, not yours. The next two things you should watch for are:

1. No piano next time you come into the bedroom

2. A request that you model your Victoria Secret stuff to make sure it fits okay. In this case I would say, "These boots are made for walkin," and get out before he starts his course on mattress magic

ASK THE AUTHOR
—
NO. 318

Dear Don:

I am a thirteen-year-old boy taking lessons from an older man. My lesson is an hour long. Lately when I start my lesson, my teacher disappears into the bedroom. I can see in the hall mirror that he has a naked young lady in there. Every now and then he comes out all sweaty and holding his chest. He is always out of breath and I'm afraid someday he'll die right on the spot. If he does, do I go home or finish the lesson and pay the lady?

~ Watching and Waiting in Weedsport

Dear Watching and Waiting:

Stay for the full hour. As soon as you're sure the teacher has passed on, go to the young lady. Tell her you've got some time left and cash in your pocket. She may give you a lesson you did not expect.

ASK THE AUTHOR

—

NO. A-170

Dear Don:

I live in Savannah. My teacher does not have air conditioning at his home studio. It gets very hot in there in the summer. How little can I wear during my lesson?

~ Sweating in Savannah

Dear Sweating:

Despite hot or humid weather, it is not socially acceptable for you to take your piano lesson in your underwear. That applies whether you are at home or in the studio for the lesson. Also, it is wrong for teachers to teach in their underwear for any reason at any location. It is okay, however, for both student and teacher to undress at the same time if some sort of payment plan has been arranged in lieu of cash. This should be done after the lesson is completed.

ASK THE AUTHOR

— NO. A-192

Dear Don:

I am the wife of a wealthy businessman. He has purchased a gorgeous baby grand piano for me and I am taking lessons. I can't play when the kids are napping and when they are awake they are forever pestering me. What can I do about this?

~ Pestered in Palisades

Dear Pestered:

You are in good shape here. A grand piano is the perfect babysitting tool. Children three and under can be placed inside the piano head first. Stick them in about halfway. Close the cover, leaving the legs exposed. As long as their legs keep moving, they are alive. Besides, being that close to the music, they might learn something.

ASK THE AUTHOR
—
NO. A-395

Dear Don:

I recently learned that piano keys can be different lengths. I have three children all taking piano lessons and their fingers are different lengths. The younger ones can't seem to reach the black keys. Do I need three pianos?

~ Interested in Indiana

Dear Interested:

DEFINITELY NOT! There are several ways to deal with short fingers:

1. The Devonshire Model FS9 Finger Stretcher (a fine machine)

2. If the black keys seem hard to reach, take a power saw and cut an inch off the front of the white keys—that will bring the blacks closer

3. Have your children wear thimbles to lengthen their fingers by a half inch

4. THROTMORTON SPECIALTY PIANOS:
   Model A - Has black keys which come out even with the white keys; the white keys are half as wide to accommodate the blacks
   Model B - All white keys are standard width and the blacks come out between them; this enlarges the keyboard by twenty-two inches and although you correct the short finger problem you may have to stretch the kid's arms

   P.S. You might want to move the bench.

AMATEUR PIANISTS

**Unskilled? Untalented? Inexperienced?
Don't know what to charge?**

"Hey, we got a spot for you!"

AMATEUR PIANISTS

As we embark upon the performer section of this book we will be dealing with two distinct groups: the AMATEUR/BEGINNER; and the PROFESSIONAL PIANIST. We will not touch on the concert pianist since this is a level that very few ever achieve. Although they might play in much nicer surroundings, to people who actually pay to come to hear them, they are subject to much greater scrutiny and many higher demands. Bless you who have achieved this status. You have indeed arrived and paid your dues to get there.

To get a basic overview of what separates the amateur from the professional let's look at ten basic comparisons.

1. AMATEURS usually have one job at a time.
   PROFESSIONALS have more repetitive engagements.

2. AMATEURS can stop playing whenever they want.
   PROFESSIONALS have scheduled sets and hours.

3. AMATEURS don't worry about tips.
   PROFESSIONALS often make it part of the salary or pay.

4. AMATEURS don't have a dress code.
   PROFESSIONALS usually have a specific wardrobe.

5. AMATEURS earn little or no money.
   PROFESSIONALS would lead you to believe that's the case with them too.

6. AMATEURS have a limited repertoire.
   PROFESSIONALS think they know it all.

7. AMATEURS retain no agents or attorneys.
   PROFESSIONALS don't make a move without them.

8. AMATEURS are not fussy about the instrument.
   PROFESSIONALS scream bloody murder if it's not just so.

9. AMATEURS don't give a shit what people think or say.
   PROFESSIONALS are devastated if they don't get rave reviews, handshakes, back pats, flowers, and bigger offers.

10. AMATEURS play for any silly thing, anytime, anywhere.
    PROFESSIONALS book in advance, scope out the place, need specific lighting and sound systems and set terms.

The AMATEUR is usually the person playing at functions that the professional will not. Not because the professional is above it. Usually the professional has already done it and vowed to suck on a bus exhaust pipe before ever doing it again. Someday the amateur will graduate out of it too and a whole brand new bunch of wannabees will come along. They always do!

If you are currently operating in the amateur mode we may be able to shed some light on what you may be facing and the type of people who ask you to play – usually for little or nothing.

They will tell you that it is good exposure and you can have all you want to eat and drink. The catch in that line is that you have to eat and drink while you are playing or after you're done. You are not expected to be any part of the actual function socially. To this end the host will always tell you what a great job you are doing. The host will also tell you everyone is raving about your music. All this is merely hot air to keep you in your seat, inflate your ego and keep the free music coming. If you break for a pee call, the silence will immediately set off an alarm to the host who will tell you, "Hurry back, everyone is waiting for you to play some more." That only serves to make you feel guilty about even relieving yourself.

There is always an approximate start time for these amateur gigs but the finish time is never defined.

The piano you will be playing is nearly always furnished by the host who has no knowledge of its condition but nonetheless expects you to do a bang-up job regardless. If you should be so brave as to request that the piano be tuned, they will tell you: the tuner just can't get to it before the party; you won't be playing all that long; and, this is not a professional performance so it doesn't matter.

There is no end to the settings for an amateur. You will be asked to play on fire trucks, hay wagons, low trailers, high trailers, boat trailers, pickup trucks and horse drawn floats. A word of caution about working behind a horse. Always be sure you are seated higher than the tail and preferably upwind. If your float is being pulled by an old car or truck you may expect them to overheat. Get ready for an afternoon of carbon monoxide fumes and oil smoke. The only way to keep those oldies running is to keep gunning the engine and all that exhaust blows directly under the float. Also remember that if the car or truck stalls you will no longer be playing up on the float. You will be on the street helping to push the float. You may also be asked to wear any silly-ass costume the host can dream up.

People do not limit their demands to land. You may be asked to play on a barge, boat, boat deck, raft or canoe. Avoid canoes at all costs. If you are on a raft be sure there is a suitable balance between you and the piano, and that the piano is tied down. If you dive off to relieve yourself the last thing you need to see is the piano sinking to the bottom of the river as you are coming up. Also, never let six to eight people hang on the side of the raft where the piano is located. It will roll over on them and surely someone will drown.

While out on the water, never accept a glass of anything that looks like beer or ginger ale unless you see it opened before your very eyes. People do strange things while swimming.

As much fun as it may appear, working on a raft is still subject to the laws of gravity and science. Primarily you are dealing with the problem of balance. If the piano somehow falls off the raft into the lake or river, you should dive off the other side, swim to land, dress and leave the party at once. Let the host deal with the commotion, lack of music and task of retrieving the piano. Do not accept phone calls from the host on the next day. They are going to tell you the piano is almost dried out and should be good as new by 6 P.M. They'd like you to play again tonight at 8 P.M. (In the back of your mind it would also be good to think about things like sea-gull shit, sunburn, high winds, lightning and rain. Party goers are oblivious to these things and they expect you to ignore them as well.)

While playing out on the water it is a good idea to reject any plan which would include generators, lights and sound systems. Once again science has taught us that electricity and water are about as compatible as shrimp and hot chocolate. Remember this: If you do get electrocuted on the job they will probably get someone else to finish the gig. You can only hope on behalf of your family that they will do something logical with your body other than leaving it in a boat or on shore for later. After all, you are dead. What's the rush? The mind set is geared for entertainment right now. No need to have the coroner putting a damper on the festivities.

THE HOUSE PARTY

Probably the most common amateur venue is the house party. This is just what the term implies. It is a party confined to several rooms of a residence. Usually the piano will be in the living room or den. Once in a while it will be in a basement rec room and occasionally in a garage. The advantage of this setup is the elimination of weather-related problems.

Having said that there are several downside tradeoffs which you may have to deal with instead. People at a house party will behave as the majority dictates. If the host gets loose or stoned or behaves in a stupid fashion, the guests will take that as a green light to do the same. If a guest does something whacky or obscene and everyone thinks that's cute, it is like opening the door on a cage of frustrated no-talents who now feel an overwhelming compulsion to perform and outdo the other person.

Although most homes will have a spinet or upright piano for you to play, you occasionally will find a baby grand. That will take you up a notch as equipment goes but grands bring with them a few inherent problems. Generally, once everyone has lost all respect for the furnishings in the home they will begin to use the flat top of the grand piano for a food court. Glasses, dishes, and bottles will begin to gather there. Some full, some empty. Once that situation has been cleared up the top of the piano now appears to some folks as a great elevated dance floor. Perhaps some self-appointed showstopper will ask you if you mind if she dances on top of the piano. You can spot this one at a glance. She will be the one wearing the tall stiletto heels with the small metal tip on the bottom. She will not take off the shoes since she feels that they add sex appeal to her act. This will cause unrepairable damage to the finish of the piano top in about ten seconds. She may start off singing but will probably end up swinging her pantyhose over her head, trying to lasso a male guest. The very best deterrent here is not to let the lady get started to begin with. Try this when confronted with this issue.

SHE: "Do you mind if I dance on top of the piano?"

YOU: "Certainly not. Do you mind if I take a shit in your purse?"

This reply may give the would-be dancer pause for thought and it will give you the fifteen seconds necessary to excuse yourself from the piano, cooling the act.

You will always find somebody who wants to sit on the bench with you while you play. They will hinder your full use of the keyboard and in some cases the bench may collapse. Always use a stool or chair. This applies even when the sitter is a beautiful babe. Facts show that she is already there with someone else and when she's done pestering you she will return to that person.

If you are playing dancing style music always carry an aerosol can of air freshener with you. Frankly speaking, a few dozen people dancing in a room with their shoes removed can really stink up the place. Spray the aerosol right at their feet at close range. Maybe the implications will wake them up. Highly concentrated foot stink can cause you to black out.

You may encounter the lady virtuoso who will ask if she can sing along. It is usually some obscure thing that you don't know and when she realizes that, she will suggest that it may be better if she accompanies herself. At this stage of the game you are out of the loop as soon as she gets the bench. Best remedy here is to drop a live frog into her bra. That usually will break her concentration and often times she will have to stand up to dislodge the frog. The instant she clears the bench you should dive in and reclaim it. In the end you may even be the hero in this setting.

Although you may not have been given a specific time to finish your performance, there are telltale signs, statements, and situations which should raise the red flag and dictate that parties are over. If your host is oblivious to these subtle hints, you could either bring them to their attention or ask to be excused to go to the john and just go home instead.

1. When the people start talking about carrying the piano out to the pool

2. When the State Police arrive with a cease and desist order signed by the governor, charging the owners with disturbing the peace and operating a disorderly premise

3. When the drunken buffoon with the lamp shade on his head is now wearing nothing but the lamp shade (and he ain't cute)

4. When you hear someone holler, "Hey, we're out of booze"

5. When the host's children are standing at the base of the stairs, dressed for Sunday school

THE PENTHOUSE PARTY

Once in a blue moon, if you are an upscale amateur almost ready to turn pro, you might be asked to play a "Penthouse Party." In this case let's say that your socially active aunt has moved into a posh high-rise. In her zest to meet the movers and shakers in the building she has bandied your name about the premises, raving about your prowess at the piano. Somewhere she crossed the line and took the extra step of volunteering you for a very special party in the penthouse occupied by the owners of the building. This is probably the only way she'll ever get into that apartment since the occupants have a preconceived notion that they are totally above everyone else and anyone invited to their functions can consider themselves blessed for life.

Usually one penthouse party with real social snobs should cure you of ever wanting to do that again. First key thing here is that your services have been volunteered and that word FREE goes over big with people who have millions. Although you will see no revenues from this job you will be expected to rent a tuxedo for the occasion.

Your aunt has set it up and the scenario unfolds as follows: You arrive just a bit early and your aunt arrives late. Therefore you know no one at the party. There are men in tuxedos and women in cocktail gowns. The hosts are seated on a couch and don't bother to get up when you arrive, rather allow their butler to introduce you to them. She is clad in a bejeweled gown of regal splendor. She has a steel gray, pompadour hairdo and is drenched in diamonds. She is a victim of failing sight and she observes everyone and everything through prescription opera glasses on a long gold rod.

He is senile and eccentric, everyone but you knows that, and no one pays any attention to him. He is wearing a green blazer with no shirt and white boxer shorts with green dollar bills all over them. His fat, hairy legs and bunny slippers seem to go unnoticed.

Next to them is their prize-winning dog. (Of course no one else in the building is allowed to keep pets.) The dog is one of a kind. He's a cross between a border collie and a turtle. The dog has nice long hair but it's green. Although the dog did take first place at the Madison Square Garden Dog Show, it has never been able to reproduce because no other dogs will come near it. The best sex this dog can look forward to is finding a near-sighted, horny turtle. It is often said that a dog looks somewhat like his owner or master but in this case the dog resembled neither one. I believe the dog came out the winner in this situation.

She said good afternoon and he grunted and smiled and that was the last communication from them all afternoon. The butler showed you to the piano. Your aunt came in a half hour late with her date. He was posing as a doctor but you found out later that he was co-owner of a shop that specialized in renting belt-sanders and rug shampoo equipment. In the two hours you were there your aunt spent ninety seconds introducing you to Kirby, her date, and thanking you for showing up. There was no ashtray on the piano. You asked for one three different times but none came. Plus, you went through two hours of nicotine withdrawal, no one offered you a drink, and no one thanked you when you left—including your aunt.

Your total assessment: these people were well dressed but not pretty; talkative but not interesting; educated but boring; rich but ugly; pretentious; and self-centered. Definitely not your choice for a group bus tour from New York City to Los Angeles.

YES, it was a fine nine-foot concert grand.

NO, you don't care if you ever see it or play it again.

SNOB JOBS - BEWARE!

I think the top snob job I can recall is the case of Derwood Musketball. He was an up and coming amateur who took a job to play for the socially elite Kittenbarf family. They were residents in the very exclusive high-rise Tingblitz Towers. It was a dream that Derwood had envisioned – a few hours to mingle with actual billionaires.

On the day of the job he reported to the Towers and after proper clearance by the front desk he was whisked to the twenty-sixth floor by a uniformed elevator operator. A business agent for the Kittenbarfs was screening people as they came off the elevator. Derwood introduced himself and a butler was summoned. The butler took Derwood down a hall to a blank door. When opened, it gave access to a gray hall and gray steel stairs leading to the roof. Once on the roof, the butler introduced Derwood to two men in gray work uniforms and immediately disappeared. The two men turned out to be Toby and Lorenzo Lintnavel. They were the owners and operators of Clearview Window Washing Corp. The Kittenbarfs had rented their window washing scaffolding for the day. As they escorted Derwood to the roof's edge the setup came into view.

A spinet piano had been fastened to the aluminum scaffold deck. Along with that there was a plastic cooler full of soft drinks and a sandwich wrapped in tinfoil. There was a small sound system and a shower curtain had been mounted on two poles with an iron cross bar.

Derwood asked Toby, "What's the shower curtain for?"

"You draw that in case you have to pee off the scaffold. The Kittenbarfs don't want you embarrassing their guests."

"How's this going to work?" asked Derwood.

"Lorenzo's got a cell phone. When they're ready for you they'll call him and we'll belt you onto the bench and lower you down to the front of the penthouse sundeck. When the job is over they'll call again and we'll bring you back up."

"Holy shit," exclaimed Derwood. "I get nervous when I'm up on a step ladder."

"Nonsense," said Toby. "We do this every day of the week without thinking a thing about it. Just don't look down."

"Hey, look down or not, I'm still twenty-six goddamn floors off the ground."

"In the nine years we've been on this job the scaffolding only failed once and we only dropped fourteen floors before the safety lines took over. The fire department had us down in five hours and we were back to work the next day," said Lorenzo with a grin.

"I don't think I want to do this," said Derwood.

"I think you better think it over," said Toby. "You are scheduled to go down in about eight minutes and you just don't say no to the Kittenbarfs. They'll smear your name from here to London. I'd say you should do it."

It was a sunny day and virtually breeze-free, even at this height. Derwood thought about the smear campaign and inched his way onto the platform. He was holding Toby's hand so tightly that both hands were white. Although he was told not to do it, Derwood had to take one fast glance down while he still had someone to hang onto. The cars looked like ants and a transit bus at the corner looked like a cigarette butt. He was scared shitless and shaking. He got onto the bench and Toby strapped him to it. Simultaneously the phone on Lorenzo's belt began to ring. He picked it up and nodded as he listened. "It's showtime," he said to Toby.

"Okay, hang on, dude. You're going down," Toby said to Derwood.

The humming of the lift motors let Derwood know that this was no test. This was the real thing. Although he only had to descend about twenty feet, it might as well have been 2000. He was so scared he didn't even know if he could play when he did get there. In a moment he was at the edge of the sundeck. A butler reached across the railing and attached an extension cord to the sound system. Several guests were already out on the deck and half a dozen or more came out once they heard the music. They had to view this oddity. Timidly, Derwood placed his hands upon the keys and began to play—staring first at the sky and then at the guests. His first number was far from his best. This was going to take time. His foot on the damper pedal was trembling and sweat ran into his eyes.

Derwood had heard of class segregation before but this was the absolute height of it. Hiring a piano player and not even letting him in the building. Seems a bit much. He was only six feet from the railing but it might as well have been the length of a football field. Nobody on that porch would grab him if he started to fall. His right leg began to cramp a bit and he instinctively began to move the bench. It slid back on the aluminum deck and that felt better. It felt better until he deduced that he was strapped to the bench but it was just sitting free on the scaffold deck. HOLY SHIT! That really grabbed some space in his head.

Tune after tune rolled from his sweaty hands, not one of which he could recall immediately after finishing them. He was completely absorbed in this ridiculous situation. Maybe a soft drink would help. A little sugar and caffeine. He slowly turned and reached down to the cooler. He grabbed a can of cola out of the cooler. It was wet and cold. Carefully he turned back, snapping the tab and putting the can to his lips. He started to shake again and the can slipped from his grip. It bounced off the deck and rolled over the edge. With the can still about ¾ full he could only assume that somewhere twenty-six floors below the can would find its mark and blast through the sunroof of a Mercedes, killing both occupants. He would be charged with involuntary manslaughter.

Several of the guests requested tunes and that was a welcome distraction. Soon he had completed the first of his two hours and a minor degree of calmness was coming over him. So far, nothing had gone wrong and the scaffold had remained pretty stable. It was shortly thereafter that three birds buzzed his head and once again his heart was pounding. The excitement made it necessary for him to pee, real soon. Only now did he realize that he was expected to unhook his safety belt, get up and slide alongside the piano, pull the shower curtain and stand on the edge of the scaffold deck peeing over the outside edge. The very thought of that maneuver scared him so badly that he pee'd down his leg at once, smiling to the guests as it happened.

At the end of the two hours the butler appeared on the sundeck, grabbed the electric cord and unplugged the sound system in the middle of a tune.

"You, my good man, are history," he said. "The Kittenbarfs asked me to thank you for your performance."

He picked up a cell phone from a glass-topped table on the deck and pushed some buttons. He mumbled into the receiver and instantly and without a sound you could feel the scaffolding rise again. Once again, Derwood's heart was in his mouth and banging like a jackhammer.

Reaching the solid feel of the rooftop again, Derwood was helped back off the scaffolding.

"Now wasn't that a breeze?" asked Toby.

"You sadistic son-of-a-bitch. I hope you drop 139 floors on your next day out," said Derwood. "I'm out of here."

His rubbery legs took him down the service stairs to the hallway below. Once in the lobby he began to shape up. He wanted to go someplace and just get shitfaced and tell somebody this story. I'm sure it would have been easier to get drunk than to get anybody to believe the story.

THE LAWN PARTY

Perhaps the most challenging and unpredictable function that an amateur can encounter is the lawn party or family picnic. It will definitely require the utmost of intestinal fortitude. Unlike the house party, which is conducted in a defined area within walls, the lawn party is a much bigger venue. This constitutes inside and outside partying as people go from the lawn to the inside bathroom and kitchen areas. Behavior patterns at one of these parties are extremely varied, the age range is extended and social graces all but disappear. The pianist's exposure to aggravation and all the "curves in the road" can almost be guaranteed. The people who ask you to play one of these will conjure up a picture of fun, frolic, free time and fantastic foods. Watch your ass on this deal. Even the host has no idea what's going to happen. There is way too much unsupervised area and once it's dark, anything goes.

Although I played a few of these parties, I learned quickly to avoid them when I could and it has been many years since I've done one. But a good friend of mine who is now on the professional circuit has a much clearer rundown of one he did not that many years ago, just as he was peaking as an amateur and just before he turned to the professional life. Over a delightful dinner of marinated portibello mushrooms, whalemeat sandwiches and lots of good red wine, Madison Dungshovel recounted the saga of his last lawn party.

"Don, this is the best I can recall. I've tried like hell to forget it all but it still haunts me".

My name, of course, is Madison Dungshovel. As an amateur pianist I worked other jobs to support myself. I was big into making designer kindling wood and also had a kite dealership. I played in a novelty band on a tour boat named 'The Bambi Z' until we were sunk by hostile fire from a pirate ship at Disney World. I now have my own band, The Dungshovel American Reformation Ethnic Ensemble. Mostly we play at Ellis Island to entertain the tourists.

This party was about my last adventure in the amateur world. I am quite sure this took place in early August. It was a hot Saturday and the skies were sunny and bright when I arrived. The job was sort of a favor for Parnell Pugwallop and his brother Slade. Parnell is a bowling ball repairman and his brother, Slade, is a sucker wrapper at the local plant of Sorority Sisters Sucker Service. I met Parnell when I was having my balls reworked. We got chummy and he knew I played piano. I told him I would play their picnic in exchange for his handling of my ball problem. The original deal involved only a few hours in the afternoon. He had borrowed a piano from Shannon Weezelblat who had a dance studio in the same plaza as Parnell's ball hospital. He handled the move and all I had to do was show up in any casual attire I desired. I chose clamdigger pants, a loose short-sleeved shirt, sandals, and sunglasses.

We had talked about a sound system. He said his nephew was a member of a rock band and that he would loan us some speakers, an amp and mikes. That took all the heat off me for equipment.

The party was at Slade's house. A suburban setting on two and a half acres. The house was an older one but tastefully remodeled. Lots of lawn, trees, bushes and flower beds. There was a three-car garage somewhat removed from the house and white fencing around all the rear yard. A small tent had been erected between the house and the garage.

When I arrived shortly before 2 P.M. Parnell took me into the tent and we tossed back a few brews and he showed me the setup. The piano was on a wooden deck about twelve to fifteen inches above the grass. It was sort of an extension of the back porch of the house. He set me up there to get power to the speakers. I took a look at the speakers; they looked like two refrigerators covered in cloth. They were huge. There was a big amp box tied to the top of the piano with clothesline. The back of the piano was at the edge of the deck along a hedgeline and a mike and stand were tucked in behind the piano next to the bushes. I would be sitting out in the sun.

There were several dozen people already milling around the yard and more came in by the carload for the next hour. I was introduced to a few people but their names did not register and I forgot them in minutes. My goal was to get this debt paid off in a hurry and depart this function ASAP.

I started playing just about 2 P.M. as we had agreed and I had to put the speaker system volume down as low as I could. Even then I suspected you could hear the piano a block away and in fifteen minutes it was hurting my ears.

From time to time Parnell would pass by with a few folks and introduce them. Aunts, uncles, cousins, friends and even a priest. They all meant nothing to me and I played on. By 3 P.M. I figured the crowd had swelled to sixty or seventy people with kids all over the place—all ages and sizes. They were the first group of aggravating piss pots that I would encounter that day.

There were frisbees flying over my head, a kite string got tangled around my throat, and I got a blast of sticky mist from a pair of kids shaking pop bottles and squirting each other. In a short period of time I was getting edgy. To top that off, their Labrador came by and took about a four-pound dump right beside the piano stage. The kids all laughed and the dog looked at me like I was intruding on his hallowed ground. That was not to be my last run-in with the dog. Later on he pissed on the leg of the piano bench and I'd swear to God that I heard him laugh.

Somebody wheeled a very old lady up to the piano. She was in a chrome wheelchair and despite the 80° heat, she was covered with a blanket. Her skin looked like a closed accordion and I figured she should have been put to sleep about eight years ago. The lady pushing her was living proof that in old age everything shrinks but your ass. The lady in the chair leaned over and said something to me. It sounded like, "Burp me if you will." Well I wanted no part of that shit so I said, "I don't think so."

The lady pushing the chair said, "Everybody knows that."

"Did I miss something here," I asked.

Just then the old lady's son showed up. He was in his late sixties and a perfect example of a diet program gone wrong. He was carrying a baseball bat and had a ball cap on backwards. He was smoking a cigar that looked and smelled like a flammable knockwurst. He bent down to speak to his mom seated in the wheelchair.

"How ya doin' Mom? Do you like the music?"

She nodded and then whispered in his ear.

"Oh, I'm sure he does," answered the son. "Didja ask him?"

She nodded again.

He looked at me and said, "Hey pal, run off Deep Purple, will ya?"

Well now, "Deep Purple" and "Burp Me If You Will" are two entirely different things so I proceeded to start the song. The old lady started to wave her arms around. Once again the son bent down to talk to her.

"Too loud, Ma. Is that what you said?"

Once again she nodded.

"Hey pal, can you cut that sound back? It's too loud."

This picnic covers two and a half acres but these fools have to wheel granny right up to the speaker and then she bitches. I shook my head no. I'd have wheeled her off the end of a dock right about now. They took the hint and moved her away.

A very light skinned, freckle-faced lady came by the piano looking a bit weak and unstable in her gait. Turns out she was having some sunstroke. She ducked behind the piano and threw up in the bushes. There's nothing more melodious than someone going through a full scale upchuck. Seeing her wobble off toward the house proved that vomiting was not the answer.

Of course, most of the people at that party were just plain folks. The kind you could lose in a crowd in a heartbeat. But there were a few that really hit me. Although it took me the whole day to get the scoop on them, I'll tell you all I remember about them now.

There was a kid there who turned out to be Slade's oldest son, Freeman. He was wandering around aimlessly part of the time and the rest of the day he sat in a rocking chair on the back porch. He was smoking a lot and had some corny hat on his head. I found out that he went completely bald at the age of twelve and was constantly shy about that. I only talked to him once and my take on this kid is that he was critically stupid. Didn't say much and what he did say had no continuity, made no sense and was virtually inaudible. The greatest portion of the day he occupied that rocking chair on the porch, staring at me and smoking. Turned out he was conducting an independent study to see if it was possible to smoke too much pot.

Another standout was a young Marine in full uniform. He was apparently home on leave and had come by to say hello to the family. Great looking stud but hour by hour he was pounding the beers pretty good.

The standout of the day was a gal named Christina Nightflasher. She was a real knockout. Probably late twenties with a dynamite tan. Unlike the rest, she was very fashionable. She had full makeup, $1500 designer low rider jeans, heels and a leather bra. I found out that she was a hooker who had just completed counseling. She was apparently trying to quit but then decided the picnic might be a nice place to conduct her "going out-of-business" sale. As time passed she zeroed in on the Marine and she became overwhelmed with spontaneous sexual combustion. She had those gorgeous blue eyes, sort of like the color of toilet bowl cleaner—they could entice you to enter a burning building. Word had it that she set up shop on a leaf pile on the far side of the garage and was running a "no charge" fertility clinic all day. I think the Marine got the best bargains in that deal.

Anyway, as 4 P.M. came around I decided that I had filled my obligation. I shut down the sound system and wandered into the tent to find Parnell. Since no one

240

but the kids, the dog, an old lady and the heaving woman had come by the piano, I figured my departure would create no issue. I told Parnell I was leaving. He insisted that I stay for the food. They were about to fire up the grill and tons of salads and stuff were showing up on the long tables in the tent. I made a grave error. I figured that I might as well get a free meal out of this. Should have left right then, but I didn't. For the next two hours I had a bunch of beer and stuffed myself with food. Burnt hot dogs, some underdone hamburger, potato salad, goulash, corn on the cob, a few brownies, pie, and something that looked like a red Chia-pet. It tasted like cinnamon so I ate it. I was full to my gum line.

A little after 6 P.M. Parnell says, "Why don't you give us a short set before you leave? I'm sure everyone would like that. In fact, why don't we move the piano into the tent, that way folks can gather around you and sing along."

Half a dozen guys disconnected the sound system, took the amp off the top of the piano and lugged the piano into the tent. There was no electricity in there so it was a bit darker. The sunshine had given way to clouds by now and it was also getting very humid. I was full of food and drink and I just wanted to find a couch and take a nap.

They set me up next to the beer table. The ground was soggy and the legs of the piano bench dug into the wet grass. The smoke from the dying fire in the grill made the air thick and hard to breathe. Up on the platform earlier, no one had hung out around me. Now they were hanging all over me and I hate that. Some asshole was eating corn on the cob and the hot butter was dripping down the back of my neck. The grandma's son was back again with another one of the bad cigars. This one smelled like a burning car seat. Not only were people behind and beside me, but now they also were behind the piano and looking across it. The combination of me being full, the humidity picking up, and all these people making it impossible to get any air made me start to sweat. I'd play one song and while I was doing it there would be someone else singing another song in my ear to see if I knew it and would play it next. Somebody brought out some soup spoons and they began to accompany me. The more spoons they brought, the worse the din. Nobody had any meter and it was just chaotic and very distracting. They thought it was cute. I watched as some guy downed a glass of Chardonnay with two flies in it. When he was done they were gone. This was turning into a circus. There was a hula hoop contest going on, some guy was spitting his tobacco juice right near my feet, and a kid with a profuse nosebleed came to hug his mother for comfort. She was standing right next to me and next thing I knew there was blood on my white pants. As darkness crept in, so did the flies, mosquitoes and moths. A lady managed to find about six of those candles that repel insects. She put them all over the piano. (That stuff also repels people, pets, and any other living things.) People were starting to pile everything on the piano – glasses, cups, ashtrays, bottles and food. A half eaten slice of watermelon fell off a dish sliding down on the keyboard. I gave it a hefty slap to the left side and it flew into someone. Not that I gave a shit. Then someone said, "Hey, it's dark. Time for Slade to do the fireworks."

That meant that maybe I'd get a break. Slade came over and asked me if I would mind getting up for a minute. Hell, I'd have gotten up for three days at that point. I was tired and full. As I stood up, Slade popped the cover of the piano bench up. The whole bench was stuffed full of fireworks. I had been sitting on a bomb all day and didn't know it.

Slade laughed when he saw the look on my face. "It was the only place we could figure to hide this stuff from the kids. Figured with you sitting on the bench all day there was no chance they'd ever open it."

That did it for me. I told Parnell I was leaving and before he could utter another word, I was gone. The last thing I can remember as I went to my car was the scene in the driveway. The cops were there. One plainclothesman, perhaps a detective, was drawing a white chalk outline around the Marine who was apparently lying dead in the driveway. I noticed he did have a smile on his face. Christina, the hooker, was perched atop a car hood, being questioned as she wept.

I vowed right then that before I'd ever do that again, I'd take a chance at repairing my own balls.

⇒◆◄

TO THE AMATEUR PIANIST:

CONSIDER BALANCING THE OVERWHELMING DESIRE
FOR EXPOSURE WITH THE NEED TO BE SOMEWHAT
SELECTIVE AND HAVE THE GUTS TO SAY NO.

THEY CAN'T FIRE YOU!!!

AGENTS

**Don't worry about the fine print.
Just sign here...**

"...we'll do the rest."

AGENTS

As a professional piano player you may come to a point when you feel you have exhausted most of the good jobs in your area. You might be considering a change of venue or even a move to a new area, but are unable to make things happen. This is the point that often requires a booking agent. It is the agent's job to seek out new and better jobs for you and to secure contracts with suitable pay.

Both men and women are involved in this field. Some work on their own and some are associated with larger agencies much like lawyers in a law firm. Some are very flamboyant and love to be in the limelight twenty-four hours a day while others may be reclusive, tending only to a few superstars. Many are very well tuned in to the movers and shakers of the business while the newer ones are still on a hit or miss basis trying anything and everything to see what will fly.

Some agents are specialty people booking only one type of act such as a singer, dancer, model, band, novelty act, etc. Others will take any client who shows promise in the hope that the agent will be rewarded through commissions as that person climbs to the top. You might get in touch with an agent by a referral from a current client or an ad in a trade paper. For the newer agents, word of mouth is their only road to bookings.

You are a thirty-two-year-old male pianist. Your technique and repertoire are polished and you feel as a bachelor you can take a shot at some out of town work. Like many musicians on the way up, you have a day job. Until you are secure in the knowledge that you have a good music job tied down, you do not want to take too much time off to look around. You have some demo tapes and have let it be known in the local music community that you are a man looking to move onward and upward.

You receive a call from someone you know who says she has run into a young gal who is booking newcomers. She seems to be very outgoing and is around all the clubs in town. She has shown an interest in you and your friend gives you the agent's phone number. Phoenix 2-1212, ask for Amanda.

You decide this is worth the call and the following night you speak to her. She asks for your number and will set up a meeting. You agree and then a week goes by with no further contact. You suspect she might be a dud but you resist the urge to call her again. Let's not show too much interest to start. Play it cool.

On Friday afternoon she calls you, all excited. She may have a slot for you this very night, are you available?

"Yes, my day job is Monday through Thursday so I'm free today," you tell her, "but I have to play my regular job tomorrow night."

"Let's deal with tomorrow tomorrow," she says. "Where do you live?"

"I'm in the Abraham Fernbaum Apartments on Jefferson."

"Great, I'll pick you up at 6 P.M. and we'll take a ride."

"Okay, what should I wear?"

"Whatever," she answers. "See ya." The phone call is over and she has not even mentioned what the job entails. And in your excitement you lost it too and never asked. Oh, what the hell, it never hurts to look.

Since it is summer you dress casually with a short-sleeved shirt, chino pants and loafers. You grab a bite to eat at 5 P.M. and are down in front of your apartment at 5:45 P.M. In five minutes a blue metallic Plymouth Valiant comes screaming down the street and slides to the curb in front of you. A woman at the wheel honks the horn and she motions for you to come to her window. She sticks her head out and asks, "Are you Ballard Wienerbun, the piano guy?"

"Yes, I am."

"Jump in, honey, we've got to roll along."

You are now forming your first image of your first ever agent. You eye the aging blue Valiant noticing that the door on her side is black and there are easily a dozen spots that have been sanded and coated with gray primer – this obviously to arrest the rust that is fast overtaking the car. As you walk around the back you see a white banner with three inch red lettering stretched across the top of the rear window. It reads: "Chill Baby – I'm Runnin' Flat Out Already." There is a good deal of smoke in the back and the low rumbling tells you that the muffler has blown.

You walk around to the passenger door and after a tug or two it creaks open. The inside of this car is unbelievable. It is cluttered full to every corner but the center of your attention is drawn to what appears to be a small child in the front seat. Bigger than a baby but still very young. The back seat is crammed full of empty pop cans, pizza boxes, costumes, and hat and wig boxes. And there is some sort of a machine there too but you can't figure out what it is. You settle into the passenger seat with great reservation. Right off the top she says, "Hi. I'm Amanda Amander, glad to meet you." She hands you a pad and says, "Sign here."

"What is this I'm signing?"

"Just an agent's agreement. Simple standard form, no biggie."

The area where you print and sign your name is spacious but the rest of the print on the sheet is about the same as a label on an aspirin bottle and you really wonder what it says.

"Just a formality," she says. "Can't tell you about this job unless I'm representing you."

The pressure she is putting on you works and you sign it and hand the pad back to her.

246

"Do I get to keep a copy of that?" you ask.

"No need, there'll be time for that later."

She takes a quick glance into the side view mirror and roars away from the curb. You are now taking in all there is to see in this car.

First off, this baby has not made a sound and as you study it you can tell now that the baby is not real. Maybe you should let her bring that up so you take time to study her instead.

She is probably thirty—maybe Italian, Spanish or Greek. Olive complexion, dark flashing eyes and black hair piled high up on her head. In her hair there is a golden butterfly near the top and she has on a headband from the Grateful Dead. Her lipstick and eye shadow seems to be blue or purple. Her outfit consists of a white silk blouse with patterns of roses, a metallic red mini-skirt, stockings that appear to be black on black with more roses and a pair of god-awful Jesus sandals. The kind that have the huge black leather straps and a sole and heel with three-inch rubber blocks. Her necklace, bracelets and rings look like copper but the metal adorning her pierced ears, nose, lip and who knows what else appears to be gold.

She starts talking a mile a minute. She is shouting because the car is roaring. You notice she has it floored and you are only going 30 m.p.h. She says, "Don't mind the noise. The transmission is stuck in low and I have to wind it up pretty good to get anywhere. Do you play any keyboard at all?"

"A bit. Not real well but I've done it," you yell.

"Good. That's a start. Want a beer?"

"No need to stop on my account. I just ate," you say.

"Oh, I'm not stopping. I got it here in the car."

You look around to see where it could be. The three of you are in the front seat and the back is full of junk.

"Well, if you're having one I'll have one."

"Okay, just suck on the baby's arm."

"I beg your pardon?"

"Lean over and suck on the baby's arm," she says.

"What does that do?" you ask.

"This is my special invention," she says. "There's a quarter keg of beer inside this latex baby. I just stretch her over the keg to disguise it. Looks real, don't it?"

"I'll say. You really had me going there for a minute. How does it work?"

"I got a compressor and refrigeration unit in the trunk with lines running to a distribution box behind my seat. When I push her nose the pump kicks in and pushes the beer out two lines in the arms of the baby. All you have to do is suck on her hand and bingo! Cold beer. Cops have never figured it out in three years."

Totally out of curiosity rather than thirst you lean over, wipe off the baby's right hand with your hankie and take a draw. Sure as hell the beer is right there and cold as ice. If this broad can dream this up she surely can book you somewhere. She is now having a beer out of the left arm and laughing.

She stops at a signal and the roar subsides for a minute. She kicks off her left sandal and curls her left leg up onto the seat and sits on it. A rather unorthodox method of driving to your thinking but she must have done this before.

"What's this job you want me to see?" you ask.

"A new band I'm representing. Hell's Angels New Revival Gospel Quintet Plus One. Their fuse is lit and they're going to the top."

The light changes and once again the deafening roar of the car makes it almost impossible to talk. It sounds like a huge rock truck coming up out of a quarry and people are gazing at the car from both sides of the street.

She is weaving in and out of traffic and sucking on the "beer baby." Now she pulls open the ashtray which is filled with pills of every color. It is a drug drawer with enough stuff in it to make this car a pharmaceutical clearing house. She pops a few and has another suck on the beer baby. "Help yourself, there's a little of everything in there."

"No thanks," you reply. "I'll hang with the beer."

This driving, drinking and drugging is giving a whole new meaning to the term "Rolling Blackout." You thought up to this point that it had to do with the California electrical dilemma. You hope you don't die before you get to the job—if there is one. You also wonder is she knows where the job actually is and you suspect she may have been a Chicago cab driver sometime in her past.

Soon the car roars into a stone parking lot, heaving and rocking as it flies through the potholes and skids to a stop next to a pink Buick hearse. "It looks like Abbott is here. Not too many pink hearses around," she says.

The hotel bar at which you have arrived is painted in about fifty psychedelic colors and has a wooden front porch with a picket railing along it. There are neon beer signs in all the windows and more metal beer signs nailed to the railing. The peaked rooftop and shuttered windows give it a homey effect and your interest to see the interior is piqued.

"Let me lay the ground work for you, Ballard. This group is playing here tonight but the keyboard guy got injured. They really need someone to jump in and help out.

I'm hoping you will make it happen. They get a good crowd here and the pay is okay. We'll discuss that later." She reaches in her purse and pulls out a piece of paper with a bunch of scribbling on it.

"Here, read this over to familiarize yourself with everyone in the band. It will save time inside and you can keep that 'cause I got copies."

"Amanda, let me ask you this. Is this a one-nighter or what's the deal?"

"The keyboard guy got hurt and we don't think he'll be back anytime soon. He was watching a demolition job and got whacked in the head with a 4000-pound wrecking ball. So far he can only count to three and he has to stamp his foot to do that. He keeps rambling on about having breakfast with General "Black Jack" Pershing and his eyes were never crossed before. I think there's some room for you on this one."

You ask, "Are you going to hang around tonight to see how it goes?"

"For a while. I got a few other clubs to hit but I'll be back before the job is over to pay you and take you home."

You can just envision what shape she'll be in four hours from now. Well, let's take this one step at a time. You read over the band roster sheet and it's a colorful selection of folks. You notice she has also made notes about each member for her own information.

CLIENT: HELL'S ANGELS NEW REVIVAL GOSPEL QUINTET PLUS ONE

LEADER: AXEL SKATEKEY 29 Egg Crater
GUITAR HOME: San Francisco, CA
NOTES: *Needs to clean up language, polish shoes, remember more lyrics.*

DRUMMER: NIGEL WAGENSCHMALTZ 26 Shoe Lace Salesman
DRUMS HOME: Nigeria, Africa
NOTES: *Should learn to speak English, ditch the turban and robe bit.*

KEYBOARD: MERLE HINDERWIPE 47 Rock Climbing Instructor
PIANO/KEYBOARD HOME: Horner's Corners, TX
NOTES: *Got to stop calling his mom on my cell phone, needs new teeth (at least in front). May be an alcoholic, watch him.*

SAXOPHONE: DELPHINO NIGHTCRUISER 19 Hell's Angel/Biker
SAX/CLARINET HOME: Brooklyn, NY
NOTES: *Cannot play in NJ, WVA or FLA – warrants pending, does not want pay by check, should not wear shoulder holster and gun during the show, sometimes abusive to management.*

BASS: ABBOTT TOADFAT 77 Seasonal Potato Farmer
BASS/TUBA HOME: Teetlesnart, ND
NOTES: *Good beat while awake, remember to keep toupee on straight. Bad knees and back, eyesight poor, frequent urination on and off stage (may need Depends).*

PICCOLO: MARIGOLD RAVENBREATH 41 Retired Druggy/Biker
PICCOLO/FLUTE HOME: Hotwaters, NJ
NOTES: *Seems to attract a lower class of clientele, takes long breaks, often goes to car, may be dealing. Might have to teach band sign language. Get her to eat more, possible anorexic, more makeup.*

The side notes which Amanda has put with each person tells you a bit more about this group and you know this will be no ordinary job. She continues to rattle on as you scope out this bio.

"Band's been together about three months but they just seem to click and I'm sure they're going to take off. They've got lots of original material. This place is just a showcase for me to bring other owners in to get a look at them in action."

"You know, Amanda, I am a dedicated acoustic piano man. I like to work alone on non-electric pianos in a lounge setting."

"Nonsense, Ballard. You are a musician. What you like and what you got to do to earn a buck are not necessarily connected. Honey, in this racket we all do what we gotta do. Do you think half of these people in this band like their day jobs? Hell, no. They're dying to have me shoot them into the fast lane. Big bucks. Pretty people."

As this conversation goes on, more cars are pulling up and a mini-parade of people are tramping by the car. Between the beer sucking, pill popping and smoke from the car you are just happy that the ride is over and you suggest that it's time to go meet the band. You know she is relaxing just now because she is sitting there cleaning her toenails with an exacto knife. This is the first time you noticed that there were no bottoms in her stockings. Weird! Also, one tidbit that you overlooked earlier was a round metal badge stuck in the headliner of the car which, reads: "I'll Drive – St. Christopher Never Had a License."

Her final comment was, "Look, Ballard, this keyboard thing could springboard you into the big time. Don't knock it until you've tried it. Give me some latitude here, honey, work with me on this one."

You both exit the car and proceed to the door of the club. Lettered on the glass of the door in gold leaf, is the following:

THE BARFBUCKET CLUB
Cy Barfbucket, Owner
No Minors
No Solicitors
Doors Open - 5 P.M.

As you enter the foyer, the smell of aromatherapy candles and marijuana smoke is overpowering. The place is as dark as a well digger's ass and the lighting is super dim, aided only slightly by a candle on each table. Also, there are some kind of birds flying through the room. They don't appear to be bats but whatever they are they don't appeal to you. Maybe if you were an ornithologist it would be different, yet even then it would be too dark for any photography.

The crowd seems to number near one hundred and people are still coming in behind you. You both make your way to the bandstand. She looks at you and says,

"About half an hour 'til showtime. They're just setting up. Plenty of time to meet the crew and discuss your part. Come on, I'll introduce you."

The guitar man is unpacking at the edge of the stage.

"Axel, this is Ballard. He's your keyboard man tonight. Looks like Merle is still incoherent from the smack on the bean."

You shake his hand and move onto the stage where two guys are setting up the drums. The first one you meet is Delphino, the sax player. You shake his hand and introduce yourself. He tells you the other guy is Nigel, the drummer. He is wearing a turban, has on a pink and purple robe with leather things running down both arms from his elbows to his wrists. You shake his hand gently and he nods. Del tells you that Nigel has just had surgery on both wrists and can only play every third number until he gets well. Also, he speaks no English.

At the edge of the stage, an old man is asleep in a chair with his string bass laid over his legs. Del shakes him and he opens his eyes. You are introduced and he nods off again.

Axel will fill you in, man. Glad to have you here. Do you need a hand with your keyboard?"

"What do you mean?" you ask.

"You know, do you want help dragging it in from your car?"

"I came with Amanda," you reply. "I don't have a keyboard here or anywhere else for that matter."

"Don't freak me out, Dude. You're spinning a tale, right?"

"No shit, Del. I don't have one," you reply.

"Well, you're gonna be doin' a lot of hummin' cause we don't have one either. Merle's is at his house."

He takes you by the hand and pulls you over to talk with Axel and Amanda.

"Dude says he's got no keyboard," says Del.

Axel, turns in astonishment, "What do you mean, no keyboard? How the hell are you going to do your job with no keyboard?"

You are now just a little bit pissed. You're being blamed for something you didn't know anything, about.

"Hey, strings, back off. Don't be raggin' on my ass when nobody told me anything, okay?"

Axel turns to Amanda. "What about this shit, no keyboard?"

"Thought you had one, Toots. I'll make some calls."

You stride from the stage to the bar and order up a whiskey and water. In two minutes the bass player is there to join you.

"Got yourself in trouble already, eh?" he says.

"Not me, it's that nitwit broad, Amanda," you reply.

"Yeah, she could screw up a one-car funeral."

"What do you know about her, Abbott?" you ask.

"She's a divorcee," he says. "Thinks she's hot shit. In fact, she wouldn't know it was daytime unless the sun was out. If it was overcast she couldn't be sure. I think she's stoned half of the time."

"What's her credentials? How did she get to be an agent?"

"Her ex-old man, Sal Amander is a booking agent with Windowwash, Barnburner, Hogbeater, Nightcrawler and O'Banion. She caught him boffing a starlet and they split up. She got some dough in her pocket and started hanging out in clubs. She ran across a guy named Cromwell Nash. He's a junior partner in a booking firm called Niederpreme, Flintlock, Needleweaver, Terracetile and Nash. She mostly did it to get back at her ex cause Nash's company is her old man's biggest competitor. As time went by Nash threw her a few crumbs letting her showcase some talent which he didn't want anything to do with and now she thinks she's God's gift to the talent pool."

"Well, she seems like a loose cannon to me," you say. "I just met her but I'd say she's fried in the penthouse."

"Yeah, sometimes she says stuff that makes no sense. She thinks because she talks fast and uses them buzz words that folks will think she has something going. They call her 'turbo-tongue' and most nobody listens to her after a while."

"Well, she's got me in a mess. I'm supposed to play the keyboard and there's none here. I don't know what to do."

"Let her and Axel deal with it. Want another drink?"

"Sure, what the hell, why not."

"Two more the same way," Abbott says to the barman.

As you sip your drink a commotion starts over by the stage. Abbott motions to you and you both walk over there. Axel is lying on the stage and everyone is gathering around him. There is a girl kneeling beside him and Amanda is standing there staring at him. He seems to be choking.

"What happened here?" asks Abbott.

Amanda turns to him and says, "He was putting a string on his guitar and holding the pick between his teeth. Del came up behind him and slapped him on the back and he swallowed his pick. I think it's caught in his throat. Marigold just got here and she's working on him."

"Anyone call 911?" asks Abbott.

"I don't know," says Amanda.

"Better do it cause he's checkin' out fast. Look at his face turning colors."

You grab Abbott and pull him aside. "Look man, this thing is going downhill in a hurry. What do you think I should do?"

"Hang in a bit, my man. Let's see how it plays out."

"Who's the skinny chick kneeling there?" you ask.

"That's Marigold, the piccolo player," says Abbott.

"Somebody should tell her to give mouth-to-mouth or do a Heimlich maneuver," you say.

"Can't tell her jack shit, she's deaf," says Abbott.

"Deaf? How the hell does she play piccolo in a band if she's deaf?"

"She just plays whatever she wants and we all follow her."

"I thought Axel was the leader," you say.

"He's the leader on paper. She's the money in the band and the one who thought up the idea and bankrolled the band to get started."

"What's her story?" you ask.

"She was with the Hell's Angels. She and a gang were drag racing bikes through an abandoned military ordnance camp and she ran over an unexploded mine field. Blew her to hell and back and she came up deaf. I guess she was in the hospital a year or so. Sued the government and got an out-of-court settlement. The Angels dropped her like a hot potato. She thinks she's a pretty good piccolo player, but that's 'cause she can't hear herself. We just follow her and get paid. At my age that's all I care about."

You both look back to the man on the floor. His face is ashen and Marigold is standing over him in tears, shaking her head. Del is walking around in circles and comes over to you and Abbott.

"Geez, all I did was pat him on the back. I didn't know he had a goddamn pick in his mouth."

254

"How could you?" asked Abbott, "Don't be too hard on yourself, Del."

"Did, anyone try to give him mouth-to-mouth?" you ask.

"Nobody wanted to. He's got crud in his mustache."

Now the police have arrived and right on their heels a team of paramedics sail through the door.

The cops are onstage and one hollers, "Alright, everybody get down off this stage. Give the medics some room to work here."

You and the rest of the band move back to the bar.

The crowd is having mixed reactions. Some of the stoners think this is a live stage play of ER. The others want to know why there is no music.

Now you are standing next to Marigold. She is as thin as a match stick and about five-foot-four. She is scribbling her drink order on a napkin to make the bartender understand. You have often heard on TV that somewhere in the world you can feed a child for 80¢ a day. This is the first time that you have actually seen one. You bet if she had two hummingbird wings on a Ritz cracker she'd have to pass on the salad and dessert.

One of the paramedics comes to the bar. "Who's the leader here, who's in charge?"

Everyone points to Marigold and Abbott says, "She's deaf."

The paramedic stands face-to-face with her and points to the stiff on the stage who is now completely covered with a dark blue blanket. "The medic gives her the time out sign used in football and walks away. A cop standing next to him says, "No one on that stage until the coroner comes. Got it?"

You are looking around to see how Amanda is taking all this. She's A.W.O.L. You stroll over to the front window and notice that the Valiant is gone, too. Great. You're here at the murder mystery theater with $20 in your pocket, a bar tab and no ride home. Unless the coroner can play the guitar and has a keyboard in his meat wagon this show is exhibiting signs of deterioration. The house music has come on at an ear shattering level and the patrons seem to be indifferent to the morbid activity onstage.

Abbott says, "Don't guess there'll be a show, what with Axel going down. You probably won't be needed here." He then strolled away into the crowd.

You take one last glimpse at the stage. Axel is still under the blue blanket with a cop standing over him. Half a dozen birds are perched on his chest and two more are circling. In the absence of vultures this is probably a token symbol of finality. You move to the foyer to find a pay phone.

After calling a cab you notice the easel with the showcard for the band. There is an 11"x14" glossy of the group.

There's Axel up-front smiling. In the back you see keyboard man Merle Hinderwipe and the drummer Nigel in a white robe and turban. The sax player in this photo is much shorter than Delfino and he is standing on a wooden crate marked "Explosives" so his sax won't drag on the floor. Abbott is to his right leaning on the bass with his eyes closed and right up front, dead center, is Marigold. She is so thin if she stood sideways and stuck out her tongue she'd look like a zipper.

On the bottom of the photo was the inscription: "Bookings by Amanda – Come Fly With Me."

Soon the cab arrived and you tell the driver your address and forewarn him that you are a $20 fare —tip included. He nods his head and runs the first half of the trip with the meter turned off. He knows exactly what to do with your $20.

You reflect on Amanda, the car, this scene and the keyboard issue. You decide she has a long way to go before she will be an agent. With her brain fried on beer and pills, her idea of the good old days is probably last Tuesday and Wednesday.

You are home by 8 P.M., out $20 and a little bit buzzed from the drinking. You check your answering machine and there is a message there from the girl who hooked you up with Amanda.

"Ballard, got a lead for you. There's a new agent in town signing up all kinds of talent. Call, Weedeater 9-3215. That's the offices of Windchime, Dragonhunter, Sapsucker, Seersucker and Jinx. Ask for Jake Jinx. I slept with him last night and he seems like a real nice guy."

Your options are threefold. Call him tomorrow, call him next year or call no agent ever and keep on doing what you're doing. Tomorrow is Saturday. You will be safe at your weekly gig and that sounds just fine for now. For the rest of the evening you do sketches of how to rig up a "beer baby" in your Camaro.

PROFESSIONAL PIANO PLAYERS

If you expect the audience to shut up and listen to you...

"... get out of the business."

THE PROFESSIONAL PIANO PLAYERS

As this book enters its last chapter, Professional Piano Players, I wish to congratulate those people who have turned pro. God knows we need music in our lives. The material in this chapter is not meant to discourage the newcomer to the professional piano game. I wholeheartedly endorse and encourage this form of employment. There is no end to the fun and people this work will bring into your life. In addition, the contentment of mastering your instrument will bring you great joy.

The next pages are but a series of road signs along the highway of melodies. If you know there is a curve coming you can slow down. If you know the bridge is out you'll find another way to get there. Whatever you have to do to get it done, don't miss a single opportunity to see these whackos in operation. Forewarned is forearmed. You will be able to recognize the setup and take it in stride, making it an education rather than an aggravation. Remember, these people will not be the same two days in a row. In many of the more subdued piano jobs, none of this may ever occur. But for some of you on the front lines, get ready. These looney people and situations may be waiting for you the next time you sit down to play. And oh yes, don't forget your camera. Some of this stuff is suitable for framing.

There comes a time in the life of everyone who plays the piano when decisions must be made. They mostly boil down to whether or not you wish to enter the field of professional piano playing in order to derive compensation. There are several steps to this progression, exemplified by these individuals:

1. The people who learn to play at a young age and then find that as they mature the piano no longer holds any attraction for them and they drop it altogether

2. The person who learns at a young age and, although not a constant player, retains the skills and plays from time-to-time for his own enjoyment

3. The person who has gone as far as she will ever go, a closet player who will play in front of no one

4. The player who, on occasion, if all factors are just right, will entertain for small groups such as family or friends—the appearance is usually brief

5. The person who will play for parties because he is probably just as drunk as the others and will not remember doing it or care how it sounds

6. The person who has tried his best and had the shit scared out of him at a recital or public performance when all did not go right and vows never to play in public again

7. Those who try to play in public and, because of the abuse inherent in playing many jobs, just don't want the hassle and so they return to home playing

Having eliminated thousands if not millions of players in the first seven groups, we now turn to those who will actually turn pro and play in exchange for money. Depending on how high up the ladder you go, you have made a deal with the devil in that you relinquish one more brick from the wall between you and the public for each notch you climb. The money will sometimes be great and most times not. In some cases you will never be paid enough for the aggravation and bullshit that you have to endure in order to do something which you otherwise find enjoyable. It is like being a pro football player and show up for the game on Sunday then are told that all the doors to the stadium are locked, but if you can scale the outside wall and get inside, they'll let you play.

Many professional players are not high profile. They ply their trade in small bars and clubs everywhere in the world. A Friday or Saturday job or perhaps both. The money is only fair and the clientele is usually the same people. Some of them revere you, others talk nicely about you and the balance of them will tolerate you. But some players stay in one place far too long. There are even cases of people working the same room for ten years or more, making them totally boring to the repeat crowd. These players have no motivation to move onward and upward. They have found a home, management doesn't bother them and they are not giving up the piano unless physically asked to leave the premises. Their pay has remained the same for ten or fifteen years and they are frankly scared to try anywhere else.

Others who are younger or more aggressive or inquisitive will move along through the venues in their area, and even venture to new places within driving range of an hour or two. Some are soloists and some play with bands. They are still in the middle of the road with jobs to augment their income. They have never considered the piano as a sole means of support and would probably have to travel a great deal more in order to make it work. This could involve agents or business advisors and that gets you into the next level which is where the "rubber meets the road."

There are those who have purposely set out from the beginning to try their hand at professional piano work. Some will be in a teaching position, some will be entertainers or band members. All will be subjected to the wills and whims of managers, customers, critics, agents, and the media in general. You may be destined to the loft of a church to play a great organ. Yes, you're at work for the Lord but you have to put up with the choir and 500 parishioners who feel your work should be flawless. You may grace the stages of America and Europe but you will be at the mercy of the sound man, the lighting man, the stage director and every other self-proclaimed expert who will tell you everything you are doing wrong and overlook any type of compliment lest he or she be judged soft hearted or sympathetic. They feel that the loud voice, the authoritative stance and the glare of a chain saw killer is their only tool to convince you to do what they say or there is no redeeming value to your act in any form. You have to get up pretty far on the ladder to get over these people and the pile of bodies will number in the hundreds before that moment comes.

When assuming your place in the professional ranks you have also opened up another can of worms. Not only are you seeking out work, negotiating wages and trying to live on the money, but you are now in a constantly competitive environment. You may think you are the greatest pianist since Horowitz until a totally unknown guy from Nosepick, Kansas comes to your place and asks to sit in. You figure him to be a schmuck and his bad playing can only make you look better. You get up, he sits down and you are looking for another job. There is no way that you are going to regain your chair with any degree of authority that night and the manager will now realize that what he thought was good was in reality only fair. This new guy has studied under a rock in a dark spot for many years and has only now realized that he can really play in public and the public likes it. It has overwhelmed him and he intends to do it hard and often. Just unlucky for you that his first strike hit your place. Just like lightning, you never know when you're going to get hit or whether you'll live through it.

The entertainment industry devours musicians by the thousands every year. The rise to fame is long and hard and the place at the top of the hill is cold, windy and constantly under attack by someone else who wants to be there. You may be better than the next guy but you and your people have to make believers out of the general public. It's not what you can do; it's what you can earn that drives a manager or publicity director to keep plugging you and shoving your face onto TV screens and magazine covers and getting your CD into every store on the planet. They have no love for you. They are better actors than you'll ever be and when the bucks stop so do their services. The professional life is a good time when it's good and when it's bad, it's badder than a junk yard dog.

Having said that, and knowing there are dozens of levels at which to get off, let's look at some of the things that can and will happen to you as you slide along on your professional bobsled.

As a professional pianist you have the option of seeking your own jobs or booking through an agent. Some of the clubs will not work without an agent and an agent will cost you part of your income. The agent, however, may save you from the daily grind of searching out a job.

Let us assume for now that you have elected to go for it on your own and will shop the available work. You will now find a new group of people to deal with in life. They will be the club owners and managers. When you appear on your own, they figure they know much more than you and that they have you at a disadvantage from the start. It boils down to one thing. They've got the job and you need the job.

In the case of the agent, he is paid to haggle and call and deal with delays, excuses, con games and other crap. It is his stock-in-trade. When you get into that merry-go-round yourself you are losing valuable time for every repeat visit or call. It is a common trick of the clubs to wear you down. You know you are good but they will always tell you of someone better who will work for less and is available sooner.

In this case you have spent over a month diddling back and forth with a club manager named Rollie Davenpratt. He is evasive, obnoxious and bold. It would be far more pleasant to just eliminate him from your agenda and move on but the club he operates is a gold mine. It is busy every night and the customers are upper class people who tip. The piano is a seven-foot grand less than a year old. You really want this job.

Mr. Davenpratt knows this and has been beating you up on price for a month. Finally there is a meeting of the minds and he has asked you to come in to talk about his rules concerning entertainers. The conversation goes something like this.

First, the lady at the reservation desk buzzes the office to announce your arrival.

"Mr. Davenpratt, there is a Mr. Foster Frazzleding here to see you about the piano playing job."

"Send him in," says Davenpratt.

You enter his office, having been there several times before.

"Sit down Frazzleding, I'll be with you in a bit," he says.

He now fumbles through some papers and puts a few things into his desk drawer. He seems in no hurry to talk with you and does not glance up. This is a tactic to make it seem that this meeting is not very urgent to him. In about five minutes he shoves the balance of the papers to one side and leans back in his chair.

"Frazzleding, I've decided to give you a shot here but I have some things you'll have to know in order to work for me. First, and foremost, I am the boss. All issues while you are in this club are between you and me. I don't want you doing your dirty laundry or beefing to any of the help. If I happen to be off the premises you may talk to the hostess, Wilhemina Vomitsmock, but any decisions will be finalized by me. Got that so far?"

"Yes, I follow you so far."

"Alright, now this is the picture. Your basic job is to play forty-five minutes on and fifteen off. I want you to play only songs the people know. I want you to play slow

262

songs but not too slow. You will play loud enough to be heard but not so loud as to bother the customers. If you do play a song with a faster tempo, make it short. Do not smoke at the piano and don't bring any drinks to the piano. I don't want you salting your tip jar with larger bills. My customers will determine what you're worth. On your breaks you are not to go to the bar and mingle with the customers. You can take your break in the kitchen, the men's room or the parking lot. If anything breaks on the piano while you are playing, it is your fault and you will be expected to pay a part or all of the repairs. If you move the bench, pick it up. Don't slide it on the hardwood floor. When you're done at night, leave the building. I don't want to see any business cards or slingers with your name on them either. I'll keep your contract in my safe at all times while you're working here in case we have a problem. Your checks will be mailed on Wednesdays."

Having said all this, the manager will usually end the meeting by telling you that you were not their first choice but you are better than nothing. He will also remind you that you are on probation for the first week. If you really like your work and your skin is thick, none of this should deter you from your goal. There are a few other things you should hammer out in club work.

In the event of a speaker or award presentation you will be expected to be quiet but available. In some cases they may try to deduct the speaker's time from your time and thus the four hours you are there may not equate to a four-hour pay. If you are a United States resident playing in a Canadian club, be sure you know what currency you are receiving or what bank and type of funds your check is being drawn on. All checks should be U.S. funds.

If you are on a short job or one-nighter in a club which you might deem second rate you should know that many of the people who hire you have a split mentality. Although they remember the exact time and date of your job, they have selective amnesia when it comes to the part about how much you are to be paid and when. Some have a habit of disappearing about thirty minutes before you finish and nobody knows their whereabouts when you are standing around at the end of the night waiting for your pay. Someone usually says, "Why don't you call him tomorrow." When you do that, he says, "I'll send you a check." It arrives ten days later, for the wrong amount, always less. You are hung out to dry!

Now that you know the pitfalls of the initial booking process, let's wander the world of the professional. There is absolutely no way to predict the behavior of the public and when alcohol is introduced into the equation the people will change by the hour. Let's just see what can happen (and does).

We can cover a lot of ground by starting off with MURPHY'S LAW FOR PIANISTS.

1. Ten minutes before you are ready to quit, a party of ten who are personal friends of the owner will come in from a wedding reception and want to sing 200 songs

2. The song you hate the most will be the most requested

3. The bigger the crowd, the softer the piano plays

4. Somebody in the crowd will always know "Heart and Soul" and want to do a duet

5. Someone will always want to screw around on the piano when you take a break

6. The person with the worst voice and usually the loudest is the one sitting closest to you at the piano bar

7. No matter what time you take your break, the people always say, "Gee, you just sat down a few minutes ago"

8. If you accept a drink from a patron, you are a lush

9. Whatever you are smoking when you are playing is also what somebody at the piano bar is smoking, but they forgot theirs—they will bum all you have

10. A professional singer comes in after her job with half a dozen guests in tow and will always ask you for a weird song in an even weirder key; she will then tell the guests that she can't sing because the piano player doesn't know the tune—this is to cover up the fact that the singer is either blitzed or no good to begin with

11. The coldest or hottest spot in the building is generally where the piano is located

12. If you are using a microphone the customers will automatically determine that it is also for them to use at their will

13. Everybody knows a song they like, but they can't remember the title or the words and can't hum it, but God help you if you don't come up with it anyway

14. Any drink spilled within fifty feet of you will hit you, or fall onto the keyboard

15. The rag the waitress brings to you to help you wipe off the keys always has more goo on it than you are trying to remove

16. The more romantic you play, the louder the drunks talk

17. If you are wearing exposed suspenders everyone will want to pull on them and snap them into your back

18. Anyone talking to you assumes you are deaf and they have to put their tongues in your ear to be heard

19. Most requests coming to you on napkins are spelled wrong, are illegible, are for songs that don't exist, and will include no tip

20. The person who wants his song right away because he is leaving will be the last one out of the bar at the end of the night

We could only hope that Murphy's Law has covered any eventuality that might befall the piano player. Well, sad to say there are more potholes in the road to completing your musical night.

As a piano player working at floor level with your audience you are inviting trouble. Unlike the athlete who is out on the field, the actor up on a stage, or a television personality who acts for the camera, you are vulnerable. You have no stage, no fence around you, and if you are playing a piano bar you are actually inviting the people to sit with you. While the audience can be your friend, it can also generate your biggest enemies and pests. You just never know!

GUEST ARTISTS

Millions of people have jobs and most take their jobs very seriously. They want to do it in a professional manner and if a boss or client is waiting for their finished product they don't want any excuses or interruptions for something that is less than one hundred percent. If you are a tour bus driver you don't let someone sit in and drive a few miles just for fun; if you are a master bricklayer you don't let some joker off the street lay a row or two for you; if you are a dentist, you don't let someone from the waiting room stroll in and help out with the extraction. Professional people do professional things and they do them well and they do them alone. Why is it then that night after night, week after week, for years on end, people think nothing of asking a professional piano player to let them sit in and play the job? The pianist is also a working pro, earning a wage to perform a service for an audience that has come to enjoy the finished product. It is very unlikely that sit-ins can play as well as you, and frankly they don't give a rat's ass anyway because they can screw up your room and leave. The sit-ins come in all shapes, sizes, ages and talents. You must be keenly aware of what your audience or the management will tolerate, and more importantly, what you can stand yourself. If someone sees you let a person sit in, the word will get out sure as hell and each week someone else will be in there. The people will say, "Well, we were here last week and you let Johnny Smith play. Our son is better than he was. How about it? Just a tune or two?"

Many times they will not even wait for you to take a break. They expect you to give up the bench in the middle of your set. They don't wait until the quieter time of the evening but want to sit in just when you have the crowd on a roll and loving what you're doing. In the case of an adult sit-in, you should always ask if you can get a six pack and a pizza and come sit in where they work.

Piano players must be ever vigilant about sit-ins. Some are good and some are not and you'll never tell just by looking. The ones who are good know it and have no desire to show off. The ones who are bad are notorious for hamming it up and stealing valuable time from your show while bombarding the ears of your crowd with frivolous bullshit. Also, the people who tie up your time and chase out your good customers are those who inevitably will not tip you.

Let's see if we can break these guests into groups to make it easier for you to spot.

Child Piano Student

This one is coaxed by the family to play "one tune." The kid doesn't want to and repeats over and over that he can't play without the music. The parents in turn discount that fact and badger the child to tears with lines like, "Oh sure you can, remember that one song that mommy likes? Remember what your teacher showed you, darling. Ardella dear, I know that you know that one by heart, now play it." The culmination of that display generates three lines of "Twinkle Twinkle, Little Star" with some questionable meter and ends in prolonged applause by the family.

The Middle-Aged Player

He "used to" fool around with the piano and is now being encouraged by some of his cronies to sit down and play one song. (Notice it always starts out with one song.) As soon as you see this person come to the piano with drink in hand, one song ain't gonna be the end. Now the problem is, how the hell do you get them off? If their mundane display goes on for any length of time, the people who came to see you will no doubt hit the street, and the people with the person sitting in will leave after he's done with his run. That leaves you with nothing.

The Elderly Person

This guy was sensational fifty years ago but has now developed terminal arthritis. His hands are shaped like they are holding onto a grapefruit and his hearing has long since dropped to a .02 on a scale of 50. He sits down and his first comment is, "Oh, I don't remember much anymore, what will I play?" The people who have encouraged him to sit in will mention five songs that don't ring a bell and then perhaps one that does generate a mild spark. Then starts the search for the right key. Fifty years of training now funnels into one production number while all present pray that the player will live through the whole tune. Out of courtesy, everyone applauds and the whole thing cycles again and again turning your whole show into a live version of "Can You Name This Tune?'

The Conservatory-Trained Pianist

This person does not want to play but has been described to you as the greatest thing since Paderewski and now you even ask him to play. Upon finally getting him to sit down, the piano bursts into a concert barrage of the best of Beethoven, Mozart and who knows what else. The intensity of the player is magnified because he is playing with his eyes shut and his face about twelve inches off the keyboard. He has no idea that he has played twenty minutes already, that his music has nothing to do with the type of show you are trying to put on, and since he is used to practicing eight hours a day, the thought that he might run another half hour does not seem impossible. It is evident from his extreme level of concentration, that you could blow off an explosive device three inches from his ear and he would have no idea it even occurred. You started this, only God knows when it will end. So it will have to be your decision when to pull the plug.

The Job Hunter

This is, by all means, the person you have to be on the lookout for. This person is hanging around, listening to your tunes and picking out the ones that you have already played that he also knows. He may have been in several times before, written down some of your best received numbers and gone home and practiced them to perfection. These may well be the only tunes he knows. Now, when you take a break, he might ask you if you mind if he tries a tune or two. Smart money tells you to say NO. But most entertainers wish to be admired and thought of as good-hearted people so you decide to let him play. Unaware that you are dealing with the enemy, you graciously surrender the bench and in five minutes you are listening to your previous show all over again. The player is now trying to show the listeners that someone can do the same tune better, louder, or faster and hoping that the club manager hears it and agrees. Oddly enough, some business cards with his name on them have appeared at the piano and in the bar area in hopes that management will see them. You must get back to your bench as soon as possible and discourage any further playing by this person. Ever! Any relaxation of this rule on your part and you could well become the audience rather than the entertainer. If your kidneys are good and you can pull it off, you can usually outwait the frustrated takeover artist. They are so wired up to play that sitting for two hours without being asked will drive them somewhere else to harass yet another piano player—or they will get blasted at the bar while waiting and be unable to function when their turn comes at last.

The Accompanist

This person cannot play a single tune alone but figures that anything they add to whatever you are doing will certainly make it much better. Usually they will slowly come nearer and nearer to you during your performance. At first they are glancing over your right shoulder. Then the hand appears on the upper end of the piano. Coming in about four bars into what you are doing, they're in the wrong key and unable to get the tempo correct. This will surely lead back to "Heart and Soul" and "Chopsticks" and will blow your customers away faster than grain through a goose. This interloper will eventually ask to do one song alone and if you let him, he will usually blow it all to hell while laughing about it from start to finish.

Having given you the task of being alert at all times for the sit-ins, we will travel on a random tour to uncover other things you might encounter as a professional.

There Are Three Occasions

When a Lady Bares Her Soul

———

To a doctor before surgery

To a priest in the confessional

To a piano player late at night

KARAOKE IS JAPANESE FOR "TONE DEAF"

ASK THE AUTHOR

—

NO. A481

Dear Don:

Last week at my piano bar some drunk flicked his cigar ashes into my tip jar thinking it was an ashtray. It lit my bills on fire and all my tips went up in smoke. I'm probably out $30 and the jerk offered me $5. Can I sue him in small claims court for the rest?

~ All Ablaze in Austin

Dear All Ablaze:

If the guy was drunk he probably won't even come up with the $5. Sorry to say you may have to eat this one. In the future you may want to work a no-smoking bar but if that's out, get yourself one of those big glass fish bowl tip jars and fill it with water. The bills will dry out soon enough and change won't rust. Also, if you see the guy again you may want to casually set fire to his suit. This may afford you some closure.

ASK THE AUTHOR

—

NO. A502

Dear Don:

I am a forty-four-year-old Greek male, classically trained on the piano. Normally I work for the Philharmonic but I do take other jobs. I was asked to fill in for a band and when I arrived I found out it was an all-girl band. They wanted me to wear a wig, dress, and heels. I refused and they're taking me to court. Do I have a leg to stand on?

~ Dressed Up in Daytona

Dear Dressed Up:

I checked into this job and indeed it was all girls, and Afro American gals as well. Getting you dressed up would have accomplished nothing unless you shaved off your mustache. As to whether you have a leg to stand on, if you are still wearing those stiletto heels, keep both feet on the ground. Good luck in your case.

ASK THE AUTHOR
—
NO. A-484

Dear Don:

I am a middle-aged female cocktail pianist working a piano bar at a nice club. The other night a man gave me $10 to play him a love song. I played it and sang it too. As the song ended his date came back from the restroom. She threw her car keys and an ashtray at me, then came over and poured her drink in my hair and flicked hot ashes down the back of my blouse. She also placed a napkin on the keyboard which said, "Take a break or I'll kill you." Obviously she was a tad distraught but I was only doing my job. How will I deal with this in the future?

~ Startled in Sacramento

Dear Startled:

Sometimes piano bars get rough. The rule of thumb is to be sure you can whip the snot out of the guy's date before you play him a love song. The guy can be uglier than a wet dog but after a few beers his woman always thinks someone is trying to steal him away. And also remember, $10 doesn't go very far in the emergency room.

ASK THE AUTHOR

—

NO. A202

Dear Don:

I am a twenty-nine-year-old man working as a cocktail pianist in a fancy restaurant. The night hostess dresses in very provocative clothing which always shows plenty of cleavage. Whenever she comes to talk to me she virtually shoves her chest into mine. It is very hard for me not to stare at her breasts. How do I deal with this?

~ Staring in Springfield

Dear Staring:

The best way to conquer this embarrassment is to stare down between her breasts and tell her how much you like her shoes.

For those of you ladies who are playing cocktail piano in a lounge setting, you are probably at a grand piano bar. It may not actually be a grand piano but the bar top will make it seem as if it was. That setting is special. Unlike the cocktail waitress or standup singer who is seen head to foot, you are only seen from the waist up as long as you remain seated. That means as long as you have a nice blouse and necklace, you could be wearing a thong and sandals and no one would know. The only people who see your legs or feet are those patrons who have been reduced to crawling around the floor on their hands and knees or the occasional drunk who has passed out under the piano. (He probably remembers nothing by this time.) Customers may be prone to slipping currency into your cleavage. Remember that a tightly folded ten dollar bill is as sharp as a straight razor, so beware. Notice also that while guys are watching you, their girls are watching them to be sure they don't get too interested. If you are prone to smoking on the job, stick to cigarettes. Piano ladies smoking cigars seem to convey a whole different image and sometimes the party gets rough.

It is only natural to assume that a piano player plays to be heard. This seems basic enough in theory, but in the real world it doesn't work that way.

"QUIET AND TALKING"

As a professional player you must remember rule number one. No matter how proficient you are at your craft, your playing will always be less important than the customer's need to talk. Even trivial bits of bull cannot wait the three minutes of your current melody, but must be shared at once, lest the impact of the revelation be lost through poor timing. Those folks that tell you they were only whispering learned to whisper in a sawmill. It has been further proven that location means nothing. Sawdust saloon or high society club, the talking continues at all levels. There is a difference between crude and rude but where and when each kicks in often shifts from night to night. With the advent of the cell phone the pianist has a whole new aggravation to deal with and a whole new group of people who fancy themselves so damned important that they have to have that phone with them 24/7/365. It may be on the bar, it may be on the table or it may be in a purse or suitcoat, but it's there. Incoming calls to adults are usually in three forms:

1. The babysitter wants you to know that the Fire Department has taken care of the housefire and that she had nothing to do with it. She and her boyfriend were up in your bedroom when it started. She is going home now because she is upset. There was no mention of the children.

2. Your son is calling to tell you that your two-week-old SUV will need a bit of body work real soon and you might want to stop by the 24th Precinct on your way home, possibly with your Automobile Club bail bond card.

3. Your stockbroker just called to tell you that your 500 shares of Amalgamated Toilet and Screen Door just dropped 755 points when the CEO was charged

with bank fraud and embezzlement on national television. He just didn't want you to read it in the morning paper and think that he wasn't on top of it. He closes with the statement, "You and the missis have a nice evening."

On the other hand, outbound calls are for completely different reasons:

1. A wife is calling her mother to tell her that she is out with her husband and he's drunk and abusive. What are the instructions from the mother about this? Is it legal to kill him under the circumstance, should she walk out without any notice or should she look around and pick up someone better while she's there?

2. That same lady's husband is calling around to his buddies to find out if he is missing some action somewhere else.

3. A single guy is still calling his date's house to find out where the hell she is. They were supposed to be out together tonight and she is now four hours late.

4. A single babe is calling her girlfriend to find out if she should sleep with this guy she's with on the first date. These two girls have been friends since 1982 and they can't do anything alone. It goes without saying that anything they do together is probably wrong anyway.

5. An employee who has just come to the conclusion that he is too drunk to make it to work tomorrow has just made the mistake of calling his boss at home at midnight to tell him (with piano and full bar noise in the background) that someone in the family has just died and they are at the hospital now making arrangements for the funeral.

In all of these situations, you as the entertainer have been put down to priority two or less and the only time you will get a shot at having them shut up is if they ask you to play a song for them. It is now and only now that they become quiet (yet sometimes they'll even talk through their request). They will, however, become offended if anyone else talks during their request.

Only in the world of concert piano are you moderately assured of some valid attention and quiet. You are no longer in the bar and club scene and therefore you have already eliminated some of the problems. Now you only have to deal with coughing, sneezing, late arrivals, and those damn cell phones brought in by people who are very important. There is also the stage hand who drops a case of 750-watt lightbulbs which all explode at once on impact.

Therefore, take this into consideration; seventy five percent of the people are not really listening; the twenty percent who are don't really know what you're doing (but it's better than the juke box); and the other five percent are trying to find fault with your work. This is so they have something to talk about which might make them seem intelligent, but it doesn't. Bottom line here, learn to play all the songs you like best because you are the only one who will know what you played by the end of the night.

For those of you who are vocalists as well as pianists it is well to note that you are supposed to know every word to every song that has ever been written and be able to play it in every key so that folks are comfortable singing along. Furthermore, it is not considered proper to have to refer to sheet music or books during your show. The customers reason that if you have to look at the music you are not paying full attention to them even if they are not paying attention to you in the first place.

One last thought on people talking during your act. There is one time they will all be quiet. That is when you make your only mistake of the evening.

FURTHER CAUSAL OBSERVATIONS & WARNINGS

Things to avoid:

- Piano jobs playing for the hearing impaired.
- Playing the piano in a bar where the dart players must throw across the piano.
- Pool players with their ass in your face.
- Playing next to an open door in the winter.
- Playing near an open door in the summer when carbon monoxide and dust will overcome you.
- Playing in a bar where there is wire mesh between you and the crowd.
- Crying babies placed on your lap while the parents go to the bar.
- Air conditioning blowing on your back.
- Bar owners who tell you, "There are five or six keys which don't work, just play around them; we had this tuned just before Arnie went into the Navy."
- Playing for a crowd of 200 without a sound system.
- Tourists flashing cameras into your eyes from four feet away.
- A piano with ivories missing from the keys. This creates a cheese grater effect and you'll notice the keyboard turning red as the night progresses—that red is blood from your hands.
- Showing up at a job to find no piano. They thought you always brought your own.
- Any bar that tells you they must keep the television on and they also need to run the blenders, listen to the scanner, and blow an air horn every time the bartender gets a tip.
- One special thing to watch for: in older bars without air conditioning they may have a large floor-mounted fan. These fans have a wire guard around the blade. Inventive patrons, however, will find a way to toss things up on the fan that will slip past the guard and into the whirling blades. Things like cake, french fries, spinach, chipped ice and chicken bones. Once chewed up by the fan blades these items will be converted into a spray of crap showering both you and the piano.

A WORD TO THOSE WHO PLAY WEDDINGS

What ever happened to the nice music that used to be played at weddings? You never hear young people whistle anymore. What in the music of today could they possibly whistle? Old tunes like "You Made Me Love You," "Deep Purple," "Feelings" and "Twilight Time" are gone. Nowadays you will hear someone announcing: the bride and groom have selected as their wedding song a new hit single by Lloyd Finsterbang. Mr. Finsterbang originally was the lead singer and choreographer for the rap band Lavatory Canary and now has his own group called Tinfoil Tricycle. Let's have a round of applause as the new Mr. and Mrs. Harley Rasmussen glide onto the floor to the song "Almost Nearly Arrested." What a memorable moment. Fellow pianists, get geared up for this moment.

Note: When you are playing at a wedding and someone throws up from too much food, booze and fast dancing, it is not polite to stop the music and point.

WORDS OF CAUTION

Do not smoke cigars under a smoke alarm.

Do not have a nine-candle candelabra under a sprinkler head.

Be sure, if someone's dentures fall out while they are singing, you do not call attention to it even while they are crawling around under the piano trying to find them.

Probably the most requested song of all is "Happy Birthday." Did you ever notice that no matter what key you play that song in, no one can sing in that key? Furthermore, no matter what tempo you use, no one can follow the tempo either. Once you have struck the first note, the race is on and the song is just not long enough for even the best pianist to overhaul. Just ignore it—it's not your fault.

Do not become upset when someone asks you to play a song you do not know. They'll probably say, "God, everybody knows that song." Just rest comfortably in the knowledge that you probably know 500 songs that they've never heard and that makes you the silent winner.

There are those establishments which will hire you as just background piano to play for brunches and cocktail hours. They may place you in a remote location, away from the guests and while you perform they may execute a taping operation without your knowledge or approval. With about a month of your stuff on tape they will then tell you the house has decided to go to canned music and your services are no longer required. If this happens to you, your best bet is to find the raunchiest party tape you have ever heard, return to the restaurant and seek out the place where the tapes are being played, then insert your party tape just before the Sunday brunch. Turn it to full volume. They probably won't check the tape or volume before punching the play button. That should set a whole new tone for the diners. Be sure you retrieve your piano tapes in the process, leaving them high and dry.

For those expecting a Utopia of lifelong, high-paying piano jobs, you may want to peruse the next few typical encounters.

When you think that this job will be the greatest and that everything is going really well...

IT ISN'T.

"Your check is in the mail."

OH, FOR A SUNDAY IN SUMMER

"Did you ever see a sea gull smile?"

It is mid-summer and along the river the boats are plentiful. Relaxation abounds in the forms of water skiing, fishing, and underwater explorations of a few old barge wrecks. You have taken to the front porch and are pondering the thought of getting in on some of these pleasant diversions to break up your busy schedule. The ringing of the phone interrupts this thought. It is your old friend Harry. He is in a predicament and needs your help. He has been asked to stand up for a wedding. The groom is a very good friend of many years and Harry would like to attend. However, he cannot return in time to play his Sunday gig on the river. Could you cover for him? Harry is a great guy and has done you some favors in the past and you answer, "Sure, I can do that."

He fills you in on the deal. "The place is called MA SWEENEY'S WHARF and is located at the foot of Claremont Street. It is a red and white wooden building located next to the bait store. You can park at the tavern if you get there early. The job starts at 3 P.M. but lots of folks get there ahead of time between 1:30 and 2:00 P.M. If the lot is full, drive across the street and park among the trucks at the city refuse transfer station. There's nobody around there on Sundays and you'll be okay.

"The job is solo piano from 3 to 7 P.M. playing sing-along tunes in the back room. Ma Sweeney is there herself and will pay you in cash at the end of the job. No big costume deal—wear a white shirt with red arm garters. The owner has hundreds of styrofoam imitation straw hats that she gives away and you can wear one of those for the afternoon. The piano is pretty decent and they have a great sound system. The people are middle-aged, older beer drinkers who like to have fun and sing-along. The pace is moderate and the crowd is sort of laid back. You may encounter the occasional spoon and kazoo player so just humor them. They don't last long. Basically that's it in a nutshell. It's your average Sunday afternoon with some great folks."

Sunday arrives. It is a gorgeous and very hot day. You are a little bit tired from playing a back-to-back Friday and Saturday job downtown but by Noon you are getting mentally set to do this job. You dress casual in your chino pants, white shirt and garters and your most comfortable sneakers. You don't go too early and you are gambling that the garbage truck deal will work for parking.

You are in the saloon by 2:35 P.M. and you meet Ma Sweeney. She is a real waterfront gal. Weathered skin and great blue eyes over an even greater smile. Her wardrobe consists of a white T-shirt, blue jeans, a yacht captain's hat, and sneakers. She draws two draft beers and you walk together into the back room with your mugs. She shows you the little stage area, unlocks the piano that has already had the front panel removed to expose the hammers, and plugs in the sound system. You stand next to the stage and gaze out onto the river. The dock in front of this place must be 150 feet long. Boats are already tying up to it as you stand there sipping your beers. There is a gorgeous forty-foot cruiser tied up directly in front of you and you can hear a party aboard already in progress.

Ma Sweeney gives you the balance of the rundown.

"Give me forty to forty-five minutes on and fifteen off. Have a beer whenever you want one as long as you don't get wasted and blow the job. If you want one brought to you catch Beth as she comes around. She's in a sailor suit and works this part of the room. The first two drinks are on me and the rest are on your tab. If the crowd really gets rolling I expect you to work the crowd and not your watch. Any questions?"

Seems like a cut and dried set of rules that you can live with for one afternoon. You tell her all seems okay and proceed to arrange the stool and test the microphone.

It is human nature for an entertainer to size up the room and you spend a few minutes scoping out the current attendees. As you gaze at the crowd a few things catch your eye. A lady quite near the stage is breast-feeding her son. In today's society this is becoming more acceptable and you would dismiss it entirely except that her son is twenty-three years old. Oh well.

A man near one window is eating raw clams dipped in hot sauce. He is dropping the shells into a beer pitcher on the next table. That would be Okay if the pitcher were empty. It is not, and the blind man drinking from it seems to think the waitress is dropping ice cubes into his beer to keep it cool. His seeing eye dog is watching a good-looking dog in the rear of the room atop a pile of empty beer cases and he misses the clam shell caper entirely.

The man directly in front of your window is decked out in his summer best. The only thing wrong with this outfit is its size. He actually should have been wearing a canvas boat cover. You judge that he is heading for 400 pounds if he hasn't already hit his mark. His belly rolls over the top of his shorts and his T-shirt is trying to get halfway down to his navel. The tattoo on his arm with the inscription "Mother" conjures up an image of what she must have looked like now that you have seen him.

Near the doorway you notice a lady seated calmly at a table. She is rather elderly and her male escort is face down on the tabletop. You assume that he is already drunk until you hear someone telling someone else that she is waiting for the medical examiner and the coroner to arrive. She must have been ready for this. She shows no emotion and is drinking her drink as well as his.

You think back to the phone call with Harry. Yes, this job is just filled with average run-of-the-mill nice folks. Nothing out of the ordinary here.

You are at the keyboard with a fresh mug of beer at 3 P.M. sharp. You start playing some easy stuff. At 3:10 P.M. Beth drifts by for the first time and flashes you a big smile. You guess she's in her early twenties. She has legs up to her earrings and a great tan. She is wearing a blue mini-skirt with a white sailor blouse. A white sailor hat sets off her frosted brunette hair to a tee. The scenery is great already.

You proceed with some old standards and keep the pace moderate. There are a few singers here and there and now Beth brings you a little note with a dollar. It seems that this place has little pink forms that you can write on to request songs from the piano player. They are placed around on all the tables, and the waitresses, three in all, bring them up to you. Apparently it is understood that a tip should accompany each request. Sounds great as long as you don't get tipped for songs you don't know. Well, let's not cross that bridge right now.

The piano is working well and the room is filling. Probably a hundred people are seated along the windowed wall overlooking the dock. The early birds have taken the best seats, but even those seated away from the windows get a view. The hot sun beating down on the roof combined with the crowd is causing heat to build in the room. You notice that all the windows are being opened for fresh air. GREAT! The smell of the river permeates the room. So do the flies. You also see that the two windows near you have no screens. That explains the flies.

By 4:30 P.M. the sing-along is starting to gather momentum. You have had one break and three beers so far. You have received nine requests and $9. You have known every tune requested so far and it appears you will be able to satisfy the patrons. You also reason that you may be able to pay your bar tab with the tips and refrain from digging into your base pay. That idea sets well with you. The party on the cruiser outside is in full swing. They have their own music blasting so you turn up the sound system in self defense. Several scantily clad women are running along the outside walkways of the boat, much to the delight of the older guys seated by the windows.

By 5:30 P.M. the sing-along is going big time and everyone is into the booze and having a great time. Kazoos and spoons appear as predicted, along with a washboard player and a guy who is strumming a washtub bass. Where that came from you have no idea. You have had some beers and although you are still very aware of your assignment, you are feeling pretty loose. Time is flying.

You hear all the hooting and hollering and look over your shoulder frequently to keep an eye on the action behind you. Some folks are now dancing and you want to keep the beat to accommodate them. There is one high-pitched squawk that you can't identify until you turn back to your piano and spot a sea gull sitting on top. You are a city boy by nature and not a waterfront dude or visitor to bird sanctuaries. A tiny sweat forms on your forehead. This bird is two feet from your face. He has a beak and you have a cigar. This puts you in a rather secondary position.

It is 6:10 P.M. There is a bit of commotion which distracts you and now you see what the crowd sees. Two voluptuous babes are poised on top of the cruiser and are preparing to dive into the river. They are wearing bikinis which look like gaily colored dental floss. They are being egged on by six guys who look like they have been in the sun for eight weeks and into the gin for eight hours. SPLASH! The girls take the plunge. There is a round of applause. You feel a strange sensation in your sneaker. The sea gull is now a floor walker and is parading over your foot on his way to a table. You assume he is cruising for some lunch. This is great!

Someone at the next table is eating a hot dog and breaks some of the roll into pieces and throws them on the floor. The sea gull spots them. A sea gull can spot a tiny piece of bread from 700 feet on a moonless night and soon there are four sea gulls on the floor. The people are having a ball with them. You had not planned on this.

The girls who went swimming have now climbed back up the ladder on the rear of the cruiser and one of them is involved in a very sensuous embrace with one of the sun gods. They are quite visible to us and all at once some guy seated near the window stands up and shouts:

"Son-of-a-bitch! That's my daughter! She said she was going to a flea market today! That lying tramp! Let me get at that guy. I'll break his neck!"

Between the beer and the rage there is no time for him to think about going all the way to the front door. He mounts his chair and jumps through the open window.

The inner edge of the dock is about four feet away from the building. Dad drops over the window-sill through the opening between the dock and the building into a murky combination of dead fish and seaweed. The fact that he can't swim adds to the scenario.

People are clambering to the windows crawling over one another to get a glimpse of who went where. The gals on the boat beat it into the galley. Beth is now telling Ma Sweeney what happened. You are pounding on the piano trying to make this all go away. Your personal sea gull is now back on top of the piano and the other three are on the floor. Ma Sweeney and some guy from the bar appear on the dock with a rope. The guy in the water is screaming bloody murder so they undertake the rescue operation.

You get up from the piano because the crowd at the window is pushing at your back. As you get up some guy falls over backwards onto a table. There are four ladies seated there. They jump up just as the table tips completely upside down and their drinks cover the floor amidst the sounds of breaking glass. You look at this mess and notice that there is only one sea gull on the floor and one on the piano. Hmmmmmmm. Yes! The other two have been smashed under the overturned table and gone to bread crumb heaven. The waitresses appear with a cop who starts pulling people away from the windows.

You think back to your phone conversation with Harry. To the best of your recollection this never came up.

Beth and her helper Allison now have broom and dustpan in action removing broken glass from the floor. People bump into them as the cop forces everyone back to the tables. The guy who tipped over the table is still trying to get up because he is smashed and has no equilibrium. Allison turns over the table and spots the two birds. They are flatter than a sheet of waxed paper and she starts to scream, "Who did this?" The four ladies point to the drunk on the floor and Allison whacks him with the broom. The old ladies yell, "Kill the murdering bastard!" This encourages Allison and she gives the guy a few extra shots.

The Coast Guard has shown up at the dock and the irate father is standing there with them. He is soaking wet, hair in his eyes, and draped with seaweed like a bad looking mermaid. He is spitting out what appears to be water but considering where he just came from you can't count on it. The big cruiser is now revving up both diesel engines and pulling swiftly away from the scene. Dad is not aware of this.

It is now 6:40 P.M. and things seem to be getting back to a dull roar. You glance at your watch and notice there are only twenty minutes left on the job. You decide to play it out until 7 P.M. You return to your piano and the sea gull is still there. You have never seen a sea gull smile but this one is smiling at you and instinctively you smile back. You sit back down at the piano and are about to play when you notice something strange. On all the pianos you have ever played there are black keys and white keys. Now all the keys on this piano are white—and gooey. It is true that you are no bird expert but you do know what this is all about. You place your styrofoam hat on top of the piano and, leaving your beer behind you, walk through the bar where Ma Sweeney is pouring beers for the Coast Guard. Seeing no need to stop, you go directly to your car.

Did you ever sit in your car on a hot summer evening, smoking a cigar, surrounded by thirty garbage trucks, and just watch the sunset? All the while wondering what the hell else can go wrong today? And you think out loud—

SUNDAY—SUMMER—SHIT!

EPILOGUE

Harry brought your pay a week later. Thanked you for playing the job and hoped you had enjoyed yourself. Not one word about anything that went on that day. You would have told him if you thought for one moment that he would believe you. On the other hand you wonder if he hadn't already been told and was just hoping you wouldn't say anything. It's true that good friendships are sometimes really tested.

ASK THE
AUTHOR
—
NO. A136

Dear Don:

I am a forty-three year old housewife. I love to cook for my family and we have a full dinner almost every night about 6 P.M. For the last several years, our piano tuner, a nice older man, has consistently scheduled his tunings at 5:30 or 6:00 in the afternoon. He insists that this is the only time he has available but I know he wants to be invited to join us at the dinner table. He often neglects showering and once seated he talks for hours. How can I discourage this habit without offending him?

~ Cooking in Connecticut

Dear Cooking:

Warn your family the day of the tuning. Let them eat out. You will then be cooking for the tuner. Fry up some dog poop, put it over a three-week-old English muffin on a bed of leaves. Include a nice tall glass of castor oil. If your guest is still seated at the table for dessert may I suggest a dead robin with chocolate or mint sauce. This should be the "Last Supper!"

THE SILENT MOVIE JOB

*Seventy-Five Indians chasing a train
is definitely not a love scene!*

It is the most publicized event of the year. Following three years of expensive and detailed renovation, the Park Avenue Opera House, a 1910 theater, is about to reopen. The work has been spearheaded and primarily funded by Olivia J. Backstabber. She is a society matron and heiress to the Backstabber Fudge fortune. Known far and wide, Ms. Backstabber is no stranger in Newport, the Hamptons or Palm Beach. And at five-foot-two, 265 pounds she is no stranger to fudge either.

One of the highlights of the event will be the showing of a 1910 silent film that was premiered in this very theater when it opened in 1910. Now they are in need of a piano person to accompany the film. Although you can't figure out how they got your name, you got the call.

Ms. Backstabber had mentioned the need for a pianist at dinner one night. Her sixteen-year-old daughter, Poinsettia, picked up on that and figured if she could deliver the name of a piano player to her mom, perhaps she might get to drive her mom's new Porsche. She knows that her girlfriend, Zawina Tubrounder, is secretly dating the music teacher at River Rock High. She hits Zawina for the favor and Zawina approaches Mel Stringpuller, the teacher, and promises him a no-holds-barred all nighter at the Frog's Croak Motel if he can fill the order for a piano player.

Several years ago, you volunteered to address the middle school band on the importance of reading music. It was one of Mel's classes and you stupidly gave him your card. You also said if there was ever anything else you could do for him he should just give you a jingle. Never dreamed he'd actually call.

Mel is now calling you like he is on the red phone at the White House. He is thinking about the Frog's Croak Motel all nighter and will tell you anything to get this job covered. He starts by telling you there is pay involved and that the piano has just been completely rebuilt and is in mint condition. The manager of the Park Avenue Opera House has located an old folio of the silent movie *Mood Music*, and since you are a good reader, this job should pose no problem.

The job lasts only fifteen minutes but you will get scale for four hours. Moreover, there will be a lot of patron-of-the-arts type people there who use piano players at their house parties. This could be a great door opener for you to break into the inner social circle. Your name will be in the program, and if you'll do him this favor he will personally pay for a quarter page ad with all your information in it. That little tidbit does it for you and Mel figures $25 for an ad in exchange for an all nighter romp at the Frog's Croak Motel is a worthwhile investment. There will be one rehearsal, but it will be relatively short.

The job is on a Sunday afternoon and you have nothing planned. You accept.

About a week prior to the job, you meet with Mel and the newly appointed theater manager, Otto Fingerfiler. He has been recruited by Ms. Backstabber from a summer stock theater in Newport. You try the piano and it is just as Mel had reported—just like new. The screen will be to your right and you can see it fairly well. Otto turns on the sound system and you speak into the mike. It is both startling and magnificent. It will easily fill this theater with sound and you will not have to hammer on the keys to service the 400 seats. Even the seats in the balcony are wrapped in sound. This job is looking like a winner.

Now they run the film for you to watch. You have the music folio from Acme Picture Works. It is original and although frayed, it is legible. The index clearly tells you what songs to play for what moods and this looks like a no-brainer. You even devise a system for yourself.

At your request they run the film two more times and you meticulously document every scene by seconds and minutes. This gives you the necessary notations to know when to change to what without actually looking at the screen. You need only work up a time schedule next to which you will sync the proper mood music. By having a stopwatch on the piano, you can flawlessly implement the correct tune at the correct time and have it in the bag. What a great idea. Now you won't have to take your eyes off the piano for a second.

At home you devote some time to learning the various mood music selections. Actually, there are only seven basic tunes with some variations in meter. This is getting to be fun because it is both novel and challenging, as well as a diversion from your regular grind. You also think about your quarter page ad and the big bucks down the line from the society set.

Sunday, May 11 arrives. Show time is at 2:00 P.M. and you are at the theater at 1:30 P.M. You are wearing a gay '90s outfit which you rented at your expense to show them that you really care. Otto and Mel are there to greet you. Otto also introduces his twenty-two-year-old stepdaughter, Brandy. She is bleary-eyed and smells like she just came from leading a raid with Elliott Ness. Otto announces that Brandy wanted to be a part of this thing but because of her condition he will hide her in the projection booth. Brandy will run your movie! Otto had Brandy in the booth at lunchtime and went over everything with her. She understands that when you play the introductory theme she is to push the "ON" button. When the film says, "THE END" she is to push the "OFF" button. This she can do.

What nobody knows is that Brandy ran the film at about 1 P.M. as a test. It broke about four minutes into the picture but she was scared to tell Otto. He was already pissed because she showed up blasted. She didn't know how to make any repairs so she rewound it and took that reel off. Using her feminine charms she convinced a stage worker that the film had never been threaded originally and she did not want to bother Otto because he had so much on his mind. She grabbed another film and was able to convince the kid to get it ready to roll. The film was marked, *Old Time Favorites*, and to her an old movie is an old movie so what the hell.

The time is now 2 P.M. sharp. The theater is filled to capacity with the cream of the crop from the social register. Tuxedos and gowns abound and there is an air of anxiety in anticipation of the gala event. The M.C. mounts the stage and introduces Ms. Backstabber and Otto, the manager. They give their respective opening remarks amid a flood of camera lights and return to the floor. Next the spotlight is on the piano player and the M.C. announces your name for all to hear. A rousing round of applause and you swell with pride. Your are confident that this is your pinnacle show—the crowning achievement of your musical prowess.

You check the cue card to be sure it is in place. In the back of your mind you think of Brandy in the projector room and hope that she is still among the lucid. Yes, yes, yes. Here we go. You hit the stopwatch to activate the sweep hand. The cue notes are right beside it to tell you the exact times for change and the songs to play.

Your first song is a love song since you are expecting the leading lady to be meeting her boyfriend in the park. As you start to play this song there is a low level of laughter from the crowd and you do not equate this with a love scene. What can be funny about that? You steal a glance at the screen and you see seventy-five Indians chasing a train. HOLY SHIT!

You switch to Indian music and as you do the entire U.S. Cavalry is shown. Quickly you switch to the *William Tell Overture* amidst further laughter since the villain is now tying the leading lady to the railroad tracks. Beads of sweat are running down your forehead and into your eyes. Things are starting to blur up a bit and you can't take your hands off the piano to correct the problem. You have switched to villain music because that is the last frame you saw before your eyes clouded up. The current scene however is that of a nun holding a baby near a covered wagon. It is becoming blatantly obvious that you do not have your act together.

Otto is standing there speechless behind the side curtain. Mel is there too and he's crying. Otto wants to kill Brandy and Mel is thinking that he may sleep alone at the Frog's Croak Motel tonight.

You are beside yourself trying to get synchronized to a film you've never seen before. At the risk of leaving a hole in your score you lift one arm and swipe it across your face and eyes. You are into a rousing version of "Yankee Doodle Dandy" and there is now a closeup of the villain. You change to villain music as swiftly as you are able just in time to accompany a closeup of the train engineer looking out his side window. You think a good train song would be "Alabamy Bound" and just as you get into that the nun is back. She is now pushing the baby in a stroller and according to you she is going to push it all the way to Alabama. BAD NEWS.

The laughter in the theater has given way to some boos. You hope they are booing the villain but deep in your heart you know it is you they are booing. The hero has now appeared on the screen and is cutting the heroine loose from the railroad tracks. For a split second you go completely blank because you have not prepared yourself for this event and don't have a clue what to play. Your mind reverts to your regular repertoire and before you know what you are doing you are playing "Please Release Me." Nice song if it hadn't been written sixty years after this film was produced.

The villain has been watching from the trees. As the heroine is released from the tracks the villain wrestles with the hero and grabs the leading lady. He swings her up onto his horse and they ride off toward town. You are still fooling with "Please Release Me" and by the time you glance at the screen again the villain is entering the doorway of a house with heroine in tow. The image of the house catapults you into a beautiful rendering of "There's No Place Like Home." Of course you missed the two-second closeup of the sign over the door to that house which read: "NELLIE CAFFERTIE'S SPORTING HOUSE."

After what seems like an eternity the film ends. You grab your watch and head your ass for the side door. The collective laughter and boos prove that you have accomplished your job. You definitely motivated the viewers, but hardly as planned.

You never receive a check. And you hear through the grapevine a few weeks later that Mel never went to the Frogs Croak Motel and Otto is back in Newport.

THE PARADE—CRUISIN'

A wet piano is not a good piano.

You are a twenty-year-old girl. You have just completed your senior year as a piano major at a musical conservatory and this summer you have decided to hang around and take advantage of the nearby river and beaches. To get some income you have made it known that you are available for private parties and one night jobs. You have run a small ad in the weekly shoppers and pennysaver newspapers. You have also tacked up some tear sheets in a few of the supermarkets and laundromats around the school area.

One day in July a man calls you. He identifies himself as Trent Bemis III. He is in need of a piano player who can read. You would be filling in with a Dixieland Band. You know you can read anything, so that part of the job doesn't bother you. You are also sure that one of your friends will have a Dixieland fake book of tunes you can borrow. When Mr. Bemis describes the job he also mentions the address. You know this is a big money neighborhood along the river. He also tells you that although the actual playing will only be a few hours, they would like you there from Noon on. You can join them for lunch and you will be paid for eight hours. The money sounds great, the hours are early, and in that neighborhood this should be a classy party. You accept the job. He tells you the dress code is to be casual. He would like you in white slacks and sneakers with a white top. No problem. You've got all that. The deal is set.

SUNDAY, JULY 9 - You are up early, well rested and looking forward to making some great money for a limited amount of work. Usually, when you have long hours with not too much playing time, it means you are either alternating with another group or you may be playing early, then breaking for the dinner hour and playing again. It could also mean that there are some speeches or announcements or even another act of some sort. There could be a dozen variables. Although split work can be boring at times, it is on the clock and the money is good.

You have your wardrobe in order. White clamdigger pants, white sleeveless blouse, red and white belt and white sneakers and socks. You decide to wear your hair up with barretts and a headband. That way you can let it down later if you want.

This outfit should be exactly what the doctor ordered. Nothing too sexy but clean. You bring along a handbag with just the basic essentials and a fake book which you have borrowed. By 11 A.M. you have left your apartment just off campus. You stop for a coffee and donut and make the thirty minute trip to the jobsite, locating it without incident. You can just see the roofline of the house. It is set back from the road and protected from view by dozens of trees and tall shrubbery. There is a curving 800-foot driveway ending at a circle and a three car garage. Ten or twelve vehicles are parked on the blacktop and grass. You park alongside a bronze SUV and get out.

The houses in this section are perched atop a bank some fifty feet above the river. You walk up to the house and knock on the door. A nice looking woman in a maid's uniform answers. You ask for Trent Bemis. She tells you that everyone is down at the boathouse and points to another small blacktop drive which you did not notice when you arrived. You thank her and make your way over to it which leads downhill to a landing below. There is another small parking area with a jeep and another SUV sitting there. All the grassy grounds around the lot and down the hill abound in beautiful floral settings. To the left is a huge boathouse that appears to be new. It's white with dark green trim—flowers and shrubs line its wall. At the water end are three tall, steel rollup doors. As you walk along this bottom lot you can hear voices which seem to be coming from an open door on the side. You enter and see at least a dozen people swarming over a large cabin cruiser. It has been decorated with large posters of movie stars, ribbons, balloons, and some sort of big smoke stack on its roof. You ask the first person you meet about Trent Bemis and he tells you that you will find him out on the front sundeck. You thank him and make your way past three slips and out another door onto a redwood sundeck. It is extremely spacious, tastefully decorated with matching umbrella tables, chairs and swing sofas. There is a barbeque grill at one end and a small bar along the wall. Small groups are milling about with drinks in hand. You ask again for Trent Bemis and for the first time you meet him. Mr. Bemis is a full-fledged yuppy. His gray hair is combed perfectly and is probably sprayed with lacquer. He has silver-rimmed glasses with clip-on sunglasses and as he speaks to you, you detect a slight Oxford accent. You peg him at about fifty-years-old and very proper. You introduce yourself and he says he is happy to have you there. He asks you to join him at a table to talk about the job. As the two of you sit down, another man joins you. He is fortyish and looks like last night did not treat him well. A bit of a beard but nothing fancy, brownish blonde hair and ears that seem to be too big for his head. Sort of dippy looking. His name turns out to be Dirk Dork and you figure the shoe fits.

Trent begins to tell you the whole story. The local yacht club, WHITE SAILS MOTOR YACHT ASSOCIATION, is celebrating its 75th anniversary and has organized a boat parade especially for the occasion. Your host is the owner of the big cruiser in the boathouse and a past commodore of the club. His name is Doyle Dinkrubber but his friends call him "the Commodore." He has invited some friends to come along on his cruiser, "The Sea Bitch." They have in turn all helped to decorate it with the theme "SHOWBOAT." He hopes to grab a prize with this theme. There is also a category for best NOVELTY CRAFT.

"In 1925," says Trent, "there was a Dixieland Band at the club. My grandfather and Dirk's grandfather both played in that band, and we thought it would be great to re-create the band. Since we are both in a band these days, we got the guys to agree to play this job with us. Our piano man got sick on Friday and can't do the job with us. This is where you come in."

So far, so good. You don't see a problem with this setup.

PIANO and WATER

THE BIGGEST ENEMY OF ANY PIANO IS MOISTURE!

Trent continues, "We thought we'd have the band right up on the front deck of the cruiser but Doyle found out that the upright is 800 pounds and Bob, the piano man weighs 370. Then he wanted no part of the band on his boat. So we came up with an even better idea. Two years ago when all this landing and boathouse construction was going on, the contractor built a huge raft. He used it for sandblasting and painting all the sheet steel piling. It was in the water for two years and at the end of the job it was so heavy and waterlogged that the contractor couldn't lift it out of the water. He didn't want to pay for a crane so he gave it to Doyle. Doyle lets the kids play on it and swim from it. Since it has a little outboard motor to move it around the harbor, we decided to make it into a separate parade float. We're going to enter it as a novelty float and we're sure to be a winner."

Now you are wondering about the sanity of this man. All the while Trent has been talking Dirk has just been nodding, smiling, and sipping on some sort of a mixed drink.

You ask Trent, "And just where is this raft?"

He raises his arms and points his thumb over his shoulder toward the river side of the sundeck. The deck is about seven feet over the water and you can't see anything. He gets up and motions you to follow him to the railing. Now you have your first glimpse of the jobsite.

The raft is ten feet wide and twenty-two feet long. It is made from five timbers, twenty-four inches square, bolted together. It has huge metal eye bolts at all four corners. As it rests in the water the deck level is about six inches above the water level. There is a table obviously taken from the sundeck and six wooden chairs all sitting on the deck. Someone has built a half-ass wooden framework out of two-by-fours. It spans the entire front of the raft and has an oilcloth banner stapled to it. The lettering says: "SEA OTTERS JAZZ BAND." Now your eyes move to the piano. A plain brown upright with no front panel on it. On both sides someone has taped paper signs reading "1925 RETURNS." A three-and-a-half horsepower Firestone outboard motor is mounted on the back.

The image of a fine waterfront party with smooth operators and glitzy ladies has now been reduced to a suicide ride on a hunk of wood with a bunch of shit-faced musicians. Water is not your biggest interest. You have done some swimming in the school pool, you love the beaches, you'd love a ride on that big cruiser, but this raft deal is not high on your priority list. You have seen *Jaws* twice. You know if a shark can eat a fishing boat it can surely raise hell with a raft. Then you remember there are no sharks in the river. Okay. Compose yourself. Don't freak out just yet. Remember the money, honey.

People are sitting around on the sundeck and you hear a voice calling, "Alright, everyone. Foody, foody. Get your lips around some fine snacks before we leave."

Trent turns around and then tells you to turn and meet your hostess, Loretta Dinkrubber, the Commodore's wife. She is downing a Bloody Mary as Trent introduces her. "Loretta, this is Gail Wind. She will be playing the piano on the raft." Mrs. Dinkrubber gives you the once over and looks at Trent.

"You got a girl to replace Bob? There was no girl in the original Sea Otters Band. You sure you're doing the right thing? Could cost you points on authenticity. Bob looked like a real piano man."

She walked away without ever speaking to you. You feel crushed. She hasn't even heard you play. What's her problem?

You comment, "Well, I can see she doesn't want me around."

"You must understand that Bob is her favorite," said Trent. You would find out later that Bob really does weigh in at 370 pounds and she only likes him because he outweighs her by two pies.

"Just let it be, Gail. She has a lot on her mind getting this party organized," said Trent.

No, this woman has aggravated you. It seems a trait of human nature that we accept people we like at face value, overlooking oddities or shortcomings. But let someone get your goat or cut you short, and you are prone to think bad thoughts and make degrading comments—even pick them apart and make fun at their expense. On this occasion you are thinking these thoughts about this tub of tuna lady. You wish one or more of your school chums were here to share some laughs and sooth your damaged pride.

Trent has momentarily walked to another part of the deck, leaving you alone to ponder Mrs. Dinkrubber. She is probably sixty. Freckled and tanless with snow white skin. She is wearing a two-piece swim suit, chartreuse with nautical flags all over. There's enough material in those two pieces to make a sun cover for a new Volkswagen. She has dark sneakers, sort of grayish black. You wonder if they might have been earthmover tires. They're about the same color and just the right ticket for that payload. As she turns toward you, her face is fully rounded with a double chin. You surmise that at one time she was kidnapped and held hostage in an "ALL-YOU-CAN-EAT" restaurant, chained to the buffet table. She was forced to eat day and night until the ransom was paid which took two years while the Commodore took time to weigh his options. Getting a full view of her, you also note that her knees are red and blotchy. Probably irritated when she was crawling around in the backyard, grazing. You think about her standing in front of a bank surveillance camera and hearing it shift up to wide angle. Then her face comes onto the screen and the camera just shuts off. And speaking of cameras, wouldn't her wide white back be a great home movie screen? Better yet, how about plastering a big Budweiser decal on it. The kind you see on the bottom of swimming pools. Oh well, screw her. You have a job to do. You take one last look at her. She's walking away from you and it looks like her ass is chewing gum. Where's Trent?

You find him at a table with four other men. One of them is Dirk Dork. Trent grabs you by the hand and introduces the other band members. They are Forrest Shortsox,

Ned Nod, and Quentin Roadramp. They are average looking men and nothing sets off any internal alarms. You tell them of your schooling and show them the fake book of *100 Dixieland Favorites* which you have borrowed. They all nod in approval and look through it. Then you find out that these guys are in a polka band and they've never played Dixie either. It was Trent's theory that the band could practice while en route to the job. You ask about this "en route" term.

It seems the club is located eight miles upstream and the Commodore has decided that he will tow the raft behind the cruiser to get there. Once upstream from the judge's stand, we can use the little motor to power us past the review board.

"Okay," says Trent, "time to get the jackets and hats. They're inside next to the changing room door." Inside there is a clothes rack with six red and white candy striped suit jackets. Each one has a name inside and they hand you the one marked Bob. This must be a joke. Bob is 370 pounds and you are 140. There's enough material left over to make a main sail for the Kon-Tiki. You call their attention to the very obvious misfit. They laugh and say, "A tuck here, a fold there and no one will be the wiser." Quentin calls to a young woman standing nearby. She walks over to your group and he introduces her to you.

"This is Bebe Wasserman. Mr. and Mrs. Dinkrubber's daughter."

She is rather attractive and you wonder how the sea cow could have produced this creature. You also think you have seen her somewhere before.

Quentin says, "Bebe honey, Gail has to wear Bob's jacket. It needs a few tucks. Could you help her out?"

"Sure, Quent. Come on honey. I've got some stuff in the bedroom on the cruiser."

"We'll be out on the raft when you're done," says Trent. "Don't forget your hat." There are half a dozen styrofoam imitation straw hats in a box on the floor and everyone grabs one as they exit. You take yours to avoid forgetting it later.

Bebe is decked out in pink shorts and a pink halter top. The shorts are set off by a silver metal belt that looks like a big watch band. She has white sneakers and pink socks rolled down at the top. Her walk indicates that she knows she has something to display and is not missing any chance to flaunt it. You both climb aboard the cruiser. She sweeps her arm like a model showing a refrigerator on a quiz show.

"This is Daddy's newest boat. It is two years old, forty-six feet long, has all the bells and whistles, diesel power, flying bridge, and sleeps eight. We just love it."

Below deck you step into the master bedroom. She opens a drawer in the dressing table and pulls out a plastic box. You see needles and thread and scissors and safety pins. She tells you to stand straight and still and starts pulling together a bunch here and there, pinning as she goes. You finally remember where you saw her. She was a lackluster actress on a TV commercial. It was for some beauty cream made of muskrat sweat and rose petals. The ad ran in the 3 A.M. time slot and you saw it on your way to the bathroom that night you fell asleep with the TV on.

"Okay, Gail, I've done what I can. It's not perfect, but it's a lot better than it was."

You ask her to take a few rolls on the cuffs and to pin them also. You exit the sleeping quarters and make your way up to the main seating area. You are amazed at how much space there is inside this boat. Wide aisles, oversized chairs in the dining area and all sorts of room on the rear deck. Then you flash back to the wife and everything falls into place.

As you walk through the boathouse, you and Bebe pass the sea cow. This time she has her right hand up to her mouth. Something she has probably done three million times before. You assume she is eating a pie with her hands. She mumbles something to Bebe, who asks to be excused. You thank her for her help and go out to the sundeck. You notice that many of the people are starting to get into show biz costumes. The Commodore, however, is dressed as the Commodore and he probably never gets out of that outfit. The light gray trousers, white shirt, blue blazer with the club crest on it and his white captain's hat with the black bill covered in gold braid. He is a tall, wiry man with curly gray hair. He is handsome for his age. You guess he is married to the Misses either because she's swimming in cash or because he got drunk at the club and signed on as an active member of a "Save the Whales" movement.

Down at the end of the sundeck you spot one of the band members. It is Quentin, standing with a very shapely and attractive brunette. He introduces you to his date, Spacey Notthome. She is a performer in the circus. She does tightrope, trampoline and Quentin. She is in town for a two-week visit.

A gate is open in the railing. It gives way to a wooden ladder fastened to the steel breakwall. Apparently it is used by the swimmers to get up and down from the deck. Today it is the raft's boarding ladder. Quentin says that Spacey has helped him to carry all the band stuff down the hill to the boathouse.

You look for a minute and think you would have paid $10 to see Mrs. Dinkrubber come down that hill. You picture her breaking the crest and picking up speed until her chubby legs are a blur, like the driving arms connected to the wheels of a speeding locomotive. It's a wonder she didn't shoot right off the end of the breakwall into the river. They probably had a pickup truck in front of her to retard her descent. You are positive it will take a pickup truck to get her back up to the house.

"Your turn, Gail. Here, I'll give you a hand," says Quentin.

You climb down the ladder and drop onto the deck of the raft. Now you are really aware of how low this thing is sitting in the water. You figure about six inches between the plane of the deck and the level of the river. Good thing it's calm.

Since you first set eyes on the raft much has been added. There is a nine by twelve-foot oriental rug on deck. Why a rug? Because there is a mossy slime on deck. The rug helps keep the chairs and table from sliding around. Two guys are hoisting a twenty-foot pole called a skittering pole. It has the U.S. flag, the boat club flag, and a third flag with three musical notes on it. They are tying that to the wood frame up front for the banner. There are two big plastic coolers near the band area. Three of the chairs have metal music stands in front of them. There is also a microphone near the chairs. The cord for the mike stand runs along the deck to an amplifier. The amp is on top of your piano with two speakers that are so big they hang over the sides. There is a small gasoline-powered generator tied to one leg of the piano. A gas can is also tied to the same leg and is tucked inside the leg to keep it out of the hot sun. There is no stool or bench, instead there is a beer keg with a pillow on top. You are told that big Bob preferred the keg to avoid breaking the wooden seats. The piano is set up so that you are looking over the rear of the raft; if you could see over the top of the upright, which you cannot. That means you are sitting up with your back to the band. You strike a few notes on the piano. Seems in tune but for sure it is no powerhouse. You can feel the greasy slime on your sneaker bottoms now and you walk carefully. You step around behind the piano and see a mike wired to the backside. You notice that the power cord for the amp is plugged into the little generator receptacle box. You have your fake book with you but with all the garbage on top of the piano, there is no room for it. You lay it on the piano just above the keyboard. Now you realize that with no front panel on the piano there's no place to rest the book even if you did want to use it. So much for that idea. You sit down on the barrel. The pillow is really not that thick; you can feel the steel outer ring of the barrel against your butt. You put on your hat and find that with your hair piled up it is too high for the hat. You figure it would look like a soup bowl on an elephant's ass. Time to talk to Trent.

You walk carefully over to the band members. They are unpacking the instruments from their cases and two of the music stands now have fake books placed on them. Those are the books that give you the basic chord changes for the tunes. Trent apologizes that your book is at Bob's house and they need theirs so there is no spare.

"Not to worry, Trent," you say. "I've got no place to put it anyway."

"Well, tell you what," he says, "if we keep the generator going all the time, the amp will be on. When we play into our mike you can hear it over the speakers and follow along."

"Great!" you reply.

You now peek into a large cardboard box. It's full of strings of colored Christmas lights, extension cords, clotheslines, and a few tools.

"What's all this?" you ask.

"Oh, that's for tonight. There are two judgings. One is in the afternoon and the other is after dark. For the best lighting effects."

It's only a little after 1 P.M. and he's already talking about an after dark light show. This being mid-summer, that would be sometime about 9 P.M. tonight. What the hell kind of a job have you gotten yourself into here?

Forrest is already pulling a beer can out of the cooler. Stacey and Quentin are playing tonsil hockey up on the sundeck. Dirk has his shoes and socks off and is smoking a cigarette which looks suspiciously like a reefer. Now Stacey is climbing down the ladder with a camera. "Kodak moment guys," she says. You decide that if you are going to be in the photos, you are going to drop your hair. Removing your hat, you snap the barrett and take off your headband. Your auburn hair falls over your shoulders. You reach into your pants pocket and grab your short comb. You run that through your hair a few dozen times and you are all set. You replace your hat, put the thin elastic tie down under your chin and it feels great. No one really noticed you fooling with your hair and when they do spot you all the guys can say is, "WOW! Looks great, but now the judges will know you're a girl for sure."

You decide to ignore that observation. With this size sixty jacket you're wearing, the judges will probably think you are a balloon on loan from the Macy's Thanksgiving Day parade. Stacey takes five group photos aboard the raft and three more from the sundeck railing. In the last three you are all looking up with hats in hands and laughing. As Stacey closes and locks the gate above the ladder you realize that this is now the real thing. You are actually going to sea with these nitwits. You secretly hope that God will remember all the good things you have done in your life and that He will protect you on this journey. You think it would be cute to holler "weigh anchor!" but you have observed that there is none. This is the first time you gave that any thought. Also, no life jackets, no fire extinguisher and no toilet. You pretty much know what these guys are going to do if they have to pee. Your options as a girl are to pee your pants or jump overboard into the river. You try hard not to dwell on that issue just now.

Two of the guys are untying the ropes from the breakwall and as they push off they are moving the raft with a hand-over-hand operation along the wall and into the deeper waters. You hear a muffled roar as white smoke comes from an open doorway at one of the boathouse slips. The cruiser is backing out into the same area. It looks great as the sun hits it—very colorful indeed. You spot the Commodore up on the bridge and watch him carefully maneuver the large craft around. Soon he has it in a position enabling him to back up to the front of the raft. You are watching a line of ducks swim by the raft. The mother and eight little babies all in a single line. You smile as she proudly parades her family in review. (You seldom take into consideration that this same mother duck when flying over your head could be as lethal as a bomber over Pearl Harbor—and just as accurate.)

The cruiser inches its way back to the raft and some men throw white nylon lines to the band members up front. They tie each line into a front steel eyebolt on the two front corners. This done, the cruiser moves slowly forward until the ropes are tight— the men on board the cruiser working to equalize their lengths. You observe that the lines are about twenty-five feet long. The ropes are now fastened securely to the rear cleats on the cruiser and a small wash comes up from behind the cruiser as power is sent to the propellers. Slowly the cruiser pulls you out between the tall wooden pilings which mark the channel and now you are in the river and the raft is moving upstream. Everyone seems pleased with the setup and the men of the band return to their chairs. The sixth chair is for you, but Trent suggests that you go to the piano and get organized for the practice session. You move carefully from the rug to the piano and plop your fanny on the barrel. You decide for the moment to rest your back against the keyboard and watch the towing operation and see what the band is going to do. They have a cornet, trombone, clarinet, banjo and guitar. Ned Nod is on guitar, which actually turns out to be an electric bass. He sets it on the chair and comes back towards you dragging an electric cord. It will not reach from the generator to him so he takes an extension cord from the box full of Christmas lights and adds it to make the connection.

"Are you ready Trent?" he asks. "Yeah boy, give us some juice."

Ned leans over the generator, gives three pulls on the starting cord and it springs to life. Tied to the piano leg it vibrates a bit and you can feel it in the small of your back as you lean against the wood. Next a voice comes from the speakers. "Testing, one, two, three, four, testing." It is Trent speaking into the mike in front of the band. You swing around and run a few chords on the piano but you don't hear it over the speakers. "Hey Trent," you shout, "I'm not coming over the speakers."

"Maybe your mike's not turned on. Check it out."

Your start around the piano to check the mike on the backside and realize it is a whole new ballgame walking on this slime when the raft is in motion. One slip and you are "man overboard." You inch your way back to the mike and sure enough you see that the button is in the "off" position. Now you ask yourself, "Do I touch this metal mike with my bare hands while my sneakers are wet and the generator is running?" You extend one finger and jab the mike once or twice to see if you get a spark or a jolt. There is none, and you move the button to the "ON" position and return to your seat. You play a few more chords and this time you hear your music over the speakers.

Trent again. "Turn up the knob so we can hear you better."

Sure. He's letting you touch all the electrical shit now that you're at sea. You move the dial until there is a squeal from the speakers and then back it off two notches. Again you strike some notes and now the piano is really hefty. Lots of sound. You can also hear Ned tuning up his electric bass. The others are screwing around too, but no song has been called as yet. It seems to you that the raft has picked up a little speed. You turn around and look forward to the cruiser. The wake coming from the rear of the cruiser seems bigger now. You can also smell the diesel fumes in the air.

Two more revelations: One, you notice that your feet are getting soaked; and two, because this raft has a square nose, it does not cut through the water like the cruiser. It plows through the water and what it cannot push aside comes washing over the deck. The oriental rug is under a few inches of moving water and all the guys in the band are also experiencing the "wet foot" syndrome. Somebody did not think this towing project through. All the people on the cruiser seem relaxed, and nobody is watching the raft anymore.

You also observe that the cruiser and raft are not the only vessels around today. A lot of boats are passing by and gawking at you. After all, from a distance it looks like the whole band is just sitting on the water. A person would have to get up close to actually see the raft itself. Trent calls to you over the mike.

"We're going to try 'The Memphis Blues' in 'B' flat."

You have never heard "The Memphis Blues" in your life. Maybe you can fake your way along. Once they start it off you are convinced that they have never heard it either. You won't be able to follow at all. You grab the fake book you brought and check the index. Good news. "Memphis Blues" page 74. Now, how do you look at the book and play? There's no place to set it and if you don't hold the book open it flops shut. As you sit there listening to the band fumble their way through the song, you spot the strip of duct tape wrapped around the amp. There must be some on board. The only supply box you can see is the Christmas tree light box and you get up to look in there. As you get up, the pillow sticks to your butt and then falls on the slime covered deck awash with water. You grab it as quickly as you can but it has instantly soaked up a good bit of water and it is soggy. You drop it back on the keg and move to the box. That has also soaked up some deck water. The box is about thirty inches tall and the dark water marks are about halfway up. Yes, there is a partial roll of duct tape and you grab it. Taking the fake book you open it to page 74 and see that the tune continues over to page 75 so you will get most of it. You hold the book up and tape the corners to the front edge of the piano top so it will hang in front of you. Not the best way perhaps, but today it is the only way. You walk up to Trent and ask if they would start over once you get back to the piano. You take your place at the piano and when they think you are ready, they start again. You play your part but it sounds like shit. It dawns on you that the band is playing in 'B' flat and your version is in 'E' flat. If you want to do this tune, you'll have to mentally transpose to their key as you go. It would help if you had ever heard this song. You do your best, taking special care to listen to the cornet and the bass to get the melody and the beat. There seems to be some disturbance or interference on the speakers. After listening closely, you realize that your mike is also broadcasting the sound of the generator engine.

Trent decides that the group should try a different song and he calls for "The Darktown Strutter's Ball" in 'C'. You try to remove the duct tape from the book and the corners of the pages rip off. Oh well, move on to page 20 and re-tape. Good, this time the book version is also in 'C'. Boats are now pulling alongside to hear the music. Their engine noises interfere and their waves, however small, are contributing to the deck wash. You also notice in this number you can't hear the bass notes. You look over your shoulder to see why you can't hear Ned. It's because his guitar is on the chair and he is busy with the clothesline tying the chairs together and anchoring them to the table. Another sign that all might not be well. As he finishes, he runs the end of the line up to a front corner and ties it into one of the big steel eyelets. You watch him go back to his guitar and the song starts over again. This time it doesn't go too badly. Trent calls for yet another run through and you feel that this one is a keeper.

Someone walks by. It is Forrest going back behind the piano to take a leak. With the other boats nearby this is like pissing in the middle of the Thruway. Apparently he is far enough along with his drinking that his social graces have been compromised. You now notice that your butt is wet too. The water has soaked all the way through the pillow.

The cruiser and raft are running up the middle of the river. You stand up to unstick your wet pants from your butt. You glance ahead to the cruiser and notice a virtual armada of small boats not too far ahead. In the distance you see what looks like a tall structure on a dock. Maybe it's the judges' stand. The band is on a break and Forrest has rejoined them.

You are once again resting your back against the keyboard when a huge cloud bursts forth from the smokestack atop the cruiser's roof. It is pure white against the bright blue sky. A group of sea gulls escorting the boat makes a hasty retreat to avoid instant asphyxiation. The resulting cloud hits its peak height and then due to your forward motion it settles down right on top of the raft. What is this shit? The guys in the band are laughing like hell so you move up there to see what you are missing. Your first question to Trent is, "What is all that smoke?"

"Neat, huh? They have a large industrial compressed air bottle hooked up to a 300-pound sandblasting pot. They've filled the pot with white flour and soap flakes and they're blowing it through a large rubber hose and up the smoke stack. It looks great but I think they have to regulate the quantity a bit."

You fail to see the humor in this and go back to the piano which now looks like there is an early morning frost on it. The white stuff is everywhere. On the keys too, damn it.

Trent calls for another number. You are losing your interest already. Your butt's wet and you are feeling nausea from the diesel fumes. You don't have anything to wipe off the keys either. You rip the tape from your fake book and of course it takes off another two corners on pages 20 and 21. You look for the newest selection, "Bye Bye Blackbird," and you don't have it in the book—you'll have to fake this one. This tune sounds like the boys know what they're doing and you halfway get the gist of it. It is in the key of 'F,' an easy key to work with.

Out of the corner of your eye you see something big and white moving past. You glance over to behold a sightseeing boat two decks high that must be 200 feet long. It is traveling in the opposite direction of the raft and people are standing all along the upper and lower railings looking at the raft and decorated cruiser. Although you are going rather slowly, the sightseeing boat is not. It is throwing about a three foot wake as it passes. Not an unusual wake for a boat that size but for a raft sitting six inches above the water it's a big deal. You prepare for the inevitable wash. Pushing the keg barrel back a bit you put your feet up on the keyboard. In a short time the wake catches the raft from the side. The waves pass just under the keyboard and you can even feel your barrel moving a bit. As soon as it has stopped you turn around to look at the band. They are all in a circle, instruments on their laps and holding hands. Drifting out in the water you can see two plastic coolers and the remnants of the cardboard Christmas tree light box. Yes, this surely was a great idea—this raft thing.

As everyone settles down, it seems more quiet and serene. What was different before? Oh yeah, the generator was running. Now it's not. It must have submerged and quit. There doesn't seem to be a need to practice any more tunes. In your opinion, this trip is now becoming more a question of survival. Soon the cruiser is slowing and the continual wash along the raft's deck has stopped. As you look forward there must be fifty or sixty boats of all sizes anchored in front of the club. Apparently this is the spectator group which was not confined to land viewing of the parade. There are eight or ten orange buoy's floating in a long line. They are about seventy-five to one hundred feet out from the dock and you assume they are marking the parade route. A large coast Guard vessel is there as well. It has a big crane thing on the back and you figure the Commodore probably paid them to bring it there in case Loretta falls overboard.

The clubhouse is a long, rambling wooden building sprawling across more than half the grassy lot. A long dock extends from the bulkhead, splitting the man-made boat harbor in half. The end of the T-dock goes in both directions for about sixty feet. Then there is that tall structure you spotted earlier rising about fifteen feet into the air. It is all wood with a peak roof on it. Half a dozen people are up there and you assume they are the judges. The cruiser continues to tow you slowly upstream—everyone on it completely oblivious to your recent swamping.

There are large slips on both sides of the dock filled with big cruisers. Along the outer edges of the harbor are more docking facilities. Small catwalks on pipes jut out from the concrete breakwalls—apparently used for smaller craft.

Once you have all settled down, Trent and Ned come back to see how you are doing. You let them know that you are concerned. They assure you that the raft has come this far and things will calm down. Just ahead, several dozen cruisers are gathered in groups of two and three. Some are tied to each other and anchored in place. Others are running and maneuvering to hold their position against the current. This, after all, is not a lake with still water but rather a river with a downstream current of about 5 m.p.h. The parade will head downstream to the judging stand with the aid of the current when the time is right.

As the cruiser pulls you up to the head of the pack it slows even more. Two men are at the rear of the cruiser hollering for someone to untie the ropes from the raft. "You can use your outboard motor to make your way into line for the parade," one man shouts. Trent moves to the front of the raft while Ned is behind the piano getting the motor started. Surprisingly it starts right up and he gives it full power to move upstream to the rear of the cruiser, where the lines are cast off. The little motor barely moves the raft against the current. With the lines removed, you and the crew are on your own. A small outboard boat operated by a man and woman pulls alongside the raft and the woman hands you a large card. It is about two-feet square and has a large number twenty-four in black on a white background. You take it from the lady and she says, "Show this card as you pass in review." As the outboard pulls away and approaches the Sea Bitch, you see her hand them a card also.

Ned is now trying to get the raft into position to wait for the parade to begin. The problem is that he cannot sit or kneel to move the arm that steers the motor and be able to see forward over the piano. He's flying blind! Another well conceived part of this cockamamie plan. He asks you to be his eyes and tell him what to do. Occasionally he stands up to look over the piano, but most of the time he is kneeling next to the little motor. The green slime on the deck has stained the knees of his white pants.

The cruiser is standing still in the water as the Commodore plays with the throttles to maintain his position. Ever so slowly you pass him and head upstream. Everyone comes to the side and cheers you on. As a special salute they blow the air horn and POOF! another white cloud blows from the stack. Yes, another rain of flour and soap flakes. This time there is no water coming over the deck to wash it away and in two minutes the whole deck is covered with white film. You can feel it in your hair and on the keyboard. Several more minutes of upstream fighting and Ned steers the raft hard left to start his swing, hoping to get the nose pointed downstream. This swing takes about five minutes and now the raft is in position. It is within the channel boundaries marked off by the orange buoys, the club dock, and the judges' stand. All there is to do now is wait for our turn to enter the parade.

Soon there are green flags flying from the reviewing stand—apparently the "GO" sign. You hear Ned swearing and step back to ask him what's wrong.

"The goddamned current is taking us downstream and I don't have an anchor."

"Gosh Ned, what can we do about this?" you ask.

"I guess I'll have to reverse the engine," he answers.

This is an old motor and does not have a reverse gear selector. When you want to reverse this motor, that's exactly what you do. You turn the whole motor backwards. This puts the steering handle out toward the river and you put your hands around the rear engine cover to steer it. Ned puts full power to the motor and spins it around. Three-and-one-half horsepower might be neat at the boathouse, but it's a pain in the ass in this current.

The little outboard boat with the man and woman is anchored a few hundred feet downstream from the raft. They are holding up duplicate cards with the big numbers and as your number comes up, you are to move into line and proceed to review. These folks are also dictating the spacing of the boats.

The little motor is screaming its ass off to hold the raft in position. You find a free moment to leave Ned and tend to the piano. The signs on the sides of it now say nothing. They are just dozens of vertical tears of red sign paint destroyed by the splashing water. You try to brush off the keys with the cuff of your jacket. You play a few chords. The water is getting to the piano because some of the wooden keys have swelled up and when you push them down, they don't come back up. GREAT!

You walk up to Trent and ask him what he is going to do for a tune while we are parading.

"I think the 'Darktown Strutter's Ball' in 'C' would be a good one," he replies.

"What about the generator and the speakers?" you ask.

"Oh yeah, shit. I completely forgot about that. Let me see if I can get the generator going again."

Both of you return to the side of the piano and he leans down and gives three or four tugs on the starting cord. No response. He leans around in back of the piano and asks Ned how to get the thing going again.

"Probably have to dry off the spark plug," Ned shouts over the motor noise. "It's down on the side of the motor."

Trent takes a look and spots the white porcelain of the plug. Pulling a handkerchief from his pocket, he takes the plug wire off and attempts to dry the plug. He gives the starting cord a few more pulls. Still no response.

You look at him and say, "Probably should hook the wire up again."

He looks at you with a sheepish grin and reattaches the wire. A few more pulls and the motor starts. You are back in business. You glance downstream to the card boat and they are showing number eight. Cruisers and speedboats full of people are taking their places as directed and the parade is underway. Ned is doing his best to keep the raft still and it seems to be holding its own. A few large boats come past and all the folks aboard give you thumbs up and cheer. A speedboat pulls alongside with four young guys in it. They stick out a paddle which they have screwed on a cup holder with a cold beer. Without a second thought you grab it and laugh. They pull away waving to you. You wonder who on this float deserves this cold beer now that the coolers are gone? You also wonder if any of them saw you take it. You take a few sips yourself and give the rest to Ned. He's going to need it.

Flocks of sea gulls are circling overhead, apparently attracted by all the activity and the possibility that some bird lover will toss bread or other food over the side. The show cards now call for number seventeen—your time is drawing near. You go up to Trent and ask when you will start playing.

"I think we'll save it until we get near the reviewing stand. We are not as good as I had hoped, and there's no use wasting time playing stuff we don't know just to pass the time and perhaps embarrass ourselves." You agree with that theory.

In a few minutes the Commodore pulls the Sea Bitch alongside—Bebe at the rail. "What number do you have, Gail?"

"Twenty-four," you shout.

"Okay, we are twenty-three so we'll go ahead."

You wonder how they got twenty-three after you got twenty-four. Oh well, what's the difference?

Twenty-three comes up in the card boat and the Sea Bitch begins its run down parade lane. You step behind the piano and tell Ned that the raft is next. You will let him know when they flash the card. It seems to you that the decks are very slippery. The soap flakes have soaked up the deck water and made a fine paste which is slicker than hell.

Card number twenty-four comes up and you give Ned the word. The Sea Bitch is now about 200 feet downstream. Ned swings the outboard motor around to forward position. The combination of the motor and the current starts you on your way downstream rather quickly. You are hollering for him to move out to the center of the lane. With the motor revving he is trying to change the line of travel. The raft is very heavy and it responds slowly. Soon you have gained more speed and are on the right track. You are thinking about playing now and suddenly you ask yourself, "If he is steering and I am helping by watching, who is playing the bass and piano?"

"Ned, how are you going to run the motor and play the bass too?" you ask.

"I can't. We should have had someone to run this motor, but I'll have to do it. You get on the keys. I'll try to look over the top of the piano now and then. We should be okay, it's not that far."

Filled with apprehension, you take your place at the piano. Now both the noise of the generator and the outboard motor are coming over the speakers. Trent hollers, "Show time!" You listen for the first note and you will blend in from there. The band starts with the intro and you strike your first chords. About eight keys do not come back up. You play a few more chords and now twelve keys are stuck down. You are playing full chords with your hands but only a few notes are coming out of the speakers. No time to make any changes, you must do the best you can. At the conclusion of the tune you turn around to look downstream.

The Sea Bitch is now in front of the reviewing stand and it looks like it is stopped. Apparently the Commodore wants everyone to hear the show tunes blasting over the boom box and he'd also like to get off one good blast of "smoke." One problem. The raft is now traveling about 10 m.p.h. and closing in fast on the Sea Bitch. You run around the piano and holler to Ned. "Better slow down, we're coming up on the Commodore!"

Ned stands up and realizes he must reverse the motor to avoid a collision. He swings it around and implements full power. Nothing happens. The momentum and tremendous weight of the raft are more than the little motor can overcome. A state of panic is setting in, calling for emergency action. Knowing he can't count on the cruiser pulling ahead in time, Ned decides he has to pass it. Can't go left, too many boats in the spectator line. Got to go right, between the dock and the cruiser. Looks like about a forty foot wide gap. He leaves the motor at full power and swings it to a position which should steer them to the right. The reaction seems to take forever but slowly the raft is turning toward the dock and it appears it will miss the cruiser.

Just as the raft is about to pass, someone on the cruiser alerts the Commodore, who panics and throws the Sea Bitch into full power ahead to make room. Now the raft is slowly heading for the end of the dock. Ned swings the motor around to turn the raft to the left. It starts to turn, but the huge wash thrown by the Sea Bitch pushes the front of the raft to the right. The raft just grazes the last piling on the main dock. The overhanging deck planking on the dock rips down the two-by-four upright holding the oil cloth banner and also drops the skittering pole back onto the deck.

The little motor is still screaming and contributing to the continued forward motion of the raft. You stare in horror as you realize the raft is going to hit the outermost catwalk across from the dock. People on the catwalk are already starting to scatter to make room for the oncoming raft. Ned now has the motor in full reverse, which is like taking a piss on a warehouse fire.

Forrest and Quentin are the first two to abandon ship—instruments in hand. Dirk is next, running to the rear, past you, and diving off.

Trent runs to the rear and joins you and ashen-faced Ned behind the piano. You are riding an armor-free dreadnought. The raft plows into the steel pipe supporting the catwalk and snaps the 'C' clamp holding the pipe to the wood like it was plastic. The pipe bends down but does not break, and the raft rides its left side up the pipe and stops abruptly. This is just enough to have it list to the right. The impact snaps the clothesline retaining the left side of the piano and it swings around to the right. You all grab for it at the same time but with all the soap on the deck it is to no avail. The piano rolls over the side into the river. It takes with it the generator and gas can which were tied to the leg and all the sound equipment sitting on its top. In fifteen seconds the harbor water is clear and calm. The only trace of this horrific experience is the empty beer keg stool floating around. The raft is under the catwalk with the oil cloth banner and framework laying back on the deck. The chairs and table have all slid to the front but are still on board. Two motorboats are there in a flash. One is helping Forrest out of the water. Dirk has swum to the raft and is now hanging on to the back end. Quentin is at the second catwalk and people are helping to pull him from the water. Apparently no one upstream knows about this yet and the parade of boats keeps moving by. The man in the second boat takes you on board and throws a line to Trent and Ned. They are still shaking. He tells them to hook the line to an eyebolt and he will tow the raft into the harbor. In a few minutes the raft is alongside the concrete retaining wall and you are safely back on land.

A crowd has gathered. Stacey appears from the throng with Quentin on her arm. He looks like a drowned rat. The other boat pulls alongside the raft and Forrest climbs onto the raft and then onto land. He does not have his trombone. A pair of medics have also come to the scene and are asking about the injured. Fortunately, that applies only to the band's pride.

The Commodore is now aware that something bad has taken place but he cannot cross the parade line because of the tightly packed row of spectator crafts. He is forced to go up river and return via the parade line. Soon he turns the Sea Bitch into the club harbor and noses back toward the raft. He turns the cruiser sideways so it is parallel to the raft and everyone comes to the side to gaze. They are anxious to see any damages and also to check on the welfare of the band/crew members. The Commodore comes down from the bridge, and as he moves to the stern he motions to Trent who comes to the side of the cruiser. They engage in some heated conversation, then Trent shakes his head and walks away. As he turns, Loretta, with drink in hand, hollers over to him, "I told you that broad would bring you bad luck."

You can't help overhearing this comment and secretly you think how much fun it would be to tie a line to her ankle and fly her past Macy's on Thanksgiving Day, letting go of the line.

There is still a considerable amount of confusion around the raft. Stacey comes to your side and says, "I've got my car here. Why don't I take you guys back to the house? I pretty much think your job is over."

Soon you are making your way to the club parking area with Stacey, Forrest, Quentin, Dirk and a few oddball spectators who are tagging along just to gawk. You are resigned that there is nothing more that you can do here at the club since playing the piano in twelve feet of water is a bit beyond your contract.

Fortunately, Stacey has a large car and the five of you fit in without the big squeeze. Conversation turns to the lighter side now that you are all on terra firma.

"I wonder if there is a trophy for best accident?" asks Dirk.

"If there is we sure should win that one," says Quentin. Stacey glances at her inside mirror to look at the three men in the back seat and says, "You definitely win for the most blessed. You all could have drowned in that dumb-ass setup."

"Well dear, it's all wet that ends wet," says Quentin.

"I'd feel that way too, but I lost my trombone in the harbor," says Forrest. "Who do you suppose is going to pay for that?"

"Maybe the divers will find it when they go down for the piano," says Stacey.

"I'm not playing something that's been filled with slime and boat water," he says.

You laugh a bit and add, "Gee, I hope my fake book is okay."

You get an across-the-board chuckle for that one statement.

"By the way," you ask, "where did that piano come from?"

"Ned's brother borrowed it from the Knights of Columbus dance hall. He told them it was for a lawn party and he'd have it back there tomorrow," answered Quentin.

"Not likely," said Forrest .

Then you say, "Probably a poor time to bring this up, but who's gonna pay us for this pleasurable afternoon?"

"Jeez," answered Dirk, "I don't even know if we were judged. We were out of control when we passed the reviewing stand and we weren't playing by that time either. The Commodore was going to split the costs with Trent but now there's a lot of new expenses to be considered. The piano will have to be replaced, the generator went down with its engine running so it's probably whacked, and I don't even know whose sound equipment that was on top of the piano. I'm sure Trent's homeowner's insurance won't want to hear this story, and the Commodore has already lost his sense of humor. We're all in our own band together and I guess we'll probably wind-up eating this one to help out Trent. That's no reason for you to get punished though. Why don't you write down your name and phone number and when all this dies down I'll have Trent give you a call."

Stacey pulls up the long driveway to the house and you get out of the car. You go to your car and get a slip of paper to write your name, address and phone number. You give it to Dirk because he's the one who suggested it but you really have second thoughts about this dork having your information. Standing there you realize that through all this chaos you still have your oversized jacket. You shed that and hand it to Forrest. Everyone shakes your hand, tells you what a good sport you've been and how much fun it was, and then they make off for the boathouse. You climb into your car and just sit there for a moment. It is not yet 3:30 P.M. and your sneakers are green with slime, your hair is matted with flour and soap flakes, and you owe your friend a new $20 fake book. In addition, you have no money to show for the day. It seems that gin and tonic was invented for just such a day and with that in mind you drive home to change, hit a local watering hole, and lick your wounds. All the way home you are imitating Barbra Streisand as you sing, "Please Don't Rain on My Parade."

SUMMARY

As a hired professional piano player, be sure you fully understand that nobody else except another musician will ever be able to understand why you do it. They will never fully comprehend how you love it, how much your instrument has become a part of you, and the disruptive feelings that come over you when there is any prolonged period during which you cannot play.

Your spouse may see your playing as a threat and a cop-out. You are using it as a means to get out of the house, go carousing about, mingle with new and interesting people, and most of all escape the obligation of a weekend at home or springing for dinner and a movie now and then.

Be careful, however, when you tell a customer how much you love to play. They will deduce that you don't even need an intermission break. And God forbid the club manager should find out how much you love your job. He will immediately think in terms of reduced wages or no wages at all in lieu of drinks.

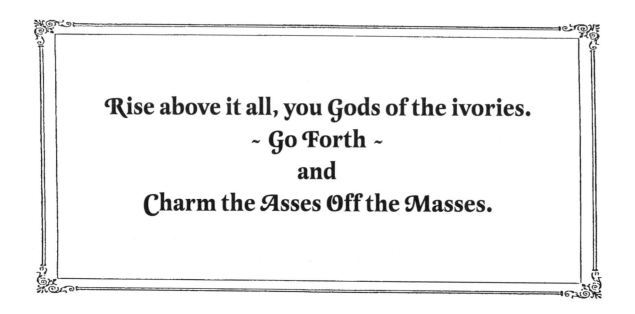

Rise above it all, you Gods of the ivories.
~ Go Forth ~
and
Charm the Asses Off the Masses.

This book will make a great gift for all those wildly, whacky Piano People in your life. Don't Wait...

GIVE THE GIFT OF LAUGHTER

Use the order form below or visit our website at

www.sundown-canyon.com

QUANTITY DISCOUNTS AVAILABLE
For Inquiries Call Toll Free 1-866-577-4266

CUT ALONG THE DASHED LINE AND TEAR OFF AT THE PERF ON THE LEFT

$25 INTRODUCTORY OFFER INCLUDES ALL SHIPPING & HANDLING
NY RESIDENTS ADD SALES TAX

PIANO PEOPLE

UPRIGHT GRAND
DOWNRIGHT NUTS

by **DON BURNS**

Name:

Address:

City: State: Zip:

Number of books ordered at $25.00 each (U.S. Funds only):

Make checks payable to Sundown Canyon Productions Inc. Send to: P.O. Box 572 • Grand Island NY 14072

☐ Money Order   ☐ Check   ☐ VISA   ☐ Master Card   ☐ Discover

Card Number: Card Expiration Date

☐☐☐☐ - ☐☐☐☐ - ☐☐☐☐ - ☐☐☐☐ | ☐☐ - ☐☐

Visit our website: www.sundown-canyon.com or call Stephanie Camden at Sundown Canyon Productions: 1-866-577-4266

CUT ALONG THE DASHED LINE AND TEAR OFF AT THE PERF ON THE LEFT

$25 INTRODUCTORY OFFER INCLUDES ALL SHIPPING & HANDLING
NY RESIDENTS ADD SALES TAX

PIANO PEOPLE

UPRIGHT GRAND
DOWNRIGHT NUTS

by **DON BURNS**

Name:

Address:

City: State: Zip:

Number of books ordered at $25.00 each (U.S. Funds only):

Make checks payable to Sundown Canyon Productions Inc. Send to: P.O. Box 572 • Grand Island NY 14072

☐ Money Order   ☐ Check   ☐ VISA   ☐ Master Card   ☐ Discover

Card Number: Card Expiration Date

☐☐☐☐ - ☐☐☐☐ - ☐☐☐☐ - ☐☐☐☐ | ☐☐ - ☐☐

Visit our website: www.sundown-canyon.com or call Stephanie Camden at Sundown Canyon Productions: 1-866-577-4266

© 2002 Donald Burns. All rights reserved